William A. Knight, Society Wordsworth

Wordsworthiana

A selection from papers read to the Wordsworth Society

William A. Knight, Society Wordsworth

Wordsworthiana
A selection from papers read to the Wordsworth Society

ISBN/EAN: 9783337275327

Printed in Europe, USA, Canada, Australia, Japan

Cover: Foto ©Andreas Hilbeck / pixelio.de

More available books at **www.hansebooks.com**

WORDSWORTHIANA

A SELECTION

FROM PAPERS READ TO

THE WORDSWORTH SOCIETY

EDITED BY

WILLIAM KNIGHT

London

MACMILLAN & CO.

AND NEW YORK

1889

PREFACE.

'THE WORDSWORTH SOCIETY' was founded at Grasmere on the 29th September 1880.

The original idea, which sprang up amongst a few friends in 1879, was to form a small and semi-private Club, consisting of one or two families, who wished to become more familiar with 'the English Lake District as Interpreted in the Poems of Wordsworth'; and it arose partly out of the publication of a little book bearing the above title. The intention was that an annual excursion should be made to the English Lakes, with the view of carrying on and completing the work begun in that volume. As soon as the scheme took definite shape, however, it was found that so many persons wished to join in it, that the idea of a private Club was abandoned, and a more public Society took its place.

After various suggestions had been made, and arrangements discussed, a meeting was held at Grasmere, in the late autumn of 1880, at which the following Constitution was adopted :—

'I. That a Society, to be called "THE WORDSWORTH SOCIETY," be formed, for the following purposes, viz.: (1) As a bond of union amongst those who are in sympathy with the general teaching and spirit of Wordsworth. (2) To promote and extend the study of his Poems—in particular, to carry on the literary work which remains to be done in connection with the Text and Chronology of the Poems, and the local allusions which they contain. (3) To collect for preservation and, if thought desirable, for publication, Original Letters and un-published Reminiscences of the Poet. (4) To prepare a Record of Opinions, with reference to Wordsworth, from 1793 to the present time, and to investigate any points connected with the first appearance of his works.

'II. That the officials of the Society be an Honorary President, Secretary, and Treasurer, with an Executive Committee; and that an Annual Meeting of the Society be held, at a place, and date, to be fixed by the Committee.

'III. That it be in the power of any member to transmit communications, bearing upon the work of the Society, to the Honorary Secretary, to be read and considered at the Annual Meeting.'

The Right Rev. the Bishop of St. Andrews was elected President for the year 1880, Professor Knight, St. Andrews, was elected Secretary, and G. Wilson, Esq., Murrayfield House, Midlothian, Treasurer.

The Society existed for seven years, from 1880 to

1886. The annual meetings were held, for the first two years, at Grasmere ; and subsequently, for the convenience of the majority of members, in London. A volume containing the *Transactions* of the Society was drawn up by the Secretary, privately printed each year, and issued to the members. It included a report of the meeting, the papers read, and others which had been sent to the Secretary but had not been read, as well as several that had been prepared for publication only. As the membership increased, however,—and beginning with half-a-dozen enthusiasts, the Society in 1886 included 344 members,—those who had subsequently joined wished to possess copies of the earlier publications ; and, as only a limited number had been printed, the *Transactions* of some of the earlier years were exhausted long before the Society ceased to exist. Numbers I., IV., and VI. of the *Transactions, e.g.* are wholly out of print, while many copies of Numbers V., VII., and VIII. still remain. It has been thought desirable, therefore, to meet the demand for copies of the *Transactions*—which exists both amongst the former members of the Society and the general public,—to issue a new volume, containing a Selection from the Papers read.

It has been a somewhat difficult task to select from these papers, but those I have omitted are chiefly those prepared by myself, such as the Bibliography, and the Chronological Table of the Poems, the Rydal Mount library catalogue, and the letters from Wordsworth, his wife, and sister, to various correspondents. All the important papers, critical or expository, which were read to the Society, have been republished in this volume, which, for want of a simpler title, I have called *Wordsworthiana.* They are printed in the order in which they were written.

A brief account of the several meetings of the Society, and of its *Transactions,* may conclude this short prefatory note.

At the second annual·meeting, held at Grasmere, on the 20th July 1881, the recommendations of the Committee, which were to the following effect, were adopted : (1) That the Society should issue a full Bibliography of the Poems of Wordsworth, published during his lifetime, with illustrative notes. This Bibliography to form No. I. of the Society's publications. (2) That an engraving, or etching, of one of the portraits of Wordsworth should be issued. (3) That the members should be requested to send to the Secretary any information they may possess, first, as to the Letters of Wordsworth—whether in MS. or published—stating where they are to be found ; and second, as to critical notices of the poems which may not be easily accessible, so as to form the materials for a Bibliography of Criticism, to be subsequently issued by the Society.

Twelve short papers, written by members of the Society and others, in this country and America, were read by the Secretary at this meeting. They included 'Wordsworth on Don Quixote,' by A. J. Duffield; 'The Platonism of Wordsworth,' by J. Henry Shorthouse; an article on Wordsworth's Tyrolese Sonnets, by Alois Brandl; Wordsworth's petition to Parliament on the law of Copyright; and six unpublished poems, in MS., or privately printed, by Wordsworth and his sister. It was resolved by the Society to erect a memorial stone at the parting-place of the brothers John and William Wordsworth, at Grisedale Tarn, inscribing on it the last stanza of the *Elegiac Verses* by the Poet. This was carried out during the following year. Lord Coleridge was elected at this meeting as President for the year 1881; as also the Executive Council, which was to consist of the President of the Society, the Honorary Secretary, and the Treasurer, and the following members: the Bishop of St. Andrews; Lord Houghton; Mr. Robert Browning; the Principal of Brasenose College, Oxford; the Very Rev. The Dean of Salisbury; Professor Campbell Fraser, Edinburgh; Professor Edward Dowden, Dublin; Professor Edward Caird, Glasgow; The Rev. Stopford Brooke, London; Mr. Richard Holt Hutton, London; and Mr. R. Spence Watson, Newcastle-on-Tyne.

In 1883, the Rev. Alfred Ainger, The Temple

Church ; the Rev. H. D. Rawnsley, Keswick ; and Mr. Heard, Fettes College, were added to the Committee.

No. I. of the *Transactions*—issued shortly after this meeting—contained the Bibliography of the Poems referred to.

The third meeting of the Society was held in the Freemasons' Tavern, London, on the 3d of May 1882. The Chair was taken, first by Mr. Robert Browning, and afterwards by Lord Coleridge, the President for the year. Papers were read from Professor Dowden on 'Wordsworth's Modernisations of Chaucer,' by Mr. Hutton on 'The Earlier and Later Styles of Wordsworth,' by the Secretary on 'The Portraits of Wordsworth,' and by Mr. Rawnsley on 'The Reminiscences of Wordsworth amongst the Peasantry of Westmoreland.' Of two papers by Mrs. Owen of Cheltenham, one on 'Wordsworth's View of Death,' the other on 'The Seeming Triviality of some of Wordsworth's Subjects,' the former was read, and both were published in the *Transactions*, along with a paper by Mr. Hutchinson of Kimbolton on 'The Structure of the Wordsworth Sonnet.'

Nos. II. and III. of the *Transactions* contain most of the above papers, and others, including a letter from Professor Bonamy Price, on the *Ode on Immortality*. No. IV. of the *Transactions* contained five portraits of Wordsworth, reproduced by photography, along with a letterpress description of them.

The fourth annual meeting was held in the College Hall at Westminster, on the 2d of May 1883. Mr. Matthew Arnold was President, and addressed the Society. The Secretary read a paper by Mr. Aubrey de Vere, on 'The Personal Character of Wordsworth's Poetry'; Mr. Stopford Brooke read one, on 'Wordsworth's *Guide to the Lakes*'; and the Dean of Salisbury read another on 'Wordsworth's Position as an Ethical Teacher.' In a fourth, Mr. Rawnsley explained the nature of a proposed permanent Lake District Defence Society. In addition to those papers,—which are published in No. V. of the Society's *Transactions*,—that volume contains some 'Notes on the Localities of the Duddon Sonnets,' by Mr. Herbert Rix; a letter from Mr. F. C. Yarnall on 'Wordsworth's Influence in America'; a 'Bibliography of Review and Magazine Articles on Wordsworth,' by W. F. Poole of Chicago; an account of a Mountain Ramble by the Poet and his Sister in 1807, written by Dorothy Wordsworth; letters from Sara Coleridge, Lamb, and Emerson on Wordsworth; a Poem by Whittier upon him; and a 'Local Note on *Hart Leap Well*,' by Mr. Hutchinson of Kimbolton.

The fifth annual meeting was held in the Library at Lambeth Palace, on the 10th of May 1884, the

American Minister, Mr. J. Russell Lowell, in the Chair, who delivered an address as President. After the Archbishop of Canterbury had moved a vote of thanks to the President, the Honourable Roden Noel read a paper on 'The Poetic Interpretation of Nature'; Mr. Heard read one on 'Wordsworth's Treatment of Sound'; Mr. R. Spence Watson on 'Wordsworth's Relations to Science'; and the Rev. Alfred Ainger on 'Wordsworth and Charles Lamb.' The Secretary also read some unpublished Letters of Wordsworth to Walter Savage Landor.

No. VI. of the *Transactions* includes, along with these papers and addresses, a series of sixteen Letters from Wordsworth to John Kenyon, and the Rydal Mount Library sale-catalogue.

The sixth annual meeting was held on the 8th of July 1885, at the residence of Lord Houghton, who delivered an address as President for the year. Some portions of the unpublished canto of *The Recluse* were then read by the Secretary, and a paper by Mr. Harry Goodwin on 'Wordsworth and Turner'; after which Mr. James Bryce, M.P., Mr. R. H. Hutton, and others, spoke. Along with a Report of this meeting, and the papers read, No. VII. of the *Transactions* contains a revised Chronological Table of the Poems of Wordsworth, and a new Bibliography.

The final meeting of the Society was held in the

Jerusalem Chamber, Westminster Abbey, on the 9th July 1886, Lord Selborne presiding. An address from the President was followed by a paper from Professor Veitch on 'The Theism of Wordsworth,' one from Mr. Ainger on 'The Poets who helped to form Wordsworth's Style,' one from Mr. Rawnsley on 'The Humanity of Wordsworth,' and a speech from Mr. Aubrey de Vere. No. VIII.—the final number of the *Transactions*—contains, in addition to these papers, the Letters of Wordsworth, his wife and sister to Henry Crabb Robinson, and a letter from the Honorary Treasurer to the Secretary of the Society.

Reports of the annual meetings of the Society were printed in the newspapers of the day, and need not be republished. An account of the first meeting, however, given in the *Spectator* of October 16, 1880, may be reproduced in part, as it contained the only report of the remarks of the first President of the Society :—

'A singularly interesting meeting took place in the Rothay Hotel, Grasmere, on the afternoon of Wednesday, September 29th, to inagurate the Wordsworth Society, the Bishop of St. Andrews presiding. Bishop Wordsworth said :—"Our assemblage here to-day represents a company spread, I may venture to say, almost throughout the civilised world ; and, embracing, as it does, several very notable Wordsworthians, is amply sufficient 'for the purpose which has brought us

together.   That purpose, as I understand it, is to plant a
sapling, which shall grow into a great tree, in honour of the
poet's memory, and which shall enable future generations
of his admirers—sitting, as it were, under its branches—to
understand his works more thoroughly, and to study them
with greater pleasure,—like the yew-trees which he himself
planted in the neighbouring churchyard, and which are now
flourishing over his grave.   With such an object before us,
the occasion is one for action rather than much speech; and,
in order that we may proceed to action with the least delay,
and with the best effect, I shall presently call upon our Secretary, Professor Knight—who, as the originator of the movement, is most competent to do it justice—to explain to us
what his ideas and wishes are concerning it.   Indeed, I feel that
I should be guilty of something like an act of petty larceny,
and should be putting my sickle into my neighbour's corn,
if I were to attempt to forestall the remarks which he will
make, with far greater propriety.   I shall therefore only add
one word to express the satisfaction which I feel in observ-
ing that, among the company here present, there is a happy
mixture of pilgrims from both sides of the Border, English
and Scotch, reminding us of the time when Walter Scott and
William Wordsworth mounted up Helvellyn together; and
reminding me more particularly of the occasion when I
had the honour of accompanying my uncle to Abbotsford,
on the memorable visit which he paid to Sir Walter in 1831,
just as he was on the point of setting out for Italy,—an
occasion which produced 'Yarrow Revisited,' and also the
well-known sonnet, first murmured by the poet while I was

walking by his side, in the following week, on the banks of
Loch Katrine."

'Professor Knight said the story of the origin of the proposed
Society was very easily told.   Some time ago it occurred to
one or two friends that there was some work still to be
done in reference to Wordsworth, both with a view to the
minute and systematic study of his text, and also to the preservation of any memorials of the poet which were of a perish-
able character, and which, if not soon rescued from oblivion,
might be lost to posterity.   Although a very great deal had
been done by critics and editors, there were many points that
remained for elucidation ; and it occurred to those friends
that this might be done more effectively by the co-operation
of several associated together than by solitary labour.   It
seemed to them that in the case of all the greater poets, a
time came when this work had to be done ; and that it was
specially needed in the case of one whose poetry was so intimately associated with locality.   Then there was the question of the chronological order of the poems, which it is not
always easy to determine ; and also the question of the best
text as all students of Wordsworth are aware that he altered
his text probably more than any other English poet.   Well, a
few friends had agreed to form a private, or semi-private Club
for these purposes ; and they originally conjoined with it
the idea of an annual meeting in this Lake District of England, which is so peculiarly identified with the poet.   Some
of the original members, however, suggested their friends as
associates ; while others, hearing of the proposed Club,
wished to be admitted to it.   It was thus very soon evident

that if a Club was to be formed, it could not be a private one; and it then seemed to some of its promoters that it would be well to make it as wide and representative as possible.

'The names of those who had joined the Society were then read, including Lord and Lady Selborne, Lord Coleridge, Robert Browning, James Russell Lowell, Leslie Stephen, Stopford Brooke, Lady Richardson, the Principal of Brasenose College Oxford, the Dean of Salisbury, John Ruskin, Edward Dowden, Aubrey de Vere, R. H. Hutton, Alfred Hunt, Mrs. Augusta Webster, Mrs. Emily Pfeiffer, the Bishops of Lincoln and St. Andrews, Professor Campbell Fraser, Professor Edward Caird, Professor Nichol, Professor Carpenter, J. M'Whirter, H. O. Holiday, F. J. Furnivall, William Wordsworth (Eton), William Wordsworth (Bombay), R. Spence Watson, George Wilson, J. Hutchinson, J. P. Graves, etc.

'Before mentioning the definite work which the Society might undertake, Professor Knight stated that he had an unpublished MS. poem of Wordsworth's, and two poems of his sister Dorothy; but that after conference with their President, the Bishop of St. Andrews, he had thought it more expedient not to bring these before the present meeting, which was mainly a business one. Referring to the work which the Society might undertake, there was, first, the systematic and detailed study of the poems, to which the younger members might devote themselves, with a view to determine certain critical points which remain unfixed. For example, there were many interesting questions in reference to the origin of the poems, which he illustrated by quoting the very sentence in Wilkinson's "Tours to the British Mountains" on which the poem of "The Solitary Reaper" was founded. Then, he thought that a valuable bit of work might be done in collecting a history of opinion with reference to Wordsworth, from the year 1793 to the present time, showing its fluctuations, etc. There were many essays and notices of the poet scattered in obscure corners, which might be lost to posterity, and which, if collected together, would form a most interesting literary record.

'He had just read, for example, an admirable criticism by Mrs. Browning, who made up for the omission of Wordsworth from her *Visions of Poets*, by one of the finest and most appreciative notices of him elsewhere. More than one correspondent had referred to this as work needing to be done, in particular Professor Dowden, of Trinity College, Dublin, who also urged the publication, by the Society, of all such writings of Wordsworth (poems, letters, etc.) as still remain in MS., and may be deemed suitable for publication. The letters scattered through various books might be brought together, or at least an index of them made, in chronological order, stating where each letter may be found. Then, it had been suggested that a short monograph might be written on the portraits of Wordsworth, and a portrait engraved for the members of the Society. It had also been proposed that the Society might, by-and-by, issue a selection of Wordsworth's poems bearing upon the Lake District of England, which, without note or comment, would be of great value. Membership of the Society was not to be re-garded as implying literary partisanship. He himself refused to be called a Wordsworthian, if that implied that he belonged to a literary party, or was the enrolled disciple of any literary school. One of his friends and correspondents—himself a distinguished writer on Wordsworth—had not joined the Society, because he thought it might imply partisanship. Now, there were many members of this Society who felt the truth of what the hostile critics say of Wordsworth,—that he lacks humour, and that he has no passion, at least of the tumultuous kind, that his constructive power is feeble, etc. ; but then, they feel that no poet gives us everything, and that all these defects in Wordsworth are compensated for by his great meditative depth, and by that feature which he alone amongst poets possessed in a super-eminent degree, viz., his power of teaching us, when the tumult of passion had passed, by insight into the symbolism of Nature —an imaginative and rational insight—which connects his poetry in so remarkable a manner, at once with the genius of Plato, and with the latest and most elevated philosophy of Europe.

' Extracts from several letters were then read giving suggestions as to the work of the Society,—in particular from Mr. Ruskin and Mr. Dowden. After making his suggestions, Professor Dowden said,—" There is a real work to do, and a sufficient work. Minor things may be done by the way, as they arise. My conception of the Club, as existing to do a definite piece of work, involves the idea of its ceasing to exist when that work is done. I should not like the Club to languish, or to seek a factitious ground of existence in the curiosities of a scholarship which has exhausted all that is real and living. Wordsworth's poetry goes furthest, like a voice among his own mountains, in quiet and solitude. When the purpose of the Club has been achieved, all external hindrances will have been removed from the way of Wordsworth's influence; all natural aids will have been afforded to it, and his poetry may be left to do its own work, side by side with that of other great writers,—in a silent, spiritual way, like that of light; in an untrammelled, invisible way, like that of the winds, blowing where they list."

'The Resolutions [1] were then proposed for consideration by the meeting.

'The Principal of Brasenose College, Oxford (Dr. Cradock), entirely concurred with Professor Knight's programme. The prejudice against Wordsworth, which was once so general, was largely diminished, but not abolished, and the Society would do good work by making Wordsworth even more widely known. Some years ago, in a large public school, there were not three boys who knew a line of Wordsworth beyond those which are quoted in *English Bards and Scotch Reviewers*. He felt that Wordsworth could not be properly appreciated without some knowledge of the Lake Country. He proposed that the resolutions should be adopted, in the form in which they had been submitted. This was agreed to unanimously. The Bishop of St. Andrews was elected President, Professor

---

[1] As printed at pp. v. vi.

Knight, Secretary, and Mr. George Wilson, Murrayfield House, Midlothian, Treasurer.'

I may add three things—*First*, that complete copies of Nos. II., III., V., VII., and VIII. of the *Transactions* can still be obtained by those who wish them—*Second*, that many of the papers in the present volume are considerably altered and enlarged ; the essay on the Portraits of the poet has been rewritten, and important changes and additions have been made in others ; so that, while this volume of *Wordsworthiana* is in one sense the publication of what has hitherto been issued privately, it is also to a certain extent a new contribution to the literature of the subject—*Third*, that many unpublished fragments and memoranda relating to Wordsworth still exist, which I have not been able to make use of in the three Volumes of his Life, which will soon appear, and which—had the Wordsworth Society continued to exist—I would have placed in subsequent volumes of its *Transactions*. Should this volume awaken any general interest, these may be collected and issued in a subsequent one.

Since the paper on the portraits of Wordsworth was printed off, I have seen a design by Mr. Woolner, for a seated statue and part of a monument, prepared by him in 1852, when the Wordsworth memorial was placed in the Baptistery at Westminster Abbey. As the design was not selected, the work was never executed. It is, however, extremely interesting, and by the kind permission of Mr. Woolner is reproduced in this volume. Within the last few weeks I have also seen a miniature in oil of Mrs. Wordsworth by Miss Gillies, which has great interest. It was taken in Mrs. Wordsworth's old age, and is now in the possession of Mrs. Charles Lewis, Cambridge Terrace, London.

I should add that Mrs. William Wordsworth, the poet's daughter-in-law—referred to frequently in the course of this paper—has passed away since it was written ; and that the portraits mentioned as belonging to her are still at 'The Stepping Stones,' Ambleside, but are now the property of her family.

WILLIAM KNIGHT.

THE UNIVERSITY, ST. ANDREWS,
  December 1888.

CONTENTS.

THE PLATONISM OF WORDSWORTH.

By J. H. SHORTHOUSE.

A

THE PLATONISM OF WORDSWORTH.[1]

[The reader will perceive that no allusion is made in this Essay to the general religious opinions of the Poet. The writer has simply attempted to trace certain lines of thought which seem to him to exist in Wordsworth's philosophic poetry.]

To write of Wordsworth would seem futile. Wordsworth is himself; to paraphrase or parody his words or characters is unspeakably painful; nay more, it is useless, it will convey no adequate idea to the man who is ignorant of Wordsworth's poetry. It is the perfection of certain passages which induces the wish to call attention to them, but this perfection leaves nothing to be desired or added; nor can any want of variety be pleaded as an excuse for using any words other than the poet's own. The stage is crowded already. Think of the press of fairy folk who throng upon your memory as you turn over his pages in your recollection—the miller and his maids on their island platform in the river—that strange woman and her no less weird mate beneath the tower of Jedburgh—the stealthy mystic form of the leech-gatherer—the stately march of figures which fill the pathways of *The White Doe*—the valleys and hill-slopes gay with blithe or hallowed with solemn figures which delight our fancy in the pages of *The Excursion*—the churchyard where the brother sleeps—the mountain sheepfold where

---

1 Read to the Society, July 1881.

Michael toiled and sorrowed—the foot-plank which bore the last impress of Lucy's feet—the dusty highway along which the Cumberland beggar moved, and will move now for ever—the ghastly fellowship that haunted the prosaic everyday walks of the travelling potter, Peter Bell—Matthew, the schoolmaster, and his mysteriously provoking witty rhymes—Simon Lee—old childless Timothy and the hunt, and that exquisite apologue which genius heard even in the chance echo of the cuckoo's cry—

> unsolicited reply
> To a babbling wanderer sent.

Wordsworth was a leader of men in the truest sense. On his guidance the jaded and perplexed intellect may safely depend; he possessed a power of cheerful calm, clear as the dawn and unvarying as the stars.

> That, when time brings on decay,
> Now and then may I possess
> Hours of perfect gladsomeness;
> Keep the sprightly soul awake,
> And have faculties to take
> Even from things by sorrow wrought,
> Matter for a jocund thought;
> Spite of care and spite of grief
> To gambol with life's falling leaf.[1]

> It is the spirit of Paradise,
> ——————————a spirit strong,
> That gives to all the selfsame bent
> Where life is wise and innocent.[2]

It may be that there are lines of thought which the Poet merely indicated, but which it is possible to trace out more

---

[1] *The Kitten and Falling Leaves*, p. 130, Ed. 1849.
[2] P. 121, Ed. 1849.

clearly, and to follow further on, not only to our own delight and advantage, but also to the appreciation of the poet.

It has been suggested that one of these lines of thought is the similarity of Wordsworth's teaching to that of Plato. I have said the *similarity* of Wordsworth to Plato, because it is not asserted that Wordsworth consciously Platonised; on the contrary, it is not likely that he ever read the *Dialogues.* It is not impossible that Coleridge may have talked to him upon the matter. We know he discoursed at length to him upon Spinoza, and Mr. Frederick Pollock fancies that he can trace the effect of those conversations in the Poet's work.

I should suppose that any ordinarily educated man would, if asked, describe Wordsworth as a poet of nature, and he has with the utmost emphasis described himself as a 'worshipper of nature;' nevertheless it would seem that Wordsworth is essentially the poet of *Man.* He is in fact less of a poet than of a Seer. It is *man* whom he chiefly busies himself about. It is the emotions and thoughts of *men* which fill his thoughts. Nature is the type of permanence and reality, man is transient and ever changing; nevertheless nature is ever subservient to man. Seen by man's intellect inanimate nature becomes 'an ebbing and a flowing mind.'[1] It is intellect projected upon the bleak side of some tall peak 'familiar with forgotten years,' that gave to it its 'visionary character.'[2] It was the transitory nature of the being that stood upon its bank that gave to the flowing stream its lesson of 'life continuous—being unimpair'd.'[3] By these forms of nature, 'in the relation which

---

[1] *The Excursion :* 'The Wanderer,' p. 447, Ed. 1849.
[2] P. 449.   [3] ' Despondency Corrected,' p. 482.

they bear to man,'[1] are evoked 'the spiritual presences of
absent things, convoked by knowledge.'[2]

> Amid the groves, beneath the shadowy hills
> The generations are prepared.[3]

> Their manners, their enjoyments and pursuits,
> Their passions, and their feelings ; chiefly those
>   -   Essential and eternal in the heart.[4]

But though man consecrates nature, nature elevates
man—man and nature act and re-act. That glorious universe, the intelligent succession of conditioned existence,
has

>   meanings which it brought
> From years of youth.   Which like a Being made
> Of many Beings, it has wondrous skill
> To blend with knowledge of the years to come ;[5]

and thus to lure mankind from a superstitious Manichæism
into a state of abiding and gracious calm, in which he is at
last able to recognise the eternal unity which pervades all
things, the synthesis of thought and matter, the clear dawn-
ing of the perfect intellectual day.

>   'Tis Nature's law
> That none, the meanest of created things,
> Of forms created the most vile and brute,
> The dullest or most noxious, should exist
> Divorced from good—a spirit and pulse of good,
> A life and soul, to every mode of being
> Inseparably link'd.[6]

---

[1] ' Despondency Corrected,' p. 487.   [2] *Idem*, 1st Edition.
[3] *The Excursion :* ' The Churchyard,' p. 504, Ed. 1849.
[4] *Idem :* ' The Wanderer,' p. 449, Ed. 1849.
[5] *Idem :* ' The Wanderer,' p. 450, Ed. 1849.
[6] *The Old Cumberland Beggar,* p. 425, Ed. 1849.

If this is the nature of Wordsworth's poetry, what is the result? He has himself told us that he did not intend to found a system ; but the effect produced by his teaching is a sacred peace, in the presence of pure and absolute Being. The petty troubles of existence vanish before the passionless face of nature, and in the presence of invariable Law an entrance is won into the kingdom of the pure Intellect,

> by mystery and hope,
> And the first virgin passion of a soul
> Communing with the glorious universe.[1]

> Immutably survive,
> For our support, the measures and the forms,
> Which an abstract intelligence supplies ;
> Whose kingdom is, where time and space are not.[2]

Now let us turn for a moment to the banks of the Ilissus and we shall find something of the same character.

Standing under the shady plane-trees, which have long since vanished, groups of earnest-looking young men are discussing those themes which, as the years roll on, generation after generation will discuss ; while among them a queer-looking little man whom all reverence, and make way for, and listen to, walks about asking questions, and showing each one of them, to his own satisfaction, how great a fool he is. Plato's dialogues, just as much as Wordsworth's poems, form a volume of Philosophical Romance. For his groundwork he seized upon a wonderful and unique man. His philosophy is based upon the story of a life and death, his pages are crowded with men ; without the aid of narrative he can create character : but story is not wanting.

---

1 *The Excursion :* 'The Wanderer,' p. 449, Ed. 1849.
2 *Idem :* ' Despondency Corrected,' p. 476, Ed. 1849.

Anecdote and incident, apologue and poetry enliven the page. The trials, the difficulties, the follies and aims of men are his theme. Nor does he stop here, his philosophy (transcendental, as it has been called) is human, his ideas are those of earth. Unlike Aristotle and the Schoolmen, he does not occupy himself with Existence, Substance, Attribute, Essence, Eternity, but with matters of every-day life; in the first place destroying false and pedantic notions, and then basing his idealism upon recognised facts, such as love, hatred, strength, and even horses, dogs, and mud.

Let us endeavour to trace this likeness still more clearly by two examples before we attempt to realise the meta-physic result, and the particular mode in which it forced itself on the Poet's imagination and by which he is still enabled to communicate it to us.

He speaks of

another gift
Of aspect more sublime ; that blessed mood
In which the burden of the mystery,
In which the heavy and the weary weight
Of all this unintelligible world
Is lighten'd : that serene and blessèd mood
In which the affections gently lead us on
Until, the breath of this corporeal frame,
And even the motions of our human blood,
Almost suspended, we are laid asleep
In body, and become a living soul ;
While, with an eye made quiet by the power
Of harmony and the deep power of joy
We see into the life of things.[1]

---

[1] *Tintern Abbey*, p. 160, Ed. 1849.

Such an extract as this has said everything that need be said on the subject. It covers all possible ground. Let us remain silent, and turn to the other master:

> And what think you would happen were it given to any one to behold beauty itself, clear as the light, pure and undefiled, not daubed with human colouring, nor polluted with human fleshliness, and other kinds of mortal trash ; so that, in its singleness of form, he were able to see the beautiful and the godlike in one. Think you that the life of a man would be of little account if he look thitherward (without fear) and has such fellowship as this ? Do you not see that to him alone will power be given (who alone has the power to behold the beautiful) to beget, not the deceitful show of virtue, as not being tempted by deceitful shows, but the truth itself as one who embraces a reality :—and so begetting virtue (as a lovely daughter) and bringing her up, it will happen to him to be God-beloved, and, if any man can be, immortal.[1]

Apart from all the distracting terminology of metaphysic, then, the meaning of the English poet and the Greek philosopher seems to be this: The forces of life, which we call intellectual, may be actually of similar birth with the physical, but phenomenally they stand out in clear distinction. Love, self-sacrifice, and self-denial, courage, and the other virtues are so far immaterial at least that they are indestructible, invisible, invariable, in action, unregulated by the laws which attach to matter. So long as the race endures they are eternal. But a difficulty seems to present itself at the outset. Love and self-denial, courage and the rest, are all that you state them to be, but so are hatred, revenge, fear, and the like. Will, then, the eternal world of Pure Intellect, which an abstract intelligence has peopled, prove

---

[1] Plato, *Symposium*, XXIX. E. Ed. Stallbaum.

nothing more than a repetition of this?—with all its unintelligible gloom, its perplexities, its cruelties, its Sphinx-riddles which lead to despair and death?

To grapple with this difficulty Plato fell back upon what may be called a principle of excellence, which rules the formation and government of all animate and inanimate things. What this principle was he was often at a loss to decide, but he appealed boldly to the experience of his hearers to acknowledge that there was such a principle, and to pronounce upon the success or failure of any Work or Being in proportion as it adheres to or departs from it. This being so, it follows that all temporary, accidental, and unsuitable adjuncts being eliminated, nothing but the pure idea of the perfect object will exist in the intellect; so that to the perfectly instructed man there would be no such thing as evil or bad workmanship in the world. Indeed this is really the case in the pure intellect, in which alone all things exist (all things, that is, in their perfect form), and which is God.

The general truth of this, I think, will not be denied. The latest efforts of modern speculation have declared that the world of thought, and that alone, is subjective and objective at once, and that all conceivable attributes turn out to be objective aspects of thought itself. 'The ultimate elements of thought are not merely correlated with the ultimate elements of things : they are the elements of things themselves.'[1]

Nor is Platonism antagonistic to any older or later form of philosophic thought. You may make matter as eternal as you like. You may deny the argument of design, and conclude that no evidence exists of a Creator, beneficent or

---

[1] *Vide* Mr. Fred. Pollock's *Spinoza*, pp. 176-9.

otherwise. You may endow matter with such vital energies and such faculties of thought as you may require. You may satisfy yourself that force, or motion, or extension is the immanent cause of all things : but the Platonic theory can never be antiquated or impossible.

From every phenomenon you will always be able to eliminate the transitory and the accidental, until you arrive at an abstract idea which exists only in the pure intellect. It is into this world of ideas that the Platonist forces his way. In this fourth dimension of intellectual space he finds himself in a world familiar and yet wonderful. Into this world neither change, nor corruption, nor decay can enter. This is the true eternal life. Of all earthly things the ideas are eternal, and this pure intellect, this world in which they live and move and have their being, and some portion of which we have each of us received, is none other than the all-perfect, all-containing intellect, the mind of God.

In what way, then, does Wordsworth speak of this world ? Under what aspect did its eternal glories present themselves to him ? He tells that

> The power
> Of nature, by the gentle agency
> Of natural objects, led me on to feel
> For passions that were not my own, and think
> On man, the heart of man, and human life.[1]
>
> .   .   .   .   .
>
> How exquisitely the individual mind
> ————————————to the external world
> Is fitted, and how exquisitely too
> The external world is fitted to the mind.[2]

---

[1] *Michael*, p. 96, Ed. 1849.
[2] Preface to *The Excursion*, p. 445, Ed. 1849.

> From that bleak tenement
> He many an evening to his distant home
> In solitude returning, saw the hills
> Grow larger in the darkness ; all alone
> Beheld the stars come out above his head,
> And travell'd through the wood with no one near,
> To whom he might confess the things he saw.
> So the foundations of his mind were laid
> In such communion, not from terror free.[1]
>
> .   .   .   .   .
>
> While yet a child, and long before his time,
> Had he perceived the presence and the power
> Of greatness : and deep feelings had impress'd
> Great objects on his mind, with portraiture
> And colour so distinct, that on his mind
> They lay like substances, and almost seem'd
> To haunt the bodily sense.[2]

I venture to think that these lines deserve the closest study. They seem to me to contain the key not only to Wordsworth's Platonism, but to that peculiar conception of his that an entrance into the world of abstract thought may be won by the help of material objects.

'The presence and the power of greatness'—this is that 'principle of excellence' in which Plato believed. This expression includes all that can be conceived of absolute perfection—of immutable morality, absolute in itself—independent of space and time, of locality and temperament. It includes that power within us which, in Mr. Matthew Arnold's phrase, 'makes for righteousness,' that consciousness which assures us that, in the Divine Intellect, love must rule and not hatred, confidence and not fear.

By deep feeling, the Poet goes on to tell us, this greatness

---

[1] *The Excursion :* 'The Wanderer,' p. 447, Ed. 1849.
[2] *Idem*, 1st Ed., p. 10.

is impressed upon our mind, so that its attributes lie like substances upon us and haunt the bodily sense. It is evident, I think, that he uses the word 'substance' in this place not in the strict metaphysical sense, but in that secondary sense which has vitiated all the terms which express essence or reality, popular use and wont invariably attaching these two last terms to that which is not essential or real. The poet evidently refers to that lower substantiality which belongs to matter, and which is perceived by the senses. He seems to affirm that by the help of the vast objects of nature, perceived in silence and in solitude, we are enabled to understand and to conceive the great realities of abstract thought, and to

> Breathe in worlds
> To which the heaven of heavens is but a veil.[1]

> But in the mountains did he feel his faith ;
> There did he see the writing—all things there
> Breathed immortality, revolving life,
> And greatness still revolving ;—infinite.
> There littleness was not, the least of things
> Seem'd infinite : and there his spirit shaped
> Her prospects.[2]

This is that 'divine hope of pure imagination,'[3] that 'fittest to unutterable thought,'[4] 'the passing shows of being.'[5]

> 'The silence and the calm of mute insensate things.'

> ' Where earth and heaven create one imagery.'[6]

---

[1] Preface to *The Excursion.*
[2] *The Excursion :* 'The Wanderer,' 1st Ed., p. 14.
[3] *Idem*, p. 497. Ed. 1849.   [4] *To H. C., Six years old.*
[5] *The Excursion :* 'The Wanderer,' p. 455, Ed. 1849.
[6] *To H. C.,* p. 62.

Matter therefore is a thought of God.   The rural gods of Greece would seem to have occupied a similar position in the mind of the Platonist as did these 'spiritual presences of absent things,'[1] 'This soul imparted to brute matter,' in the poet's 'pure imaginative soul.'[2]

> We live by admiration, hope, and love.[3]

>   A spirit hung,
> Beautiful region ! o'er thy towns and farms,
> Statues and temples, and memorial tombs ;
> And emanations were perceived ; and acts
> Of immortality, in Nature's course,
> Exemplified by mysteries, that were felt
> As bonds.[4]

The means are not very different, the result is the same. This absolute being is described as including within itself, as the sea its waves, all adoring and conscious and apprehending existence :

> —— Life continuous, Being unimpaired,
> That hath been, is, and where it was, and is,
> There shall be—seen, and heard, and felt, and known,
> And recognised—existence unexposed
> To the blind walk of mortal accident ;
> From diminution safe, and weakening age ;
> While man grows old, and dwindles, and decays,
> And countless generations of mankind
> Depart ; and leave no vestige where they trod.[5]

>   Thou, thou alone
> Art everlasting, and the blessed Spirits
> Which thou includest, as the sea her waves :
> For adoration thou endur'st ; endure

---

[1] 'Despondency Corrected,' p. 487, Ed. 1849.
[2] 'The Parsonage,' p. 523.
[3] 'Despondency Corrected,' p. 482.
[4] *Idem*, p. 482, Ed. 1849.
[5] *Idem*, 1st Ed.

> For consciousness the motions of thy will ;
> For apprehension those transcendent truths
> Of the pure intellect, that stand as laws
> Even to thy Being's infinite majesty ! [1]

The inborn conscience of humanity has recognised the perfection of Being in a variety of forms—by diverse myths and it may be grotesque imaginations at which a misdirected intellect may sneer. The 'secret spirit of Humanity' [2] has consented with a marvellous unanimity to conceive of a world where wrong is made right, where suffering is turned to joy, where inequality is removed, and the rough places of misery and oppression made smooth—where the poor and the afflicted who have seen or felt little in this life to delight or elevate may find existence somewhat more worthy to be lived. That this blessed consummation may never arrive in the form religionists have dreamed may be true : but that the idea can never be aught else than true and righteous is impossible.

> The life where hope and memory are as one,
> Earth quiet and unchanged, the human soul
> Consistent in self-rule, and heaven revealed
> To meditation in that quietness. [3]

Miserable indeed would the world become were this ideal of righteousness ever entirely lost.

> Who in this spirit communes with the forms
> Of nature, who with understanding heart
> Doth know and love such objects as excite
> No morbid passions. [4]

---

[1] 'Despondency Corrected,' p. 476, Ed. 1849.
[2] 'The Wanderer,' p. 455, Ed. 1849.
[3] 'Despondency,' p. 469, Ed. 1849.
[4] 'Despondency Corrected,' 1st Ed., p. 195.

> The light of Love
> Not failing, perseverance from his steps
> Departing not, he shall at length obtain
> The glorious habit by which sense is made
> Subservient still to moral purposes,
> Auxiliar to divine.[1]
>
> Thus deeply drinking in the soul of things,
> He shall be wise perforce, and while inspired
> By choice, and conscious that the will is free,
> Unswerving shall he move, as if impelled
> By strict necessity, along the path
> Of order and of good.   Whate'er he see,
> Whate'er he feel of agency direct,
> Or indirect, shall tend to feed and nurse
> His faculties, shall fix in calmer seats
> Of moral strength, and raise to loftier heights
> Of love divine his intellectual soul.[2]

It would be easy to go on.   This synthesis of thought and matter is the key-note of every line in the poem.   But the line of thought has been sufficiently laid down; who will follow it up?

'He excels,' says Jewish proverb, when at loss for words of highest praise, 'He excels upon Sheminith'—the eighth string of the world to come which shall be added to the Kinnor of the Sanctuary when Messias begins His reign. Listening, weary and sad, amidst the rustling echoes of the *selva selvaggia* of metaphysical tradition, we may catch from these two master-singers, as Dante heard in the stately rhythm of the volume he so long had conned, the clear resonance of this mystical string.

---

[1] ' Despondency Corrected,' p. 196.   [2] *Idem*, p. 197.

WORDSWORTH'S SELECTIONS FROM CHAUCER MODERNISED.

BY EDWARD DOWDEN.

B

WORDSWORTH'S SELECTIONS FROM CHAUCER MODERNISED.[1]

Wordsworth's *Selections from Chaucer* aim at rendering Chaucer's verse into plain, modern English, only slightly coloured by archaic words or phrases, and retaining the ancient accent only "in a few conjunctions, such as *alsò* and *alwaỳ*." Almost any writer of the present day would retain several words having a savour of antiquity which Wordsworth thought it right to reject, and doubtless the verse would approach somewhat nearer to Chaucer's manner. It may be questioned, however, whether the simplicity of Chaucer's style (where it is simple, which is far from being always the case) is not best preserved by Wordsworth's method of modernisation, which is at once frank and faithful.

The selections are *The Prioress's Tale*—the story of the little Christian boy murdered by Jews of Asia ; a passage from the fifth book of *Troilus and Creyseyde* describing the love-sorrow of Troilus during Cressida's absence ; and the poem (erroneously ascribed to Chaucer) *The Cuckoo and the Nightingale*. These were written in the winter of 1801 ; but remained long in manuscript. *The Prioress's Tale* was first published in 1820 (*The Miscellaneous*

Poems of William Wordsworth, vol. iii.). The remaining two modernisations were given as a present to one of the contributors to the interesting little volume, *The Poems of Geoffrey Chaucer Modernised* (London, 1841), in which Leigh Hunt, Elizabeth Barrett, and Mr. R. H. Horne assisted. Was the contributor to whom Wordsworth ¸presented his versions Mr. Thomas Powell?[1] In Mr. Powell's *Poems* (1842) are two sonnets relating to Wordsworth, one beginning thus :

> Wordsworth, my heart rose as I heard you say,
> ' There is a spirit in the hearts of men,
> Which had from God its wondrous origin,
> And while a man lives ne'er can pass away.'

The other, *On a Portrait of Wordsworth, painted by Margaret Gillies*, closes with the lines—

> Here I seem to gaze
> On Wordsworth's honoured face ; for in the cells
> Of those deep eyes Thought like a prophet dwells,
> And round those drooping lips Song like a murmur strays.

In 1849, Mr. Powell emigrated to the city of New York. Does he still live? I have not been fortunate enough to see Mr. Powell's volume, *The Living Authors of England* (New York, 1849), reprinted, I suppose, as *Pictures of the Living Authors of Britain* (London, 1851). It might possibly yield something of interest to lovers of Wordsworth.

In a letter to Professor Reed of Philadelphia, Wordsworth writes : 'Mr. Leigh Hunt has not failed in the Manciple's Tale, which I myself modernised many years ago.' It would be interesting to ascertain whether Words-

---

[1] Professor Knight has since ascertained that this conjecture was correct.

worth's version of this tale (which he considered unsuitable for publication) still exists in manuscript.

Wordsworth's modernisations of Chaucer may be read with pleasure even by those who know the originals. But they ought to be read with a recognition of their defects as well as of their merits. In a few instances errors seem to have arisen either through ignorance of Chaucer's English, or through inattention, or from a faulty text. Thus the Christian boy who sings in praise of Mary all through *The Prioress's Tale,* is described by Chaucer as 'a little clergeon,' which Wordsworth renders by 'a little scholar;' but '*clergeon*'[1] means, not merely a young clerk, as Tyrwhitt says, it specially means 'a chorister-boy.' Again, when Troilus would visit secretly the deserted home of Cressida, we read—

> And therewithalle, his meynye for to blende
> A cause he fonde for in towne for to go ;

'*his meynye for to blende,*'—that is, to keep his household or his domestics in the dark. But Wordsworth writes—

> And therewithal to cover his *intent*,

possibly mistaking '*meynye*' for '*meaning.*'

In the following instance it would be pleasant to suppose that there was a printer's error, but the metre forbids such a conjecture. When Troilus sees the shut windows and desolate aspect of his lady's house, his face grows blanched, and he rides past with speed—so fast, says Wordsworth,—

> That no wight his *continuance* espied.

---

[1] Professor Skeat in his Clarendon Press *Selections from Chaucer*, cites Du Cange : '*Clergonus,* junior clericus vel puer choralis ; jeune clerc, petit clerc ou enfant de chœur ;' and Cotgrave, '*Clergeon*, a singing man, or Quirester in a Queer.'

But in Chaucer he rides fast in order that his white face may not attract notice—

> And as God wolde he gan so faste ride
> That no wight of his *contenaunce* espiede—

'*Countenance,*' not '*continuance.*'   On the other hand it is to Urry's text, or whatever other text may have been before him, that we must ascribe the error in Wordsworth's version of Troilus's despairing love-song—

> Toward my death with wind *I steer* and sail,—

which ought to be—

> Toward my death with wind *in stern* I sail—

Troilus's bark careering towards death, with all sails set, before a fierce stern-wind.

Two instances may be noted in which the simplicity and innocence of Chaucer are lost, and with these, in one case, some of his pathos.   The little chorister who has so miraculously sung the praise of Mary is buried with due honour,—

> And in a tombe of marble stoones clere
> Enclosede thay this[1] litel body sweete.

'*This litel body sweete*'—how tender as compared with Wordsworth's—

> And in a tomb of precious marble clear
> Enclosed his *uncorrupted* body sweet,

where the word '*uncorrupted*' casts an unpleasant suspicion across the meaning of the adjective '*sweet.*'   And yet the change was wilful, for nothing could be easier or more obvious than the version in modern English—

> Enclosèd they this little body sweet.

---

[1] '*His* litel body,' in several MSS. and in Tyrwhitt.

Again, Chaucer's lines describing the boy martyr at his lesson in school—

> This litel child his litel book lernynge,
> As he sat in the schole in his primere,

lose in Wordsworth's—

> This little child, while in the school he sate,
> His primer conning with an earnest cheer.

That 'earnest cheer' is a poor exchange for—

> This litel child his litel book lernynge.

Besides, the pious boy cared not for the secular learning of his primer; his heart being set on Mary's praise, he by and by looked forward to being shent for his primer; even to being beaten for his neglect of it thrice in an hour.

There is a fine extravagance, or perhaps I should say, a vigorous realism towards the close, which Wordsworth has toned down. The murdered boy must sing in his chorister's treble, 'O Alma Redemptoris Mater,' as long as the miraculous grain lies upon his tongue. To hear the boy singing thus with throat cut to the neck-bone is blissful, but it is also ghastly; and it were well if his spirit could depart. In Chaucer, the holy Abbot with passionate action plucks forward the boy's tongue—

> His tongue out-caught and took away the greyn.

Then the little child gives up the ghost full softly, and, with tears streaming like rain, the Abbot falls right along upon the ground, grovelling—

> And gruf he fil al plat upon the grounde.

We see the vivid gesture, the extreme abandonment of body to a sudden wave of emotion, as in some mediæval picture. In Wordsworth's corresponding stanza the Abbot 'touches' the tongue, and takes away the grain ; he 'drops on his face' upon the ground, but hardly with the prone abandonment of Chaucer's

> And gruf he fil al plat upon the grounde.

I wish all this had taken place in Wordsworth's poem not 'before the altar,' which might be the communion-table of an Anglican church, but, as in Chaucer, before the 'chief altar.' I like to imagine the little boy's body in a great cathedral where are many shrines ; it lies in no side-chapel, but before the high altar, in presence of the Host :

> Vpon his beere ay lyth this Innocent
> Biform the chief auter while the masse laste.

There are two passages in which Wordsworth makes, as it were, open confession of failure. One is the concluding stanza of *The Prioress's Tale,* the address to 'Yonge Hew of Lincoln,' where Wordsworth destroys the stanza by a change in the rime system, and, indeed, leaves the second line unrimed. The other is the ninth stanza of the same poem. Chaucer writes :

> Thus hath this widow her litel child i-taught
> Our blisful lady, Cristes moder deere,
> To worschip ay, and he forgat it nought ;
> *For sely child wil alway soone leere.*

that is, '*for a happy child will always learn soon.*' Wordsworth renders it thus—

> For simple infant hath a ready ear,

and adds a needless generalisation—

> Sweet is the holiness of youth ;

extending the stanza to receive this addition from seven to eight lines, with an altered rime system.

Here may be noted a curious added epithet, which does not appear in the selection from *Troilus and Cresida*, as first printed in Mr. Horne's volume of *Chaucer Modernised*, but which is found in *The Poetical Works of Wordsworth*, 1849-50, and in later editions. Troilus sings of his absent lady, in Chaucer:

> With a softe vois, he of his lady deere
> That absent was, gan sing as ye may heere.

And in Wordsworth's earliest text it is—

> With a soft voice, he of his lady dear
> That absent was, 'gan sing as ye may hear.

Are we to ascribe to the printer the odd reading of the later text, ' with a soft *night* voice, he,' etc. ?

It is true the song addresses the departed lady as a lost star, and was probably sung in the same hour when Troilus would tell his trouble to the moon. Hence, perhaps, Wordsworth's 'soft night voice,' if Wordsworth's it be.

It may be questioned whether an expression from *Hamlet*·ought to have been imported into a version of Chaucer. Troilus has fancies that he is paling, pining, and about to die; but they are mere fancies :

> And al this nas but his melancolye
> That he had of hym self swich fantasye.

Wordsworth, haunted by Shakespeare, wrote—

> All which he of himself conceited wholly
> Out of his weakness and his melancholy.

Every one knows—and no one better than Wordsworth knew—that Chaucer did special reverence to the daisy. In *The Cuckoo and the Nightingale*, a poem long ascribed to Chaucer, it is the third of May[1]—a date corresponding

---

[1] This paper was read before the Wordsworth Society on May 3, 1882.

almost to mid May, according to our present reckoning. The poet, after a wakeful night, rises, and goes forth at dawn; he comes upon a 'laund' or plain 'of white and green:'

> So feire oon had I nevere in bene,
> The grounde was grene, ypoudred with daysé,
> The floures and the gras ilike al hie
> Al grene and white, was nothing elles sene.'

A beautiful description of what it was possible to see before patent mowing-machines made havoc of beauty, and ground our quietude into discord, far different from the pleasant swish of the scythe,—short green grass, and the daisies and the grass of equal height. Unfortunately in the text which Wordsworth followed the description is sheer nonsense—

> The floures and the greves like hie.

The daisy flowers are as high as the groves! Wordsworth retained the groves but refused to make the 'wee crimson-tipped flowers' of equal height with them :

> Tall were the flowers, the grove a lofty cover,
> All green and white, and nothing else was seen.

It must be left for those who love the dawn to decide whether the first birds get sleepily or briskly out of bed. There seems to be a half-hour of tentative song, during which the little throats are tuning for the day. Perhaps the old poet who describes their first motions in the dewy dawn as 'creeping' is not wrong :

> There sat I doune among the feire floures,
> And saw the briddes *crepe out of her boures*
> Ther as they had rested hem al the nyght.

But Wordsworth, whose observation is declared to be in-fallible, has it—

> There sat I down among the fair fresh flowers,
> And saw the birds *come tripping from their bowers*,
> Where they had rested them all night.

Perhaps they come quickly, but, like passengers from the cabin to the deck at morning, one by one, and so their gradual arrival appears to an onlooker a slow proceeding.

It is to be noted here that Wordsworth follows the author of *The Cuckoo and the Nightingale*, in changing the sex of the baser bird at pleasure; now the Cuckoo is male, now female;[1] but the love-loyal Nightingale is always *she*.

Chaucer, Burns, and Wordsworth are lovers of the daisy. All poets are lovers of the nightingale, including even Mr. Allingham, a native of the unhappy country where there is no 'Nightingale Valley.'[2]   In the old poem, after the cuckoo, bird unholy, has said his evil say, the nightingale breaks forth 'so lustily'—

> That with her clere voys she made rynge
> Thro out alle the grene wode wide.

Wordsworth has taken a poet's licence with these lines :

> I heard the lusty nightingale so sing,
> That her clear voice made *a loud rioting*,
> Echoing through all the green wood wide.

This 'loud rioting' is the characteristic Wordsworthian interpretation of a song which has impressed various imaginative minds in various ways—as melancholy, or glad almost to madness.   It is akin to that other passage so well known :

---

[1] Would Chaucer have shown this carelessness ?

[2] See a beautiful Ode by the compiler of *Nightingale Valley*, entreating the birds to come back to the West,—

> For Ireland's furious days are past.

> O Nightingale thou surely art
> A creature of a fiery heart ;
> These notes of thine they pierce and pierce,
> Tumultuous harmony and fierce !
> Thou sing'st as if the God of wine
> Had helped thee to a Valentine.

In 1827 Wordsworth added to his note prefixed to *The Prioress's Tale*, a critical remark worth quoting before we end : 'The fierce bigotry of the Prioress forms a fine background for her tender-hearted sympathies with the Mother and Child ; and the mode in which the story is told amply atones for the extravagance of the miracle.' Yes ; Madame Englentyne would weep if she saw a mouse caught in a trap 'if it were deed or bledde ;' she would weep if one of her small hounds were dead,

> Or if men smot it with a yerde smerte.

How piteous therefore must her heart grow for the little martyred boy with his fair, carven throat ! But for the cursed race of Jews, no pity ! That serpent Sathanas has his wasp's nest in their hearts. And so the amiable Prioress relates, with a *gusto* in that pretty voice of hers, how the Provost drew the guilty Jews with wild horses—

> And after that he heng them by the lawe.

Wordsworth's modernisations of Chaucer are sufficiently good to deserve that we should know their faults. And as it is better to know definitely the weak points in the character or conduct of a friend than to have our feeling towards him undermined by a vague suspicion, so it is better to read Wordsworth's renderings with an exact knowledge of their defects than with a general impression that because they are modernisations they must therefore be unfaithful.

ON THE PORTRAITS OF WORDSWORTH.

By WILLIAM KNIGHT.

ON THE PORTRAITS OF WORDSWORTH.[1]

I.

THE earliest portrait of Wordsworth, of which there is any
record, was taken in 1797,—during the Alfoxden days,—by
an artist then living at Stowey. It was a half-length figure
(14 in. by 10), and is mentioned by Joseph Cottle in his
Early Recollections chiefly relating to S. T. Coleridge, vol. i.
p. 317. It represented Wordsworth as he was in his twenty-
seventh year.

Nothing seems to have been heard of this picture for
ninety years, till it turned up at Sotheby's saleroom in
London, in July 1887. It is now in the possession of
Mr. George, bookseller, Bristol. Its artistic merit is not
great, but its historical interest is considerable.

II.

In the following year (1798) Robert Hancock took a
drawing in black chalk for Joseph Cottle. This was engraved
by R. Woodman for Cottle's *Recollections*, along with
portraits of Coleridge, Southey, and Lamb—all drawn by
Hancock—in the years in which each published his first
volume of poems. The originals are now together in the
National Portrait Gallery at South Kensington, having been
purchased by the trustees in May 1877. Like all the rest,
Wordsworth's is on a small scale. He is represented as
wearing a dark buttoned coat and white cravat, seated in

---

[1] Read to the Society in May 1882.

a wooden chair.   The face is seen in profile, turned to the left; the complexion tinted with red.   Of this picture Cottle says, 'The portrait of Mr. Wordsworth was taken also by Hancock, and was an undoubted likeness, universally acknowledged to be such at the time.'   Referring to the four portraits together he adds, 'The time in which these four men of genius were drawn was perhaps the most advantageous for exhibiting their genuine characters; in which case the likenesses contained in the following work are those which might most faithfully and favourably descend to posterity.'[1]   This picture of Wordsworth passed from Cottle to his daughter, Mrs. Green; thence to Messrs. Fawcett and Noseda, after which it was bought by Colonel Francis Cunningham, and sold at his sale in 1876 to Mr. De la Rue, from whom the Trustees of the National Portrait Gallery bought it in the following year.   When Dora Wordsworth, the poet's daughter, saw this picture of her father in 1836, she remarked that it 'reminded her of her brother John.' In Henry Crabb Robinson's Diary, August 29, 1836, the following allusion to this picture occurs, 'In Cottle's house at Bristol, my attention was drawn to five miniatures, rather say small portraits of Southey, Coleridge, Lamb, and Wordsworth. . . . W. resembles E. Lytton Bulwer more than himself now.   All (C. assures me) were excellent likenesses.'

III.

In the year 1803 a portrait of Wordsworth was painted by Hazlitt (the literary critic and artist).   Of this picture Southey wrote to his friend Richard Duppa, from Keswick,

---

[1] See *Early Recollections chiefly relating to S. T. Coleridge,* by Joseph Cottle.   London, 1837.   Preface, p. xxxiii.

December 14, 1803 : 'Hazlitt has been here. . . . He has painted Wordsworth, but so dismally—though Wordsworth's face is his ideal of physiognomical perfection—that one of his friends, on seeing it, exclaimed, " At the gallows—deeply affected by his deserved fate, yet determined to die like a man ; " and if you saw the picture, you would admire the criticism.' (See Southey's *Life and Correspondence*, vol. ii. p. 238.)

I may add that almost all the portraits of that period were artistically bad.

On June 11, 1804, Southey wrote to Coleridge, 'I went into the Exhibition merely to see your picture, which perfectly provoked me. Hazlitt's does look as if you were on your trial, and certainly had stolen the horse ; but then you did it cleverly—it had been a deep, well-laid scheme, and it was no fault of yours that you had been detected. But this portrait by Northcote looks like a grinning idiot, and the worst is, that it is just like enough to pass for a good likeness, with those who only know your features imperfectly. Dance's drawing has that merit at least that nobody would ever suspect you of having been the original.' (See his *Life and Correspondence*, vol. v. p. 291.)

IV.

For fifteen years after this—*i.e.* from his thirty-third to his forty-eighth year—no portrait seems to have been taken of Wordsworth ; but about the year 1818, Edward Nash (who was a friend of Southey's, and had painted several portraits of the Southey family) took a likeness of Wordsworth for Southey.[1] Mrs. Joshua Stanger (of Fieldside,

---

See *Life and Correspondence of Southey*, vol. v. pp. 50, 51.

Keswick), who now possesses it, bought this picture at the Greta Bank sale of Southey's effects, and an engraving of it is prefixed to *The Prose Works of Wordsworth.* It is a pencil drawing (9 in. by 7 in.); three-quarters length; and the face is three-quarters turned to the left. The figure is seated, the head resting on the right hand, the right elbow on a table; and the left hand is placed inside the waistcoat.

V.

In the summer of 1817 Mr. Richard Carruthers visited Rydal Mount, and took a sketch for a picture in oil, which was finished in November of that year. The artist himself, in writing to Mr. Thomas Monkhouse, mentions the dates. This picture is now in the possession of the Rev. Thomas Hutchinson, the Rector of Kimbolton, Leominster, in Herefordshire, a nephew of Mr. Monkhouse, and also of Mrs. Wordsworth. It is a half-length picture, three-quarters face, turned to the right. The figure is in a sitting posture, with the back against the trunk of a tree, the right elbow leaning on a rock. In the background are mountain tops and a rapid mountain stream. The dress is a black coat with ruffled shirt. The left hand is thrust into the waistcoat, *more suo.* Carruthers's picture was engraved by Henry Meyer, and published by Henry Colburn, Conduit Street, London, in the *New Monthly Magazine*, Feb. 1, 1819. It was also engraved by J. T. Wedgwood for the Paris edition of Wordsworth's Poems, published by Galignani in 1828. The latter is not nearly so good a reproduction of the original as Meyer's, published eight years before. A copy of this picture by E. Hader—taken not from the original, but from the engraving in the Paris edition—has recently been photographed in Germany.

In October 1821, Wordsworth, writing to Henry Crabb Robinson, said of Carruthers, ' He is an amiable young man, whom a favourable opening induced to sacrifice the pencil to the pen, not the pen of authorship—he is too wise for that,— but the pen of the counting-house, which he is successfully driving at Lisbon.' Of Meyer's print in Colburn's Magazine, Southey wrote to Sir George Beaumont (Feb. 1819), ' Wordsworth may be congratulated upon coming off so well in the Magazine. The print is not so good as the drawing in my possession, because it does not so well represent his capacious forehead ; but on the whole it is a respectable likeness, and would be thought excellent by those who are not intimate with his face.'

VI.

Mr. Carruthers took a copy of this picture, which is now, I understand, in the possession of Mrs. Drew, the daughter of Mr. Thomas Monkhouse.

VII.

Writing to Henry Crabb Robinson from Rydal Mount on the 24th June 1817, Wordsworth says, ' I have not lately . . . seen any one new thing whatever, except a bust of myself. Some kind person—which persons mostly unknown to me are—has been good enough to forward me this.' Of this bust I can discover no trace whatsoever. Probably it had no merit.

VIII.

Benjamin Robert Haydon seems to have painted Wordsworth at least four times. The first portrait was taken in

1817; and was a sketch intended for the head of a by-stander, in his picture of Christ's Entry into Jerusalem. Of this sketch Hazlitt said, ' Haydon's head of him, introduced into the Entry of Christ into Jerusalem, is the most like his drooping weight of thought and expression.'

It is thus that Haydon writes, in his *Autobiography* of his ' Jerusalem,' as he called it : ' During the progress of the picture of Jerusalem, I resolved to put into it (1816), in a side group, Voltaire as a sneerer, and Newton as a believer' (vol. i. p. 358). ' I now (1817) put Hazlitt's head into my picture, looking at Christ as an investigator. It had a good effect. I then put in Keats into the background, and re-solved to introduce Wordsworth bowing in reverence and awe. Wordsworth was highly pleased, and before the close of this season (1817) the picture was three-parts done. The centurion, the Samaritan woman, Jairus and his daughter, St. Peter, St. John, Newton, Voltaire, the anxious mother of the penitent girl, and the girl blushing and hiding her face, many heads behind, in fact the leading groups were accomplished, when down came my health again, eyes and all' (vol. i. p. 372). Wordsworth's head is again referred to in the artist's account of the successful exhibition of this picture in London : ' Wordsworth's bowing head ; Newton's face of belief; Voltaire's sneer; the enormous shouting crowd,' etc. (p. 404). The Entry into Jerusalem was sold in September 1831 to Messrs. Child and Inman, of Philadelphia. Its departure from England was a heavy blow to the painter. ' September 23, 1831.—My Jerusalem is purchased, and is going to America. Went to see it before it was embarked. It was melancholy to look, for the last time, at a work which had excited so great a sensation in England and Scotland. It was now leaving my native country for ever' (vol. ii. p. 314). This picture is now in the Roman Catholic Cathedral at Cincinnati.

Henry Crabb Robinson, in his Diary, May 11, 1820, writes: 'The group of Wordsworth, Newton, and Voltaire is ill-executed. The poet is a forlorn and haggard old man; the philosopher is a sleek, well-dressed citizen of London; and Voltaire is merely an ugly Frenchman.'

The original study by Haydon for this head of Wordsworth is now in the possession of Mr. Stephen Pearce, 54 Queen Anne Street, Cavendish Square, London, who writes to me as follows: 'The portrait I have of Wordsworth is the original study in black chalk, by Haydon, the painter. They were great friends. The head is larger than life, most carefully drawn, and was executed for the purpose of being placed in Haydon's large picture of Christ's Entry into Jerusalem. It was his general plan with all the principal heads in his pictures to make chalk studies, and then, I believe, to paint from them. In that large picture Haydon painted several of his eminent friends, using them as models. The face and expression of the head of Wordsworth are those of one bowing in reverence to Christ. It is on tinted paper, and beneath the head in Haydon's writing is—

> ' " Wordsworth.
> For Entry into Jerusalem, 1817." '

This Haydon drawing was bought by Mr. Pearce at the sale of some of Haydon's effects in 1852, and has been in his possession ever since.

IX.

The second picture by Haydon was drawn during the following year, while the artist, according to the testimony

given below, was staying at Rydal Mount.   I find no trace
of this visit to Rydal in Haydon's own autobiographical
memoranda; but his records of the years 1818 and 1819
are extremely meagre, and the date of the drawing is undoubted.   The original is in the possession of Mrs. Walter
Field, the only daughter of the late William Strickland
Cookson, Esq., Hampstead, and was given to him by Mr.
Wordsworth's sons.   Mrs. Field writes to me of it, ' The
sketch in my possession is a crayon drawing on tinted paper,
made by Haydon while staying at Rydal Mount, and presented by him to Mr. Wordsworth.   It was, I believe, employed in the picture you name.   It has on it, in Haydon's
writing, "B. R. Haydon, in respect and affection, 17th June
1818;" and in Wordsworth's writing, "Wm. Wordsworth,
1818."'

It was engraved by Thomas Landseer, Southampton
Street, and published by him on May 1, 1831.

It is a three-quarters face, with a large turn-down collar,
showing the throat.   The face looks somewhat over the
right shoulder to the spectator's left, and shows an outline
of the back of the head.   It has the appearance of never
having been quite finished, but the massiveness of the head
is well rendered.

A living artist, commenting on this picture, writes to me
thus :—

June 26, 1882.

I have seen the Haydon 'Wordsworth.'   I distrust its
merits as a piece of draughtsmanship; and I suspect that
there is too much Haydon in it to make it valuable as a
likeness.   It was taken when Wordsworth was forty-eight
years of age.   If it is rightly drawn, Wordsworth must have
had a very great development of the back of the head.   I

cannot imagine how such a head and face could ever grow into anything like the head and face which Miss Gillies painted in 1841. That portrait strikes me as lacking in the representation of the strength and stubbornness which must have been evident in Wordsworth's face, but I feel that there is a likeness in it. It is very delicately and carefully done. . . . There is a want of thoroughness and of humility, as it appears to me, in that sketch of Haydon's.

Wordsworth, I am told, used to speak of this as the likeness of 'the brigand.'

X.

In 1831 Sir William Boxall painted a small half-length likeness, which was engraved by J. Bromley, and subsequently by R. Roffe, for the frontispiece to the twenty-sixth . volume of *The Mirror*, published in 1835. The original is now at the Stepping Stones, Ambleside, in the possession of Mrs. William Wordsworth, the poet's daughter-in-law. It was also engraved by J. Cochran.

XI.

In or about the same year, Wilkins published a lithograph in his series of *Men of the Day*, including Lockhart, Allan Cunningham, Rogers, etc. This likeness was nearly life-size. The print of it, which I have seen, has these words underneath: 'Printed by C. Hullmandell. Drawn from life, and on stone, by Mr. William Wilkins, 20 Newman Street. Published as the Act directs, by J. Dickinson, 114 New Bond Street.' The poet himself, however, used to call it the portrait of 'the stamp-distributor.'

XII.

I may place beside this a medallion in wax by William
W. Wyon, A.R.A.—a companion to one which Wyon did
of Southey.   It was taken in 1835, the same year as that in
which Southey's was done.   (See his *Life and Correspondence*,
vol. vi. p. 273.)   It is now in the possession of Mrs. William
Wordsworth, the poet's daughter-in-law.   Wyon was an engraver and designer of coins and medals; and held the
post of second engraver to the Mint, from 1816 to 1851.

XIII.

In the year 1837, when Wordsworth was in Rome along
with Mr. Crabb Robinson, his portrait was painted by Severn,
the friend of Keats.   It is a small picture (13 inches by 9).
Miss Caroline Fox tells us that Hartley Coleridge thought
this the best of all the portraits.   It is now in India, in the
possession of the grandson of the poet, the Principal of
Elphinstone College, Bombay, who writes thus to me of it:—
'April 18, 1882.—I possess the portrait painted in Rome;
but I neither consider it a pleasing picture, nor a satisfactory
likeness. . . .   The artist has, I dare say, conveyed a
sufficiently faithful representation of what Wordsworth was,
in his less inspired moments, about the year 1836.   He is
represented seated, with an umbrella in his hand, with the
air and attitude, as I have always thought, of an elderly
citizen, waiting for a 'bus,' or some public conveyance.   I
think I have heard that Wordsworth himself said that it
made him look more like a banker than a poet; perhaps
he ought to have said a stamp-distributor.'   Wordsworth
writing to his sister from Albano, during the Italian tour of
1837, says, 'Mr. Severn, the friend of Keats, has taken my

portrait, which I mean to present to Isabella.[1]   I fear you will not, nor will she, be satisfied with it.   It is thought, however, to be a pretty good likeness as to features; only following the fact, he has made me look at least four years older than I am.'

XIV.

Next in order come the five pictures painted by the Pickersgills, father and son.   The first (which may be numbered twelfth in the list) was painted at Rydal Mount, but finished in London, by H. W. Pickersgill, R.A., for St. John's College, Cambridge, at the request of the Master and Fellows.   It is three-quarters length, and represents the poet in a black cloak lined with red.   It originally hung in the Combination Room, but has been transferred to the Dining Hall at St. John's College.   It was engraved by W. H. Watt for the stereotyped edition of the poems, issued in 1836; and also by C. Rolls in 1838, and published in *The Modern Poets and Artists of Great Britain*, edited by S. C. Hall (London: Whitaker and Co., 1838).   It was this picture that gave rise to the not very appropriate sonnet, beginning—

> Go, faithful Portrait ! and, where long hath knelt
> Margaret, the saintly Foundress, take thy place.

The following description of it is by the Rev. Alexander Freeman, M.A., Fellow of St. John's College, Cambridge: —'William Wordsworth, Poet, by H. W. Pickersgill, R.A.; canvas 5 feet by 4 feet 4 in.; lake scenery in background; seated under a high bank; black cloak, lined with red, thrown open; left hand rests on some papers, holding pencil.   Painted in old age, at Rydal Mount, for St. John's College, about 1831 ; grey hair, rather sharp

---

[1] His daughter-in-law, his son John's wife.

features, three-quarter face, turning over right shoulder, three-quarter length.'—*The Eagle*, vol. xi. No. 61.

Mr. William Wordsworth, the poet's son, told me that it was painted in London in 1830. The above sonnet was written in 1832. But in a postscript by Dorothy Wordsworth to a letter of her brother's to Sir W. Rowan Hamilton, written on June 13, 1831, she says, 'This very moment a letter arrives, very complimentary, from the Master of St. John's College, Cambridge (the place of my brother William's education), requesting him to sit for his portrait, etc.' She adds, 'of course my brother consents, but the difficulty is to fix on an artist. There never yet has been a good portrait of my brother. The sketch by Haydon is a fine drawing, but what a likeness! All that there is of likeness makes it to me the more disagreeable.'

I do not think this picture of Pickersgill's was painted till 1832. Wordsworth, writing to Dr. Arnold on Sept. 19, 1832, speaks of having had Pickersgill down with them for the purpose of painting it. Henry Crabb Robinson wrote in his Diary of May 30, 1833, 'I went to Pickersgill's to see his painting of Wordsworth. It is in every respect a fine picture, except that the artist has made the disease in Wordsworth's eyes too apparent. The picture wants an oculist.'

Wordsworth writing to Mr. Moxon, October 10, 1836, refers to the print of this portrait by Pickersgill, and complains of 'an air of fulness spread through the whole, which is the more felt, from a fault in the original picture, of a weakness of expression about the upper lip.' And again (in October 20, 1836), 'I am still of opinion, in which others concur, that the attitude has a look of decrepitude, in consequence of the whole person not being given. It appears to me to be beautifully engraved.'

XV.

A copy of this picture was painted by Pickersgill junior (H. Pickersgill), for Mrs. Quillinan, the poet's daughter. It was partly taken from one or two fresh sittings, and partly from his father's previous portrait. In Henry Crabb Robinson's Diary of March 3, 1835, the following occurs: 'Walked with the Wordsworths to Pickersgill, who is painting a small likeness of the poet for Dora.' Again, March 14, 1835 : 'Called on Wordsworth by appointment at Pickersgill's. The small picture is much better than the large one. W. walked with me to see the bust at Denman's. He thinks it a good likeness.'

XVI.

Another copy of the St. John's Pickersgill, drawn by the artist's son for the poet's brother Christopher—the Master of Trinity College, Cambridge—is now in the possession of the Bishop of St. Andrews.

XVII.

In 1840, the elder Pickersgill took a likeness of the poet for Sir Robert Peel, to be placed in his Gallery of Living Authors at Drayton Manor. Wordsworth wrote thus of it to Mr. Reed, Philadelphia :—'Jan. 13, 1841.—Pickersgill came down last summer to paint a portrait of me for Sir Robert Peel's Gallery at Drayton Manor. It was generally thought here [*i.e.* at Rydal] that this work was more successful as a likeness than the one he painted some years ago for St. John's College, at the request of the Master and Fellows.' On the 1st of Sept. 1840, Wordsworth wrote thus of this picture to the artist Haydon, ' I am this moment (while dictating this letter) sitting to Mr. Pickersgill, who has kindly come down to paint me at leisure, for Sir Robert Peel, in whose gallery at Drayton the portrait will probably be hung.'

An engraving of this later picture of Pickersgill's, by T. Skelton, is published in the *Memoirs* of the poet, written by the Bishop of Lincoln.

XVIII.

A replica of this, also by Pickersgill, may be seen in the South Kensington National Portrait Gallery. The catalogue informs us that it was purchased by the Trustees in 1860; and the Director and Secretary, Mr. Scharf, informs me that it was purchased from Mr. Pickersgill himself.

XIX.

Following the five Pickersgills come the five pictures by Miss Margaret Gillies, which were taken on ivory. In reference to these, I quote the artist's own statement, sent to me in 1882 :—'Miss Gillies visited Rydal Mount in 1841, at the invitation of Mr. and Mrs. Wordsworth, to make a miniature, which was commissioned by Mr. Moon (the publisher) for the purpose of engraving. The engraving from this by Edward M'Innes was published on the 6th of August 1841, and republished Feb. 15, 1853, by Miss Boyd, 467 Oxford Square. The original was sold many years afterwards, and is now in America.' [A few years ago it was repurchased, and is now in the possession of Sir Henry Doulton, Lambeth.]

XX.

'The second portrait was similar in position to the first; the Wordsworths being so pleased with the one done for

Moon, as to wish it repeated for themselves, with the addition of Mrs. Wordsworth at the poet's side in one picture.'[1]

XXI.

'A copy of the same was subsequently taken for Miss Quillinan, and is now in her possession at Loughrigg Holme.

XXII.

'The third portrait was a profile. It was also from life. It was engraved by Armitage, and published in a book entitled *The New Spirit of the Age* issued by Smith and Elder in 1843 or 1844. Miss Gillies does not know what became of the original of this profile. She considers it, as a likeness, the most satisfactory of the three. The engraving from the first portrait was not, in Miss Gillies's judgment, a very good representation of her picture.'

The original of the profile is in the possession of Mrs. William Wordsworth, and is by far the best likeness of the three. The engraving, which has been often reproduced in popular editions of the Works, does no justice to it. Wordsworth, writing to Mr. Thomas Powell in 1841, says, 'I think you will be delighted with a profile picture on ivory with which Miss Gillies is at this moment engaged. Mrs. Wordsworth seems to prefer it as a likeness to anything that Miss G. has yet done.'

Mr. Powell published a volume of poems, in which there is one *On a Portrait of Wordsworth painted by Miss Margaret*

---

[1] This picture descended to the poet's grandson, William Wordsworth, Elphinstone College, Bombay, and was accidentally burnt.

Gillies.   Judging, however, by the following extract, I think
that he refers to the first portrait painted by her :—

Here I seem to gaze
On Wordsworth's honoured face ; for in the cells
Of those deep eyes Thought like a prophet dwells,
And round those drooping lips Song like a murmur strays.

XXIII.

Miss Gillies painted another portrait, of the poet and his
wife—a copy of the one burnt in India—for Mr. William
Wordsworth.   It is now at the Stepping Stones, Ambleside.

XXIV.

In 1842 Wordsworth again sat to Haydon at the painter's
urgent request.   In a letter to Professor Reed of Philadelphia, written in January 1841, Wordsworth says, 'Haydon
is bent upon coming to Rydal next summer, with the view
of painting a likeness of me, not a mere matter-of-fact portrait, but one of a poetical character, in which he will
endeavour to place his friend in some favourite scene of
these mountains.   I am rather afraid, I own, of any attempt
of this kind, notwithstanding my high opinion of his abilities;
but, if he keeps in his present mind, which I doubt, it
would be in vain to oppose his inclination.   He is a great
enthusiast, possessed also of a most active intellect ; but he
wants that submissive and steady good sense, which is absolutely necessary for the adequate development of power,
in that art to which he is attached.'

It does not appear, however, that Haydon did visit Rydal
Mount in 1842.   In that year Wordsworth was in London,
and Haydon painted him in his own studio there.

In the *Autobiography*, already referred to (see Nos. VIII. and IX.), edited by Mr. and Mrs. Taylor (second edition, vol. iii. p. 223), the following occurs under date June 14, 1842 : 'Wordsworth sat, and looked venerable, but I was tired with the heat. . . . I made a successful sketch. He comes again to-morrow. 16th.—Wordsworth breakfasted with me, and we had a good sitting. He was remarkably well, and in better spirits.' Further on, in this *Autobiography*, we read that 'He [*i.e.* Haydon] sent, at the request and pressure of Miss Mitford, to her friend Miss E. B. Barrett (now Mrs. Browning), the portrait of Wordsworth on Helvellyn, painted this year' (p. 237). The portrait inspired this sonnet by Mrs. Browning :—

ON A PORTRAIT OF WORDSWORTH BY B. R. HAYDON.

> Wordsworth upon Helvellyn ! Let the cloud
> Ebb audibly along the mountain-wind,
> Then break against the rock, and show behind
> The lowland valleys floating up to crowd
> The sense with beauty. He with forehead bowed
> And humble-lidded eyes, as one inclined
> Before the sovran thought of his own mind,
> And very meek with inspirations proud,
> Takes here his rightful place as poet-priest
> By the high altar, singing praise and prayer
> To the higher Heavens. A noble vision free
> Our Haydon's hand has flung out from the mist !
> No portrait this, with academic air !
> This is the poet and his poetry.

One of the last entries in Haydon's diary, June 18, 1846, —six days before his death, when hard pressed by his chronic embarrassments,—is to this effect: 'I sent . . . Wordsworth, . . . to Miss Barrett, to protect.'

Haydon represented Wordsworth in this picture as if ascending Helvellyn, and composing the sonnet addressed to himself (to Haydon) on his portrait of the Duke of Wellington upon the field of Waterloo. This sonnet was written in 1840, and the portrait represents Wordsworth in his seventy-second year. It was bought at the sale of Haydon's effects by Mr. Cornelius Nicholson of Ventnor, Isle of Wight, in whose possession it now is. It was engraved by Thomas Lupton in 1848, and has been recently lent by Mr. Nicholson for the purpose of being etched for the edition of the poet's works which is being published by Mr. Paterson, Edinburgh., Of this picture by Haydon, Wordsworth wrote to the artist, Jan. 24, 1846: ' I myself think that it is the best likeness—that is, the most characteristic, that·has been done of me.'

XXV.

Mr Francis Bennoch, 5 Tavistock Square, London, tells me that he possesses a portrait of Wordsworth *seated* on Helvellyn, by B. R. Haydon. It is, he says, ' on canvas, about four or five feet square, and was painted on the occasion when the poet was last in London, prior to the artist's death. The head was sketched with infinite care, and is altogether the most characteristic likeness I have ever seen of him. He sat for it two or three times, but it was never finished. The general idea of the scene is clearly indicated, though rough exceedingly. From the elevated point on which Wordsworth is seated, the shimmering on the surface of the lake is seen far beneath, while overhead an eagle is perched on a crag. . . . The head of the poet, however, is the only part really worth preserving.'

XXVI.

In 1844, Mr Henry Inman, an American artist (1802-1846) was commissioned by Professor Reed, of Philadelphia, to paint a likeness of Wordsworth for him. Mr. Inman, while in England, took portraits of Macaulay and Chalmers, as well as of Wordsworth, and amongst his landscapes was one of Rydal Falls. His portrait of Wordsworth belongs to Mr. Reed's widow in Philadelphia. Mr. Yarnall, of Wynndown, Overbrook, Montgomery Co., Pa., wrote to me of this picture, Feb. 14, 1881 : 'Not having seen it for several years, I made a careful examination of it within a few days. It is in perfect condition, evidently represents the poet at his best, and is a singularly clear and beautiful work of art. It is not quite but almost a profile—the face indicating perfect health—the features rather large, the complexion very clear, and the large grey eyes with that far-off look that gaze into the future, which has so often been described. I think the expression of the eyes is the most noticeable characteristic of this picture, of which Mrs. Wordsworth wrote, "In my opinion . . . Mr. Inman's portrait of my husband is the best likeness that has been taken of him." In 1845 Mr. Inman himself wrote as follows of the picture : "His [*i.e.* Wordsworth's] wife, son, and daughter, all declared their approval of my work. He told me he had sat twenty-seven times to various artists, and that my picture was the best likeness of them all."'

Mr. Yarnall wrote, on June 27, 1882 : 'The other portraits are more or less *conventional*—while the true man, Wordsworth as he was, as he lived and moved among the sons of men—not perhaps the ideal poet, but the somewhat rustic dweller among the hills—speaks in the

Inman picture. It is a likeness. It is the man, with the far-off gaze, who wrote the poems. Do you need more than that? To my mind its simplicity is its charm.'

The following is Mr. Inman's letter to Professor Reed, describing his picture of the poet :—

NEW YORK, *June* 23, 1845.

MY DEAR SIR,— . . . Mr. Wordsworth's reception of me and the brief professional and social intercourse I enjoyed with him and his excellent family, furnish me with none but the most pleasing recollections. He seemed to be much gratified with your request for his portrait ; and though his house teems with tokens of regard from his countrymen, he evidently had a peculiar value for this transatlantic compliment to his genius. On a fine morning (I think it was on the 20th of August 1844) I made my first visit to Rydal Mount. I found the house of the poet most delightfully situated—a long, low cottage almost buried among trees and clustering vines. It is built upon a small eminence called Rydal Mount, and behind the house the cliffs of Fairfield Fell rise in picturesque beauty; and from its rocky ravine issues forth a pleasing waterfall or 'Force' called Rydal Falls, whose waters precipitate themselves in two sheets a few hundred yards from the house.

Mr. Wordsworth received me with unaffected courtesy; and my first close and technical observation of him did not fail to note the peculiarly genial smile which lights up a face full of intelligence and good-nature.

I took sittings of him nearly every day, and in the presence of Mrs. Wordsworth and his daughter and a son (a fine-looking young man, holding some Government appointment, I believe, at Carlisle).

It was delightful to mark the close and kindly sympathy

that seemed to bind the aged poet and his wife together. They had known each other from the early period of infancy, having gone to the same school at three years of age. She sat close at his side when the sittings were taken, and the good old man frequently, in the course of a conversation mainly addressed to myself, turned to her with an affectionate inquiry for her opinion respecting the sentiment he had just expressed, and listened with interest to her replies. . . . The poet accompanied me twice on my sketching excursions, and pointed out various points of view, which seemed favourable as subjects for the pencil. In walking over his own grounds, he would pause occasionally to invite my attention to some fine old tree, whose '*verdurous* torso' (that was his phrase) chanced to strike his imagination as worthy of remark. He would point to its gnarled and tortuous trunk with the same gusto with which the statuary might scan a fragment from the chisel of Phidias. His gallery of gems were all from the hand of Nature—the moss-covered rock, the shining cascade, the placid lake, or splintered mountain pinnacle, seemed each to constitute for him a prideful possession—and well they might, for his footstep has during a long life pervaded every marked point of interest in that picturesque region.

When the picture was finished, he said all that should satisfy my anxious desire for a successful termination to my labours. His wife, son, and daughter, all expressed their approval of my work. He told me he had sat twenty-seven times to various artists,[1] and that my picture was the best likeness of them all. Pray excuse this irregular and hasty scrawl, and believe me, your obliged and obedient servant,

H. INMAN.

---

[1] I have only been able to make out twenty-six up to the date in question.

XXVII.

Of the last-mentioned picture Mr. Inman made a replica, which was presented by Mr. Reed to Wordsworth, and which hung at Rydal Mount ever afterwards during the poet's lifetime. It is now, I believe, in the possession of his grandson, the Rev. John Wordsworth, Gosforth Rectory, Carnforth, Cumberland.

XXVIII.

While staying at Rydal Mount, Inman also made a pen-and-ink sketch of the residence and grounds, which he afterwards painted on canvas, introducing the figure of the poet; but he died before the picture was finished. Mr. Yarnall tells me that he has seen both the sketch and the unfinished picture, and that both are very good.

XXIX.

In 1847 a Carlisle artist, Carrick, took a miniature in water colour, some time before he took one of the poet Rogers. It is in the possession of Mr. William Wordsworth; but it is a poor likeness. Mr. Wordsworth told me that the late Lord Bradford had a copy of this picture of Carrick's taken by himself. Wordsworth, writing to Rogers on March 10, 1848, says he forwards a letter from Carrick, requesting to be allowed to take Rogers' portrait, and Wordsworth adds, 'He took my portrait, when I met him not long ago at his native place, Carlisle. If you should comply with his request, I should be gratified, and should deem it an honour to be associated with you in this way.'

XXX.

I now come to four busts of Wordsworth. The precise date of the earliest I have not been able to ascertain. It is one of the most interesting of the busts at Coleorton Hall, near Ashby-de-la-Zouche, in Leicestershire, where Wordsworth was a frequent visitor of the late Sir George Beaumont, and where he spent the winter of 1806 and part of the summer of 1807. Sir George Beaumont, who was himself an artist—and whose picture of Peel Castle in a Storm gave rise to some of the finest stanzas Wordsworth ever wrote—commissioned Chantrey to take the bust, which was certainly executed before the year 1821, and which was engraved for the 8vo edition of the Poems, 1845. Henry Reed tells me that the poet told his father in 1845 that when he sat for this bust he chanted the lines,

But who is he with modest looks, etc.

It has been said that Wordsworth himself wished to be known to posterity by this statue; and some have pronounced it 'a very noble idealisation.' Mr. Thrupp considers it 'too smoothly shaven and chiselled, and without mental expression.' Hazlitt said of it, 'It wants marking traits.' 'The bust flatters his head' (*Noctes Ambrosianæ*, No. 11.). Coleridge remarked of Chantrey's bust that it was 'more like Wordsworth than Wordsworth was like himself.'

XXXI.

Mr. Angus Fletcher (a brother of Lady Richardson of Lancrigg)—who studied under Chantrey, and who executed busts of Mrs. Hemans and Joanna Baillie—also took one of Wordsworth. The year is uncertain, but it was either in

1842, or between that year and 1844. Of this bust, which is at Lancrigg, a niece of the artist writes to me:— 'The Wordsworth head is very like in air and expression, and much more like than the medallion in the Church, although there is no comparing the two artists. But then Mr. Woolner had never seen Wordsworth, whereas my uncle had opportunities of seeing him daily.'

XXXII.

Then there is the medallion just mentioned, designed by Mr. Woolner for Grasmere Church.   In reference to it Mr. Woolner writes :—

29 WELBECK STREET, W.,
January 26, 1882.

DEAR SIR,—I was staying with the Tennysons in the autumn of 1850 at Coniston Lake, and while there was introduced to Mrs. Fletcher of Lancrigg, and her son Angus, Dr. Davy (brother of Sir Humphry), who married a daughter of Mrs. Fletcher, and to other friends of Wordsworth ; and I feel sure it was in the following year, 1851, that I was asked to prepare a design for the tablet which is in Grasmere Church.

Angus Fletcher, Dr. Davy, and Mr. Quillinan (son-in-law of Wordsworth), were the persons who assisted me, and with whom I corresponded on the subject.   Unhappily, they are all now dead, and the affair seems to me more like a circumstance I had read of, than anything that I was ever personally connected with.

One of the plants on the tablet is the lesser celandine ; and I found myself scolded in the *Gardeners' Chronicle* about a year ago for mistaking it for the greater celandine, an entirely gratuitous assumption on the writer's part, as I had no intention of representing the greater, that being a flower wholly unsuited to my purposes.

.   .   .   .   .   .

The tablet was executed for his friends.—Ever truly yours,

THOS. WOOLNER.

XXXIII.

In 1852, Mr. Frederick Thrupp designed the statue which is now in the Baptistery at Westminster Abbey. The model in plaster, from which the marble in the Abbey was done, is at the Crystal Palace, Sydenham. Of this statue Mr. Thrupp writes :—

232 MARYLEBONE ROAD, LONDON, N.W.

DEAR SIR,—In answer to your note, I beg to inform you that I am the sculptor of the statue of Wordsworth which is in the Baptistery of Westminster Abbey. Soon after his death it was proposed and subscribed for by public contributions, brought forward chiefly by Sir John Coleridge. The present Lord Chief-Justice, with Sir W. Boxall and Mr. J. Spedding, were Secretaries and the Executive Committee. There was a general competition among sculptors for the statue. I made four models varied in position, and the present statue was preferred as giving his contemplative character. As regards the clothing of the figure adopted, it is really just what he wore, his ordinary dress, covered by a plaid, such as he was wont to wear, or a cape. A visitor to my study related to me how he, travelling in Switzerland, came to an hotel, in the grounds of which he saw a man sitting, and just as my statue has represented him. On joining the company of the stranger, and conversing with him, he soon discovered that he was talking with William Wordsworth. To obtain a likeness I depended on a cast of his face taken in plaster during his lifetime; also on Haydon's painting and drawing, which perhaps, like all the painter's heads, is rather too strongly featured about the mouth. He habitually thickened the lips, and curled them overmuch.

Chantrey's bust is too smoothly shaven and chiselled, is done in his most mannered style, without mental expression.

Pickersgill's portrait is a mild likeness, and without fervour or power of thought.—I remain, dear Sir, yours faithfully,

FREDERICK THRUPP.

Mr. Thrupp's bust was moulded from a mask of which some casts were taken. Of what he calls the 'unsophisticated mould,' Sir Henry Taylor remarks in his *Autobiography*, p. 60, 'It is admirable as a likeness, in my opinion, and to my knowledge in that of Mrs. Wordsworth; and there is a rough grandeur in it, with which, if it were to be converted into marble, posterity might be content.'

XXXIV.

Mr. Jacob Thompson, a Cumberland artist (born 1806, died 1879), and a friend of Wordsworth, took several drawings connected with the poet—one of Rydal Mount; another, a view from the Mount; a third representing the stone in the grounds of the Mount that had been spared 'at Wordsworth's suit' 'from some rude beauty of its own;' a fourth, a view of the poet's grave in Grasmere Churchyard. 'Later on,' according to the account given by Mr. Llewellynn Jewitt, 'Jacob Thompson designed two illustrative pictures which he himself drew on the wood, and presented ready for engraving to his friend Mr. Hall, for his *Social Notes*. The first of these, commemorative of Wordsworth, bears in the circle an original portrait of the Laureate, and a composition of landscape which includes in the middle distance the home of the poet, Rydal Mount, Rydal Water, in the distance the mountains, and, in the foreground— evidently by the side of the stone, which at his suit was spared—one of the poet's own creations, the simple pastoral of Barbara Lewthwaite and her pet lamb.' The portrait represents the head and bust (clothed) in advanced middle life. It is a three-quarters face, turned to the left.[1]

<h2 style="text-align:center">XXXV.</h2>

Mr. Stephen Pearce, of 54 Queen Anne Street, Cavendish Square, who possesses one of the Haydon drawings of Wordsworth (see No. VII.), writes to me of a life-sized paper profile by Sir George Beaumont, also in his possession. On this is written in Haydon's autograph—

' Wordsworth, a profile sketched and cut out by Sir George Beaumont, when I was going to have a bust of him.'

Mr. Pearce says, ' This profile was evidently first drawn in pencil by Sir George Beaumont, and then cut out with a knife or scissors by Sir George Beaumont also.

' Haydon writes in his Autobiography, April 13th, 1815 : " I had a cast made yesterday of Wordsworth's face." It was on that occasion, I expect, that Sir George Beaumont drew Wordsworth's profile in pencil, and then cut it out ; and Haydon evidently valued it, as he preserved it.

' I do not believe that Haydon had anything whatever to do with the drawing of it, or the cutting out of it. I expect

---

[1] See *Life and Works of Jacob Thompson*, by L. Jewitt, 1882, pp. 102-106.

that Sir George Beaumont was present when Haydon was going to have a cast made of Wordsworth's face ; and, as they were all great friends, Sir George sketched Wordsworth's profile, and then cut it out. Haydon may have suggested improvements to Sir George as he was doing it.'

XXXVI.

This cast of Wordsworth's face, taken by Haydon in 1815, may stand as likeness No. xxxvi. Mr. Thrupp tells me that he made use of it in his construction of the Wordsworth statue, now in the. Baptistery of Westminster Abbey.

XXXVII. AND XXXVIII.

Samuel Lawrence made two very interesting sketches of Wordsworth's head, which now belong to Mr. Dykes Campbell, who writes of them thus :—

I am unable to assign any probable date, but they were evidently made when Wordsworth was an elderly if not quite an old man. They are in charcoal. . . . One day when I was showing the whole of these sketches by Lawrence to Mrs. Proctor, she identified many of the heads, and was particularly struck by the two of Wordsworth, as being so like him, as she remembered him. Lawrence was perhaps the most faithful reproducer of men's features of his day, and he had sketched, as he had known (with more or less intimacy), all the best literary men of the period. Mr. Browning told me, looking at my sketches of Carlyle by Lawrence, that Carlyle had told him more than once that Lawrence was the only man who had ever made a thoroughly satisfactory portrait of him.'

XXXIX.

There have been several attempts, since Wordsworth's death, to produce a likeness of him, founded upon previous portraits and descriptions of his appearance. Whatever their artistic merits, they are of no great value as likenesses. But two exceptions may be made. The first is Mr. Armitage's fresco drawing at University College Hall, Gordon Square, London. This painting was designed to commemorate the late Mr. Henry Crabb Robinson. On one side are grouped his German, and on the other his English friends. Wordsworth is seated with Coleridge, Southey, Lamb, and others near him. Of this fresco Mr. Armitage writes :—

3 HALL ROAD, ST. JOHN'S WOOD,
June 29, 1882.

DEAR SIR,—The likeness of Wordsworth in my mural painting at University Hall was certainly not taken from life, and I really cannot recollect exactly from what portrait of the poet I constructed my version of him.

I fancy my authorities were an engraved portrait of him in a book, and a medallion profile, but I cannot be sure ; and Mr. Edwin Field, who exerted himself to get me the most trustworthy data for my portraits, has been dead many years.—Yours very truly, E. ARMITAGE.

XL.

Another reconstruction of Wordsworth worthy of notice was by Thomas Faed, R.A., in his picture representing Sir Walter Scott and his literary friends at Abbotsford. It was engraved by James Faed, and published by James Keith, Edinburgh, on the 2d of January 1854. This likeness of

Wordsworth is evidently based on the Pickersgill portrait in St. John's College, Cambridge. He is represented as seated in the centre of the group of Sir Walter's friends, between Jeffrey and Lockhart.

XLI.

There was a pen-and-ink sketch of Wordsworth taken by Alfred Croquis, and published by James Farmer, 215 Regent Street, London, to which no date is assigned; but as the poet's name is printed below, 'Wm. Wordsworth, author of the Excursion,' I infer it may belong to some year between 1820 and 1830. It has no great merit.

XLII.

I have heard of a sketch of the head of the poet, taken in Rydal Church, in the year 1845, by a living artist, an eminent portrait-painter; but, as it has been lost for the present, description of it in detail is unnecessary.

I have also seen a portrait—which is said to be original, but is of little value—at Brinsop Court, Herefordshire; and another in a private house at Kendal.

On the whole, I am inclined to think that the best likenesses are two of those by Haydon (Nos. VIII. and XXIV.), the profile by Miss Gillies (No. XXII.), Inman's picture (No. XXVI.), and the busts by Angus Fletcher and by Thrupp (Nos. XXXI. and XXXIII.).

ON WORDSWORTH'S TWO STYLES.

By R. H. HUTTON.

ON WORDSWORTH'S TWO STYLES.[1]

THE essential feature of Wordsworth's Poetry has been described by the greatest of our living critics in language that none of our Society is at all likely to forget. After speaking of Goethe's experience of the Iron Age, Matthew Arnold says of Wordsworth :—

> He, too, upon a wintry clime
> Had fallen, on this iron time
> Of doubts, disputes, distractions, fears.
> He found us when the age had bound
> Our souls in its benumbing round ;
> He spoke, and loosed our heart in tears.
> He laid us as we lay at birth
> On the cool, flowery lap of earth,
> Smiles broke from us, and we had ease ;
> The hills were round us, and the breeze
> Went o'er the sunlit fields again ;
> Our foreheads felt the wind and rain,
> Our youth returned ; for there was shed
> On spirits that had long been dead,
> Spirits dried up and closely furled,
> The freshness of the early world.
> Ah ! since dark days still bring to light
> Man's prudence and man's fiery might,
> Time may restore us in his course
> Goethe's sage mind, and Byron's force ;

---

[1] Read to the Society in May 1882.

> But where will Europe's latter hour
> Again find Wordsworth's healing power?
> Others will teach us how to dare,
> And against fear our breast to steel;
> Others will strengthen us to bear;
> But who, ah! who will make us feel?
> The cloud of mortal destiny,
> Others will front it fearlessly,
> But who, like him, will put it by?

I think this is rightly chosen as the characteristic of Wordsworth's poetry, that he puts by for us the 'cloud of mortal destiny,' that he restores us the 'freshness of the early world;' that he gives us back the magic circle of the hills, makes us feel the breath of the wind and the coolness of the rain upon our foreheads; and touches both the vigour of youth, and the peace of age, with more of that serene lustre which dew gives to the flowers, than any other poet. But the same great critic has assured us that, properly speaking, Wordsworth has no style, 'no assured poetic style of his own;' and this though he freely admits that 'it is style, and the elevation given by style, which chiefly makes the effectiveness of *Laodamia*. For my part, I should have said that as to Wordsworth's blank verse Mr. Arnold is right; that in his blank verse Wordsworth is so dependent on his matter, that he runs through almost all styles, good and bad. But in his rhymed verse, I should have preferred to say—though the admission may, perhaps, be used on behalf of Mr. Arnold's drift, that Wordsworth had two distinct styles—the style of his youth and the style of his age —the elastic style of fresh energy, born of his long devotion to Nature's own rhythms, and the style of gracious and stately feeling, born of his benignity, of his deep-set, calm sympathy with human feeling,—the style of *The Solitary*

Reaper, and the style of *Devotional Incitements.*   Surely the style of the verse,

> Alone she cuts, and binds the grain,
> And sings a melancholy strain ;
> Oh ! listen, for the vale profound
> Is overflowing with the sound,

is Wordsworth's, in as true a sense as the style of

> After life's fitful fever, he sleeps well,

is Shakespeare's.   Or again, is there not the personal stamp of Wordsworth indelibly imprinted on every line in the *Song at the Feast of Brougham Castle?*—

> No thoughts hath he but thoughts that pass
> Light as the wind along the grass !
> Can this be he who hither came
> In secret, like a smothered flame ?

Less personal, certainly less indelibly branded with Wordsworth's hand, is what I call the later style.   Still, I think such lines as these, in the *Devotional Incitements*, describing the comparatively slight power of Art, when compared with Nature, to excite reverence, have on them an indelible impress of Wordsworth's developed genius, in its gracious, pure, and serene solemnity :

> The priests are from their altars thrust ;
> Temples are levelled with the dust ;
> And solemn rites and awful forms
> Founder amid fanatic storms.
> Yet evermore, through years renewed
> In undisturbed vicissitude
> Of seasons balancing their flight
> On the swift wings of day and night,
> Kind Nature keeps a heavenly door
> Wide open for the scattered poor.

E

The most characteristic earlier and the most characteristic later style are alike in the limpid coolness of their effect,—the effect in the earlier style of bubbling water, in the later of morning dew.   Both alike lay the dust, and take us out of the fret of life, and restore the truth to feeling, and cast over the vision of the universe

> The image of a poet's heart,
> How bright, how solemn, how serene !

But the earlier and the later styles, even in their best specimens, do this in very different ways, while the inferior specimens of each are marked by very different faults.   As models of the two styles at their best, I would take, for instance, *The Daffodils* for the earlier, and *The Primrose of the Rock* for the later; *Yarrow Unvisited* for the earlier, and *Yarrow Revisited* for the later; *The Leech-gatherer* (or as Wordsworth rather cumbrously called it, *Resolution and Independence*) for the earlier, and *Laodamia* for the later style.   The chief differences between the two styles seem to me these :—That objective fact, especially when appealing to the sense of vision, sometimes utterly bald and trivial, though often very commanding in its effects, plays so much larger a part in the earlier than the later; that the earlier, when it reaches its mark at all, has a pure elasticity, a passionless buoyancy (passionless, I mean, in the sense of being devoid of the hotter passions) in it, almost unique in poetry; and lastly, that in the greater of the earlier pieces emotion is uniformly suggested rather than expressed, or, if I may be allowed the paradox, expressed by reticence, by the jealous parsimony of a half-voluntary, half-involuntary reserve.   In the later style, on the other hand, objective fact is much less prominent; bald moralities tend to take the place of bald realities; and though the buoyancy is much diminished, emotion is much more freely, frankly and tenderly expressed, so that there is often in it a richness and mellowness of effect quite foreign to Wordsworth's earlier mood. The ruggedness of the earlier style is what one may call one of knots and flinty protuberances; there is an occasional bleakness about it; the passion with which passion is kept down, though often exalted, is sometimes hard; there is a scorn of sweetness, an excess of simplicity, which frequently touches *simplesse*; and though the depth of feeling which is dammed up makes its surging voice heard in the happier instances, yet in the less happy instances the success of the operation is only too great, and leaves us oppressed with a sense of unexpected blankness.

In the later style, all this is changed. The keenness of sheer objective vision is still felt, but is less dominant; while emotion, no longer restrained, flows naturally, and with a sweet and tender lustre shining upon it, into musical expression. I may illustrate the difference between the two styles so far as regards the degrees of their direct expressiveness, by a characteristic change which Wordsworth made in his later editions in the beautiful poem entitled *The Fountain*. The poet, it will be remembered, there remonstrates with the schoolmaster, whom he calls Matthew, for speaking of himself as unloved in his old age:

> ' Now both himself and me he wrongs,
> The man who thus complains !
> I live and sing my idle songs
> Upon these happy plains ;
>
> And, Matthew, for thy children dead
> I 'll be a son to thee.'
> At this he grasped his hands, and said,
> ' Alas, that cannot be ! '

In the later editions, Wordsworth altered this to—

> At this he grasped my hand, and said
> ' Alas, that cannot be ! '

The earlier reading looks like hard fact, and no doubt sounds a little rough and abrupt. But I feel pretty sure, not only that the earlier version expressed the truth as it was present to Wordsworth's inner eye when he wrote the poem, but that it agreed better with the mood of those earlier years, when the old man's wringing of his own hands, in a sort of passion of protest against the notion that any one could take the place of his lost child, would have seemed much more natural and dignified to Wordsworth, than the mere kindly expression of grateful feeling for which he subsequently exchanged it.

Now, I will go a little into detail. Contrast the power, which is very marked in both cases, of the poem on *The Daffodils*, with that on *The Primrose of the Rock*. You all know the wonderful buoyancy of that poem on the daffodils, —the reticent passion with which the poet's delight is expressed, not by dwelling on feeling, but by selecting as a fit comparison to that 'crowd' and 'host' of golden daffodils the impression produced on the eye by the continuousness of 'the stars that shine and sparkle in the Milky Way,' the effect of wind, and of the exultation which wind produces, in the lines,

> Ten thousand saw I at a glance,
> Tossing their heads in sprightly dance ;

and in the rivalry suggested between them and the waves :

> The waves beside them danced, but they
> Outdid the sparkling waves in glee.

You all know the exquisite simplicity of the conclusion when the poet tells us that as often as they recur to his mind, and

> —— flash upon that inward eye
> Which is the bliss of solitude,

his heart ' with pleasure fills, and dances with the daffodils.'

The great beauty of that poem is its wonderful buoyancy, its purely objective way of conveying that buoyancy, and the extraordinary vividness with which 'the lonely rapture of lonely minds' is stamped upon the whole poem, which is dated 1804. Now turn to *The Primrose of the Rock*, which was written twenty-seven years later, in 1831. We find the style altogether móre ideal,—reality counts for less, symbol for more. There is far less elasticity, far less exultant buoyancy here, and yet a grander and more stately movement. The *reserve* of power has almost disappeared; but there is a graciousness absent before, and the noble strength of the last verse is most gentle strength :

> A Rock there is whose homely front
>   The passing traveller slights ;
> Yet there the glow-worms hang their lamps,
>   Like stars, at various heights ;
> And one coy Primrose to that Rock
>   The vernal breeze invites.
>
> What hideous warfare hath been waged,
>   What kingdoms overthrown,
> Since first I spied that Primrose-tuft
>   And marked it for my own ;
> A lasting link in Nature's chain,
>   From highest heaven let down !
>
> The flowers, still faithful to the stems,
>   Their fellowship renew ;

> The stems are faithful to the root,
>   That worketh out of view ;
> And to the rock the root adheres
>   In every fibre true.
>
> Close clings to earth the living rock,
>   Though threatening still to fall ;
> The earth is constant in her sphere ;
>   And God upholds them all :
> So blooms this lonely Plant, nor dreads
>   Her annual funeral.

It will be observed at once that in *The Daffodils* there is no attempt to explain the delight which the gay spectacle raised in the poet's heart.   He exults in the spectacle itself, and reproduces it continually in memory.   The wind in his style blows as the wind blows in *The Daffodils*, with a sort of physical rapture.   In the later poem, the symbol is every-thing.   The mind pours itself forth fully in reflective gratitude, as it glances at the moral overthrow which the humble primrose of the rock,—and many things of human mould as humble and faithful as the primrose of the rock,— has outlived.   In point of mere expression, I should call the later poem the more perfect of the two.   The enjoyment of the first lies in the intensity of the feeling which it some-how indicates, without expressing, of which it merely hints the force by its eager and springy movement.

Now, take the earliest and latest Yarrow, and note the same difference.   How swift, and bare, and rapid, like the stream itself, as Wordsworth chooses to describe it :

> A river bare
> That glides the dark hills under,

is the verse in which he depreciates the reality, in order to enhance the treasure of an unverified vision !   Yarrow is represented as a fit home chiefly for the country-people who go to market at Selkirk, and for the wild birds and ground game which fly and burrow beside it:

> Let Yarrow folk frae Selkirk town,
> Who have been buying, selling,
> Go back to Yarrow, 'tis their own ;
> Each maiden to her dwelling !
> On Yarrow's banks let herons feed,
> Hares couch, and rabbits burrow !
> But we will downward with the Tweed,
> Nor turn aside to Yarrow.

The charm of that is the charm of a perfectly bare representation of a perfectly simple scene, enhanced by the suggestion which lurks everywhere that the common facts of life are pretty certain to seem common, unless, indeed, you bring an imagination strong enough to transfigure them; while if you do, the poet insists that the true magic is in you, and not in the scene, since it is independent of the actual vision on which the mind seems to feed. The beauty of the verse is almost all confined to the thought itself; the only touch of extraneous beauty is the careless suggestion that 'the swan on still St. Mary's Lake' may, if it pleases, 'float double, swan and shadow,' without tempting them aside to see it ; and even that seems put in only to suggest, as it were, how greatly the power of vividly imagining even such a sight as this exceeds in significance the power which the mere eyes possess of discerning loveliness even where they have taken in the forms and colours which ought to suggest it. The whole beauty of the verses is in their bareness. The poem may be said to have for its very subject the economy of imaginative force, the wantonness of poetic prodigality, the duty of retaining in the heart reserves of potential and meditative joy, on which you refuse to draw all you might draw of actual delight :

> Be Yarrow stream unseen, unknown !
>   It must, or we shall rue it ;
> We have a vision of our own ;
>   Ah ! why should we undo it ?

And the style corresponds to the thought ; it is the style of one who exults in holding over, and being strong and buoyant enough to hold over, a promised imaginative joy. A certain ascetic radiance,—if the paradox be permissible, —a manly jubilation in being rich enough to sacrifice an expected delight, makes the style sinewy, rapid, youthful, and yet careful in its youthfulness, as jealous of redundancy as it is firm and elastic.   This was written in 1803.   Turn to *Yarrow Revisited,* which was written twenty-eight years later, in 1831.   The rhythm is the same, but how different the movement; how much sweeter and slower, how many more the syllables on which you must dwell, sometimes with what the ear admits to be an over-emphasis; how much richer the music, when it is music ; how much more hesitating, not to say vacillating, the reflection ; and how the versification itself renders all this, with its sedate pauses, —pauses, to use another poet's fine expression, 'as if memory had wept,'—its amplitude of tender feeling, its lingerings over sweet colours, its anxious desire to find compensations for the buoyancy of youth in wise reflection !—

> ·Once more, by Newark's castle gate,
>   Long left without a warder,
> I stood, looked, listened, and with thee,
>   Great Minstrel of the Border !

Grave thoughts ruled wide on that sweet day,
  Their dignity installing
In gentle bosoms, while sere leaves
  Were on the bough, or falling;
But breezes played, and sunshine gleamed—
  The forest to embolden;
Reddened the fiery hues, and shot
  Transparence through the golden.

For busy thoughts the stream flowed on
  In foamy agitation;
And slept in many a crystal pool
  For quiet contemplation:
No public and no private care
  The free-born mind enthralling,
We made a day of happy hours,
  Our happy days recalling.

.   .   .   .   .   .

And if, as Yarrow, through the woods
  And down the meadow ranging,
Did meet us with unaltered face,
  While we were changed or changing;
If, *then*, some natural shadows spread
  Our inward prospect over,
The soul's deep valley was not slow
  Its brightness to recover.

The expression there is richer, freer, more mellow; but the
reserve force is spent; all the wealth of the moment—and
perhaps something more than the wealth of the moment,
something which was not wealth, though mistaken for it—
was poured out.   One cannot but feel now and again that,
as Sir Walter said of his aged harper,

His trembling hand had lost the ease
Which marks security to please,
And scenes long past of joy and pain
Came wildering o'er his aged brain.

Mr. Arnold places almost all the really first-rate work of Wordsworth in the decade between the years 1798 and 1808. I think he is right here. But I should put Wordsworth's highest perfection of style much nearer the later date than the earlier; at least if, as I hold, the *Song at the Feast of Brougham Castle* touches the very highest point which he ever reached. *The Leech-gatherer* was written in the same year, though its workmanship is not nearly so perfect. Let me contrast its style with that of *Laodamia*, of which the subject is closely analogous, and which was written only seven years later, in 1814; though these seven years mark, as it appears to me, a very great transformation of style. Both poems treat of Wordsworth's favourite theme,—the strength which the human heart has, or ought to have, to contain itself in adverse circumstances, and the spurious character of that claim of mere emotion to command us by which we are so often led astray. *The Leech-gatherer* has much less of buoyancy than the earlier poems, and something here and there of the stateliness of the later style, especially in the noble verse :

> I thought of Chatterton, the marvellous Boy,
> The sleepless Soul that perished in his pride ;
> Of him who walked in glory and in joy,
> Following his plough along the mountain-side ;
> By our own spirits are we deified :
> We Poets in our youth begin in gladness ;
> But thereof come in the end despondency and madness.

But on the whole, the poem is certainly marked by that emphatic visual imagination, that delight in the power of the eye, that strength of reserve, that occasional stiffness of feeling, and that immense rapture of reverie, which characterise the earlier period, though it wants the more rapid and buoyant movement of that period. Take the wonderful description of *The Leech-gatherer* himself:

> Himself he propped, limbs, body, and pale face,
> Upon a long grey staff of shaven wood :
> And still, as I drew near with gentle pace,
> Upon the margin of that moorish flood
> Motionless as a cloud the old Man stood,
> That heareth not the loud winds when they call ;
> And moveth all together, if it move at all.

Or take the description of the reverie into which the old man's words threw Wordsworth :

> The old Man still stood talking by my side ;
> But now his voice to me was like a stream
> Scarce heard ; nor word from word could I divide ;
> And the whole body of the Man did seem
> Like one whom I had met with in a dream ;
> Or like a man from some far region sent,
> To give me human strength, by apt admonishment.

In turning to *Laodamia*, we see that a great change of style—a great relaxation of the high tension of the earlier power—and with it a great increase in grace and sweetness has come. When Protesilaus announces that his death was due to his having offered up his own life for the success of the Greek host, by leaping first to the strand where it was decreed that the first comer should perish, Laodamia replies :

> ' Supreme of Heroes—bravest, noblest, best !
> Thy matchless courage I bewail no more,
> Which then, when tens of thousands were deprest
> By doubt, propelled thee to the fatal shore ;
> Thou found'st—and I forgive thee—here thou art—
> A nobler counsellor than my poor heart.

' But thou, though capable of sternest deed,
Wert kind as resolute, and good as brave ;
And he, whose power restores thee, hath decreed
Thou shouldst elude the malice of the grave :
Redundant are thy locks, thy lips as fair
As when their breath enriched Thessalian air.

' No Spectre greets me,—no vain Shadow this ;
Come, blooming Hero, place thee by my side !
Give, on this well-known couch, one nuptial kiss
To me, this day, a second time thy bride ! '
Jove frowned in heaven, the conscious Parcae threw
Upon those roseate lips a Stygian hue.

' This visage tells thee that my doom is past :
Nor should the change be mourn'd, even if the joys
Of sense were able to return as fast
And surely as they vanish.   Earth destroys
Those raptures duly—Erebus disdains :
Calm pleasures there abide—majestic pains.

' Be taught, O faithful Consort, to contrôl
Rebellious passion : for the Gods approve
The depth, and not the tumult, of the soul ;
A fervent, not ungovernable love.
Thy transports moderate, and meekly mourn
When I depart, for brief is my sojourn.'

There is certainly an air of classic majesty and a richness
of colour about this which contrasts curiously with the
strong sketch of the lonely Leech-gatherer, though there
seems to me a fitness in the fact that the style of the poem
which paints the excess of unregulated feeling is full of
almost artificial grace, while the style of the poem which
paints the humble self-reliance of desolate fortitude is
for the most part cast in the mould of a bare and almost
bleak dignity.

But I must come to an end. The later style has, I think, this advantage over the earlier, that where its subject is equally fine,—which, as I admit, it often is not,—the workmanship is far more complete, often almost of crystal beauty, and without the blots, the baldness, the dead-wood, which almost all Wordsworth's earlier works exhibit. Where, for instance, in all the range of poetry, shall we find a more crystal piece of workmanship than the sonnet—written I think, as late as 1827, and addressed to Lady Beaumont in her seventieth year—with which I may conclude this paper :—

> Such age, how beautiful ! O Lady bright,
> Whose mortal lineaments seem all refined
> By favouring Nature and a saintly mind
> To something purer and more exquisite
> Than flesh and blood ; whene'er thou meet'st my sight,
> When I behold thy blanched unwithered cheek,
> Thy temples fringed with locks of gleaming white,
> And head that droops because the soul is meek,
> Thee with the welcome Snowdrop I compare ;
> That child of winter, prompting thoughts that climb
> From desolation toward the genial prime ;
> Or with the Moon conquering earth's misty air,
> And filling more and more with crystal light,
> As pensive Evening deepens into night.

REMINISCENCES OF WORDSWORTH AMONG THE PEASANTRY OF WESTMORELAND

By H. D. RAWNSLEY.

REMINISCENCES OF WORDSWORTH AMONG THE PEASANTRY OF WESTMORELAND.[1]

HAVING grown up in the immediate vicinity of the present Poet-Laureate's old home in Lincolnshire, I had been struck with the swiftness with which,

> As year by year the labourer tills
> His wonted glebe, or lops the glades,

the memories of the poet of the Somersby Wold had faded 'from off the circle of the hills.' I had been astonished to note how little real interest was taken in him or his fame, and how seldom his works were met with in the houses of the rich or poor in the very neighbourhood.

It was natural that, coming to reside in the lake country, I should endeavour to find out what of Wordsworth's memory among the men of the Dales still lingered on,—how far he was still a moving presence among them,—how far his works had made their way into the cottages and farm-houses of the valleys.

But if a certain love of the humorous induced me to enter into or follow up conversations with the few still living among the peasants who were in the habit of seeing Wordsworth in the flesh, there was also a genuine wish to endeavour to find out how far the race of Westmoreland and Cumberland farm-folk—the 'Matthews' and the 'Michaels'

---

of the poet as described by him—were real or fancy pictures, or how far the characters of the dalesmen had been altered in any remarkable manner by tourist influences during the thirty-two years that have passed since the aged poet was laid to rest.

For notwithstanding the fact that Mr. Ruskin, writing in 1876, had said 'that the Border peasantry (painted with absolute fidelity by Scott and Wordsworth)' are, as hitherto, a scarcely injured race,—that in his fields at Coniston he had men who might have fought with Henry v. at Agincourt without being distinguished. from any of his knights,—that he could take his tradesmen's word for a thousand pounds, and need never latch his garden gate, nor fear molestation in wood or on moor, for his girl guests ; the more one went about seeking for such good life and manners and simple piety as Wordsworth knew and described in fell-side homes, or such generous unselfishness and nobility among the Dale farmers as would seem to have been contemporaries of the poet, the more one was disappointed to find a characteristic something faded away, and a certain beauty vanished that the simple retirement of old valley-days of fifty years ago gave to the men amongst whom Wordsworth lived. The strangers with their gifts of gold, their vulgarity, and their requirements, have much to answer for in the matter. But it is true that the decent exterior, the shrewd wit, and the manly independence and natural knightliness of the men of the soil is to a large extent responsible for raising expectations of nobility of life and morals, the expectation of which would be justified by no other peasant class in England, and which, by raising an unfair standard for comparison, ought to be prepared for some disappointment.

One's walks and talks with the few who remember Wordsworth, or *Wudsworth* as they always call him, have done little to find out more than the impression that they as outsiders formed of him, but it allowed one to grasp by the hand a few of those natural noblemen who by their presence still give testimony to a time and a race of men and women fast fading away, and in need already of the immortality of lofty tradition that Wordsworth has accorded them.

While these few of his still living peasant contemporaries show us the sort of atmosphere of severely simple life, hand-in-hand with a 'joy in widest commonalty spread,' that made some of Wordsworth's poems possible, I think the facts that they seem to establish of Wordsworth's seclusion, and the distance he seems to have kept from them and their cottage homes, not a little interesting. For they point to the suggestion that the poet lived so separate and apart from them, so seldom entered the 'huts where poor men lie,' or mixed with the fell-side folk at their sports and junketings, that he was enabled, in his swift selection and appreciation of the good and pure and true in their surroundings, to forget, quite honestly perhaps, the faults of the people among whom he lived.

Be that as it may, this paper aims at establishing no new doctrine or view about the man, but at simply putting on record reminiscences still in the minds of some of those who often saw him, knew his fancies and his ways (as only servants know the fancies and ways of their master), and spoke with him sixty, fifty, or forty years ago.

These reminiscences may seem worthless to many, just from the fact that they are the words of outsiders. They will seem to others of interest for that very reason. And this much must be said, they are trustworthy records from true mouths. The native love of *truth*, or perhaps better,

the native *dislike ever to hazard suggestion*, or to speak
without book, is guarantee for that. To ask questions in
Westmoreland is the reverse of asking them of Syrian fella-
heen and Egyptian dragomans. The Cumberland mind is
not inventive, nor swift to anticipate the answer you wish,
and one is always brought up sharp with—

'Naay, I wud na speak to that neäther :'

'Naay, I 'se not certain to owt o' that :'

'Might bea, but not to my knowledge howivver :'

'It 's na good my saaing I kna that, when I doant, now
then,'—and so on.

Twenty summers had let the daisies blossom round Wordsworth's grave, when, in 1870, I heard of and saw the old
lady who had once been in service at Rydal Mount, and was
now a lodging-house keeper at Grasmere. She shall be called
as first witness, but what kind of practical and unimaginative
mind she had may be gathered from the following anecdote.
My sister came in from a late evening walk, and said, 'O
Mrs. D——, have you seen the wonderful sunset?' The good
lady turned sharply round, and drawing herself to her full
height, as if mortally offended, answered, ' No, Miss R——,
I 'm a tidy cook, I know, and, "they say," a decentish
body for a landlady, and sic-like, but I doant knaw nothing
about sunsets or them sort of things, they 've never been in
my line.' Her reminiscence of Wordsworth was as worthy
of tradition as it was explanatory, from her point of view,
of the method in which Wordsworth composed, and was
helped in his labours by his enthusiastic sister.

' Well you know,' were her words, ' Mr. Wordsworth
went humming and booing about, and she, Miss Dorothy,
kept close behint him, and she picked up the bits as he let
'em fall, and tak 'em down, and put 'em together on paper

for him. And you may,' continued the good dame, 'be
very well sure as how she didn't understand nor make sense
out of 'em, and I doubt that he [Wordsworth] didn't know
much about them either himself, but, howivver, there's a
great many folk as do, I dare say.'

And here it will be well to put in a caution. The
vernacular of the Lake district must be understood a little, or
wrong impressions would be got of the people's memory of
the bard. 'What was Mr. Wordsworth like in personal
appearance?' I once asked of an old retainer, who still
lives not far from Rydal Mount. ' He was a ugly-faäced man,
and a meän liver,' was the answer. And when he continued,
'Ay, and he was a deäl upo' the road, ye kna,' one might
have been pardoned if one had concluded that the Lake
poet was a sort of wild man of the woods, an ugly customer
of desperate life, or highwayman of vagrant habit. All that
was really meant when translated was, that he was a man of
marked features, and led a very simple life in matters of
food and raiment.

The next witness I shall call to speak of the poet is none
other than the lad whose wont it was to serve the Rydal
Mount kitchen with meat, week in week out, in the poet's
days. A grey-haired man himself now, his chiefest memory
of Wordsworth is that of a tall man, 'rather a fineish man in
build, with a bit of a stoop, and a deal of grey hair upon
his heäd.'

In some of the days of close analysis that are coming upon
us, poets will perhaps be found to have depended for the
particular colour of their poems, or turns and cast of
thought, upon the kind of food—vegetable or animal—that
they mostly subsisted on. It will be well to chronicle the
fact that Wordsworth had an antipathy to veal, but was very

partial to legs,—'lived on legs, you may almost say.' But as my friend added, almost in the same breath, that the poet was 'a greät walker i' the vaäles,' he had uttered unconsciously a double truth.

The next fact that remained clear and distinct in the butcher's mind was, that whenever you met the poet he was sure to be ' quite [pronounced *white*] pläinly dressed.' Sometimes in a round blue cloak. Sometimes wearing a big wideawake, or a bit of an old boxer, but plainly dressed, almost 'poorly dressed, ya mun saay, at the best o' times.' ' But for aw that, he was quite an object man,' he added, meaning that there was a dignity that needed no dressing to set it off, I suppose, in the poet's mien and manner. It was interesting to hear, too, how different Wordsworth had seemed in his grave silent way of passing children without a word, from ' li'le Hartley Coleridge,' with his constant salutation, uncertain gait, his head on one side, his walking-stick suddenly shouldered, and then his frantic little rushes along the road, between the pauses of his thought. ' Many 's the time,' said my friend, ' that me and my sister has run ourselves intil a lather to git clear fra Hartley, for we allays thowt, ya kna, when he started running he was efter us. But as fur Mister Wudsworth, he 'd pass you, same as if ya was nobbut a stoan. He niver cared for children, however ; ya may be certain of that, for didn't I have to pass him four times in t' week, up to the door wi' meat? And he niver oncst said owt. Ye 're well aware if he 'd been fond of children he 'ud 'a spoke.'

But Mrs. Wordsworth had made her impressions too on the youth's mind. ' As for Mrs. Wordsworth, she was pläiner in her ways than he was. The pläinest woman in these parts, for all the world the bettermer part of an old farm-wife.' He intended nothing disrespectful by this simile, he only wished to say she was simple in manner and dress. But if Mrs. Wordsworth's personal appearance had impressed him, her powers of housekeeping had impressed him more. She was very persevering, and 'ter'ble particular in her accounts, never allowed you an inch in the butching-book.' It did not raise one's opinion of Lake country butcher morality to find this a grievance, but the man as he spoke seemed to think a little sorely of those old-fashioned days, when mistresses, not cooks, took supervision of the household economies.

I bade my friend good-day, and the last words I heard were, 'But Mr. Wudsworth *was quite an object man, mind ye.'*

It is an easy transition from butcher-boy to gardener's lad, and I will now detail a conversation I had with one who, in this latter capacity at Rydal Mount, saw the poet daily for some years.

. It was Easter Monday, and I knew that the one-time gardener's lad at Rydal Mount had grown into a vale-renowned keeper of a vale-renowned beerhouse. I had doubts as to calling on this particular day, for Easter Monday and beer go much together in our Lake country. But I was half reassured by a friend who said, 'Well, he gets drunk three times a day, but takes the air between whiles, and if you catch him airing he will be very civil, but it's a bad day to find him sober, this.' I explained that I wanted to talk with him of old Wordsworthian days. 'Aw, it's Wudsworth you're a gaan to see about? If that's the game, you're reet enuff, for, drunk or sober, he can crack away a deal upon Mr. Wudsworth. An' I'se not so varry seuer but what he's best drunk a li'le bit.' I was reassured, and soon found myself sitting on the stone ale-bench outside the public-house, the best of friends with a man who had been apparently grossly libelled—for he was as sober as a judge—and whose eye fairly twinkled as he spoke of the Rydal garden days.

'You see, blessed barn, it's a lock o' daäys sin', but I remember them daäys, for I was put by my master to the Rydal Mount as gardener-boy to keep me fra bad waays. And I remember one John Wudsworth, Mr. Wudsworth's nevi, parson he was, dëad, like enough, afore this. Well, he was stayin' there along o' his missus, first week as I was boy there, and I was ter'ble curious, and was like enough to hev bin drowned, for they had a bath, filled regular o' nights, up above, ya kna, with a sort of curtainment all round it. And blowed if I didn't watch butler fill it, and then goa in and pull string, and down came watter, and I was 'maazed as owt, and I screamed, and Mr. John come and fun' me, and saäved my life. Eh, blessed barn, them was daäys long sin'.'

I asked whether Mr. Wordsworth was much thought of. He replied, 'Latterly, but we thowt li'le enough of him. He was nowt to li'le Hartley. Li'le Hartley was a philosopher, you see; Wudsworth was a poet. Ter'ble girt difference betwixt them two ways, ye kna.' I asked whether he had ever found that poems of Mr. Wordsworth were read in the cottages, whether he had read them himself. 'Well, you see, blessed barn, there's pomes and pomes, and Wudsworth's was not for sich as us. I never did see his pomes—not as I can speak to in any man's house in these parts, but,' he added, 'ye kna there's bits in the paapers fra time to time bearing his naame.'

This unpopularity of Wordsworth's poems among the peasantry was strangely corroborated that very same day

by an old man whom I met on the road, who said he had
often seen the poet, and had once been present and heard
him make a long speech, and that was at the laying of the
foundation of Boys' Schoolroom at Bowness, which was
built by one Mr. Bolton of Storrs Hall.

On that occasion Mr. 'Wudsworth talked long and weel
enough,' and he remembered that he 'had put a pome he
had written into a bottle wi' some coins in the hollow of
the foundation-stone.'

I asked him whether he had ever seen or read any of the
poet's works, and he had answered, 'No, not likely; for
Wudsworth wasn't a man as wrote on separate bits, saäme
as Hartley Coleridge, and was niver a frequenter of public-
houses, or owt of that sort.'   But he added, 'He was a good
writer, he supposed, and he was a man folks thowt a deal
of in the dale : he was such a well-meaning, decent, quiet
man.'

But to return to my host at the public. Wordsworth, in
his opinion, was not fond of children, nor animals.   He
would come round the garden, but never 'say nowt.' Sometimes, but this was seldom, he would say, 'Oh! you 're
planting peas?' or, 'Where are you setting onions?' but
only as a master would ask a question of a servant.   He
had, he said, never seen him out of temper once, neither in
the garden, nor when he was along o' Miss Dorothy in her
invalid chair.   But he added, 'What went on in the house
I can't speak to ;' meaning that as an outdoor servant he
had no sufficiently accurate knowledge of the indoor life to
warrant his speaking of it.   Wordsworth was not an early
riser, had no particular flower he was fondest of that he
could speak to ; never was heard to sing or whistle a tune
in his life; there was no two words about that, 'though he
bummed a deal ;'—of this more presently.

' He was a plain man, plainly dressed, and so was she, ya mun kna.   But eh, blessed barn ! he was fond o' his own childer, and fond o' Dorothy, especially when she was faculty strucken, poor thing ; and as for his wife, there was noa two words about their being truly companionable ; and Wudsworth was a silent man wi'out a doubt, but he was not aboon bein' tender and quite *monstrable* [demonstrative] at times in his own family.'

I asked about Mr. Wordsworth's powers of observation. Had he noticed in his garden walks how he stooped down and took this or that flower, or smelt this or that herb? (I have heard since that the poet's sense of smell was limited.)   ' Na, he wadna speak to that, but Mr. Wudsworth was what you might call a vara practical-eyed man, a man as seemed to see aw that was stirrin'.'

Perhaps the most interesting bit of information I obtained, before our pleasant chat was at an end, was a description of the way in which the poet composed on the grass terrace at Rydal Mount.   'Eh ! blessed barn,' my informant continued, ' I think I can see him at it now. He was ter'ble thrang with visitors and folks, you mun kna, at times, but if he could git away from them for a spell, he was out upon his gres walk ; and then he would set his head a bit forward, and put his hands behint his back. And then he would start a bumming, and it was bum, bum, bum, stop ; then bum, bum, bum reet down till t'other end, and then he 'd set down and git a bit o' paper out and write a bit ; and then he git up, and bum, bum, bum, and goa on bumming for long enough right down and back agean.   I suppose, ye kna, the bumming helped him out a bit.   However, his lips was always goan' whoale time he was upon the gres walk.   He was a kind mon, there 's no two words about that : if any one was sick i' the plaace, he wad be off to see til 'em.'

And so ended my Easter Monday talk with the poet's quondam gardener's boy, the now typical beerhouse-keeper, who is half pleased, half proud, to remember his old master in such service as he rendered him, in the days when it was judged that to keep a boy out of mischief and from bad company it was advisable to get him a place at Rydal Mount.

I must ask you next to take a seat with me in a waller's cottage. If tea and bread and butter is offered, you had better take it also, it is almost sure to be pressed upon you, and it is of the best. I will be interrogator, only by way of introduction saying, that our host is a splendid type of the real Westmoreland gentleman labourer, who was in his days a wrestler too, and whose occupation at the building of *Foxhow* and *Fiddler's Farm* in the Rydal Valley, often allowed him to see the poet in old times.

'Well, George, what sort o' a man in personal appearance was Mr. Wordsworth ?'

'He was what you might ca' a ugly man,—mak of John Rigg much,—much about same height, 6 feet or 6 feet 2,— smaller, but deal rougher in the face.'

I knew John Rigg by sight, and can fancy from the pictures of the poet that the likeness is striking in the brow and profile.

'But he was,' continued George, 'numbledy in t' kneas, walked numbledy, ye kna, but that might o' wussened with age.' In George's mind age accounted for most of the peculiarities he had noticed in the poet, but George's memory could go back fifty years, and he ought to have remembered Wordsworth as hale and hearty. 'He wozn't a man as said a deal to common folk. But he talked a deal to hissen. I often seead his lip sa gaäin', and he 'd a deal o' mumblin' to hissel, and 'ud stop short and be a lookin' down upo' the ground, as if he was in a thinkin' waäy. But that might ha' growed on him wi' age, an' aw, ye kna.'

How true, thought I, must have been the poet's knowledge of himself!

> And who is he with modest looks,
>   And clad in sober russet gown?
> He murmurs by the running brooks,
>   A music sweeter than their own ;
> He is retired as noontide dew,
> Or fountain in a noonday grove.

And indeed, in all the reminiscences I have obtained among the peasantry, these lines force themselves upon one as corroborated by their evidence.

'He' [Mr. Wordsworth], continued George, 'was a deal upo' the road, would goa most days to L'Ambleside in his cloak and umbrella, and in later times folks would stare and gaum to see him pass, not that we thowt much to him hereabouts, but they was straängers, ye see.'

It is curious, though natural, perhaps, to find a sort of disbelief among the natives in the poet's greatness, owing somewhat to the fact that it 'was straängers as set such store by him.' They distrust strangers still, almost as much as they did in old Border-times.

But the secret of Wordsworth's unpopularity with the dalesmen seems to have been that he was shy and retired, and not one who mixed freely or talked much with them.

'We woz,' said George, 'noan of us very fond on 'im ;

eh, dear! quite a different man from li'le Hartley. He wozn't a man as was very compannable, ye kna. He was fond o' stones and mortar, though,' he added. 'It was in '48, year of revolution, one Frost, they ca'd him rebellious (Monmouth), and a doment in Ireland. I mind we was at wuk at Fiddler's Farm, and Muster Wudsworth 'ud come down most days, and he sed "it sud be ca'èd Model Farm," and so it was.'

Speaking of Foxhow, he said, 'He and the Doctor [Doctor Arnold], you 've happen heard tell o' the Doctor,— well, he and the Doctor was much i' one another's company; and Wudsworth was a great un for chimleys, had summut to say in the making of a deal of 'em hereabout. There was 'most all the chimleys Rydal way built after his mind. I 'member he and the Doctor had great arguments about the chimleys time we was building Foxhow, and Wudsworth sed he liked a bit o' colour in 'em. And that the chimley coigns sud be natural headed and natural bedded, a little red and a little yallar. For there is a bit of colour in the quarry stone up Easedale way. And heèd a great fancy an' aw for chimleys square up hauf way, and round the t'other. And so we built 'em that how.' It was amusing to find that the house chimney-stacks up Rydal way are in truth so many breathing monuments of the bard. The man who with his face to the Continent passed in that sunny pure July morn of 1803 over Westminster Bridge, and noticed with joy the smokeless air, rejoiced also to sit 'without emotion, hope, or aim, by his half-kitchen and half-parlour fire' at Town End, and wherever he went seems to have noted with an eye of love

> The smoke forth issuing whence and how it may,
> Like wreaths of vapour without stain or blot.

But if from the highland huts he had observed how intermittently the blue smoke-curls rose and fell, he was most pleased to watch on a still day the tremulous upward pillars of smoke that rose from the cottages of his native dale.   In his *Guide to the Lakes* (p. 44) Wordsworth has said, ' The singular beauty of the chimneys will not escape the eye of the attentive traveller.   The low square quadrangular form is often surmounted by a tall cylinder, giving to the cottage chimney the most beautiful shape that is ever seen.   Nor will it be too fanciful or refined to remark that there is a pleasing harmony between a tall chimney of this circular form and the living column of smoke ascending from it through the still air.'

And my friend George's memory of Mr. Wordsworth's dictum about the need of having the chimney coign ' natural headed and natural bedded, a little red and a little yallar ' is again found to be true to the life from a passage in the same *Guide to the Lakes* (p. 60), in which the poet, after stating that the principle that ought to determine the position, size, and architecture of a house (viz., that it should be so constructed as to admit of being incorporated into the scenery of nature) should also determine its colour, goes on to say ' that since the chief defect of colour in the Lake country is an over-prevalence of bluish tint, to counteract this the colour of houses should be of a warmer tone than the native rock allows ; ' and adds, ' But where the cold blue tint of the rocks is enriched by an iron tinge, the colours cannot be too closely imitated, and will be produced of itself by the stones hewn from the adjoining quarry. '   How beautiful the colouring of the Rydal quarry stone is, and how dutifully the son of the poet carried out his father's will in his recent rebuilding of a family residence near Foxhow, may be judged by all who glance at the cylindrical chimneys, or look at the natural material that forms the panels of the porch of the 'Stepping-stones' under Loughrigg.

I rose to go, but George detained me. For he was proud to remember that upon one occasion ' Mr. Wudsworth had warmly watched him as he put forth his feats of strength in the wrestling ring at Ambleside, 'in the churchyeard day after fair, forty or fifty years ago,' and had passed a remark upon him. It was in the days 'when folks wrustled for nowt no more than a bit of leather strap.' And George had 'coomed to pit,' as the saying is, and after 'coming again' one man and throwing him, and another and throwing him,' was last man in against a noted wrestler, one Tom Chapman. He had agreed for one fall. Mr. Wordsworth was 'a-lookin' on.' George and his antagonist 'comed' together, and Chapman fell. 'And I 'member that I was more pleased with Mr. Wudsworth's word than wi' the strap (or belt), for folks telt me that he kep' a saying, "He must be a powerful young man that. He must be a strong young man."'

So ends our chat with honest George, the waller. We will next interview a man who at one time, for more than eleven years, saw Wordsworth almost daily. This was in the days that Hartley Coleridge lived at the Nab Cottage, or, as our friend puts it (with a touch of menagerie suggestion in it), 'i' the daays when *he kep' li'le Hartley* at the Nab,'—for our friend was Coleridge's landlord. I had considerable difficulty here, as in almost all my interviews with the good folk, of keeping to the object or subject in hand. For li'le Hartley's ghost was always coming to the front. 'Naäy, naäy, I cannot say a deal to that, but ye kna li'le Hartley would do so-and-so. Li'le Hartley was the man for them.

If it had been Hartley, now, I could ha' told you a deäl.'
And so on.

But in this particular instance my difficulty was trebled, for my friend evidently nursed the idea that Wordsworth had got most of 'his poetry out of Hartley,' and had in return dealt very hardly with him, in the matter of admonishment and advice, while at the same time Mrs. Wordsworth, in her capacity of common-sense accountant, with a strict dislike to wasteful expenditure or indiscriminate charity, had left something of bitter in his cup of Rydal Mount memories; and the old man would gladly enough pass over a Wordsworth leaflet for a folio page of li'le Hartley. But he too would be true in his speech, and would speak as he 'kna'ed,' neither more nor less. In his judgment Mr. Wordsworth was a 'plainish-faaced man, but a fine man, tall and leish (active), and almost always upo' the road. He wasn't a man of many words, would walk by you times enuff wi'out sayin' owt, specially when he was i' study. He was always a studying, and you might see his lips agoin' as he went along the road. He did most of his study upo' the road. I suppose,' he added, 'he was a cleverish man, but he wasn't set much count of by noan of us. He lent Hartley a deal of his books, it's certain, but Hartley helped him a deal, I understand, did best part of his poems for him, so the sayin' is.'

'He would come often in the afternoon and have a talk at the Nab, and would go out with Hartley takin' him by t' arm for long eneugh. And when Hartley was laid by for the last, Muster Wudsworth com down every day to see him and took communion wi' him at the last.'

'Then Mr. Wordsworth and Hartley Coleridge were great friends?' I asked.

'Na na, I doant think li'le Hartley ever set much by him,

never was very friendly, I doubt. Ye see, he [Mr. Words-
worth] was so hard upon him, so very hard upon him, giv'
him so much hard preaäching about his waäys.'

'Well, but Mrs. Wordsworth was kind to Hartley?' I
said. 'Happen she was, but I never see it. She was' [and
here the old man spoke very deliberately, as if this was the
firmest conviction of his life]—'she was very on-pleasant,
very on-pleasant indeed. A close-fisted woman, that's what
she was.' But further inquiry elicited the reason of this
personal dislike to the poet's wife, and a narrative of it will
probably win a public verdict for the lady of Rydal Mount,
with damages for libel against the man who so faithfully
kep' li'le Hartley at the Nab, and so made his lodger's
wrongs his own.

'Well, you see,' he continued gravely, 'I remember oncst
I went up to the Mount to ask for sattlement of account,
for Mrs. Wudsworth paid for Hartley's keep, time he lodged
at the Nab, and I had fifteen shillings i' the book against
Coleridge for moneys I'd lent him different times. And she
was very awkward and on-pleasant and wouldn't sattle, ye
kna, for she thowt that Hartley had been drinkin' wi' it.
But,' he added, 'howiver, I wrote to his mother as lived in
London, and she wrote to me and telt me I was to lend a
shilling or two as Hartley wanted it, and arter that she
sattled wi' me for his lodgment hersel', but Mrs. Wudsworth
was very on-pleasant.'

I was glad to change a subject that so distressed him,
and asked how the poet was generally dressed, and of his
habits. 'Wudsworth wore a Jem Crow, never seed him in a
boxer in my life,—a Jem Crow and an old blue cloak was his
rig, and *as for his habits, he had noan*, niver knew him with
a pot i' his hand, or a pipe i' his mouth. But,' continued

he, 'he was a greät skater for a' that'—(I didn't see the connection of ideas—pipes and beer don't generally make for good skating),—'noan better in these parts—why, he could cut his own naäme upo' the ice, could Mr. Wudsworth.'

Before rising to go, I asked, 'Which roads were the favourites of the poet?'

'Well, well, he was ter'ble fond of going along under Loughrigg and over by Redbank, but he was niver nowt of a mountaineer, always kep' upo' the roäd.'

This was a bit of news I had not expected, but we will bear it in mind and test its truth in future conversations with the poet's peasant contemporaries.

Our next talk shall be with one of the most well-informed of the Westmoreland builders, and I am indebted to Wordsworth's love of skating for an introduction to him. For making inquiries as to this pastime of the poet, I had chanced to hear how that Wordsworth had gone on one occasion to figure a bit by himself upon the White Moss Tarn. How that a predecessor of my friend the builder who lived near White Moss Tarn had sent a boy to sweep the snow from the ice for him, and how that when the boy returned from his labour he had asked him, 'Well, did Mr. Wudsworth gie ye owt?' and how that the boy with a grin of content from ear to ear had rejoined, 'Na, but I seed him tummle though!'

I determined to seek out the builder and have the story first-hand, and was well repaid; for I heard something of the poet's gentle ways that was better than the grotesquely humorous answer of the boy who saw him fall.

The poet's skate had caught on a stone when he was in full swing, and he came with a crash on to the ice that starred the tarn, and the lad, who had thought 'the

tummle ' a fair exchange for no pay, had been impressed
with the quiet way in which Wordsworth had borne his fall.
' He didn't swear nor say nowt, but he just sot up and said,
" Eh, boy, that was a bad fall, wasn't it ? " And now we are
walking along briskly towards Grisedale, with the recounter
of the story: ' Kna Wudsworth ! I kent him weel,—why,
he taught me and William Brown to skate. He was a
ter'ble girt skater, was Wudsworth now ; and he would put
one hand i' his breast (he wore a frill shirt i' them days),
and t'other hand i' his wäistband, same as shepherds does
to keep their hands warm, and he would stand up straight
and sway and swing away grandly.'

' Was he fond of any other pastime ? ' I asked.

' Nay, nay, he was over feckless i' his hands. I never seed
him at feasts, or wrestling, he hadn't owt of Christopher
Wilson in him. Nivver was on wheels in his life, and wud
ratherly ha' been a tailor upon horseback happen, but he
was a gay good un upon the ice, wonderful to see, could
cut his name upon it, I 've heard tell, but never seed him
do it.'

So that the rapture of the time when as a boy on Esthwaite's frozen lake Wordsworth had

> . . . wheeled about,
> Proud and exulting like an untired horse
> That cares not for his home, and, shod with steel,
> Had hissed along the polished ice,

was continued into manhood's later day ; and here was
proof that the skill which the poet had gained, when

> Not seldom from the uproar he retired,
> Into a silent bay, or sportively
> Glanced sideway, leaving the tumultuous throng
> To cut across the reflex of a star,

was of such a kind as to astonish the natives among whom he dwelt.

My friend had known Wordsworth well, and what was better, knew his poems too. 'Here,' said he, 'is the very spot where Wudsworth saw Barbara feeding her pet lamb, you'll happen have read it i' the book. She telt me herself. I was mending up the cottage there at the time. Eh, she was a bonny lass! they were a fine family all the lot of Lewthwaites. She went lang sin and left, but she telt me the spot wi' her own lips.' As I peered through the hedge upon the high-raised field at my right, I remembered that Barbara Lewthwaite's lips were for ever silent now, and re-called how I had heard from the pastor of a far-away parish that he had been asked by a very refined-looking handsome woman, on her deathbed, to read over to her and to her husband the poem of *The Pet Lamb*, and how she had said at the end, 'That was written about me. Mr. Wordsworth often spoke to me, and patted my head when I was a child,' and had added with a sigh, 'Eh, but he was such a dear kind old man.' We passed on in silence till we were near 'Boon beck,' and opposite Greenhead ghyll, 'That,' said my companion, 'is a cottage as we used to ca' i' these parts Village Clock. One,—I 'a' forgotten his name, a shep, lived here, and i' winter days folks from far enough round would saay, "Is leet out i' shep's cottage? then you may wind the clock and cover the fire" (for you kna matches was scarce and coal to fetch in them days); and of a morning "Is leet i' winder? is shep stirrin'? then you munna lig no longer," we used to saay.' My friend did not know that this too was in the book, as he called it,—that Wordsworth had described 'the cottage on a spot of rising ground,'

> And from its constant light so regular,
> And so far seen, the House itself, by all
> Who dwelt within the limits of the vale,
> Both old and young, was named the Evening Star.

Onward we trudged, entered the pastures leading to the Grasmere Common that stretches up to the Grisedale Pass, there sat, and had a talk as follows, the Tongue Ghyll Beck murmuring among the budding trees at our feet :—

'Why, why, Wudsworth never said much to folk, quite diffcrent from li'le Hartley, as knawed the insides of cottages for miles round, and was welcome at 'em all. He was distant, ye may saäy, varra distant. He was not maade much count of at first either in this country, but efter a time folks began to tak his advice, ye kna, about trees, and plantin', and cuttin', and buildin' chimlcys, and that sort o' thing. He had his saäy at most of thc houses in these parts, and was very partic'lar fond of round chimleys.'

It was delicious this description of the path to fame among his countrymen the poet had taken, but my friend explained himself as he went on :—

'Ye see, he was one as kept his head dan and eyes upo' the ground a deal, and mumbling to himself; but why, why, he 'ud never pass folks draining, or ditching, or walling a cottage, but what he 'd stop and say, "Eh dear, but it 's a pity to move that stoan, and doant ya think ya might leave that tree ?"[1] I 'member there was a walling chap just going to shoot a girt stoan to bits wi' powder in the grounds at Rydal, and he came up and saaved it, and wrote summat on it.'

'But what was his reason,' I asked, 'for stopping the wallers or ditchers, or tree-cutters, at their work ?'

'Well, well, he couldn't abear to see faäce o' things

altered,[1] ye kna. It was all along of him that Grasmere folks have their Common open. Ye may ga now reet up to sky over Grisedale, wi'out laying leg to fence, and all through him. He said it was a pity to enclose it and run walls over it, and the quality backed him, and he won. Folks was angry enough, and wrote rhymes about it; but why, why, it's a deal pleasanter for them as walks up Grisedale, ya kna, let aloan rights of foddering and goosage for freemen in Grasmere.'

'But Mr. Wordsworth was a great critic at trees. I've seen him many a time lig o' his back for long eneugh to see whether a branch or a tree sud ga or not. I 'member weel I was building Kelbarrer for Miss S——, and she telt me I must git to kna Wordsworth's 'pinion. So I went oop to him as he came i' t' waäy, and he said, "Ay, ay, building wad do, and site wad but it's very bare, very bare."

'I mind anither time I was building house aboon Town End, with a lock of trees and planting round, and he said to me, "Well, well, you're fifty years in advance here:" he meant it was grawed up well.

'And I remember once upon a time at Hunting Stile thereaway he coomed up. "Now, Mr. Wudsworth, how will it goa?" I said. He answered me, "It'll do; but where are the trees?" and I said, "Oh, it's weel enuff for trees, it nobbut wants its whiskers." "How so?" said he. "Why, it's a young 'un," I said, "and we doant blame a young 'un for not having its hair upo' its faace." And he laughed, and he said, "Very good, a very good saying; very true, very true." But he was ter'ble jealous of new buildings.

---

[1] Readers who may chance to have seen the letter Wordsworth wrote to the local paper when he heard the news of the first railway invasion of the Lake district, will notice how accurately true this piece of testimony is.

'As for Mrs. Wudsworth, why, why, she was a very plain woman, plainest i' these parts, and she was a manasher an' aw, and kep' accounts. For ye kna he never knowed about sich things, neither what he had nor what he spent.'

As we rose to continue our climb, my friend looked at the trees in the little stream-bed below us, and said, 'In my days there was a deal of wild fruit in these parts. We had toffee feasts i' winter, and cherry feasts i' summer,—quite big gatherings at cherry feasts.'

'Did you ever see Wordsworth at one?'

'Niver, he only follered one amusement: that was skating, as I telt ye.'

'Had he any particular friends among the shepherds?' I asked.

'Na, na, not as ever I kent or heard of; but he wozn't a mountaineer, was moastly down below upo' the road.'

'But what was his favourite road?'

'Oh, round by Grasmere and Red Bank and hoam again, without a doubt. He 'ud go twice i' the day round by Mr. Barber's there. He was a girt walker round there, and a'most as girt a eater. Why, why, he 'ud git breakfast at häame, poddish or what not, and then come wi' Miss Wudsworth round lake to Mr. Barber's, and fall in wi' them, and then off and round again, and be at Barber's at tea-time, and supper up again before going häame. And as for her, why Miss Wudsworth, she 'ud often coom into back kitchen and ask for a bit of oatcake and butter. She was fond of oatcake, and butter till it, fit to steal it a'most. Why, why, but she was a ter'ble clever woman, was that. She did as much of his potry as he did, and went completely off it at the latter end wi' studying it, I suppose. It 's a very strange thing, now, that studying didn't run on in the family.'

It was, I thought, a little hard to expect that the poet should have handed on the torch, or to speak with disrespect of his sons because they only thought in prose. But it was evidence in my friend, at least, of a profound belief in the genius of the Rydal poet and tree-and-building critic of old days. And it would have been a guess shrewdly made that it was Wordsworth's brotherhood with him, in the interests of his builder life, and jealous care for architecture in the vales, that had made the bond so strong and the belief in the poet so great, and exclusive. We descended into the valley, took tea together at the Swan Inn, and chatted on : now learning that Wordsworth was a regular attendant at Grasmere Church, now that he would often in church-time be like a dazed man,—forget to stand up and sit down, turn right round and stare vacantly at the congregation. 'But I remember one time partic'lar, when he and Hartley and I coomed out of the church together. I said, "What did you think of the sermon, Mr. Wudsworth?" and he answered me, "Oh, it was very good, and very plain ;" and I said, "Saame here, Mr. Wudsworth ;" and li'le Hartly put his head on one side, and squeaked out, "Oh, did ye think it was good? well, well, I was in purgatory the whole time." '

The stars were overhead as we left all that was left—and that was little enough—of our cosy evening meal ; and, bidding good-night I went home, with more Wordsworth memories to keep me company.

It was by happy accident that I was enabled to have a chat with one of the best types of our half-farmer half hotel-keeper, only a few days before he left the Rydal neighbourhood for good, after a sojourn of sixty-five years therein. We met at the house of a friend where he had been to pay his last rent due, and as I entered the room I was conscious of a be-whiskied conversationally aromatic air that boded well for a 'reet'-down good crack.

'Kna Wudsworth! I sud kna him, if any man sud, for as a lad I carried butther to the Mount, as a growing man I lived and worked in sight of him, and I lig now upon the vara bed-stocks as he and his missus ligged on when they were first wed, and went to Town End thereaway.'

'Now tell me,' said I, 'what was the poet like in face and make?'

'Well in mak he was listyish. I dar say I cud gee him four inches, now I suddent wonder but what I could, mysen.' My informant stood about six feet four, or four and a half. 'He was much to look at like his son William; he was a listy man was his son, mind ye. But for a' he was a sizeable man, was the father, he was plainish featured, and was a man as had no pleasure in his faace. Quite different Wudsworth was from li'le Hartley. Hartley always had a bit of smile or a twinkle in his faace, but Wudsworth was not lovable in the faace by noa means, for o' he was sizeable man, mind ye.'

'But,' I interrupted, 'was he not much like your friend John Rigg in face?'

'He might bea, saam mak, ye kna, much about; but, John Rigg he's a bit pleasant in his faace at wust o' times, and Wudsworth, bless ye, never had noan.'

'Was he,' I said, 'a sociable man, Mr. Wordsworth, in the earliest times you can remember?'

'Wudsworth,' my kindly giant replied, 'for a' he had noa pride nor nowt, was a man who was quite one to hissel, ye kna. He was not a man as folks could crack wi', nor not a man as could crack wi' folks. But there was another thing as kep' folks off, he had a ter'ble girt deep voice, and ye might see his faace agaan for long enuff. I 've knoan folks, village lads and lasses, coming over by old road above which runs from Grasmere to Rydal, flayt a'most to death there by Wishing Gaate to hear the girt voice a groanin' and mutterin' and thunderin' of a still evening. And he had a way of standin' quite still by the rock there in t' path under Rydal, and folks could hear sounds like a wild beast coming from the rocks, and childer were scared fit to be deäd a'most.'

'He was a great walker, I know,' I broke in. 'Which were his favourite roads? and was he generally on the hills, or did he keep pretty much to the valleys?'

'He was a gay good walker, and for a' he had latterly a pony and phaeton, I never once seed him in a conveyance in whole of my time. But he was never a mountain man. He wud gae a deal by Pelter-bridge and round by Red Bank, but he was most ter'ble fond of under Nab, and by old high road to Swan Inn and back, and very often came as far as Dungeon Ghyll. You 've happen heerd tell of Dungeon Ghyll; it was a vara favourite spot o' Wudsworth's, now, was that, and he onst made some potry about a lamb as fell over. And I dar say it was true enuff o' but the rhymes, and ye kna they was put in to help it out.'

For the life of me, as he spoke, I didn't understand whether he meant that the rhymes fished the lamb out of the Dungeon Ghyll pool, or helped the poet out with his verses, but I suppressed a smile and listened attentively.

'But for a' he was a distant man, they was well spoke of, mind ye, at the Mount,' continued my voluble friend. 'They stood high, and he was a man as paid his way and settled vara reg'lar; not that his potry brought him in much, a deal wasn't made up in books till after he was dead. Ay, and they lived weel. Many 's the time, when I was a lad, I went wi' butter. I could ha' been weel content to be let aloan for a bit in pantry. 'Ticing things there, mind ye. And they kep' three servants. I kent cook and housemaid weel, and one they ca'ed Dixon, smart little chap as ever was seen in these parts, ter'ble given over to cold water and temperance—he woz. Coomed out of a "union," but vara neat, and always a word for anybody, and a vara quiet man, partic'lar quiet, never up to no mischief, and always sat at hoam wi' the lasses a mending and sewing o' evenings, ye kna.'

I didn't know, but guessed at once the sort of simple stay-at-home ways and happy-family style of quiet domestic service, known to the circle of maidens, who, after their day's work, sat with their needles and thread entertaining the guileless Dixon.

'And what is your memory of Mrs. Wordsworth?'

'Well, every Jack mun have his Jen, as the sayin' is, and they was much of a mak. She was a stiff little lady, nothin' very pleasant in her countenance neither.' I soon found out that the word unpleasant was being used in a double sense, and was intended to convey rather an over-seriousness of expression perhaps than any disagreeable look or ill-tempered face. 'Ye 're weel awar',' continued the former hostel-keeper, 'that we mun a' hev troubles, times is not a' alike wi' best of us ; we have our worrits and our pets, but efter one on 'em, yan's countenance comes again, and Wudsworth's didn't, nor noan o' the family's, as I ever see.'

'Did you ever see Mr. Wordsworth out walking—round Pelter-bridge way?'

'Ay, ay, scores and scores o' times. But he was a lonely man, fond o' goin' out wi' his family, and saying nowt to noan of 'em. When a man goes in a family way he keeps togither wi' 'em and chats a bit wi' 'em, but many 's a time I 've seed him a takin' his family out in a string, and niver geein' the deariest bit of notice to 'em ; standin' by hissel' and stoppin' behind agapin', wi' his jaws workin' the whoal time; but niver no cracking wi' 'em, nor no pleasure in 'em,—a desolate-minded man, ye kna. Queer thing that, mun, but it was his hobby, ye kna. It was potry as did it. We all have our hobbies—some for huntin', some cardin', some fishin', some wrestlin'. He niver followed nowt nobbut a bit o' skating, happen. Eh, he was fond of going on in danger times ;—he was always first on the Rydal, however; but his hobby, ye mun kna, was potry. It was a queer thing, but it would like enough cause him to be desolate ; and I 'se often thowt that his brain was that fu' of sic stuff, that he was forced to be always at it whether or no, wet or fair, mumbling to hissel' along the roads.'

' Do you think,' I asked, ' that he had any friends among the shepherds ? '

' Naay, naay, he cared nowt about folk, nor sheep, nor dogs (he had a girt fine one, weighed nine stone, to guard the house) not no more than he did about claes he had on—his hobby was potry.'

' How did he generally dress ? '

' Well, in my time them swaller-lappeted ones were i' vogue, but he kep' to all-round plain stuff, and I remember had a cap wi' a neb to it. He wore that most days.'

' Did you ever read his poetry, or see any books about in the farm-houses ? ' I asked.

' Ay, ay, time or two. But ya 're weel aware there 's potry and potry. There 's potry wi' a li'le bit pleasant in it, and potry sic as a man can laugh at or the childer understand, and some as takes a deal of mastery to make out what 's said, and a deal of Wudsworth's was this sort, ye kna.

You could tell fra the man's faace his potry would niver
have no laugh in it.

'His potry was quite different work from li'le Hartley.
Hartley 'ud goa running along beside o' the brooks and
mak his, and goa in the first oppen door and write what he
had got upo' paper. But Wudsworth's potry was real hard
stuff, and bided a deal of makking, and he'd keep it in his
head for long enough. Eh, but it's queer, mon, different ways
folks hes of making potry now. Folks goes a deal to see
where he's interred; but for my part I'd walk twice distance
over Fells to see where Hartley lies. Not but what Mr. Wudsworth didn't stand very high, and was a well-spoken man
enough, but quite one to himself. Well, well, good-day.'
And so we rose to go; he to his farm, I to my note-book.

I pass over sundry interviews of minor import, and will
detail as accurately as I can the result of several conversations with one who as a boy lived as page, or butler's assist-
ant, at Rydal Mount, and now himself in total eclipse (for
he is blind) delights to handle and show with pride the massy,
old-fashioned square glazed hand-lantern, that lighted his
master the poet on his favourite evening walks.

We go through Ambleside to reach his house, and call for
a moment at the shop of a man for whom on his wedding-
day Hartley Coleridge wrote the touching sonnet in which
he describes himself as

Untimely old, irreverendly grey,

and he will tell us that Mr. Wordsworth was not a man of
very outgoing ways with folk, a plain man, and a very austere
man, and one who was ponderous in his speech. That he
called very often at his shop, and would talk, 'but not about
much,' just passing the day. He will tell us that Mrs.

Wordsworth was a very plain-faced lady, but will add that, 'for all that, Mr. Wordsworth and she were very fond of one another.'

There is, as one would expect, a sort of general feeling among the dalesmen that it was rather a strange thing that two people so austere and uncomely in mere line of feature or figure should be so much in love, and so gentle and considerate in their lives. I say as we should expect, for the men of Lakeland and the women of Lakeland are notably comely, their features notably regular. I do not myself know of a single instance of a really ugly married woman among the peasants that I have met with in Westmoreland. But at the same time we must remember that the word 'plain,' whether applied to dress or feature in Westmoreland, means for the most part simple, homely, unpretending, unassuming, and is often a term of honour rather than dispraise.

We shall, perhaps, as we near the village where our blind friend lives, meet with an old man who will tell us that he helped to bear both the poet and his wife to the grave, but he will add that he was not 'over weel acquent wi' 'em, though he knas the room they both died in,' and that the time he saw most of the poet was the occasion when he conducted Queen Adelaide 'to see the Rydal Falls, and all about.'

We have got to the end of our walk, and, here, picking his way by means of his trusty sounding-staff backwards and forwards in the sunshine he feels, but cannot see, is the old man, or rather old gentleman who in former times 'took sarvice along of Mr. Wudsworth,' and was 'so well pleased with his master that he could vara well have ended his days at the Mount,' but found it was over quiet, and, wanting to see the world beyond the charmed circle of the hills, left a good place, but not before he had formed his opinion of both master and mistress, and obtained indelible impressions of their several personalities, and had conceived along with these an affection for them which glows in his words as he talks to us of them. 'Mr. Wudsworth was a plain-faced man, and a mean liver.' The description, as I hinted in the preface, would have staggered a philo-Wordsworthian unaccustomed to the native dialect. 'But he was a good master and kind man; and as for Mrs. Wudsworth, she was a downright clever woman, as kep' accounts, and was a reg'lar manasher. He never know'd, bless ye, what he had, nor what he was worth, nor whether there was owt to eat in the house, never.'

'But you say,' I interposed, 'that he didn't care much whether there was or was not food in the house.'

'Nay, nay, Wudsworth was a man as was fond of a good dinner at times, if you could get him to it, that was t' job; not but what he was a very temperate man i' all things, very, but they was all on 'em mean livers, and in a plain way. It was porridge for breakfast, and a bit of mutton to dinner, and porridge at night, with a bit of cheese, happen, to end up wi'.'

'You said it was hard to get him to his meals: what did you mean?' I asked.

'Weel, weel, it was study as was his delight: he was a' for study; and Mrs. Wudsworth would say, "Ring the bell," but he wouldn't stir, bless ye. "Goa and see what he's doing," she'd say, and we goa up to study door and hear him a mumbling and bumming through it. "Dinner's ready, sir," I'd ca' out, but he'd goa mumbling on like a deaf man, ya see. And sometimes Mrs. Wudsworth 'ud say, "Goa and

break a bottle, or let a dish fall just outside door in passage."
Eh dear, that mostly 'ud bring him out, would that. It was
only that as wud, however. For ye kna he was a very careful mon, and he couldn't do with brekking the china.'

'And was he continually at study in-doors, or did he rise
early, go out for a walk before breakfast, and study, as I
have heard, mostly in the open air?' I asked.

My friend answered at once. 'He was always at it, ye
kna, but it was nowt but what he liked, and not much desk-
work except when he had a mind to it. Noa, noa, he was
quite a open-air man, was Wudsworth : studied a deal upo'
the roads. He wasn't partic'lar fond of gitten up early, but
did a deal of study after breakfast, and a deal after tea.
Walked the roads after dark, he would, a deal, between his
tea and supper, and efter. Not a very conversable man, a
mumblin' and stoppin', and seein' nowt nor nobody.'

'And what were his favourite roads?' I asked, in an
innocent way.

'Well, he was very partial to going up to Tarn Foot in
Easedale, and was fondest o' walking by Red Bank and
round by Barber's (the late Miss Agar's house), or else
t'other way about and home by Clappersgate and Brankers,
under Loughrigg. Never was nowt of a mountaineer, and
Miss Dorothy 'companied him. Eh dear, many time I've
watched him coming round wi' lantern and her after a walk
by night. You've heard tell of Miss Dorothy, happen.
Well, folks said she was cleverest mon of the two at his
job, and he allays went to her when he was puzzelt.
Dorothy had the wits, tho' she went wrang, ye kna.'

'Then,' said I, 'Mrs. Wordsworth did not help the poet
in writing his verses?'

'Naay, naay. Why, she was a manasher, niver a studier,

but for a' that there's no doubt he and she was truly companionable, and they was ter'ble fond of one another. But Dorothy hed t' wits on 'em boath.'

'And he was very devoted to his children ?' I put in.

'Ay, ay, he was fond of children like enough, but children was niver vara fond o' him. Ye see he was a man o' moods, niver no certainty about him; and I'm not so sure he was fond of other foak's bairns, but he was very fond of his own, wi'out a doubt.'

'And was he very popular among the folk hereabouts?'

'There's no doubt but what he was fond of quality, and quality was very fond o' him, but he niver asked folk about their work, nor noticed the flocks nor nowt: not but what he was a kind man if folks was sick and taen badly. But farming, nor beast, nor sheep, nor fields wasn't in his way, he asked no questions about flocks or herds, and was a distant man, not what you might call an outward man by noa means. And he was very close, very close indeed, from curious men. He'd goa t'other side o' road rather than pass a man as axed questions a deal.'

It was a mercy, I thought to myself, that no Wordsworth Society had invited me to collect and write down the results of a cross-question tour in those days.

'But surely,' I said, 'he had some particular cottage or farm where he would go and have a crack.'

'Naay, naay. He would go times or two to farm Dungeon Ghyll way, but he wasn't a man for friends. He had some, neäh doubt, in his walk of life; he was ter'ble friends with the Doctor (Arnold) and Muster Southey, and Wilson of Elleray and Hartley Coleridge. I 'se seen him many a time taking him out arm i' arm for a talking. But he was specially friendly with Professor. I mind one time when we was driving, me and Mrs. Wudsworth and Miss Wudsworth, to Kendal, and Professor Wilson was superintending making o' a bye-road up by Elleray there, and he was in his slippers. Nowt wud do but Wudsworth must git down and fall to talkin', and we went on; but he didn't come, and Mrs. Wudsworth said, "Ye mun drive on; he'll pick us up at Kendal: no knowing what's got him, now Professor is wi' 'im." Well, well, she was right. For after putting up at Kendal, who should walk in but Wudsworth and Professor wi'out ony shoes to his feet neäther, for Wilson was in his slippers, and 'ad walk'd hisself to his stockin' feet, and left best part of his stockin' on road an' a', far enuff before they got to Kendal.'

'But it was strange,' I said again in a suggestive way, 'that Mr. Wordsworth should be so well "acquaint" with Professor Wilson, for he was a great cock-fighting and wrestling man, was he not, in his day?'

'Ay, ay, biggest hereabout,' my old friend replied. 'It's queer, but it was along o' his study, ye kna. Wudsworth was never no cock-fighter nor wrestler, no gaming man at all, and not a hunter, and as for fishing he hedn't a bit o' fish in him, hedn't Wudsworth—not a bit of fish in him.'

'I have read in his books,' said I, 'things that make me feel he was kind to dumb animals.'

'Naay, naay,' my friend broke in, 'Wudsworth was no dog fancier; and as for cats, he couldn't abide them; and he didn't care for sheep, or horses, a deal, but if he was fond of onything, it was of *li'le ponies*. He was a man of fancies, ye kna. It was a fancy of his. He was fond of li'le ponies, nivver rode a horse in his life, nivver.'

'But he went over a deal of ground in his time. Was he always on his feet?' I said.

'He went a deal over more ground nor ever he saw, for he went a deal by night, but he was a man as took notice, ye kna, never forgit what he saw, and he went slow.'

'But,' said I, 'how did he cover so much ground; was he never on wheels?'

'Ay, ay, wheels, to be sure, he druv a' times, ye kna, in cart. He, and Mrs. Wudsworth, and Dorothy and me, we went a deal by cart Penrith way, and Borradale and Keswick way, and Langdale way at times.'

'What sort of a cart?' I inquired.

'Dung cart, to be sure. Just a dung cart, wi' a seat-board in front, and bit of bracken in t' bottom, comfortable as owt. We cud go that away for days, and far enuff. Ye knaw in them days tubs wasn't known. Low-wood was nobbut a cottage, and there was never abuv six or seven ponies for hiring at Ambleside. Tubs we ca' the covered carriages, tubs wasn't known in these parts. But happen there was a tub or two at Kendal.'

'And you must have gone precious slowly,' I said.

'Ay, ay, slow enough, but that was Mr. Wudsworth's fancy, and he 'd git in and go along, and then he git down into t' road and walk a bit, and mak a bit, and then he git oop and hum a bit to himself, and then he stop and have a look here and there for a while. He was a man as noticed a deal stones and trees, very partic'lar about trees, or a rock wi' ony character in it. When they cut down coppy woods in these parts they mostly left a bit of the coppy just behint wall to hide it for him, he was a girt judge in such things, and noticed a dëal.'

'And would he,' I asked, 'tell you as you jogged along in the cart, which mountain he was fondest of, or bid you look at the sunset?'

'Ay, ay, times he would say, "Now isn't that beautiful?" and times he would hum on to himself. But he wasn't a man as would give a judgment again' ony mountain. I've heard girt folks 'at come to the Mount say, "Now, Mr. Wudsworth, we want to see finest mountain in t' country," and he would say, "Every mountain is finest." Ay, that's what he would say.'

'But I have been told that his voice was very deep,' I put in, in a happy-go-lucky way. 'Had he a loud laugh, now?'

'I don't remember he ever laughed in his life, he'd smile times or two. Ay, ay, his voice was deep one; but I remember at family prayers in t' morning he'd read a bit of the Scripture to us, and he was a very articulate, partic'lar good reader, was Mr. Wudsworth, always had family prayer in the morning, and went to church wi' prayer-book under his arm, very reg'lar once upon the Sunday, he did.' My friend added, 'He was quite a serious-minded man, and a man of moods.'

Here ended my talk with the old retainer at the Mount. But I was not allowed to go off until I had seen and handled the old-fashioned candle lantern by which, as my kind informant put it, the poet 'did a deal of his study upo' the roads after dark.'

And so must end my plain unvarnished tale. I leave my indulgent readers to form their own conclusions; merely suggesting that the collected evidence points to a simple plainness and homeliness of life such as remains indelibly impressed upon the men of Westmoreland, whose own lives are less simple in these latter days, when ostentation and vulgar pride of wealth in a class above them have climbed the hills and possessed the valleys.

The testimony of the witnesses I have been fortunate

enough to bring before you seems to agree in depicting Wordsworth as he painted himself, a plain man, continually murmuring his undersong as he passed along by brook and woodland, pacing the ground with uplifted eye, but so retired, that even the North country peasant, who does even yet recognise the social differences of class and caste that separate and divide 'the unknown little from the unknowing great,' was unable to feel at home with him. · 'Not a very companionable man at the best of times' was their verdict. But I think all the while these dalesmen seem to have felt that if the poet was not of much count as a worldly-wise farm or shepherd authority, nor very convivial and free and easy as li'le Hartley was, nor very athletic and hearty as Professor Wilson, there was a something in the severe-faced, simply habited man 'as said nowt to nobody' that made him head and shoulders above the people, and bade them listen and remember when he spoke, if it was only on the lopping of a tree or the build of a chimney-stack. 'He was a man of a very practical eye, and seemed to see everything,' was the feeling.

And turning from the poet to his wife, whilst one can see how the household need of economy in early Town End days gave her to the last the practical power of household management that had almost passed into a proverb, one can see also how true was that picture of the

> Being, breathing thoughtful breath,
>
> .   .   .   .
>
> A perfect woman, nobly planned,
> To warn, to comfort, and command.

'He never knawed, they say, what he was wuth, nor what he had in the house.' She did it all. Then, too, it is touching to notice how deep and true the constant love between man and wife was seen to be, how truly companions for life they were, and that, too, in the eyes of a class of people who never saw that

> Beauty born of murmuring sound
> Had passed into her face,

and half marvelled that the spirit wed with spirit was so marvellously closer than fleshly bond to flesh.

Upright, the soul of honour, and for that reason standing high with all; just to their servants; well-meaning and quiet in their public life; full of affection in their simple home life; so it seems the poet and his wife lived and died. Thought a deal of for the fact that accounts were strictly met at the tradesmen's shops, they were thought more of because they were ever ready to hear the cry of the suffering, and to enter the doors of those ready to perish.

I do not think I have been able to tell the world anything new about the poet or his surroundings. But the man 'who hedn't a bit of fish in him, and was no mountaineer,' seems to have been in the eyes of the people always at his studies; 'and that because he couldn't help it, because it was his hobby,' for sheer love, and not for money. This astonished the industrious, money-loving folk, who could not understand the doing work for 'nowt,' and perhaps held the poet's occupation in somewhat lighter esteem, just because it did not bring in 'a deal o' brass to the pocket.' I think it is very interesting, however, to notice how the woman part of the Rydal Mount family seemed to the simple neighbourhood to have the talent and mental ability; and there must have been, both about Dorothy Wordsworth and the poet's daughter Dora, a quite remarkable power of inspiring the minds of the poor with whom they came in contact, with a belief in their intellectual faculties and brightness and cleverness. If Hartley Coleridge was held by some to be Wordsworth's helper, it was to Dorothy he was supposed by all to turn 'if ivver he was puzzelt.' The women had 'the wits, or best part of 'em,'—this was proverbial among the peasantry, and, as having been an article of rural faith, it has been established out of the mouths of all the witnesses it has been my lot to call.

MATTHEW ARNOLD'S ADDRESS AS
PRESIDENT, 1883.

MATTHEW ARNOLD'S ADDRESS AS PRESIDENT, 1883.

AT your last year's meeting you did me the honour, although I was not then a member of your Society, to elect me your President for this year. I had declined to join the Wordsworth Society for the same reason that I decline to join other societies—not from any disrespect to their objects or to their promoters, but because, being very busy and growing old, I endeavour to avoid fresh engagements and distractions, and to keep what little leisure I can for reflection and amendment before the inevitable close. When your election of me came, however, I felt that it would be ungracious to decline it; and, as generally happens, having decided to accept it and to join you, I soon began to find out a number of excellent reasons for doing what I had resolved to do. In former days, you know, people who had in near view that inevitable close of which I just now spoke, people who had had their fill of life's business and were tired of its labour and contention, used to enter a monastery. In my opinion they did a very sensible thing. I said to myself: ' Times and circumstances have changed, you cannot well enter a monastery; but you can enter the Wordsworth Society.' The two things are not so very different. A monastery is under the rules of poverty, chastity, and obedience. Well, and he who comes under the discipline of Wordsworth comes under those same rules. Wordsworth constantly both preached and practised them. He was 'frugal and severe ;' he ever calls us to 'plain living and high thinking.' There you have the rule of poverty. His chosen hero and exemplar, the Pedlar of *The Excursion*, was formed and fashioned by the Scottish Church having held upon him in his youth, with a power which endured all his life long, 'the strong hand of her purity.' There you have the rule of chastity. Finally, in an immortal ode, Wordsworth tells us how he made it his heart's desire and prayer to live the 'bondman of duty in the light of truth.' There you have the rule of obedience. We live in a world which sometimes, in our morose moments, if we have any, may almost seem to us, perhaps, to have set itself to be as little poor as possible, and as little chaste as possible, and as little obedient as possible. Whoever is oppressed with thoughts of this kind, let him seek refuge in the Words-worth Society.

As your President, it is my duty not to occupy too much of your time myself, but to announce the papers which are to be read to you, and to introduce their readers. It was hoped that a paper would have been read by Lord Coleridge. There was an additional reason for joining your Society ! But the paper has had to be put off, alas, till next year. There is a reason for continuing to belong to you ! Mr. Stopford Brooke—whose published remarks on Wordsworth, as on other great English writers, we all know, and excellent they are—Mr. Stopford Brooke, I am glad to say, will read us a paper. Mr. Aubrey De Vere —who has given us more interesting and trustworthy reports of Wordsworth in his old age than any one except Miss Fenwick—Mr. Aubrey De Vere has prepared a paper, which will be read by our

Secretary—if he is not more properly to be called the author of our being—Professor Knight. If Professor Knight's work in founding us (I may say in passing) had even had no other result than the production of those photographs of Wordsworth which appear in the Society's Transactions of last year, that result alone would have been a sufficient justification of his work. Other matters, besides the papers which I have mentioned, will come before you, and I must leave way for them. But suffer me, before I sit down, to say seriously and sincerely what pleasure I find in the testimony afforded by the prosperity of your Society, and by the numbers present here to-day, to the influence of Wordsworth. His imperfections, the mixture of prose with his poetry, I am probably more disposed than some members of this Society to admit freely. But I doubt whether any one admires Wordsworth more than I do. I admire him, first of all, for the very simple and solid reason that he is such an exceedingly great poet. One puts him after Shakespeare and Milton. Shakespeare is out of comparison. Milton was, of course, a far greater artist than Wordsworth; probably, also, a greater force. But the spiritual passion of Wordsworth, his spiritual passion when, as in the magnificent sonnet of farewell to the River Duddon, for instance, he is at his highest, and 'sees into the life of things,' cannot be matched from Milton. I will not say it is beyond Milton, but he has never shown it. To match it, one must go to the ocean of Shakespeare. A second invaluable merit which I find in Wordsworth is this: he has something to say. Perhaps one prizes this merit the more as one grows old, and has less time left for trifling. Goethe got so sick of the fuss about form and technical details, without due care for adequate con-tents, that he said if he were younger he should take pleasure in setting the so-called art of the new school of poets at nought, and in trusting for his whole effect to his having something important to say.[1]   Dealing with no wide, varied, and brilliant world, dealing with the common world close to him, and using few materials, Wordsworth, like his great contemporary the Italian poet Leopardi, who also deals with a bounded world and uses few materials—Wordsworth, like Leopardi, is yet so profoundly impressive, because he has really something to say.   And the mention of Leopardi, that saddest of poets, brings me, finally, to what is perhaps Wordsworth's most distinctive virtue of all—his power of happiness and hope, his 'deep power of joy.'   What a sadness is in those brilliant poets of Italy—what a sadness in even the sweetest of them all, the one whom Wordsworth specially loved, the pious and tender Virgil !

> Optima quæque dies miseris mortalibus ævi
> Prima fugit—

'the best days of life for us poor mortals flee first away;' *subeunt morbi,* 'then come diseases, and old age, and labour, and sorrow; and the severity of unrelenting death hurries us away.' *Et duræ rapit inclementia mortis.*[2]   From the

---

[1] See Eckermann, *Gespräche mit Goethe,* ii. 260-2 :—' Es ist immer ein Zeichen einer unproductiven Zeit, wenn die so ins Kleinliche des Technischen geht, und eben so ist es ein Zeichen eines unproductiven Individuums, wenn es sich mit dergleichen befasst. . . . Wäre ich noch jung und verwegen genug, so würde ich absichtlich gegen alle solche technische Grillen verstossen . . . aber ich würde auf die Hauptsache losgehen, und so gute Dinge zu sagen suchen, dass jeder gereizt werden sollte, es zu lesen und auswendig zu lernen.'

[2] Optima quæque dies miseris mortalibus ævi
    Prima fugit ; subeunt morbi, tristisque senectus
    Et labor ; et duræ rapit inclementia mortis.
    VIRGIL, *Georgics,* iii. 66-8.

ineffable, the dissolving melancholy of those lovely lines, let us turn our thoughts to the great poet in whose name we are met together to-day; to our Westmoreland singer of 'the sublime attractions of the grave,' and to the treasure of happiness and of hope—

> Of hope, the paramount *duty* which Heaven lays,
> For its own honour, on man's suffering heart—

which is in him. We are drawn to him because we feel these things; and we believe that the number of those who feel them will continue to increase more and more, long after we are gone.

    .   .   .   .   .   .

Before the meeting separated, the Lord Chief-Justice proposed a vote of thanks to the Chairman. In doing so, LORD COLERIDGE said :—

I have been asked to do something which some one must do, which all of you desire should be done, and which, in one respect perhaps, there is hardly any one present who can do with greater propriety than myself, namely, to move a vote of thanks to Mr. Matthew Arnold for his address, and for being our President for the year. He has told us how very old he is, and how very grave and solemn he has become, to which every one who looks at him, and listens to him, and reads him, must at once entirely assent. He tells us that he has withdrawn from the world, that he longs to enter a cell, to go into a monastery; and he has described the charms of reflection and meditation with much personal appreciation and characteristic accuracy. But though he has done that, and come here to preside over us, I am sure none of us would have thought that these were his peculiar and characteristic qualities upon any authority less cogent than his own. For my own part, having been brought up with him from a child, I may say that the statement comes upon me as a complete, an interesting, and a pleasurable surprise. With regard to Wordsworth, however, of all living men he has probably done most to bring back and place upon its true grounds the devotion to that great Poet. I should say, moreover, that he is fitly our President, because not only is he perhaps the greatest of English critics, but because he is, if not the greatest, at any rate the most exquisite, of English poets. Those of us who have had the pleasure to live for many years in the light of his friendship know him also to be the most generous, the most steadfast, the most loyal of friends. As his oldest living friend, and as one who yields to no man in admiration for him, as well as one who has owed him much for many many years, I gladly take the opportunity of moving this vote of thanks.

ON WORDSWORTH'S *GUIDE TO THE LAKES.*

By STOPFORD BROOKE.

WE may be quite sure that when Wordsworth wished to write his *Guide to the Lakes* he would look to see what his brother poet, Gray, had said about them in the Journal written to Mr. Wharton; and it is characteristic of Wordsworth's poetic temper that he seizes on the pathetic circumstance of it being written shortly before the death of Gray. Of the natural descriptions he says that they are marked by 'distinctness and unaffected simplicity;' and we cannot better the words. These *are* the excellencies of the natural description, though here and there are phrases which recall the artificial style in which men wrote about Nature when Gray was still alive.

Rarely, if ever, the poet appears. There is one passage where he says that he 'heard the murmur of many waters, not audible in the daytime,' which seems to have in it what Wordsworth calls 'an ear practised like a blind man's touch;'—but I do not know whether I do not attribute a poetical quality to it which it has not, because of Wordsworth's observation of the same voicefulness of the streams at evening, and the lines in which he describes it—

> A soft and lulling sound is heard
> Of streams inaudible by day.

Another passage is more distinctly poetical, and were it not lifted a little too high by the academic introduction of

---

[1] Read to the Society in May 1883.

'Chaos and old Night,' would not be unworthy of Wordsworth himself: and, in its conception of the mountains as alive, and guarding their dreadful and solitary secrets, resembles Wordsworth's way of thinking

Gray is speaking of a mountain road, passable only for a few weeks by the peasants, and leading into savage recesses that ought not to be invaded. 'But the mountains know well,' he says, 'that these innocent people will not reveal the mysteries of their ancient kingdom—the reign of Chaos and old Night.'

But, after all, this single passage does not come out of any poetical conception or passion of Nature such as Wordsworth always has; it is a mere chance. Gray was not at home with wild scenery. His sense of the horror of Gordale Scar, his fear of 'the loose stones that hang in the air, and threaten the idle spectator with destruction;' his declaration that, though the impression of the place—so sublime it was—would last him his life, yet that he could not stay in it a quarter of an hour without shuddering, all prove that he had no real care for places where Wordsworth would have felt filled with joy, and content to rest in as in home.

Nay, I even doubt whether he had any direct delight in Nature for her own sake, such as we feel, or have been taught to feel, by the poets. He likes his natural scenery made artificial. It was his habit to carry about with him a square of blackened glass, such as artists use to define the limits of a landscape, and whenever he saw any scene he thought pretty, he sat down to contemplate it in this glass. 'Pray think, Doctor, how the glass plays its part in such a spot,' he writes, after an ardent description of Borrowdale. And at Grasmere, after equal ardour, he says—and the sentence marks how æsthetic rather than natural was his con-templation of Nature—'From hence I got to the Parsonage, a little before sunset, and saw in my glass a picture which, if I could transmit to you, and fix it in all the softness of its living colours, would fairly sell for 1000 pounds. This is the sweetest scene I can yet discover in point of pastoral beauty.'

I do not depreciate Gray's 'distinctness and unaffected simplicity,' as Wordsworth has it ; but the difference between this manner of seeing and feeling Nature, and that of Wordsworth, is quite immeasurable. We are in another world altogether when we open the *Guide to the Lakes.* Wordsworth was at home with,—his life from a child was interwoven with,—wild Nature. He loved and talked to it, as a man loves and talks to a friend, and it would be un-natural—considering the inevitableness of the poetic passion —if, even in a Guide-Book, his love did not appear. It does appear. The descriptions in this book glow with re-collected love, and with the indignation which companies with love, when that which is dearly loved is injured or made less beautiful.

There are many passages of anger against those who dared to injure, or to make artificial the wild and fanciful play of Nature. There is a long indictment (not without a little of that humour which the force of indignation some-times attains) against the larch-tree, for its want of sympathy and organisation, and its gross individualism ; thousands and tens of thousands of 'separate individual trees obstinately presenting themselves as such.' But the indignation is little, and the love much. Mark the minute affection, the long contemplation of love in this passage—and there are many more. He is talking of the lake shores.

'Along bays exposed to the setting in of strong winds,' we see the 'curved rim of fine blue gravel, thrown up in course of time by the waves, half of it gleaming from under the water, and the corresponding half of a lighter hue; and in other parts bordering the lakes, groves, if I may so call them, of reeds and bulrushes, or plots of water-lilies, lifting up their large target-shaped leaves to the breeze, while the white flower is heaving on the wave.'

This subtle essence of love, rising again and again through the quiet argument and detail of the book, like the voice of a hidden stream heard at intervals from the road on which we walk, is part of the charm of this book.

Again, Wordsworth was first the poet, a poet also with certain fixed ideas on which his imagination always built; so that another part of the charm of this book is the continual emergence of these poetic ideas through the prose. There is, also, the apparition of the Poet himself, speaking the poetic tongue; more than in his letters, more than in the prefaces, does he here lift his head above the sober-moving waves of prose.

The first of these fixed ideas is, that in the universe there was a living Will,—the soul as it were of its body,—which had pleasure in its own doings, and which could harmonise itself with Man. Some say that this was only a poetic sentiment. It may be so to them; it may be so in itself. But it was not so to Wordsworth. It was his deepest faith concerning what we call Nature, and there is not a single poem which has to do with the natural world in which it does not appear.

It appears in this little book, but in a different way—and this is its interest—from the way it appears in his poetry. He is speaking, for example, of Mountain Tarns, and of their want of wood, and of 'other cheerful images by which fresh water is usually attended,' and he says that this inability in the tarn to g ve furtherance to the meagre vegetation excites the sense of *some repulsive power* strongly put forth, and thus deepens the melancholy natural to such scenes;' but he does not leave the Tarn to this gloomy thought, but goes on—and the added thought is the origin of one of the finest passages in his mountain poetry—to say that the imagination is tempted to attribute a voluntary power to every change which takes place in such a spot.

This talk of repulsive and voluntary powers is an apparition of his idea.

So, also, it appears in another way, when (speaking of the vapours which, exhaled from the lakes, brood on the heights, or descend to the valleys with inaudible motion) 'he is disposed to sympathise with those who fancy these delicate apparitions to be the spirits of their departed ancestors;' and, rising more and more into the poetic temper, thinks of the fleecy clouds that rest on the hill-tops as caught and detained there by some mysterious impulse of love.

Nor is this idea of a life in separate things, and of a vast, self-conscious thought, of which the phenomena of Nature are the form, the mere vague sentiment of one who did not observe the processes of Nature. Wordsworth had the eye of a field-geologist, and he describes (as Professor Geikie, writing for the popular eye, would describe) the way in which the shores of Rydal Mere were carved, or in which the outline of a wood, as it climbs a mountain, was wrought; and I do not doubt myself that close observation of this kind is behind all the transcendental passages concerning Nature in his poetry.

In this book, when he has done this accurate work, what

do we find? He is not satisfied with the statement of the natural causes. His idea comes in! and behind these causes, and present through them *as power*, he conceives of an actual Being who day by day has wrought out into beauty, for his own pleasure and for ours, the edges of the lake and of the wood. 'We never contemplate these boundaries without some feeling, more or less distinct, of the powers of Nature by which they are imposed:' and if they are defaced by man, 'such is the benignity of Nature, the scars will gradually disappear before a healing spirit.'

A second part of this idea of a universal life in the world without us, is in his conception of a co-operative harmony between the animals and Nature herself—a conception of which his poetry is full, and which is frequent in this little book.

Mr. Darwin would have been pleased, as we in this poetic assembly are pleased, with Wordsworth, when he descries 'the stately heron, with folded wings, that might seem to have caught their delicate hue from the blue waters by the side of which she watches.' Again, in his *Excursion*, he describes the straight flight of the raven over the large bay under Place Fell. And when we read, 'The waters were agitated, and the iron tone of the raven's voice was in fine keeping with the wild scene before our eyes,' we think of the lines where this prose is made poetry—

> The crags repeat the raven's croak
> In symphony austere.

The same idea fills another passage, where he describes the birds and the young lambs in the vales : 'The notes of the birds, when listened to by the side of broad still waters, or when heard in unison with the murmuring of mountain

brooks, have the compass of their power enlarged accordingly.' That is a phrase alive with Wordsworth, but this
which follows about the cuckoo is almost finer than anything
in the famous poem : 'There is also an imaginative influence
in the voice of the cuckoo, *when that voice has taken possession of a deep mountain valley*, very different from anything
which can be excited by the same sound in a flat country.'
Then he passes on to the lambs ; and we think of many a
passage in the *Doe of Rylstone* : 'These sportive creatures,
as they gather strength, are turned out upon the open mountains, and with their slender limbs, their snow-white colour,
and their wild and light motions, beautifully accord or contrast with the rocks and lawns on which they seek their food.'

Another part of his idea is that Nature takes up the need-
ful works of Man into herself and unites her work to his, so
that Man's work seems to be Nature's, and Nature's that of
Man. Yet each, while ministering to one another, are
distinct.

Every one will remember many instances of this con
ception in Wordsworth's poems.

I wish I had time to read you the whole passage in this
book in which (speaking of the mountain cottages) he
enshrines this thought; but it is enough to take two
sentences : *the first*, when he says—'that they remind the
contemplative spectator of a production of Nature, and may
(using a strong expression) rather be said to have grown
than to be erected ; to have risen, by an instinct of their
own, out of the native rock, so little is there in them of
formality, such is their wildness and beauty ;' the second,
when, after describing the work of Nature on them, clothing
them, roof and sides, with moss and ferns and flowers, he
breaks out into his complete idea : 'Hence buildings, which

in their very form call to mind the processes of Nature, do thus, clothed in part with a vegetable garb, appear to be received into the bosom of the living principle of things, as it acts and exists among the woods and fields.'

Another part of the same idea (that Nature has a life not created in her by our imagination, but separate from ours), is, that she acts upon us from without, to awaken thought, to inspire feeling,—to do, in fact, on us the work of a teacher and a friend. This idea, expanded in a hundred poems, and one of the foundation-thoughts of *The Prelude* and *The Excursion*, is not neglected in this book. Here is the passage, and though it ought to be in poetry, it is not uninteresting to find our poetic idea in prose :—

'A resident . . . must have experienced, while looking on the unruffled waters, that the imagination, by their aid, is carried into recesses of feeling otherwise impenetrable. . . . All else speaks of tranquillity ;—not a breath of air, no restlessness of insects, and not a moving object perceptible—except the clouds gliding in the depths of the lake, or the traveller passing along, an inverted image, whose motion seems governed by the quiet of a time, to which its archetype, the living person, is, perhaps, insensible :—or it may happen, that the figure of one of the larger birds, a raven or a heron, is crossing silently among the reflected clouds, while the voice of the real bird, from the element aloft, gently awakens in the spectator the recollection of appetites and instincts, pursuits and occupations, that deform and agitate the world, —yet have no power to prevent Nature from putting on an aspect capable of satisfying the most intense cravings for the tranquil, the lovely, and the perfect, to which man, the noblest of her creatures, is subject.

In this way Wordsworth is led from Nature to Mankind. It was the natural course with him; and though his abiding of thought over human life was deep, yet as deep was his brooding over the life in Nature.

According to the way in which our character is originally tempered, or is wrought at certain times, is our pleasure in the one or in the other side of Wordsworth's thinking; but he, more manifold than we, was seldom enthralled by the one without seeking, or at once seeing, the other. Hence the chapter in this book on the aspect of the country as affected by its inhabitants is full of human feeling; while at the same time he writes as if he felt that the indwellers and all their work were actual receivers, day by day, of the sympathy of Nature.

As to his own method of work, the way in which, having watched with ardent minuteness the aspects and changes of Nature during a long mountain walk, he added afterwards to these the thoughts of human life and duty that belonged to them (by right, as he would think, of pre-established harmony between the mind of Man and the mind of the Universe), you will find an example of it here, if you read the journal of the crossing of the pass of Kirkstone, and the poem wrought out of the memories of that day.

I have but two things more to say. The first is, that not only does Wordsworth express in this little book his poetic ideas, but that he cannot help frequently falling into the modes of poetry in the midst of his prose. This apparition of the poet, as I said, is very pleasant, and if you read with open eyes, you will often have the pleasure of that sight.

Phrases like these: 'Turning round, we saw the mountains of Wastdale in tumult;' 'The Scawfell cataracts were voiceless;' 'Skiddaw also has *his own* rainbows;' 'On this day the winds have been acting on the small lake of Rydal as if they had received command to carry its waters from their bed into the sky;' 'Such clouds, cleaving to their stations'—he is speaking of the fleecy clouds among the mountain-tops—'or lifting up suddenly their glittering heads from behind rocky barriers, or hurrying out of sight with speed of the sharpest edge,' are not prose, nor in the manner of prose.

Sometimes the delight he feels is so great that the prose is not only poetical in expression, but it is urged by his pleasure into rhythm. Here are two instances : 'The lake, the clouds, and mists were all | in motion, to the sound of sweeping winds'—'The Den of Wastdale at our feet | a gulf immeasurable.'

Nor, lastly, can he help, like a poet, creating or composing subjects. There are two (among a few others in this book) which, I have no doubt, Wordsworth had formed into poems in his mind ; and I will close this paper by reading them both. The first belongs to his ascent of Scawfell. They are on the top.

' "Look !" I exclaimed, "at yon ship upon the glittering sea !" "Is it a ship?" replied our shepherd-guide. "It can be nothing else," interposed my companion ; "I cannot be mistaken, I am so accustomed to the appearance of ships at sea." The Guide dropped the argument ; but, before a minute was gone, he quietly said, "Now look at your ship; it is changed into a horse." So indeed it was,—a horse with a gallant neck and head. We laughed heartily ; and, I hope, when again inclined to be positive, I may remember the ship and the horse upon the glittering sea ; and the calm confidence, yet submissiveness, of our wise Man of the Mountains, who certainly had more knowledge of clouds. than we, whatever might be our knowledge of ships.'

This is, you may think, commonplace enough. But it is a subject, isolated, and touched in for such imaginative moral treatment, with constant reference to the whole natural scene around, as Wordsworth has done in the poem of *Resolution and Independence*, when the Leech-gatherer and the Moorland are wedded together.

The other subject is more ideal; and no one but a poet could have first made the thing seem so vivid, *then* so visionary—object and subject alike; and no one, perhaps, but Wordsworth, could have so harmonised, as in the *Doe of Rylstone*, the animal, and the natural scene which accompanied it,—nor afterwards added to it his own passionate feeling of the mountain solitudes at night (with soft-sounding streams), nor finally brought all the mountains in, to embrace, with their invisible power, himself, and the quiet centre of the vision, the knoll, the dark yew-tree, and the white animal beneath it, and this :—'I shall say nothing of the moonlight aspect of the situation which had charmed us so much in the afternoon; but I wish you had been with us when, in returning to our friend's house, we espied his lady's large white dog, lying in the moonshine upon the round knoll under the old yew-tree in the garden, a romantic image—the dark tree and its dark shadow—and the elegant creature, as fair as a spirit ! The torrents murmured softly : the mountains down which they were falling did not, to my sight, furnish a background for this Ossianic picture; but I had a consciousness of the depth of the seclusion, and that mountains were embracing us on all sides; "I saw not, but I *felt* that they were there."'

This is Wordsworth, and this is half his charm. It needs the humanity, and the metrical music he would have given it, had he put it into verse, and ordered it therein; but who does not see the Poem within it ?

REMARKS

ON THE PERSONAL CHARACTER OF

WORDSWORTH'S POETRY.

By AUBREY DE VERE.

REMARKS ON THE PERSONAL CHARACTER OF WORDSWORTH'S POETRY.[1]

POETRY is frequently termed a 'creative art,' and, in a sense, the title is a just one; but it fails to express one of the most remarkable characteristics of poetry. A history, or a philosophical treatise, may also be called a creation of human intelligence; and though a first-class poem is a creation in a higher sense, standing as it does more remote from what may be called the 'handicraft' of the mind, still there remains a yet closer relation between true poetry and the poet. Byron, in one of his best poems, *The Lament of Tasso*, has made the Italian poet speak of his Christian Epic as his 'soul's *child*;' and there is a deep significance in the term. True poetry stands at the second, not the first, remove from a mere manufactured article; it is less a creation of the poet's intellect than the spiritual *progeny* of his total spiritual being. A history may reveal to us little of the writer; but the image of the poet is stamped upon great poetry, and stamped the more deeply the less the poet intended that it should be thus impressed. For this there is a momentous cause. It is not a single faculty of the mind that originates a true poem, though the imagination

---

is specially needed for that end ; it is the whole mind, and not the mind only, but the whole moral and emotional being, including those antecedent habits and experiences which fitted that being for its task. In this respect the highest poetry has some analogy to religious faith. It is this also which makes poetry such a large thing, and which constitutes the infinite variety of poetry. The circumstances which modify both the dispositions and the intellect of man are ever changing with the ages ; and therefore, even if the special poetic faculty of a Homer, a Dante, or a Shakespeare chanced to be exactly reproduced after the lapse of centuries, its poetic products would be essentially different. If the second Dante chose to imitate the first, the resemblances would be less than the diversities, for the imitator contented to be a mere plagiarist could never have been a Dante. Had he been a true poet he would have lived a true life, and by that life his genius and its products must have been substantially modified. It is this also which gives to great poetry, and especially to Wordsworth's, its extraordinary influence over all those who enter into *vital* relations with it. They find in it more than beautiful thoughts, vivid images, valuable conclusions, melodious cadences ; they find these things, and many more, not apart and isolated, but fused into a living and personal union. They find in it humanity, and a diverse humanity. It is their whole being that is challenged by a brother man, and to that challenge they respond.

The faculties of a man, though distinct faculties, yet act conjointly, not separately, and act thus more in poetry than in prose. The greatest poetry possesses most eminently this diversity in unity. In it we note, in closest union, faculties and habitudes, intellectual and moral, which might seem to stand naturally at the furthest distance apart each from each. They are thus united in poetry because they are thus united in man. Comparing poet with poet, we find that the qualities which jointly make up their several aggregates of power have been combined in very different proportions, and according to a different law. This is because in the highest poetry there is not only a human element but also a distinctly personal element. Such poetic personality is not to be confounded, as has been well observed by Mr. R. H. Hutton, with the trivial egotism which is ever displaying itself in mannerisms, affectations, and the other more direct appeals of self-love to unworthy sympathies. It is a personality to be found in the epic poet and the dramatist, who have no opportunity of thus obtruding themselves, not less than in the lyrical or elegiac poet. In this personality the universal human type is never lost or merged, while yet the individual type is differenced from other exemplars of human nature in its modes of self-manifestation—differenced by an essential, not an accidental diversity. In no modern poetry is this higher personality so strongly indicated as in Wordsworth's,—a proof in itself that he belongs to the first class of poets. It is in his higher poetry that Wordsworth is most eminently himself. Whatever he looks at he looks at in a way special to him. When he contemplates Nature, it is as the mystic of old perused the page of Holy Writ—making little of the letter, but passing through it to the 'spiritual interpretation.' If he regards man, it is not as a busy agent amid the turmoil of life, nor yet as an ascetic 'housed in a dream.' He regards him rather as a being in whom there unite countless mysterious influences both from the inner world of the spirit and from the visible creation of God, constituting, when thus combined, a creature destined for lofty contemplation, yet bound at the same time by a network of sympathies 'descending to the worm in charity.' If he looks upon human gladness, his ready sympathy with it is seldom unshadowed by a remembrance of the speed with which joy passes into sorrow; and, when contemplating sorrow, his most abiding thought is that her mission is to cleanse, to elevate, and to make free. He sees good in all things; yet in all good things he sees also some record of a higher good now lost, so that the rejoicing of man seems but the captive's harping in the land of exile. For him the smallest objects have rightful claims upon our deeper affections; yet the greatest are scarcely worthy of man's higher desires, for the *potential* excellencies in them too often are but 'things incomplete and purposes betrayed.'

It is easier to feel the strong personality of Wordsworth's poetry than to define critically in what it consists. I have suggested an approximate answer to this question, viz. that it consists—*1st*, in the unusually large number of qualities, intellectual and moral—qualities often not only remote from each other, but apparently opposed to each other—which are represented by his higher poetry; *2dly*, in the absolute unity in which these various qualities are blended; and, *3dly*, in the masterful moral strength which results from their *united* expression. This measureless strength was so deeply felt by Coleridge that in his *Friend* he describes Wordsworth's poetry as 'non verba sed tonitrua,' and elsewhere spoke of him as 'the Giant;' while admirers of a very different sort were but beginning to babble about the 'sweet simplicity' of his verse. Wordsworth did a signal injustice to his own poems when he classified them as poems of the 'Affections,' of the 'Fancy,' of the

' Imagination,' of ' Sentiment and Reflection.' There exist no poems which could less equitably be subjected to a classification so arbitrary. It but points to a partial truth, while it conceals one of primary importance. All of these faculties are doubtless found, though with diversities of proportion, in Wordsworth's poems; but they are commonly found in union, and they are found marshalled under the control of the highest poetic faculty, viz. the Imagination. *The Brothers, A Farewell,* ' She dwelt among the untrodden ways,' *Ruth,* nay, even *Laodamia,* were classed among the ' Poems of the Affections;' but there was no reason why they should not have been equally classed among those of the ' Imagination,' to which, in his later editions, many poems were transferred. On the other hand, ' She was a phantom of delight,' ' Three years she grew in sun and shower,' ' A slumber did my spirit seal,' and *Tintern Abbey,* were placed under the title, ' Poems of the Imagination :' but they might with equal justice have been referred to the category of the ' Affections ;' while the *Lines left upon a seat in a Yew-tree, The Happy Warrior, A Poet's Epitaph,* ' I heard a thousand blended notes,' and the *Ode to Duty,* might as fitly have been classed with the poems of the ' Imagination' as with those of ' Sentiment and Reflection.' It is but in a few of Wordsworth's inferior poems, such as might have been written by his imitators, that the higher faculties and impulses are found in separation. In his best poetry the diverse elements of the human intellect and of the human heart are found, not only in a greater variety, but in a closer and more spiritual union, than in any other poetry of his time; and, from that union, rose the extraordinary largeness of character which belonged to it. That characteristic was felt by the discerning, even in his earlier day, when other poets were travelling over the world in search of sensational incidents or picturesque costume, while he seldom sought a theme except among the primary relations of humanity, and those influences of exterior nature by which human nature is moulded.

The largeness that belongs to Wordsworth's poetry resulted in part from the circumstance that the numerous elements included in the poet's genius were often converse powers, which in an inferior poet would have proved antagonistic. The intelligential and the emotional parts of man's nature are often at variance, and each part has found special representatives among the poets; but in Wordsworth's poetry it is impossible to say whether the mind or the heart is the predominant power. Again, both in the mind and the heart there are energies of an almost antagonistic nature. What faculties are less like each other than those of meditation and observation? Yet to Wordsworth they belonged alike. He dwelt in meditation, as in a cavern, but one

> Not uncheered
> By stealthy influx of the timid day
> Mingling with night, such twilight to compose
> As Numa loved ; when, in the Egerian grot,
> From the sage Nymph appearing at his wish,
> He gained whate'er a regal mind might ask,
> Or need, of counsel breathed through lips divine.[1]

It will, perhaps, be as the inmate of some such holy seclusion that, in future days, those who have taken counsel with Wordsworth will most often image to themselves their master. They will picture him there as bending in meditative trance over

---

[1] *Ode to Lycoris.*

> Diluvian records ; or the sighs of Earth
> Interpreting ; or counting for old Time
> His minutes, by reiterated drops,
> Audible tears, from some invisible source
> That deepens upon fancy—more and more
> Drawn toward the centre whence those sighs creep forth
> To awe the lightness of Humanity.[1]

Yet it is certain that there was nothing by which Wordsworth was more characterised than by a gift the opposite of meditation—that of minute observation. The most delicate effects of Nature are those which he most delights in noting. He marks the autumnal leaves, 'unfaded, yet prepared to fade,' and listens to the wood-dove when its voice is

> Buried among trees
> *Yet to be come at* by the breeze.

Equally minute is his observation of those trifles by which human emotions are best indicated. Thus, of the deserted wife in her stern gloom, he says—

> And when she at her table gave me food,
> She did not look at me.

And again of her child—

> Her infant babe
> Had from its mother caught the trick of grief,
> And sighed among its playthings.

In such passages meditation and observation constitute a single intellectual act. Again, Imagination and Fancy are very different powers; yet vast and plastic as Wordsworth's imagination is, his poems include a series in which fancy predominates, while yet she ever sports under the watchful eye of the nobler power. Again, the intuitive faculties of

---

[1] *Ode to Lycoris.*

the mind are commonly contrasted with those of discursive thought: but, penetrating as is Wordsworth's 'gift of genuine insight,' he is not less remarkable for the accuracy of his logical processes, which communicates to his philosophical conclusions, and to his diction no less, that especial note of *truthfulness* which belongs to them no less than to his descriptions of Nature. Once more, what can be more dissimilar than the creative faculty whose energy moulds all things to shape, and the passive power which persistently submits itself to the influences of Nature, till it has taken in her meanings and absorbed her very soul? Early in life he wrote the lines—

> Nor less I deem that there are Powers
>   Which of themselves our minds impress;
> That we can feed this mind of ours
>   In a wise passiveness.[1]

It was this 'wise passiveness,' this poetic quietism, that drank in that power which Wordsworth put forth again in the form of creative energy. His 'passiveness' meant that profound and persistent *attention*, both of thought and will, of which but the fewest of men are capable. Where a habit of restlessness has destroyed this quiescent power, the resilient power, which should alternate with it, is dissipated before it is formed, the slender tendrils of thought having been successively snapped off before they had time to root themselves. All profound and authentic power, intellectual or imaginative, moral or spiritual, is thus stunted. Newton once said that the only difference between him and ordinary men was, that his mind could *attend* longer to a single train of thought. A great poet needs this power no less. Men who value them-

---

[1] *Expostulation and Reply.*

selves on their intellectual agility, can seldom rest upon a thought long enough to profit by it.   Between Wordsworth and Nature, and not less between him and that whole body of Truth of which he was cognisant, there were more than such nods of passing recognition,—there was a perpetual spiritual commerce.   Thence came the weight, the momentum and living strength of his knowledge.[1]

In Wordsworth's genius there were not less intimately combined certain *moral* qualities often found in antagonism to each other.   It has been said that his sympathies were rather *for* men than *with* men.   There is much truth in this remark.   In any case, his sympathies for men must have been held in check by the stately severity of his moral ideals.   But a compensation for this restriction, so far as it exists in him, is found in the circumstance that his sympathies for men were almost unlimited, as is marked by the fact that sternly as he condemned the evil-doer, he held contempt to be an unlawful sentiment, and but once expressed it in his poetry.   He affirms

> . . . . . that he who feels contempt
> For any living thing hath faculties
> Which he has never used ; that thought with him
> Is in its infancy.

Two other moral habits often found apart from each other are veneration and admiration.   In Wordsworth those two habitudes most happily united, as his imaginative soarings and exultations were blended with misgivings, his strong and fearless self-assertion with humility, his general hopefulness of disposition with moods of deep depression, his contemplative calmness with gusts of stormy passion, his

---

[1] Some admirable remarks on subjects analogous to this will be found in Principal Shairp's *Studies in Poetry and Philosophy*, pp. 47-50.

recluse and hermit spirit with patriotic ardours. It was the
vast number of these 'harmonious opposites' united in
Wordsworth, and the closeness with which they were interfused, which imparted to his poetry those characteristics of
magnanimity, of large-hearted humanity, and of vastness in
unity, which, taken together, constitute what is felt as the
personal character of Wordsworth's poetry.

WORDSWORTH'S POSITION AS AN ETHICAL TEACHER.

By THE DEAN OF SALISBURY.

WORDSWORTH'S POSITION AS AN ETHICAL TEACHER.[1]

WORDSWORTH has on the whole been fortunate in his critics.
If we leave out of sight the lucubrations of Jeffrey in the
Edinburgh Review, we have first to notice the incomparable
exposition of Coleridge, in the *Biographia Literaria*, where
the poet was for the first time placed in his proper niche.
The matured and thoughtful reflections of Sir Henry Taylor,
originally published in the *Quarterly Review*, and now reprinted in his works, give an adequate account of the energy
and force found by men of the generation now passing away
in the works of Wordsworth.   Principal Shairp, who is still
happily employed in declaring to younger Oxonians the
poetic faith of their elders, has blended biography and
criticism in an admirable essay.   If I do not make mention
of the refined and subtle teachings of Mr. R. H. Hutton,
the keen insight of Mr. Stopford Brooke, and the delightful
and characteristic introduction to the selections, which are
doing so much for Wordsworth's fame, the reason will be
apparent to the members of the Wordsworth Society.   I
venture, however, humbly to think that there are certain
points in Wordsworth's writings, taken as a whole, which
have hardly been touched upon as they deserve.   A poet

---

[1] Read to the Society in May 1883.

and a critic has said of the gifted sister of Maurice de Guérin, that 'her soul had the same characteristic quality as his talent—distinction.' If I may adapt and expand the phrase, I should say that there is in Wordsworth a distinction of moral elevation, which, when recognised adequately, discovers to us the reason why he has been a soother and guide of such spirits as John Stuart Mill, and why he bids fair to continue in the position, the unique position, of an ethical teacher as well as a great poet. In the remarkable introduction of Professor Jowett to the *Gorgias* of Plato we find these words: 'The true office of a poet or writer of fiction is not merely to give amusement, or to be the expression of the feelings of mankind, good or bad, or even to increase our knowledge of human nature. There have been poets in modern times, such as Goethe or Wordsworth, who have not forgotten their high vocation of teachers ; and the two greatest of the Greek dramatists owe their sublimity to their ethical character. The noblest truths, sung of in the purest and sweetest language, are still the proper material of poetry.' And again : 'He (the poet) is his own critic, for the spirit of poetry and criticism are not divided in him. His mission is not to disguise men from ·themselves, but to reveal to them their own nature, and make them better acquainted with the world around them.' I contend that the spirit of this instructive passage is to be found expressed in full completeness in the poems of Wordsworth which treat especially of the deeper emotions of the soul. Wordsworth himself, in the interesting reply to the letter of Mathetes, contained in the third volume of *The Friend* (edition of 1844), has revealed his own method, and the truest convictions of his matured intellect. The prose of Wordsworth possesses certain excellencies of its own. In the pamphlet on the Convention of Cintra we find some passages recalling the stately majesty of Burke. There is a letter to Walter Scott, on Dryden, in the highest vein of manly criticism. In the Essay on Epitaphs there is a certain Miltonic ring. But the answer to Mathetes, in terseness and purity, is quite admirable. In his portrayal of the temptations and intellectual pitfalls of young men there is an expression of true sympathy. And when he claims for Nature the office of 'a teacher of truth' through joy and through gladness, we have a subtle exposition of the affinity he always delights to trace between the ministrations of natural beauty and the perfect freedom of the moral faculties. Youth must return to the visible universe, to ancient books, and to those which breathe the ancient spirit. But beneath all desire for culture must reside the primary sense of duty. Man is ever to remember that to act is better than to think. The *Ode to Duty* all lovers of Wordsworth have, or ought to have, by heart. The poet evidently designs to bring into high relief the perfect play of a moral nature, wherein acts of virtue pass out of restraint into the glorious freedom and liberty which are proper to man. If it be asked, What in this and in *The Happy Warrior* constitute, in Wordsworth's eyes, the true panacea for moral ill? surely the word Self-government will supply all we are in search for. · 'Genial virtue falling back,' as Sir Henry Taylor says, 'upon severe virtue for support,' is the governing motive of the *Ode to Duty*. The conclusion of the reply to Mathetes, in which the poet speaks of the transference 'in the transport of imagination of the law of moral to physical natures, and the contemplation of all modes of existence as subservient to one spirit,' is fitly followed by the stanza which I venture to quote, familiar though it may be to all present :—

> To humbler functions, awful Power !
> I call thee : I myself commend
> Unto thy guidance from this hour ;
> Oh! let my weakness have an end !
> Give unto me, made lowly wise,
> The spirit of self-sacrifice ;
> The confidence of reason give,
> And in the light of truth thy bondman let me live !

Mr. Hutton has said, that 'Wordsworth alone, of all the great men of that day, had seen the light of the countenance of God, shining clear into the face of duty.' I am inclined to think that as the world grows older, a still greater value will attach to the ethical qualities of Wordsworth's verse. Whatever science may achieve, there will still be the stern whisper of a voice, 'Thy duty do,' and men, sated with the feverish poetry of emotion and sensation, will return to the sterner and more barren heights 'of verse that builds a princely throne on humble truth.' The attraction which the terse vigour possessed by Burns in his moral mood had for Wordsworth men will continue to find in *Michael*, *The Leech-Gatherer*, and the great *Ode*. Nowhere, perhaps, has the awful contrast between the prisoned spirit and the buoyancy of nature been brought out so fully as in the poem on the lonely Leech-Gatherer. I must not, however, be tempted into enlarging on the true lessons to thought and action to be derived from poems in the recollection of all. Again and again, as we all know, throughout Wordsworth's poetry, the outward picture is nothing to the poet unless it be connected with the freedom of duty, and the hope of immortality, where he finds the 'diviner air' in which man is destined to expatiate. Undoubtedly there are passages in *The Excursion* and *The Prelude* where we desire greater concentration of thought and expression, where the didactic impulse is hardly disguised; but from both of these poems a noble cento of passages might be extracted, all tending to indicate the true tendency of his ethical system, 'efficacious in making men wiser, better, and happier.' We are sometimes told that men are passing away from that stage of intellectual interest when the fragments of Coleridge and the poems of Wordsworth thrilled the souls of aspirant youth with a desire for a noble and dutiful life. It may be so. But I for one am still loath to believe that the hour of Wordsworth's empire as an ethical teacher and as a great poet is coming to an end. Mr. Emerson's words dwell in my memory: 'Alone in his time he treated the human mind well, and with an absolute trust. His adherence to his poetic creed rested on real inspirations. The *Ode on Immortality* is the high-water mark which the intellect has reached in this age.' May I venture to add, that his ethical teaching can never be separated from his poetic power? They are twin stars. Never by the keenest science can they be separated.

J. RUSSELL LOWELL'S ADDRESS AS
PRESIDENT, 1884.

J. RUSSELL LOWELL'S ADDRESS AS
PRESIDENT, 1884.

IN an early volume of the *Philosophical Transactions* there is
a paper concerning 'A certain kind of lead found in Germany
proper for Essays.' That it may have been first found in
Germany I shall not question, but deposits of this depressing
mineral have been discovered since in other countries also,
and we are all of us more or less familiar with its presence
in the essay,—nowhere more than when this takes the shape
of a critical dissertation on some favourite poet. Is this,
then, what poets are good for, that we may darken them
with our elucidations, or bury them out of sight under the
gathering silt of our comments? Must we, then, peep and
botanise on the rose of dawn or the passion-flower of sunset?
I should rather take the counsel of a great poet, the com-
mentaries on whom already make a library in themselves,
and say,

State contenti, umana gente, al quia,

—be satisfied if poetry be delightful, or helpful, or inspiring,
or all these together, but do not consider too nicely why it
is so.

Do not suppose that I am glancing covertly at what others,
from Coleridge down, have written of Wordsworth. I have
read them, including a recent very suggestive contribution of

Mr. Swinburne, with no other sense of dissatisfaction than that which springs from 'desiring this man's art and that man's scope.' No, I am thinking only that whatever can be profitably or unprofitably said of him has been already said, and that what is said for the mere sake of saying it is not worth saying at all. Moreover, I myself have said of him what I thought good more than twenty years ago. It is as wearisome to repeat one's-self as it is profitless to repeat others, and that we have said something, however inadequate it may afterwards seem to us, is a great hindrance to saying anything better.

The only function that a President of the Wordsworth Society is called on to perform is that of bidding it farewell at the end of his year, and it is perhaps fortunate that I have not had the leisure to prepare a discourse so deliberate as to be more worthy of the occasion. Without unbroken time there can be no consecutive thought, and it is my misfortune that in the midst of.a reflection or of a sentence I am liable to be called away by the bell of private or public duty. Even had I been able to prepare something that might have satisfied me better, I should still be at the disadvantage of following next after a retiring president[1] who always has the art of saying what all of us would be glad to say if we could, and who in his address last year gave us what seemed to me the finished model of what such a performance should be.

During the year that has passed since our last Annual Meeting, however idle the rest of us may have been, our Secretary has been fruitfully busy, and has given us two more volumes of what it is safe to say will be the standard

---

[1] Mr. Matthew Arnold.

and definitive edition of the poet's works. In this, the chronological arrangement of the several poems, and still more, the record in the margin of the author's corrections or repentances (*pentimenti*), as the Italians prettily call them, furnish us with a kind of self-registering instrument of the exactest kind by which to note, if not always the growth of his mind, yet certainly the gradual clarification of his taste, and the somewhat toilsome education of his ear. It is plain that with Wordsworth, more than with most poets, poetry was an art—an art, too, rather painfully acquired by one who was endowed by nature with more of the vision than of the faculty divine. Some of the more important omissions, especially, seem silently to indicate changes of opinion, though oftener, it may be suspected, of mood, or merely a shifting of the point of view, the natural consequence of a change for the better in his own material condition.

One result of this marshalling of the poems by the natural sequence of date is the conviction that, whatever modifications Wordsworth's ideas concerning certain social and political questions may have undergone, these modifications had not their origin in inconsiderate choice, or in any seduction of personal motive, but were the natural and unconscious outcome of enlarged experience, and of more profound reflection upon it. I see no reason to think that he ever swerved from his early faith in the beneficence of freedom, but rather that he learned the necessity of defining more exactly in what freedom consisted, and the conditions, whether of time or place, under which alone it can be beneficent, of insisting that it must be an evolution and not a manufacture, and that it should co-ordinate itself with the prior claims of society and civilisation. The process in his mind was the ordinary crystallisation of sentiment hitherto swimming in vague solution, and now precipitated in principles. He had made the inevitable discovery that comes with years, of how much harder it is to do than to see what 'twere good to do, and grew content to build the poor man's cottage, since the means did not exist of building the prince's palace he had dreamed. It is noticeable how many of his earlier poems turn upon the sufferings of the poor from the injustice of man or the unnatural organisation of society. He himself had been the victim of an abuse of the power that rank and wealth sometimes put into the hands of the unworthy, and had believed in political methods, both for remedy and prevention. He had believed also in the possibility of a gregarious regeneration of man by sudden and sharp, if need were by revolutionary expedients, like those impromptu conversions of the inhabitants of a city from Christ to Mahomet, or back again, according to the creed of their conqueror, of which we read in mediæval romances. He had fancied that the laws of the Universe would curtsey to the resolves of the National Convention. He had seen this hope utterly baffled and confuted, as it seemed, by events in France, by events that had occurred, too, in the logical sequence foretold by students of history. He had been convinced, perhaps against his will, that a great part of human suffering has its root in the nature of man, and not in that of his institutions. Where was the remedy to be found, if remedy indeed there were? It was to be sought at least only in an improvement wrought by those moral influences that build up and buttress the personal character. Goethe taught the self-culture that results in self-possession, in breadth and impartiality of view, and in equipoise of mind; Wordsworth inculcated that self-development through intercourse with man and nature which leads to self-sufficingness, self-sustainment, and equilibrium of character. It was the individual that should and could be leavened, and through the individual the lump. To reverse the process was to break the continuity of history and to wrestle with the angel of destiny.

And for one of the most powerfully effective of the influences for which he was seeking, where should he look if not to Religion? The sublimities and amenities of outward nature might suffice for William Wordsworth, might for him have almost filled the place of a liberal education ; but they elevate, teach, and above all console the imaginative and solitary only, and suffice to him who already suffices to himself. The thought of a god vaguely and vaporously dispersed throughout the visible creation, the conjecture of an animating principle that gives to the sunset its splendours, its passion to the storm, to cloud and wind their sympathy of form and movement, that sustains the faith of the crag in its forlorn endurance, and of the harebell in the slender security of its stem, may inspire or soothe, console or fortify the man whose physical and mental fibre is so sensitive that, like the spectroscope, it can both feel and record these impalpable impulses and impressions, these impersonal vibrations of identity between the fragmentary life that is in himself and the larger life of the universe whereof he is a particle. Such supersensual emotions might help to make a poem, but they would not make a man, still less a social being. Absorption in the whole would not tend to that development of the individua which was the corner-stone of Wordsworth's edifice.

That instinct in man which leads him to fashion a god in his own image, why may it not be an instinct as natural and

wholesome as any other?   And it is not only God that this
instinct embodies and personifies, but every profounder
abstract conception, every less selfish devotion of which
man is capable.   Was it, think you, of a tiny crooked outline on the map, of so many square miles of earth, or of
Hume and Smollett's History that Nelson was thinking
when he dictated what are perhaps the most inspiring words
ever uttered by an Englishman to Englishmen?   Surely it
was something in woman's shape that rose before him with
all the potent charm of noble impulsion that is hers as
much through her weakness as her strength.   And the
features of that divine apparition, had they not been
painted in every attitude of their changeful beauty by
Romney?

Coarse and rudimentary as this instinct is in the savage,
it is sublimed and etherealised in the profoundly spiritual
imagination of Dante, which yet is forced to admit the
legitimacy of its operation.   Beatrice tells him—

> Thus to your minds it needful is to speak,
> Because through sense alone they understand :
> It is for this that Scripture condescends
> Unto your faculties and feet and hands,
> To God attributes, meaning something else.

And in what I think to be the sublimest reach to which
poetry has risen, the conclusion of the *Paradiso*, Dante
tells us that within the three whirling rings of vari-coloured
light that symbolise the wisdom, the power, and the love of
God, he seems to see the image of man.

Wordsworth would appear to have been convinced that
this Something deeply interfused, this pervading but illusive
intimation, of which he was dimly conscious, and that only
by flashes, could never serve the ordinary man, who was in

no way and at no time conscious of it, as motive, as judge, and more than all as consoler,—could never fill the place of the Good Shepherd. Observation convinced him that what are called the safeguards of society are the staff also of the individual members of it, that tradition, habitude, and heredity are great forces, whether for impulse or restraint. He had pondered a pregnant phrase of the poet Daniel, where he calls religion 'mother of Form and Fear.' A growing conviction of its profound truth turned his mind towards the Church as the embodiment of the most potent of all traditions, and to her public offices as the expression of the most socially humanising of all habitudes. It was no empty formalism that could have satisfied his conception, but rather that 'Ideal Form, the universal mould,' that *forma mentis æterna* which has given shape and expression to the fears and hopes and aspirations of mankind. And what he understood by Fear is perhaps shadowed forth in the *Ode to Duty*, in which he speaks to us out of an ampler ether than in any other of his poems, and which may safely 'challenge insolent Greece and haughty Rome' for a comparison either in kind or degree.

I ought not to detain you longer from the interesting papers, the reading of which has been promised for this meeting. No member of this Society would admit that its existence was needed to keep alive an interest in the poet, or to promote the study of his works. But I think we should all consent that there could be no better reason for its being than the fact that it elicits an utterance of the impression made by his poetry on many different minds looking at him from as many different points of view. That he should have a special meaning for every one in an audience so various in temperament and character might well induce us to credit him with a wider range of sympathies and greater breadth of thought than each of us separately would, perhaps, be ready to admit.

But though reluctant to occupy more than my fair share of your time, the occasion tempts me irresistibly to add a few more words of general criticism. It has seemed to me that Wordsworth has too commonly been estimated rather as philosopher or teacher than as poet. The value of what he said has had more influence with the jury than the way in which he said it. There are various methods of criticism, but I think we should all agree that literary work is to be judged from the purely literary point of view.

If it be one of the baser consolations, it is also one of the most disheartening concomitants of long life, that we get used to everything. Two things, perhaps, retain their freshness more perdurably than the rest,—the return of spring, and the more poignant utterances of the poets. And here, I think, Wordsworth holds his own with the best. But Mr. Arnold's volume of selections from him suggests a question of some interest, for the Wordsworth Society of special interest,—How much of his poetry is likely to be a permanent possession? The answer to this question is involved in the answer to a question of wider bearing,—What are the conditions of permanence? Immediate or contemporaneous recognition is certainly not dominant among them, or Cowley would still be popular, Cowley, to whom the Muse gave every gift but one, the gift of the unexpected and inevitable word. Nor can mere originality assure the interest of posterity, else why are Chaucer and Gray familiar, while Donne, one of the subtlest and most self-irradiating minds that ever sought an outlet in verse, is known only to the few? Since Virgil there have been at most but four cosmopolitan authors—Dante, Cervantes, Shakespeare, and Goethe. These have stood the supreme test of being translated into all tongues, because the large humanity of their theme, and of their handling of it, needed translating into none. Calderon is a greater poet than Goethe, but even in the most masterly translation he retains still a Spanish accent, and is accordingly *interned* (if I may Anglicise a French word) in that provincialism which we call nationality.

When one reads what has been written about Wordsworth, one cannot fail to be struck by the predominance of the personal equation in the estimate of his value, and when we consider his claim to universal recognition, it would not be wise to overlook the rare quality of the minds that he has most attracted and influenced. If the character of the constituency may be taken as the measure of the representation, there can be no doubt that, by his privilege of interesting the highest and purest order of intellect, Wordsworth must be set apart from the other poets, his contemporaries, if not above them. And yet we must qualify this praise by the admission that he continues to be insular, that he makes no 'conquests beyond the boundaries of his mother tongue, that, more than perhaps any other poet of equal endowment, he is great and surprising in passages and ejaculations. In these he truly

> Is happy as a lover, and attired
> In sudden brightness, like a man inspired ;

in these he loses himself, as Sir Thomas Browne would say, in an *O altitudo!* where his muse is indeed a muse of fire, that can ascend, if not to the highest heaven of invention, yet to the supremest height of impersonal utterance. Then, like Elias the prophet, 'he stands up as fire, and his word burns like a lamp.' But too often, when left to his own resources, and to the conscientious performance of the duty laid upon him to be a great poet *quand même*, he seems diligently intent on producing fire by the primitive method of rubbing the dry sticks of his blank verse one against the other, while we stand in shivering expectation of the flame that never comes. In his truly inspired and inspiring passages it is remarkable also that he is most unlike his ordinary self, least in accordance with his own theories of the nature of poetic expression. When at his best, he startles and waylays as only genius can, but is furthest from that equanimity of conscious and constantly indwelling power that is the characteristic note of the greatest work. If Wordsworth be judged by the *ex ungue leonem* standard, by passages, or by a dozen single poems, no one capable of forming an opinion would hesitate to pronounce him, not only a great poet, but among the greatest, convinced in the one case by the style, and in both by the force that radiates from him, by the stimulus he sends kindling through every fibre of the intellect and of the imagination. At the same time there is no admittedly great poet in placing whom we are forced to acknowledge so many limitations and to make so many concessions.

Even as a teacher he is often too much of a pedagogue, and is apt to forget that poetry instructs not by precept and inculcation, but by hints, and indirections and suggestions, by inducing a mood rather than by enforcing a principle or a moral. He sometimes impresses our fancy with the image of a schoolmaster whose classroom commands an unrivalled prospect of cloud and mountain, of all the pomp and prodigality of heaven and earth. From time to time he calls his pupils to the window, and makes them see what without the finer intuition of his eyes they had never seen, makes them feel what, without the sympathy of his more penetrating sentiment, they had never felt. It seems the revelation of a new heaven and a new earth, and to contain in itself its own justification. Then suddenly recollecting his duty, he shuts the window, calls them back to their tasks, and is equally well pleased and more discursive in enforcing on them the truth that the moral of all this is that in order to be happy they must be virtuous. If the total absence of any sense of humour had the advantage sometimes of making Wordsworth sublimely unconscious, it quite as often made him so to his loss.

In his noblest utterances man is absent except as the antithesis that gives a sharper emphasis to nature. The greatest poets, I think, have found man more interesting than nature, have considered nature as no more than the necessary scenery, artistically harmful if too pompous or obtrusive, before which man acts his tragi-comedy of life. This peculiarity of Wordsworth results naturally from the fact that he had no dramatic power, and of narrative power next to none. If he tell us a story, it is because it gives him the chance to tell us something else, and to him of more importance. In Scott's narrative poems the scenery is accessory and subordinate. It is a picturesque background to his figures, a landscape through which the action rushes like a torrent, catching a hint of colour perhaps from rock or tree, but never any image so distinct that it tempts us aside to reverie or meditation. With Wordsworth the personages are apt to be lost in the landscape, or kept waiting idly while the poet muses on its deeper suggestions. And he has no sense of proportion, no instinct of choice and discrimination. All his thoughts and emotions and sensations are of equal value in his eyes because they are his, and he gives us methodically and conscientiously all he can, and not that only which he cannot help giving because it must and will be said. There is no limit to his—let us call it facundity. He was dimly conscious of this, and turned by a kind of instinct, I suspect, to the sonnet, because its form forced boundaries upon him, and put him under bonds to hold his peace at the end of the fourteenth line. Yet even here nature would out, and the oft-recurring *same subject continued* lures the nun from her cell to the convent parlour, and tempts the student to make a pulpit of his pensive citadel. The hour-glass is there, to be sure, with its lapsing admonition, but it reminds the preacher only that it can be turned.

I have said that Wordsworth was insular, but, more than this, there is also something local, I might say parochial, in his choice of subject and tone of thought. I am not sure that what is called philosophical poetry ever appeals to more than a very limited circle of minds, though to them it appeals with an intimate power that makes them fanatical in their preference. Perhaps none of those whom I have called universal poets (unless it be Dante) calls out this fanaticism, for they do not need it, fanaticism being a sure token either of weakness in numbers or of weakness in argument. The greatest poets interest the passions of men no less than their intelligence, and are more concerned with the secondary than the primal sympathies, with the concrete than with the abstract.

But I have played the *advocatus diaboli* long enough. I come back to the main question from which I set out. Will Wordsworth survive, as Lucretius survives, through the splendour of certain sunbursts of imagination refusing for a

passionate moment to be subdued by the unwilling material
in which it is forced to work, while that material takes fire
in the working as it can and will only in the hands of genius,
as it cannot and will not for example, in the hands of Dr.
Akenside? Is he to be known a century hence as the
author of remarkable passages? Certainly a great part of
him will perish, not, as Ben Jonson said of Donne, for want
of understanding, but because too easily understood. His
teaching, whatever it was, is part of the air we breathe, and
has lost that charm of exclusion and privilege that kindled
and kept alive the zeal of his acolytes while it was still sec-
tarian, or even heretical. But he has that surest safeguard
against oblivion, that imperishable incentive to curiosity and
interest that belongs to all original minds. His finest utterances do not merely nestle in the ear by virtue of their
music, but in the soul and life, by virtue of their meaning.
One would be slow to say that his general outfit as poet was
so complete as that of Dryden, but that he habitually dwelt
in a diviner air, and alone of modern poets renewed and
justified the earlier faith that made poet and prophet inter-
changeable terms. Surely he was not an artist in the
strictest sense of the word; neither was Isaiah, but he had
a rarer gift, the capability of being greatly inspired. Popular, let us admit, he can never be; but as in Catholic countries men go for a time into retreat from the importunate
dissonances of life to collect their better selves again by
communion with things that are heavenly, and therefore
eternal, so this Chartreuse of Wordsworth, dedicated to the
Genius of Solitude, will allure to its imperturbable calm the
finer natures and the more highly tempered intellects of
every generation, so long as man has any intuition of what
is most sacred in his own emotions and sympathies, or of

whatever in outward nature is most capable of awakening them and making them operative, whether to console or strengthen.   And over the entrance-gate to that purifying seclusion shall be inscribed :

> Minds innocent and quiet take
> This for an hermitage.

THE POETIC INTERPRETATION OF NATURE.

By HON. RODEN NOEL.

THE POETIC INTERPRETATION OF NATURE.

WITH EXAMPLES TAKEN CHIEFLY FROM WORDSWORTH.[1]

I PROPOSE to say a few words on that Poetry of Nature of which Wordsworth was High Priest—my examples being of course taken chiefly from him—though I quite feel with Mr. Arnold that the fruitful application of ideas to life is one main element in the impression he makes. But I cannot follow that fine poet and critic in his apparent depreciation of Nature-poetry, as when he dismisses Shelley as the poet of the clouds and sunsets, and says he had not got hold of the right subject-matter for poetry. It is distinctly a modern subject, no doubt; but, I should have thought, one newly reclaimed for beneficent poetic ends,— so much more fertile possession made over to the Muse, in addition to that purely human interest which has been hers from of old.

I believe that Rousseau, Wordsworth, Byron, Shelley, Keats, Coleridge, were verily prophets, to whom a new revelation was intrusted. In a time when all secrets were at length supposed to be laid bare before man's microscopic understanding, all superstitions exploded, all mysteries explained; when the universe emptied of ancient awe seemed no longer venerable, but a hideous lazar-house rather, made visible to all human eyes in every ghastly corner of it; before the Circe-wand of materialism, Love metamorphosed into a

---

[1] Read to the Society, July 1884.

sensation, Man shrivelled to a handful of dust, the Body of God's own breathing world with familiar irreverence laid upon the board of some near-sighted professor to be dissected; when the angels of Faith and Hope seemed to be deserting for ever the desecrated shrines of mankind, —then it was that these Prophet-Poets, as very ministers of Heaven, pointed men to the World-Soul, commanding them once more to veil their faces before the swift subtle splendour of Universal Life.   The moods of Nature do mysteriously respond to the moods of Man.   To the sensitive spirit the sea, the mountains, and the stars are very types and symbols of permanence, order, eternity.   Nature and man are elder sister and younger brother; she wakes intelligence and will in him; he knows himself in knowing her.   She seems to him a dumb and blind elder sister, whose laws inexorably bind him, while he imposes himself upon her, reading spiritual meanings in her face.   The chaos of our own soul, individual human degradation, of which we in the midst can but dimly divine the issue, receives a mystic interpretation from what seems the unconscious innocence of a sphere which yet manifests evil and good, strength and weakness, —though, withal, the grand universality of a Kosmos. Thence we can look up with greater trust than before even for the worms that 'sting one another in the dust.'

Why do the Arab in the desert, the Persian on his mountain, bow before the all-beholding sun?   In him is no sin, no vanity, falsehood, or vain ambition, himself veritable incarnation of one invisible Sun.   He who loses his own personality in Nature, who lays down before her, the universal mother and tomb of humanity, his own private wrongs and griefs and fevered aspirations, hereby redresses the balance so unduly weighted with the self-will and momentary longings of one restless man. For she is one who toils not nor dreams, errs not nor supposes, raves not nor repents, but calmly fulfils herself for ever.

In her general aspects, Nature, if we do not peer too closely into the minutiæ of her painful strife and struggle, looks inevitable and calm, not in perpetual spiritual conflict like ourselves; and hence she seems to offer *rest* to those who love her. The harmony of inviolable laws appears in her coöperant to an end. But I think that this inevitableness of a universal order implicitly involves the idea of rightness, that of some fulfilled obligation tinged with morality, or what is akin to it. I know this cannot be proved, but I think it may be felt.

The individual, in so far as he can assert himself against, or regard himself as out of relation with, the whole Kosmos is wrong, evil; but in harmony with all he is right. And though indeed external nature may be really composed of individuals, yet if it be so, we are not, except in some small degree as respects the animal world, in the secret of their subjectivity, and therefore cannot know them as such. Intelligences who should be unable to put themselves in conscious communication with ours might well regard human bodies as part of a fixed order of inflexible laws, without private volition or caprice, just as we now regard the inorganic. For even in ourselves private volitions are capable of being reduced to a law of averages through statistical science, which points to a real eternal order beyond and beneath our discords, resolving them into harmony. And however this be, to merge our personality in quiet or rapturous contemplation of universal natural order proves indeed heavenly relief from the too often intolerable burden of an isolated self-life.

All that is profound, eternal, impersonal in us, goes forth to wed with the profound, eternal, impersonal Heart of all. It is beyond our good and right, more than our ideal, yet justifies, sanctions, transcends, absorbs it. Universal Nature, who is one with us, constitutes, nourishes, creates us; while we in her constitute, nourish, create ourselves, one another, and her. If it be true that we form her in our image, it is also true that from her we derive the power so to form her; we are her creatures, living in and by her. Verily, it is our *privilege* to know conflict, and bewilderingly to realise some fundamental inner freedom, which is more than mere inanimate law; but the seemingly inanimate order is a revelation of still higher privilege,—that of inevitable Will, at one with unhesitating Wisdom; and this surely is the inmost verity of things, our defect and disharmony being but an isolated chord in the grand music.

Therefore, I repeat, 'the light that never was, on sea or land, the consecration, and the poet's dream' is indeed a new revelation, made peculiarly in the modern poetry of true spiritual insight, and of this Poetry of Nature Wordsworth is the High Priest. Not only does it pour fresh illuminating light upon Nature herself, but it also deepens and enlarges our comprehension of man. By means of their analogues in Nature, the human heart and mind may be more profoundly understood. Human emotions win a double dearness, or an added sorrow from their fellowship and association with outward scenes. While Nature can be fathomed only through her analogies with the desires, fears, and aspirations of the human soul, these again can scarcely become defined and articulate save through the mystic and multiform appearances of Nature. We have here then a new poetic product of priceless value; neither the external scene alone, nor man alone, but rather the spiritual child of their espousals.

It is really almost puerile nowadays to suppose that there is an absolute Nature, which science and the land-surveyor are alone competent correctly to know,—while poetry invents a world of her own wherewith to amuse her-self and other people. Spiritual imagination alone knows Nature; I don't say *adequately*, even she,—but with any approach to adequacy; though, of course, the common con-stitution of our senses and understanding presents to us an external world which, so far as superficial characteristics are concerned, is pretty well the same for all, and which quite sufficiently serves the purposes alike of science, of common intercourse, and of practical utility. But since Berkeley, Kant, and modern physiology, it is no longer permissible to doubt that even these superficial qualities, and what we call 'laws of nature,' are merely the interpretation which our sensible and mental constitution enables us to put upon the language of the Kosmos, wherein a great deal more is meant than meets the ear. Of course, one must be insane to deny that the sea is a vast quantity of salt water, or that a primrose is indeed a yellow primrose, as Peter Bell with his plain common sense sees it to be. But it is quite compatible with sanity to believe that both sea and primrose are a great deal more also. Only one must have other faculties, or faculties more highly trained, to discern the more. Poetry does not tell pretty lies for the sake of amusement, but penetrates to the heart of things. Therefore, I cannot alto-gether agree with Mr. Ruskin about 'pathetic fallacy,'—although no doubt there *is* a 'false' way of looking at things as well as a true. The nimble fancy may suggest mere points of superficial resemblance, hardly vital or essential to the objects, which the poet endows with animation and soul, rather perhaps conveying an erroneous conception of their proper and peculiar character. So far I can agree; but what I urge is that to endow them with animation and soul is not necessarily to falsify, may rather be to see more to the very root of them. I don't pretend that the poet speaks with precise accuracy in his metaphors and similes, but he suggests an inner truth of things, to which the un-imaginative are simply blind. Indeed precise accuracy belongs to the region of the understanding, which is by itself incapable of the higher truth. So that when Mr. Arnold tells us to conceive dogmas in the light of poetry, if he means with elasticity, in no hard and fast, cast-iron fashion, I can follow; but if he means as mere gracious figurative fables, I cannot.

For instance, nothing could be more realistically descriptive than Wordsworth's magnificent lines on the Yew-trees of Borrowdale :

> each particular trunk a growth
> Of intertwisted fibres serpentine
> Up-coiling, and inveterately convolved ;

but the imaginative touches are equally true ; nay, penetrate more to the heart of things :

> Nor uninformed with Phantasy, and looks
> That threaten the profane ;

then those wonderful personifications, less fanciful than Shelley's in *Adonais*, but more imaginative, how deep they go, how grand and solemn the mystery they unveil !

> beneath whose sable roof
> . . . . ghostly Shapes
> May meet at noontide ; Fear and trembling Hope,
> Silence and Foresight ; Death the Skeleton
> And Time the Shadow.

To meditative imagination, in the umbrageous atmosphere
of the yew-trees, these august Presences verily abide—more
actually, than their ancient boughs with coral berries.   The
cuckoo is no mere cuckoo, but 'a wandering voice;' a voice
of dear memories, and coming summer.   'Yellow bees in
the ivy bloom' are to the poet 'forms more real than living
man, nurslings of immortality.'   Nay, those outer things are
because these inner realities are; the former would not be
without the latter—they are images and shadows only;
the leaping lamb is on earth because the Lamb of God
is in Heaven, in the inner Holy of Holies of Humanity.
Light is in the sense, in outer space, because Light is in the
spirit, in the understanding. The perishing bread that sustains the body is by virtue of the Bread of Life.   To the
opened inner eye there is indeed a Real Presence in the
elements of the Eucharist.

I do not mean to say that the animism of savages is a
correct belief, for they simply deify phenomena without
analysis, or suspicion that these are largely subjective; nor
even do I say that the Pagan poets were correct in their
mythological beliefs; or the mediævals in their fairy-lore; yet
I believe that they were not far from the truth when they
formulated their conviction that our spiritual kinship with
Nature testifies to some spiritual beings like ourselves behind
the phenomena of Nature,—the elements, and so-called inanimate objects, being only their expression, body, or vesture.
Nor do I deem such a belief at all incompatible with a full
recognition of that ever-widening kingdom of physical law, to
which modern Science introduces us : only let science 'stick
to her own last'!   Quite certainly the ancients were never
guilty of deliberately, in cold blood, inventing a quasi-poetic,
or metaphorical diction, which the vulgar were so foolish as

to take for literal fact, as our pseudo-scientific insincerity of unbelief, and incapacity for comprehending other modes of thought and feeling, now complacently assume. On the contrary, modern Nature-poetry is reverting, though in its own fashion, and in accordance with other altered convictions of our age, to this primal conception of the ancients. For as Science—though furnishing in her fairy tales new material for poetry—affords no help to the poetic feeling of life and spirit in Nature, so neither does a theology which teaches that there is a God external to the world, who once made, and still possibly sustains it. Poetry demands God immanent in Man and Nature. So that the author of Ecclesiastical Sonnets, the High Priest of this special poetry, yet hesitating and bewildered by his dogmatic creed, as by his habit of inherited thought, startles us out of our propriety by exclaiming :

> Great God ! I 'd rather be
> A Pagan suckled in a creed outworn,
> So might I, standing on this pleasant lea,
> Have glimpses that would make me less forlorn ;
> Have sight of Proteus rising from the sea ;
> Or hear old Triton blow his wreathèd horn !

But the philosophy of idealism supplies for the logical faculty the conception needed to lift it into some harmony with the vision of children, poets, and the more primitive, less sophisticated, races. Wordsworth, however, and Coleridge seem scarcely to dare believe what to the inmost core of them they feel true. You will remember the strange passage, in one of Coleridge's philosophical poems, where he apologises to his wife for giving utterance to his conviction! Schiller, in his *Gods of Greece*, makes a melancholy lament over their extinction. And I confess that, dearly as

I love Mrs. Browning, her poem in reply to Schiller appears
to me in all respects the least felicitous of her works.   Pan
is not dead—save in this sense,—that God manifest in
Nature is now, since the revelation of our Blessed Lord
Jesus Christ, felt to be less worshipful than God manifest in
Divine Humanity.   There would seem to be three elements,
which, combined, create the world as we know it—the God
in Man, the God in Nature, and the Defect in both.   We
and the world have a common reason, and a common heart,
or we could not know the world.   The richer and deeper
our own life, the more can we enter into the life of the world,
and the more fully we enter into that, the more universal
and profound becomes our own.   Not only is our mental
life developed through perception, but physiology shows the
close correlation of our external and internal lives, so that
without the nourishment and sustainment of our bodies by
earth and sun, our soul-life in its present form would be
impossible.   Yet the Divine Reality is deeper than plummet
of human understanding ever sounded : eye hath not seen,
nor ear heard.   The outer world is but symbol and parable,
the imperfect self-manifestation to our defective apprehen-
sion of eternal Ideas, which are substantial.   That is a truth
familiar to mystics of all ages, and in recent times has been
virtually restated by two notable teachers, one a man of
science, James Hinton, the other a theologian, Cardinal
Newman.   The world, says Hinton, seems to us dead, only
on account of our own deadness.   And therefore, in proportion as we are made alive, will the life of the world
become manifest to us.   Therefore also I conceive Wordsworth's position in the immortal *Ode on Immortality* to be
thoroughly justified.   Fresh from the Fountain of his being,
the child-spirit sees most truly.   The gleam of the sanctuary

is upon him, and around : 'meadow, grove, and stream, the earth, and every common sight, to him do seem, apparelled in celestial light, the glory and the freshness of a dream.'

> Heaven lies about us in our infancy !
> Shades of the prison-house begin to close
> Upon the growing Boy,
>
> .   .   .   .   .
>
> The Youth, who daily farther from the east
> Must travel, still is Nature's priest,
> And by the vision splendid
> Is on his way attended ;
> At length the Man perceives it die away,
> And fade into the light of common day.

But—

> The Clouds that gather round the setting sun
> Do take a sober colouring from an eye
> That hath kept watch o'er man's mortality ;
>
> .   .   .   .   .
>
> Thanks to the human heart by which we live,
> Thanks to its tenderness, its joys, and fears,
> To me the meanest flower that blows can give
> Thoughts that do often lie too deep for tears.

The Child-spirit is alone immortal ; yet the Divine Child in his eternal youth looks often forth from the sadder and wiser eyes of man. The old mystics believed that when Adam and Eve sinned, the gods or angels they talked with became hidden from them, and appeared to them as trees and flowers, and common earth or sky,—beautiful indeed, but hardly animate, and they quite unable to hold intelligent converse with them as before. To Blake, the seer-poet, the sun was no mere ball of fiery vapours, but a glorious company of the Heavenly Host praising God. Yet to me it appears that James Hinton was wrong in his assumption that Man alone is fallen or defective, while Nature remains perfect. The impression one derives is rather that we have shared in her fall, or she in ours. Between us there can be no such chasm. Nay, she is 'red in tooth and claw with ravine.' A formidable indictment, indeed, has been drawn up against her in the outraged names of justice and of love! She has her moods as we have, good and evil, grave and gay, desolate and happy, cruel and kind, terrible and gentle, while we respond to her varying humour according to our own. Hence it is that poets interpret her differently according to their own characters. The grand and gloomy, the Titanic and diabolic, find their expression in Byron, but the tranquil and tender chiefly in Wordsworth. I really do not think there is much 'pathetic fallacy' in the ascription by poets of their own moods to Nature. It is rather that in these dominant moods of theirs they are able to feel the corresponding note in Nature. There is indeed in Her, as there is also in ourselves, a deep foundation of tranquillity and calm under all the roaring and unrest of loud waves,—a region of repose, an inner haven of peace; and the profoundest poet abides, or is anchored there, however he may be tossed to and fro on the upper surge. And very often have her loud pæans of rejoicing been felt by the sorrowful to be out of harmony with their sorrow. Or again, the overflowing, multitudinous joy of her springs and summers may carry consolation, and conviction that all is well, into the arid recesses of a mourner's heart. Or once again, the dreariness and desolation of her dark seas and shores, her mountains and barren plains, may unbearably overwhelm an already overburdened soul.

I have admitted with Mr. Ruskin that there is a false and

vicious metaphorical diction used by poetasters, insincerely, as a kind of 'current coin;' frigid conceits, cold artifices of mere talent, or mere jingling babble for effect, from which precisely Wordsworth came to deliver us. And doubtless a man's individual feeling may blind him to the dominant mood in Nature, at a given moment. So far he may misrepresent her.

A true poet is ever a loving and faithful observer of the external features and deportment of his mistress. But just because his look is the long look of a lover,—no passing glance,—he sees more than that. Real feeling, I hold, must put us into some vital relation with the actuality of things, though the expression of it may be but a tentative striving to body forth the truth about them. Thus when Kingsley, in his beautiful ballad, *The Sands of Dee*, calls the foam of the wave that drowned Mary 'cruel,' though indeed the foam itself may not be cruel, he gives utterance to a feeling that is inevitable, and therefore in all probability justified; for behind those engulfing seas there surely must be some pitiless and murderous Power, some Prince, or princes, of a world that 'lieth in the wicked,' however that power may be directed and overruled by a Paternal Master-Love. And when Keats, in describing the slow movement of spent shredding foam along the back of a heavy wave, characterises it by the phrase 'wayward indolence,' he fixes and determines the idiosyncrasy of this movement in a manner simply impossible to a poet who should either fail to perceive, or else resolve not to allow himself the language of analogy. There is some occult identity between spent foam and our 'wayward indolence.'

The heart of Wordsworth beats in sympathy with the sea's when he sings—

> Listen ! the mighty being is awake,
> And doth with his eternal motion make
> A sound like thunder everlastingly.

The great Apocalypse of Dante is one colossal translation of the inner truths of heart and soul into the corresponding imagery and environment of sense. When Milton calls the boat that wrecked Lycidas

> That fatal and perfidious bark,
> Built in the eclipse and rigg'd with curses dark,
> That sunk so low that sacred head of thine ;

how unliteral, inaccurate, and yet true to the inmost fact is he ! 'Stone him with hardened hearts, harder than stones,' says Shakespeare. Stones are hard because hearts are, not hearts hard because stones are, though that is not the common opinion. To arrive at the true spiritual order, you must reverse the order of experience. Metaphor is the interpretation of one thing through another. And one thing *is* through another ! Seeing it as isolated, we see it, through our own defect, imperfectly. It ever fulfils itself by analogy, developed and discerned, as by passing on into some other phase or form of existence. Everything is a Proteus. But as Keats attributes the bright mail of fish to the kisses of lovers, Wordsworth assigns to Duty the guardianship of the Ancient Heavens, and the laughter of fragrant flowers. Nor is this graceful falsehood, but vital truth.

We have in *The Thorn*—not, on the whole, a very inspired poem—some minute, faithful description, characteristic of Wordsworth. His graphic delineations of landscape place a vivid imagery before the sense, which must ever be dear to true lovers of Nature, dearer than the

N

often vaguer and more confused reminiscences, or too
phantasmal, nebulous, and unarticulated, however gorgeous,
inventions of Shelley.   But still the imaginative touch in
that poem goes deeper than all the realism—

> And she is known to every star,
> And every wind that blows.

Yet if that is false, if it hints not, in the only or best way
possible, at a vital reality, why should it give peculiar
delight?   Can what is known to be the most utterly fantas-
tic, and irrational element in the whole composition boast
such a prerogative?   Surely not, though it be quite unnecessary to define this imaginative truth more precisely.
Again, do we not thank our poet when he calls the Wye
'wanderer through the woods,' and tells us of the Thames
'wandering at its own sweet will'?

Shelley is hardly so close an observer as Wordsworth ; or,
when he is so, his observation is more limited in range.   It
is a dissolving view of cloud, and wood, and water, and
flower.   While Wordsworth spiritualises the results of
loving observation, Shelley rather etherealises vague impressions as of trance or dream.   The former is like an
inductive philosopher, setting in order, indeed often trans-
figuring into sacred glory common experience ; the latter
like a schoolman of the middle ages, expatiating in phenomena deduced *a priori* from his own inner consciousness.

While Shelley volatilises sense, Wordsworth conducts us
through its homely portal into a heavenlier and more
abiding realm.   Wordsworth and Byron, Antæus-like, win
new strength from contact with Mother Earth.   I love
Shelley too well to compare him with Icarus, or with
Phaeton ; for, if he does not soar with us to the highest, he

flies with us through a very lovely, however insubstantial, dreamland of his own fair vision.[1]

How should the uncertain trembling motion of mist about a mountain be defined better than by the lines of Wordsworth ?—

> Such gentle mists as glide,
> Curling *with unconfirmed intent*
> On that green mountain-side.

Whatever corresponds to that 'unconfirmed intent,' the kinship there is in the mist to the more vital and essential characteristics of the human soul, this surely is as much there as mechanical laws of motion in space, which are themselves but systematised perceptions of our sensuous understanding, though doubtless corresponding to some reality of sensuous perception outside ; but the very essence of those material qualities is that they are distantly akin, that they are mysteriously symbolical of more human, more intellectual, more ethical behaviour. For, as Schelling and Coleridge pointed out, a symbol is itself the superior being under inferior conditions : it is the higher essence, one may say, deprived of its ethereal vesture, and become incarnate, yet radiant still, and redolent of veiled Divinity.

Of course such poetry will never be popular, because it can be only intelligible to the few. When Nature is treated as a mere background for the figures, and merely the salient features within common observation are described, as in Sir Walter Scott, or in Thomson, descriptive verse may be

---

[1] But I have just read Mr. Stopford Brooke's introduction to Shelley, which, so far as I know, is assuredly the most pregnant and illuminating criticism of him extant. The comparison of his nature-poetry with that of Wordsworth deserves careful study.

appreciated; for most people do care for landscape in a general way; they give it a careless occasional glance in passing; but the poetry which is begotten of the ardent look of a lover is a very different affair; although there is an occult undefined influence of scenery on races, and mountaineers love their mountains. In Wordsworth the reader has not only the initial difficulty of translating words —arbitrary oral symbols—into their visual equivalents, but he must translate them also into 'the light that never was on sea or land,' the spiritual offspring of Nature and the poet's heart. Yet you may as well expect a man born blind to understand the meaning of the word 'colour.' Such poets as Wordsworth and Shelley cannot be understood by the unprepared, by the worldly-minded, or self-absorbed, though to the elect they are very clear. To reap 'the harvest of a quiet eye,' certain sensibilities are implied, and the reader must be able to recognise, feel, and re-create for himself the pictures with which the poet presents him. If he finds it too much trouble, let him shut the book, for it is a trouble he cannot be spared. Lessing's arguments against descriptive poetry are invalid, for even in looking at a scene, or a painting, you must be able yourself to put together successively the parts of what you see, in order to form for yourself an agreeable whole. And if the poet shall have preserved a unity of mood, that is enough to steep the creation in one harmonious artistic atmosphere.

And now as to the dramatic interpretation of Man through Nature.

What would the Leech-gatherer in Wordsworth's poem be without the 'lonely moor'? They coalesce to one moving image. In the meditative imagination of the poet the poor contented old man becomes transfigured, and appears as a heavenly minister, an angel from God, sent to console the poet, upon whom weighed 'the weary burden, and the mystery of all this unintelligible world.' Often indeed does the meditative rapture of Shelley and Wordsworth pass into a kind of mystic disembodiment before the face of Nature ; they are caught up into some third heaven, where sense-limits are confounded, and our poor earth-language falters 'with the burden of an honour unto which she was not born.' What would that wonderful pathos of Michael be without the unfinished sheep-fold, or the equally wonderful pathos of Margaret without the neglected garden, once so trim, or the red stains and tufts of wool on the corner-stone of the cottage porch, where the sheep were now permitted to come and 'couch unheeded'?

Let us note in conclusion a few brief instances where Wordsworth deals with the influences of Nature, and her own character as manifested to him. In that loveliest of lyrics, *Three years she grew*, we have the picture of Lucy, to whom Nature was 'law and impulse,' 'an overseeing power to kindle or restrain,' to whom the cloud lent state, and the willow grace, into whose face from the rivulets passed 'beauty, born of murmuring sound,' to whom belonged 'the silence and the calm of mute insensate things.' Remember too that beautiful passage in *The Excursion* where the old man corrects the wanderer's despondency by pointing him to the spear-grass on the wall, with the dew on it, as testifying to the clear-hearted peace which abides in the bosom of things.

There is the magical poem about the boy, into whose heart the voice of mountain torrents was borne in those intervals of blowing mimic hootings to the owls, under the starlight by the lake ; there is the dancing of the poet's heart with the daffodils, and that picture in *Nutting*, wherein 'the green and mossy bower, deformed and sullied, patiently gave up its quiet being.' The voices of sea, of mountain torrents, and of forests, are indeed the voice of Liberty, as Coleridge in the ode, Wordsworth in the sonnet, and Longfellow in the *Slave's Dream* declare. Every flower 'enjoys the air it breathes;' 'the budding twigs spread out their fan to catch the breezy air,' and can we doubt that there is pleasure? We ought indeed 'to move among the shades with gentleness of heart, and with gentle hand touch, for there is a spirit in the woods.' In all sobriety, it is true, that what the poet saw in the Simplon Pass was 'like the workings of one mind, features of one face, characters of the great Apocalypse;' in all sobriety it is true that Nature

> can so inform
> The mind that is within us, so impress
> With quietness and beauty, and so feed
> With lofty thoughts, that neither evil tongues,
> Rash judgments, nor the sneers of selfish men,
> Nor greetings where no kindness is, nor all
> The dreary intercourse of daily life,
> Shall e'er prevail against us, or disturb
> Our cheerful faith, that all which we behold
> Is full of blessings.
>
> While with an eye made quiet by the power
> Of harmony, and the deep power of joy,
> We see into the life of things.

WORDSWORTH'S RELATIONS TO SCIENCE.

By R. SPENCE WATSON.

WORDSWORTH'S RELATIONS TO SCIENCE.[1]

In his *History of English Thought in the Eighteenth Century*, Mr. Leslie Stephen says that Wordsworth 'hates science, because it regards facts without the imaginative and emotional colouring.' The statement is not correct, but it expresses the belief generally held. And that this unfounded view should be the common one is scarcely surprising when we consider the way in which Wordsworth speaks of science and her votaries in the few writings known to the general reader which contain any allusion to them. For example, in *Stanzas suggested in a Steamboat off St. Bees Head*, he declares that to Prowess, guided by the keen insight of the Genius of our age, 'Matter and Spirit are as one Machine.'

In *The Tables Turned*, he contrasts the sweetness of 'the lore which Nature brings,' with 'our meddling intellect,' which 'mis-shapes the beauteous forms of things.' In his notes upon his poems he compares the botanical names given to the plants and flowers imported from all quarters of the globe with the touching and beautiful names of our indigenous flowers, and says, 'Trade, commerce, and manufactures, physical science, and mechanic arts, out of which so much wealth has arisen, have made our countrymen infinitely less sensible to movements of imagination and fancy than were our forefathers in their simple state of society.'

---

[1] Read to the Society in May 1884.

He speaks of the better days when 'Art's abused inventions were unknown,' and 'of undue respect' for 'proud discoveries of the intellect.' In *A Poet's Epitaph*, he calls the philosopher 'a fingering slave; one that would peep and botanise upon his mother's grave;' and speaks of his 'ever-dwindling soul.' The philosopher of that day is the man of science of this, as the literary and scientific societies of this day are the children of the literary and philosophical societies of ninety years ago. Wordsworth's botanical philosopher is the man of science 'whose mind is but the mind of his own eyes,' and we have it upon the authority of our poet, and confirmed by common-sense, that such an one 'is a slave, the meanest we can meet.'

But we must remember that Wordsworth's life was a long one, and that he was born and educated before scientific inquiry had claimed the general acceptance which is now acknowledged to be her due. When the second edition of his *Lyrical Ballads* was published, in the year 1800, the Linnæan Society was the only learned body in England devoted to the investigation of a single branch of physical science. The Royal Society had existed for a century and a half, but the Royal Institution did not begin its labours until that very year; the Geological Society was established in 1808; the Institute of Civil Engineers in 1818; and the Royal Astronomical Society in 1821. The greatest triumphs of steam were still in the far future. There was much scientific speculation indeed, and often of great value, but there was as yet little patient, systematic, and widespread observation. Scientific inquiry was an individual, not a general, task. It had but little hold of the popular mind. It was looked upon with suspicion, if not with dread, by the religious world, who did not see that to strive against truth in any form was to strive against their own highest ideal. Before Wordsworth died, in 1850, the world of thought had changed, and it is no discredit to him to acknowledge that his range of vision had widened. His standpoint from time to time was different ; but I hope to show that it was always a reasonable one, always rather in advance of, than behind, the times ; the standpoint of an honest and earnest thinker, who was indeed a poet, but none the less a close observer, and a shrewd, practical, common-sense man.

I shall not attempt to exhaust the instances of the scornful way in which Wordsworth speaks of him whose life is spent in the consideration of details, and who never rises to a general view, never sees beyond 'the mind of his own eyes.' Nor shall I take account of the quality of the poetry which I cite or quote. I confine myself simply to what bears most directly upon my theme, and pass to that slightly tedious poem, in nine books, *The Excursion*, because in it Wordsworth treats frequently and fully of scientific inquiry and its results. We must listen to all he says in this poem on the subject, or we shall assuredly misconceive his rela- tions to it.

His words are frequently those of condemnation. He speaks of 'knowledge ill begun in cold remark on outward things,' and ending 'with formal inference ;' of the prying, poring, and dwindling of the men who, 'still dividing and dividing still,' would weigh the planets in the hollow of a hand ; of the philosophers who prize the human soul, with its thousand faculties and twice ten thousand interests, but 'as a mirror that reflects to proud self-love her own intelli- gence.' He describes 'the wandering herbalist,' who casts a slight regard of transitory interest upon the lofty crags and masses of rock around him, whilst peeping anxiously about

'for some rare floweret of the hills;' and 'the fellow-
wanderer,' whose road and pathway may be traced by the
scars his activity leaves behind :—

> He who with pocket-hammer smites the edge
> Of luckless rock or prominent stone, disguised
> In weather-stains or crusted o'er by Nature
> With her first growths, detaching by the stroke
> A chip or splinter—to resolve his doubts ;
> And, with that ready answer satisfied,
> The substance classes by some barbarous name,
> And hurries on ; . . .
>   . . . and thinks himself enriched,
> Wealthier, and doubtless wiser, than before !

Although Wordsworth was brought up in the pre-scientific
age, he knew that the world may be wiser, and even
wealthier in the wealth which perishes not in the possessing,
from the labours of patient and diligent observers with the
imaginative power to make their observations of worth, and
never dreamed of including such amongst those whom he
satirised. He expresses indeed his admiration of 'the
great Newton's own ethereal self;' he describes with praise
the astronomical researches of the Chaldeans, amongst whom
'the imaginative faculty was lord of observations natural;'
he lauds the 'nicest observation and unrivalled skill' of the
Greeks ; he even points out the close connection between
the higher mathematics and poetry, and tells how, 'in
geometric science,' he 'found both elevation and composed
delight ;' and his gentle satire is aimed at those, and at those
alone, 'whose mind is *but* the mind of their own eyes,' and
in geology, as in other things, the tribe is unlikely to become
extinct.

He says frequently and plainly that such alone *are* the
men he objects to, and that he objects to them because they

never rise above that which they see to that which it really is ; because they place the letter above the spirit, or perhaps do not know that there is any spirit, the light in them being darkness.   He is careful to explain that even minute scientific inquiry has not necessarily this soul-dwindling effect ; that such result depends upon the character and capacity of the individual inquirer ; that the human mole will grub into the earth, wherever you may place him, and be satisfied therewith.   'Some are of opinion,' Wordsworth writes, 'that the habit of analysing, decomposing, and anatomising, is inevitably unfavourable to the perception of beauty.   People are led into this mistake by overlooking the fact that such processes being to a certain extent within the reach of a limited intellect, we are apt to ascribe to them that insensibility of which they are in truth the effect, and not the cause. Admiration and love, to which all knowledge truly vital must tend, are felt by men of real genius in proportion as their discoveries in natural philosophy are enlarged ; and the beauty in form of a plant or an animal is not made less, but more apparent, as a whole, by a more accurate insight into its constituent properties and powers.   A *savant*, who is not also a poet in soul and a religionist in heart, is a feeble and unhappy creature.'   But he speaks of the happiness of him who, 'directed by a meek, sincere, and humble spirit,' explores not human nature only, but all natures, to the end that he may find the law that governs each, 'the constitutions, powers, and faculties,' that assign to every class of visible beings its station and its office—

> Through all the mighty commonwealth of things,
> Up from the creeping plant to sovereign man.

He does not hate science ; he only sees clearly the errors and the dangers into which an undue appreciation of

it, and a neglect of that which is outside of it, may cause its
votaries to fall.   He does not deny that it is an important
realm of the intellect; but he does not hold it to be the
most important.   Take such a passage as the familiar one—

I have seen
A curious child, who dwelt upon a tract
Of inland ground, applying to his ear
The convolutions of a smooth-lipped shell,
To which, in silence hushed, his very soul
Listened intensely ; and his countenance soon
Brightened with joy ; for from within were heard
Murmurings, whereby the monitor expressed
Mysterious union with its native sea.
Even such a shell the universe itself
Is to the ear of faith ; and there are times,
I doubt not, when to you it doth impart
Authentic tidings of invisible things ;
Of ebb and flow, and ever-during power ;
And central peace subsisting at the heart
Of endless agitation.

From such a passage we learn what it is which Wordsworth places far above scientific knowledge.   He does not
teach that poetry and science are necessarily antagonistic,
but that they are different.   He goes even further than this,
and tells us that they should not be looked upon as enemies,
but as intimate allies.   True that in a note to the Preface
to the *Lyrical Ballads* he explains that 'much confusion has
been introduced into criticism by the contradistinction of
poetry and prose, instead of the more philosophical one of
poetry and matter of fact, or science.'   But this is no more
than most men would readily admit.   It is simply a question
of more or less felicitous expression.   Wordsworth holds
that science will only be a 'precious visitant,' that it will
only be of true worth, when the loftier teachings of poetry

supplement and embrace its instruction ; that the man who neglects the imaginative side of his intellect cannot truly live ; and that scientific observation, which has no outlook beyond the naked object, will make man dull and inanimate, will chain him to that object as a slave, instead of supporting and guiding his mind's excursive power.

When he turns to the visible outcome of scientific research, and considers the results of the practical application of scientific discovery to the useful arts, he sees both sides of the case, and states them fairly.   He takes a view which is remarkable indeed for common-sense, and in it, as in the whole of his relations to science, we are struck by the unerring instinct which leads him to admire the good and eschew the evil.   He tells how the little hamlets have grown into huge continuous and compact towns ; how the furthest glens have been penetrated ' by stately roads, easy and bold :'

> And, wheresoe'er the traveller turns his steps,
> He sees the barren wilderness erased,
> Or disappearing ; triumph that proclaims
> How much the mild Directress of the plough
> Owes to alliance with these new-born arts !
> —Hence is the wide sea peopled,—hence the shores
> Of Britain are resorted to by ships
> Freighted from every climate of the world
> With the world's choicest produce.   Hence that sum
> Of keels that rests within her crowded ports,
> Or ride at anchor in her sounds and bays :
> That animating spectacle of sails
> That, through her inland regions, to and fro
> Pass with the respirations of the tide,
> Perpetual, multitudinous !

He is writing before beneficent legislation began to root out that infant slavery in England under which mere babies

worked twice the hours which grown men will now consent
to labour, and at tasks of the most fatiguing and degrading
kind.   And he looks upon both sides of the shield, and tells
also of the darker aspect of the great change which has
come over the land—

>   When soothing darkness spreads
> O'er hill and vale . . .
>   . . . and the punctual stars,
> While all things else are gathering to their homes,
> Advance, and in the firmament of heaven
> Glitter—but undisturbing, undisturbed ;
> As if their silent company were charged
> With peaceful admonitions for the heart
> Of all-beholding Man, earth's thoughtful lord ;
> Then, in full many a region, once like this,
> The assured domain of calm simplicity
> And pensive quiet, an unnatural light
> Prepared for never-resting Labour's eyes,
> Breaks from a many-windowed fabric huge ;
> And at the appointed hour a bell is heard,
> Of harsher import than the curfew-knoll
> That spake the Norman Conqueror's stern behest—
> A local summons to unceasing toil !
> Disgorged are now the ministers of day ;
> And, as they issue from the illumined pile,
> A fresh band meets them, at the crowded door—
> And in the courts—and where the rumbling stream,
> That turns the multitude of dizzy wheels,
> Glares, like a troubled spirit, in its bed
> Among the rocks below.   Men, maidens, youths, .
> Mother and little children, boys and girls,
> Enter, and each the wonted task resumes
> Within this temple, where is offered up
> To Gain, the master idol of the realm,
> Perpetual sacrifice.

Fully and earnestly had Wordsworth felt the miserable

inequalities in the conditions of existence, the depth of sadness in the lives of too many of the working poor, and the ever-increasing number of those in our great cities, where the application of scientific discovery has been carried the furthest, 'who sit in darkness and there is no light.' Nobly does he exclaim, and his exclamation claims audience of all men now as forcibly as when it was penned—

> Our life is turned
> Out of her course, whenever man is made
> An offering or a sacrifice, a tool
> Or implement, a passive thing employed
> As a brute mean, without acknowledgment
> Of common right, or interest in the end ;
> Used or abused, as selfishness may prompt.

Warmly does he protest in his latter days against the thirst for gold which would leave 'no nook of English ground secure from rash assault.' He inveighs in bitter terms against the invasion of his favourite mountain solitudes by the ruthless railway director in search of dividends. And his words have helped to save, in our own day, these last refuges of repose from the ravages of railways, saved them not only for the inhabitants of the district or for wealthy visitors, but for the toiling masses from our great centres of industry in the north of England, who, thanks to the proper application of railways, are able to escape from time to time for a few hours from the ceaseless whir and hum of machinery into these lovely and noble scenes, to 'let the misty mountain wind be free to blow against them,' and to

> Feel that this cold metallic motion,
> Is not all the life God fashions or reveals.

The two letters to the *Morning Post*, in which Words-

worth, in 1844, discussed the projected Kendal and Winder-
mere railway, are good examples of the calm, sensible, and
thorough way in which he argues a question. He does not
rave wildly against all railways, nor does he assume that all
men, whether they be rich or poor, are fitted to appreciate
the beauties of Nature. There is a good deal of Wordsworth, of Ruskin, and of humbug, in the present day's
ready-made enthusiasm for natural beauty or grandeur, led
up to by excellent roads, and not too remote from comfortable and well-ordered inns. But he puts his points strongly :
— 'The railway power, we know well, will not admit of
being materially counteracted by sentiment ; and who would
wish it where large towns are connected and the interests of
trade and agriculture are substantially promoted by such
mode of intercommunication ? But, be it remembered, that
this case is a peculiar one, that the staple of the country is
its beauty and its character of retirement.' And again :
'The time of life at which I have arrived may, I trust, if
nothing else will, guard me from the imputation of having
written from any selfish interests, or from fear of disturb-
ance which a railway might cause to myself. If gratitude
for what repose and quiet in a district hitherto, for the most
part, not disfigured, but beautified by human hands, have
done for me through the course of a long life, and hope
that others might hereafter be benefited in the same
manner and in the same country, be selfishness, then,
indeed, but not otherwise, I plead guilty to the charge.
Nor have I opposed this undertaking on account of the
inhabitants of the district merely, but, as hath been inti-
mated, for the sake of every one, however humble his
condition, who, coming hither, shall bring with him an eye
to perceive, and a heart to feel and worthily enjoy.'

Wordsworth, then, was no simple reviler of railways or of other useful scientific appliances. He felt the grandeur of the

> Motions and means, on land and sea, at war
> With old poetic feeling.

He would not judge them amiss. He had 'that prophetic sense of future change, that power of vision,' which enabled him to discover the soul which is behind even 'steamboats, viaducts, and railways,' and he sang of them—

> In spite of all that beauty may disown
> In your harsh features, Nature doth embrace
> Her lawful offspring in Man's art ; and Time, '
> Pleased with your triumphs o'er his brother Space,
> Accepts from your bold hands the proffered crown
> Of hope, and smiles on you with cheer sublime.

He is not led to hate science because many of its votaries can see nothing beyond it, nor to decry its practical application because of the many abuses attendant upon that application. On the contrary, he bursts forth into full acknowledgment of the might of the power which he will not hold all mighty—

> Yet do I exult,
> Casting reserve away, exult to see
> An intellectual mastery exercised
> O'er the blind elements ; a purpose given,
> A perseverance fed ; almost a soul
> Imparted—to brute matter. I rejoice,
> Measuring the force of those gigantic powers
> That, by the thinking mind, have been compelled
> To serve the will of feeble-bodied Man.

This surely should go far to dispel the delusion that Wordsworth hated science. You do not hate the less because you hold that it is included in the greater. You can scarcely hate that which you exult in and rejoice at.

At the beginning of the last book of *The Excursion*, we learn what, to Wordsworth, is the conclusion of the whole matter—

To every Form of being is assigned
An *active* Principle : howe'er removed
From sense and observation, it subsists
In all things, in all natures ; in the stars
Of azure heaven, the unenduring clouds,
In flower and tree, in every pebbly stone
That paves the brooks, the stationary rocks,
The moving waters, and the invisible air.
Whate'er exists hath properties that spread
Beyond itself, communicating good,
A simple blessing, or with evil mixed ;
Spirit that knows no insulated spot,
No chasm, no solitude ; from link to link
It circulates, the Soul of all the worlds.

This is that which we must remember whatever else we may forget—this spirit, this living principle, this 'soul of all the worlds.' Preached often indeed by Wordsworth, the central thought of all his poetry, but not of his alone. This same truth we find in Genesis, 'and the Spirit of God moved upon the face of the waters;' this in Proverbs, 'rejoicing in the habitable part of his earth, and my delights were with the sons of men;' this in John, 'in Him was life, and the life was the light of men;' this in Milton's 'holy light, offspring of Heaven first-born;' this in Cowper's, 'there lives and works a soul in all things;' this in Shelley's 'light whose smile kindles the universe;' this in Matthew Arnold's 'calm soul of all things;' and in Robert Browning's 'the forests had done it;' this, repeated in many forms by all true poets in all true poetry, of which it is, indeed, a fundamental truth.   And, this being so, however closely we may observe, whatever laws we may discover, however often we may 'triumph o'er a secret wrung from nature's close reserve,' we have made but a little further progress into the illimitable unknown ; we are 'groping blindly in the darkness,' until, by this talisman, we 'touch God's right hand in that darkness, and are lifted up and strengthened.'

Then we gather from Wordsworth's poems that he fully recognised the true value of science, and acknowledged the benefits to mankind accruing from scientific investigation applied to the arts of everyday life.   We gather also that he saw how the value of these benefits was diminished by their inherent dangers.   And he is careful to point out the chief danger, that of causing the soul to dwindle by centering its life upon petty, or even upon important, details, whilst neglecting the wider and higher fields of vision.

His views upon this matter are yet more directly stated in his prose writings—those writings so full of interest and of wisdom, yet so little known.   In the pamphlet usually called *The Convention of Cintra* there are many passages in which he points out the danger I have referred to, and the way in which it must be avoided.   I shall quote but one of these :—

In many parts of Europe (and especially in our own country), men have been pressing forward, for some time, in a path which has betrayed by its fruitfulness ; furnishing them constant employment for picking up things about their feet, when thoughts were perishing in their minds. While mechanic arts, manufactures, agriculture, commerce, and all those products of knowledge which are confined to gross, definite, and tangible objects, have, with the aid of experimental philosophy, been every day putting on more brilliant colours, the splendour of the imagina- tion has been fading. . . . Animal comforts have been rejoiced over, as if they were the end of being. . . . Now a country may advance, for some time, in this course with apparent profit ; these accommodations, by zealous encouragement, may be attained, and still the peasant, or artisan, their master, be a slave in mind—a slave rendered even more abject by the very tenure under which these possessions are held ; and if they veil from us this fact, or reconcile us to it, they are worse than worthless.

I do not wish to argue that physical science has any prominent place in Worthsworth's writings. That was not to be expected, for reasons already sufficiently stated. But whenever it does come across his path, and he has to notice it, he does so in a clear-sighted and sympathetic way. This is the case throughout all his writings, from the familiar letters to his friends to the formal and carefully polished sonnet ; from his youthful days to the fulness of his years. He studiously discriminates between that which is evil and that which is good, and when he condemns, his condemnation is confined to those particular points upon which our greatest scientists would cordially unite with him. As in the last quotation, he points out the practical dangers which he saw in the too complete absorption in scientific pursuits, so in the following words from his essay on the *Principles of Poetry*, he states explicitly what his views upon the relations between poetry and science really were :—

The poet considers man and nature as essentially adapted to each other, and the mind of man as naturally the mirror of the fairest and most interesting properties of nature ; and thus the poet, prompted by this feeling of pleasure, which accompanies him through the whole course of his studies, converses with general nature with affections akin to those which, through labour and length of time, the man of science has raised up in himself, by conversing with those particular parts of nature which are the objects of his studies. The knowledge, both of the poet and the man of science, is pleasure, but the knowledge of the one cleaves to us as a necessary part of our existence, our natural and inalienable inheritance ; the other is a personal and individual acquisition, slow to come to us, and by no habitual and direct sympathy connecting us with our fellow-beings. The man of science seeks truth as a remote and unknown benefactor; he cherishes and loves it in his solitude: the poet, singing a song in which all human beings join with him, rejoices in the presence of truth as our visible friend and hourly companion. Poetry is the breath and finer spirit of all knowledge; it is the impassioned expression which is in the countenance of all science. . . .

If the labours of men of science should ever create any material revolution, direct or indirect, in our condition, and in the impressions which we habitually receive, the poet will sleep then no more than at present; he will be ready to follow the steps of the man of science, not only in those general indirect effects, but he will be at his side, carrying sensation into the midst of the objects of the science itself. The remotest discoveries of the chemist, the botanist, or mineralogist, will be as proper objects of the poet's art as any upon which it can be employed, if the time should ever come when these things shall be familiar to us, and the relation under which they are contemplated by the followers of these respective sciences shall be manifestly and palpably material to us as enjoying and suffering beings. If the time should ever come when what is now called science, thus familiarised to men, shall be ready to put on, as it were, a form of flesh and blood, the poet will lend his divine spirit to aid the transfiguration, and will welcome the being thus produced as a dear and genuine inmate of the house-hold of man.

Thus, then, both from his prose and poetry, we have seen what Wordsworth thought of the relations between poetry and science, and have learned how grave a misconception it is to speak of him as a science-hater. Since he ceased to write, science has made gigantic strides, and has fulfilled some of his demands, and our true poets have not failed in some measure to recognise and avail themselves of the fact. But the dangers which he foresaw are still present with us, and in ever-increasing strength. They are actual, not imaginary dangers—dangers which affect our everyday lives; and Wordsworth's warning voice is of even greater value in our time than it was in his own.

For this is the day of specialised study—of specialised life. In all branches of human affairs, intense competition, the pressure of numbers, the desire to go far, the wish to know much, and to know it accurately, have led to subdivision of labour, to the individual man's becoming a specialist— in some instances 'a tool or implement.' In our manufactories apprentices no longer learn a trade, but one department of a multiform business. In medicine there is a strong tendency to become attached to some special form of disease or disaster; in painting, to walk along a certain path—that usually which is most economical of thought. In science it is really necessary that a man should choose his subject, and devote his life to it, if he is to make any substantial progress, but it is his work-a-day life, not his whole life, which must be so devoted. The stunting and dwindling soul-processes must be counteracted; and surely it is to poetry that we must look as to the force which can best counteract them. Specialising is in its infancy in England as compared with Germany, and in Germany it has become so universal that poetry has almost ceased to be written.

Not long ago, an eminent French critic said that, owing to the specialising tendency of science and to its all-devouring force, poetry would cease to be read in fifty years. Not English poetry, I trust and think. The belief in necessary conflict between Letters and Science hinders the general recognition of the fact that an advance in either must be a gain to both. Poetry long held the field alone, but did not necessarily benefit thereby. Ours is the transition time, or, rather, the time of development and growth. Science, which has won for mankind liberty of thought, and which has created for mankind 'new heavens and a new earth,' receives in our day her full meed of praise. But all movements which depend upon the mind of man go forward in tides, and, for the moment, the tide of science flows on to the full whilst that of art is on the ebb. It is a time when it behoves those who believe that the relations of Wordsworth towards science were true and wise ones, to be firm in upholding them, and whilst, with him, exulting 'to see an intellectual mastery exercised o'er the blind elements,' yet to keep ever before the minds of men that the higher life is that which passes beyond the realms of sense into those of spirit; that there are emotions, passions, longings, of the mind of man, which are just as truly facts, and enter just as largely into the web of life, nay, which demand to be studied, understood, and accounted for, just as faithfully, and with just as fatal consequences for neglect or misunderstanding, as any of the laws which affect the physical world.

WORDSWORTH'S TREATMENT OF SOUND.

By W. A. HEARD.

WORDSWORTH'S TREATMENT OF SOUND.[1]

Mr. STOPFORD BROOKE, in the interesting paper which he read at our meeting last year on the *Guide to the Lakes*, called attention to a noteworthy passage in which, speaking of the songs of the birds, Wordsworth remarks :—'Their notes, when listened to by the side of broad still waters, or when heard in unison with the murmuring of mountain brooks, have the compass of their power enlarged accordingly. There is also an imaginative influence in the voice of the cuckoo, when that voice has taken possession of a deep mountain valley, very different from anything which can be excited by the same sound in a flat country.' These remarks illustrate a sensibility to the sounds of nature, and an imaginative appreciation of these sounds and voices, which constitute, I think, a peculiar characteristic of Wordsworth's poetry ; and they are requoted here to introduce us to a few thoughts upon his frequent references to the utterances of nature.

It is surprising that Wordsworth did not give us himself a more explicit account of this sensibility to sound, being, as it is, one of those elements in the poetic interpretation of nature, and one of those habits of mind, which he delighted to analyse. There is little in the *Guide to the Lakes* beyond the passage quoted which bears directly, save in the way of illustration, upon the subject. Yet all his poems,

---

[1] Read to the Society in May 1884.

the sonnets, lyrics, and longer pieces, are rich in the associations of sound.

> The region of his inner spirit
> Teems with vital sounds.

We cannot penetrate the secret of a poet's art; but we
may with advantage examine and illustrate some special
detail or habit of thought; and in this case an apology is
the less necessary, because there is such a unity of spirit in
Wordsworth, that we cannot examine any particular constituent of his poetry without seeing the whole compass of
his mind. We cannot separate his sensibility to sound from
his general philosophy of nature; the one is subservient to
the other, the ear revealing to us a large part in the secret
and inward life of nature upon which that philosophy rests.

In such a subject the poet best speaks for himself; but
before giving any illustrations, it may be serviceable to sum-
marise briefly the general characteristics of Wordsworth's
treatment of sound.

As the basis or origin of all, we find that he had a
peculiarly sensitive ear. It is not only the grander tones of
the waterfall or the roaring storms that impress him, but he
treasures all the tiny sounds down to the piping of the stone-
chat or the sand-lark, and all 'the milder minstrelsies of
rural scenes.' Even silence itself is no mere negation of
sound, but a positive power, that seems at times to strain
the senses, at times to allay and lull them. This capacity is
instinctive and habitual: he does not hear sounds only
under constrained attention, but in consequence of an
unusually quick and vigilant sense. The ear seems never
to sleep: brood as the mind will, the ear always has its
message to report.

There is also a great retentiveness of sound. This is only true to Wordsworth's general capacity of mind. All that he notes in nature seems to become fixed in his thoughts; he is not a poet of fleeting impressions; the impressions once conveyed become permanent associations. Thus when he recalls the hillside or the valley, it is not only the appearance to the eye that revives in the memory, but the voices of nature's breathing life are heard in the imagination; the music of water, or wind, or trees, or birds, is an inseparable part of the retrospect. 'The memory is a dwelling-place for all sweet sounds and harmonies.'

The imagination comes into play in various ways. (1) He regards the sounds of wind, and breeze, and flood, and torrent, and brook, as the utterance or language of a living power. They are not noise, but voices; not mechanical sounds, but expressions of nature's mighty life. Nor is it these only that utter her voice. (2) The same life or power which speaks from the mountain or the ghyll thrills also all the creatures that dwell in her domain. The bleating of the lamb and the song of the birds seem to issue from the heart of nature, and, like the rushing waters or the murmuring rill, they proceed from her universal inspiration. (3) There is too a sweet concord and a spontaneous harmony in these voices. Nature is not heterogeneous; sound blends with sound, like the song of the birds in unison with the mountain brooks, 'With chiming Tweed the lint-whites sing in chorus.' (4) Another noticeable point is his habit of selecting some peculiar note or tone as interpretative of the landscape, and finding some key-note of the scene, as if nature put forth a cry as a revelation of her inmost self. (5) Further, we find that voice or utterance in Wordsworth's mind is almost inseparable from the notion of life. Partly literally, partly metaphorically, he thinks of nature as full of gentle delicate music which only those who are most in sympathy with her can catch. We must not confuse this with the music of the spheres; he is not thinking of the rhythmical movements of nature, but of nature in her abundant forms of individual life; each flower, each tree, each blade of grass has a music of its own. Lastly, we must remember throughout, that in virtue of the harmony between man and nature all her various voices become in a way intelligible to the heart. Of course we are familiar with Wordsworth's belief that nature teaches men by disclosing a spiritual presence, and satisfying with something more than a material beauty the communings of those that love her. But it is not the mere contemplation of nature that does this for us; there is another influence than that which streams through the eye; as often, perhaps oftener, the utterances of nature bring home this spiritual power— the invisible bird, the ceaseless murmur of the fountain, the echoes that through the mountains throng.

We may illustrate these remarks by quotations from the poems. We have spoken of Wordsworth as having, in a special degree, an organic sensibility to sound. He has given us himself in one of his prose essays an elaborate analysis of what he considers the innate faculties of a poet; but we may turn with advantage to his poems for a briefer, but more telling account. Speaking of his brother, whom he ventures to call a silent poet, he says:

> Thou from the solitude
> Of the vast sea didst bring a watchful heart
> Still couchant, an inevitable ear,
> And an eye practised like a blind man's touch.

The 'inevitable ear' thus essential to the poet exactly

denotes the quality of which we are speaking.   He seems almost to catch the sound of growth :

> She listens, but she cannot hear
> The foot of horse, the voice of man ;
> The streams with softest sounds are flowing,
> The grass you almost hear it growing,
> You hear it now if e'er you can.

With this we naturally couple two lines in *The Prelude* :

> Catching from tufts of grass and harebell flowers
> Their faintest whisper to the passing breeze.

It was partly in consequence of this sensitiveness of ear, and partly of his avowed preference for homely detail, that he at times revives or retains a landscape in our memory by the introduction of very familiar, yet often unnoted, sounds. The *Evening Walk* gives us happy specimens of this power. Any one who knows the lake-sides of Westmoreland or Cumberland will recognise the truth, and with all the homeliness, the power over the imagination of the details :

> Sweet are the sounds that mingle from afar,
> Heard by calm lakes, as peeps the folding star,
> Where the duck dabbles 'mid the rustling sedge,
> And feeding pike starts from the water's edge,
> Or the swan stirs the reeds, his neck and bill
> Wetting, that drip upon the water still.

From the same poem I may be allowed to make another quotation, containing more imaginative force, yet still illustrative of the same sensibility :

> The song of mountain-streams, unheard by day,
> Now hardly heard, beguiles my homeward way.
> All air is, as the sleeping water, still,
> To catch the spiritual music of the hill.

There is no doubt that in the wear and tear of life the ears of most of us <u>wax grosser,</u> and become less conscious of the myriad sounds of which the air is full. It was not so with Wordsworth. Nature at noonday and at midnight, in repose as well as storm, was full of manifold tones and voices. I believe that in this matter, as indeed in almost all others, Wordsworth will be found free from exaggeration; if we put him to the test, as I have done myself, we shall find that sounds, which we were before not conscious of, are astonishingly distinct when we stop to listen. That is just the point where Wordsworth is superior to ordinary men. He is always listening; he not only observes nature; he constantly hears nature. The landscape is, if I may say so, for the ear as well as for the eye; neither in reality, nor in the imagination, is it a silent picture; it is a living presence, and full of the utterance of life." He is surely describing himself, while he attributes to another this wondrous sensation :

> And when there came a pause
> Of silence such as baffled his best skill,
> Then sometimes in that silence, *while he hung
> Listening,* a gentle shock of mild surprise
> Has carried far into his heart the voice
> Of mountain torrents.

He is so habitually conscious of the voices and sounds of nature that at will he can turn to them, and by one stroke or touch keep before us the occasion and scene of the poem. By a little detail of sound he brings us back from the regions of reverie, and detains us upon earth. In the memorial lines upon Collins the mind is dramatically arrested by this one touch :

> How calm, how still, *the only sound
> The dripping of the oar suspended.*

Thus are we stopped and recalled to the real scene, as

we seem floating away in the pensiveness of the evening twilight.

Wordsworth might almost be called the poet of the waters. From boyhood the sounding cataract haunted him like a passion. Last winter's storm, which laid low the Fraternal Four of Borrowdale, gives a pathetic interest to the lines where he describes how he delighted

> in mute repose
> To lie and listen to the mountain flood
> Murmuring from Glaramara's inmost caves.

With that truth to nature which makes his poems so composed in tone, and so full of a reserve of strength, he does not thrust the waterfall upon us; there is no accumulation of detail. As in nature, so in his poem, the waterfall is only to be heard by the listening ear; but to the listening ear a magical power makes the plashing of the waters ceaselessly distinct. Throughout and underneath all other details and all the musings of his mind we seem to hear through the poem

> The fall of water that doth make
> A murmur near the silent lake.

The sound of waters does indeed, as he tells us, literally haunt him. The Derwent

> loved
> To blend his murmurs with my nurse's song,
> And from his alder shades and rocky falls,
> And from his fords and shallows, sent a voice
> That flowed along my dreams.

In distant cities he represents the power as felt, and far away at sea,

> Oft in the piping shrouds had Leonard heard
> The tones of waterfalls and inland sounds
>   Of caves and trees.

It was the ceaseless voicefulness of the stream that impressed his mind with the notion of the continuous life of a river, and led him to give it a kind of spiritual personality:

> It seems the Eternal Spirit is clothed in thee
> With purer robes than those of flesh and blood.

The river that sweeps so softly by him on the plain is the same that is still murmuring at its mountain source, and is conscious of life and identity:

> Mountain rivers, where they creep
> Along a channel, smooth and deep,
> To their own far-off murmurs listening.

There are two remarkable instances in *The Prelude* showing how the associations of sound remained fixed in his memory, and combined with the imagery of a scene to form an extraordinarily vital reproduction of the past. Many will remember the passage in the twelfth book in which he recounts how he went in his school-days, at the beginning of a memorable Christmas holiday, to a crag that ascends from the meeting-place of two highways to watch for the palfreys descending from Kirkstone to take him and his brothers home. A few days afterwards his father died, and the contrast between the expectation of the holiday and the bereavement that so shortly came, made this moment immortal in his memory. He recalls the scene, but note how he blends the sounds with the sights:

> And afterwards, the wind and sleety rain,
> And all the business of the elements,
> The single sheep, and the one blasted tree,
> *And the bleak music from that old stone wall,*
> The noise of wood and water, and the mist,
>
> .　　　.　　　.　　　.　　　.
>
> All these were kindred spectacles and sounds
> To which I oft repaired.

So when he records a school-boy visit to the ruins of
Furness Abbey, the particular moment becomes permanent
in the memory, chiefly in consequence of the magic song of
an unseen wren, singing to herself in the lonely pile. Here
we have to notice not only the song of the bird, but the
subsidiary sounds of rain and wind, that stir the memory so
long, and are so accurately preserved :

>   That single wren
>   Which one day sang so sweetly in the nave
>   Of the old church, that—though from recent showers
>   The earth was comfortless, and touched by faint
>   Internal breezes, sobbings of the place,
>   And respirations, from the roofless walls
>   The shuddering ivy dripped large drops,—yet still
>   So sweetly 'mid the gloom the invisible bird
>   Sang to herself, that there I could have made
>   My dwelling-place, and lived for ever there
>   To hear such music.

When we proceed to what I may term the poetic interpretation of sound, we must pause for a moment to consider
an habitual characteristic of Wordsworth's use of the imagination. The imagination is not arbitrarily exercised. There
is a notable robustness and sanity, in virtue of which,
though he casts the visionary gleam, he never obscures the
real and obvious nature of things. He discerns in this
world a spiritual life, and yet he retains its material identity.
The primrose by the river's brim is something more than a
yellow primrose, yet this spiritual addition is not a negation
of the commonplace aspect of the flower. This combination
of a fidelity to nature worthy of a naturalist, with a spiritual
transfiguration, seems to constitute the uniqueness of Wordsworth's imaginative power. We find the same power
evincing itself in his interpretation of nature's voices. Al-

ways keeping the true character of the sound before us, he yet finds in it something more than an unintelligible voice. Yet this voice is no mere echo of human emotions. It has a meaning, but it is not a mere reflection of human moods. We hear elsewhere of the mountains bursting forth into singing. If this is not merely a poetic figure, it proceeds from the subordination of nature to man, so that, having no domain of its own, it only reflects, like a cheerful home, the joy of the human inmates. Wordsworth's is a very different conception,—we are not concerned with defending, but only with stating it. He does not destroy the identity and independence of nature. Nature has a strong, real, unassailable life of her own. Yet man and nature do not stand entirely apart; there is a wedding, a blending, a sacred union of their might; both have certain inherent and indestructible qualities of their own, but these are in harmony · with each other, and thus it is that nature has an utterance for man.

We have spoken of the notion of the mountains bursting forth into singing. Let us compare with this a passage · from *The Excursion*, where he is speaking of the awful voices of the lofty Brethren of the Langdales :

> And well these lofty Brethren bear their part
> In the wild concert—chiefly when the storm
> Rides high : then all the upper air they fill
> With roaring sound that ceases not to flow
> Like smoke—along the level of the blast
> In mighty current.

The wild sound of the mountains is like the mist that creeps and shifts and variously blends and dissevers upon their lofty sides. Here we have a true rendering of the infinite tones of the hills in wind and storm, and yet they are something more than roar and noise; they are the utterance of a living power, though it is not clothed in flesh and blood. It is no Orpheus, but the mountains themselves that speak. Still less is it merely the caprice of man fantastically producing speech from brute and silent earth.

This combination of literal fact and imaginative interpretation is noticeable in another very familiar passage from *The Prelude*, the famous skating scene:

> With the din
> Smitten, the precipices rang aloud,
> The leafless trees and every icy crag
> Tinkled like iron : while far distant hills
> Into the tumult sent an alien sound
> Of melancholy.

This is true realism : nature is not inanimate, nor entirely external to man : the instinct to find in her some correspondence with the human soul is universal. The Pagan world felt the necessity, and satisfied the craving by a prolific creation of guardian deities and nymphs. With this religion of Paganism Wordsworth had unquestionable sympathy, but he had absolutely no patience with the artifices of a later age, which endeavoured in its unspiritual way to represent the correspondence between man and nature under the hollow forms of Dryads in which it did not believe. There is indeed a spiritual music in nature, but it issues from nature's genuine forms of life,—the hill, and wood, and water. So Wordsworth does not speak of nature as a harp; but with realism and spirituality combined he tells us of

> The pointed crags
> That into music touch the passing wind.

And again we have a similar blending of fact and imagination :

> When is the Orphean lyre or Druid harp
> To accompany the verse?   The mountain blast
> Shall be our hand of Music ; he shall sound
> The rocks and quivering trees and billowy lake,
> And search the fibres of the caves.

Another characteristic of Wordsworth's is that he sees nature as one living power, in which nothing is isolated and unconnected. In nature, as he says, everything is distinct, yet nothing is defined into absolute independent singleness. This is true also of the voices of nature ; they are distinct, yet they are not dissonant, but form a concord of sounds, a blending music of hill and waterfall and pine-tree. Deep answers unto deep ; the creatures, permeated by one influence, call each to the other ; the busy sounds of the air are linked in a single harmony :

> The stream, so ardent in its course before,
> Sent forth such sallies of glad sound, that all
> Which I till then had heard appeared the voice
> Of common pleasure : beast and bird, the lamb,
> The shepherd's dog, the linnet and the thrush,
> Vied with this waterfall, and made a song
> Which, while I listened, *seemed like the wild growth,*
> *Or like some natural produce of the air*
> *That could not cease to be.*

Nature being thrilled with one and the same life, one inspiration fills her manifold voices, and produces a majestic unison :

> Loud is the Vale !—the Voice is up
> With which she speaks when storms are gone,
> A mighty unison of streams !
> Of all her Voices, One !

This sympathy diffused throughout nature is sometimes

revealed to us, as in the above instances, by the blending of numerous voices in one harmony or unison. At other times, and indeed oftener, the poet detects some single tone or cry, so appropriate to the landscape, so much in keeping with its mood and character, that it seems to disclose nature's inward life. Wordsworth in nothing shows truer poetic power than in the discernment with which he selects some single object as a centre for the imagination. He dispenses with detail, and places but little material before our imaginations, yet that material is of such a kind that when we dwell upon it, the whole scene is revealed! As in

> What's Yarrow but a river bare
> That flows the dark hill under,

we have the minimum of detail, but detail pregnant with imaginative life ; so we find the same penetrativeness in the selection of some single sound or cry which gives a unity to the scene. He finds in the voice of a bird or the bleating of a lamb this unity and revealing power :

> The bleating of the lamb, I heard, sent forth
> As if it were the mountain's voice ;
> As if the visible mountain made the cry :
> *The plaintive spirit of the solitude.*

In the following passage also, though other sounds are heard, it is the voice of the solitary raven that gives us the true note of the night scene in all its solemnity :

> The whispering Air
> Sends inspiration from the shadowy heights
> And blind recesses of the caverned rocks :
> The little rills and waters numberless,
> Inaudible by daylight, blend their notes
> With the loud streams : and often at the hour
> When issue forth the first pale stars, is heard
> One voice—the solitary raven,
> An iron knell.

Notice again how he carries into our hearts the very personality of nature's solitary recesses by a lonely sound :

> There sometimes doth a leaping fish
> Send through the tarn a lonely cheer :
> The crags repeat the raven's croak
> In symphony austere.

It would be difficult to find a passage which reveals so much to the imagination, by such slight materials ; nothing could more perfectly express the solitude of this mountain tarn.

This potency of sound is specially distinct in the songs of the birds, and becomes a mysterious fascination when the bird is unseen. Wordsworth prefers not to localise sound. What indeed seems to charm him most in the sounds of nature is that they are dissociated from place or bound, and blend mysteriously with the beauty of the landscape. When the birds are singing, their joy seems to proceed from the general life of nature ; it is not the utterance of an individual thing, or the music of one grove or covert, it is the voice of nature itself. The linnet is a life, a presence like the air, the presiding spirit of the May, its song the voice of nature's gladness. In the poem *To the Cuckoo* this conception finds a still more emphatic expression :

> Thrice welcome, darling of the Spring :
>   Even yet thou art to me
> *No bird,* but *an invisible thing,*
>   A voice, a mystery.

In the lines upon the Stock-dove there is the same notion of diffusion of sound from a source not seen, lines to which the poet has appended his own comment :

> His voice was buried among trees,
> Yet to be come at by the breeze.

But in the poem on the Cuckoo there is a still greater spiritual power in the song of the bird.   Not only does the bird seem devoid of corporeal existence, but the material world itself becomes spiritualised by the voice as it passes from hill to hill, now far, now near :

> O blessed bird, the earth we pace
>   Again appears to be
> An unsubstantial fairy place
>   That is fit home for thee.

> The gross and visible frame of things
> Relinquishes its hold upon the sense,
> Yea almost on the mind itself, and seems
> All unsubstantialised.

The voice of man may also in the same way become almost a part of nature, working a human sweetness into the landscape.   In *The Solitary Reaper* we feel the song to be the very soul of the valley : it transfuses the whole scene ; it makes a new atmosphere, inseparable from the vale :

> O listen, for the vale profound
> Is overflowing with the sound,—
>   The maiden sang
> As if her song could have no ending.

The same idea underlies the familiar poem, *What, you are stepping westward?* where the evening greeting, as it falls from human lips, blends with lake, and air, and light, and sky.

In these instances the voice of man is practically impersonal, and the singer and the speaker are unconsciously parts of nature.   But when self-consciousness and self-will come into play, the voice of man may disturb the harmonies of nature and produce a discord : man's querulousness is a jarring note :

> No more shall grief of mine the season wrong.

We all know the development of the human mind in contact with nature as Wordsworth conceived it: there is first the instinctive, sensuous, unreflective, irrepressible delight; then a period of self-consciousness and self-centred aims, in which nature seems more at distance from us; lastly, a new contact and harmony between man and nature, human experience attuning our ears,

> The soothing thoughts that spring
> Out of human suffering

bringing a chastened, but more spiritual, delight in the life and utterances of nature. Moral life quickens within us a spiritual sense, so that we are more and more enabled to catch the harmonies of nature in proportion as we are truer men. Literally, and as a physical fact, he believed that a finer organ than the ear, or even the ear, if we diligently trained it, could catch a music in what we now deem the voiceless movements of nature; but he delighted to use this notion as an expression of a closer spiritual contact between nature and man. The charm of the flower is something more penetrating than the mere delight of the eye: the flowers have an utterance for us, and their beauty and fragrance conspire into a harmony:

> Flowers themselves, whate'er their hue,
> With all their fragrance, all their glistening,
> Call to the heart for inward listening.

And again:

> While flower-breathed incense to the skies
> Is wafted in mute harmonies.

So the mysterious influence of the mountains is a kind of harmony, a ceaseless language to be understood by a

spiritual ear : nature's laws have gifted them with a power
to yield music of finer frame :

> A harmony,
> So do I call it, though it be the hand
> Of silence, though there be no voice : the clouds,
> The mists, the shadows, light of golden suns,
> Motions of moonlight, all come thither—touch
> And have an answer—thither come and shape
> A language not unwelcome to sick hearts
> And idle spirits.

With this we would compare a subtle line in which he
combines the language of two senses :

> A soft eye-music of slow waving boughs,
> Powerful almost as vocal harmony.

Nature thus speaks to our minds, but her sounds and
music also affect body as well as soul. Wordsworth does
not separate the physical and the spiritual : nothing is
solely physical in its effect, everything has a spiritual result.
This combination of physical and spiritual teaching in
nature is the idea embodied in the well-known poem, *Three
years she grew in sun and shower.* One stanza is specially
apposite :

> And she shall lean her ear
> In many a secret place,
> Where rivulets dance their wayward round,
> And beauty born of murmuring sound
> Shall pass into her face.

This is not only true poetry, but it has a Platonic felici-
tousness of language as the expression of a philosophy.

In *The Prelude* we have a still more convincing testimony
to the influence, primarily physical, but also and inevitably

spiritual, of the music of nature ; a portion of the passage has already been quoted :

> For this, didst thou,
> O Derwent, winding among grassy holms
> When I was looking on, a babe in arms,
> Make ceaseless music that composed my thoughts
> To more than infant softness, giving me,
> Amid the fretful dwellings of mankind,
> A foretaste, a dim earnest of the calm
> That Nature breathes among the hills and groves.

It is hardly necessary, however, to multiply instances of Wordsworth's belief in the educating influences of nature, or in particular, of the beneficent and soothing power of her harmony.

It is no matter for surprise that he brings to other subjects the mood and language of a listener. Combining with the voices of nature he hears the still sad music of humanity, but, thanks to the tranquillity which the love of nature has instilled into his spirit, it is a music no longer harsh nor grating, though of ample power to chasten and subdue. In the seclusion of a mountain home the tones of strife are mitigated, and that which seems a dissonant clamour to those who are in the thick of the fight, is softened as it passés through the atmosphere of a life in communion with nature, into a sad, yet not inharmonious music. The same metaphorical language is elsewhere to be found, notably in two famous passages of *The Excursion*. To the ear of faith the universe resounds with hidden murmurs, like the hollow shell, which, to the ear of the curious child, betrays, by its sonorous cadences, mysterious union with its native sea. In the second passage we have a metaphor which has recently become more familiar, when he tells us how old age gives us.

> Fresh power to commune with the invisible world,
> And hear the *mighty stream of tendency*,
> Uttering, for elevation of our thought,
> A clear sonorous voice, inaudible
> To the vast multitude.

Wordsworth has written some stanzas upon the power of sound, but his admirers are perhaps not so anxious to make mention of these. What he has to tell us is not to be found there, but in fragments, touches, passing intimations, which not only reveal his thought, but are themselves a sweet aërial music like the music of his own hills. I cannot conclude better than with the true note sounded at his grave in Mr. Matthew Arnold's *Memorial Verses*:

> Keep fresh the grass upon his grave,
> O Rotha, with thy living wave !
> Sing him thy best ! for few or none
> Hears thy voice right, now he is gone.

WORDSWORTH AND CHARLES LAMB.

By ALFRED AINGER.

Q

WORDSWORTH AND CHARLES LAMB.[1]

In the *Edinburgh Review* of November 1814 appeared
Jeffrey's famous notice of *The Excursion,* beginning with
words that have since become almost monumental: 'This
will never do.' But it is less generally known that in the
corresponding number of the *Quarterly* (October 1814)
appeared a review of the same poem by Charles Lamb,
which may well be taken as a happy instance of a bane
being found in company with its antidote, like that botanical
superstition of our childhood, the nettle and the dock leaf.

Professor Knight has given us, in an appendix to the last
volumn of his excellent edition, the principal letters of
Lamb to Wordsworth that contain critical remarks on his
poetry, especially on *The Excursion*; but he has not given
any extracts from this *Quarterly* article, and it has occurred
to me that a very brief account of it might be interesting to
the Society, because, as far as I have observed, it is less
known even to lovers of Charles Lamb than most of his
other critical papers.

There is one special reason, however, why the review of
necessity does not rank with Lamb's best criticism. Just
before its appearance in print, Lamb writes to Wordsworth
apologetically on the subject, claiming indulgence on the
ground that it was the first review he had ever written. 'I
hope,' he says, 'you will see goodwill in the thing. I had

---

[1] Read to the Society in May 1884.

a difficulty to perform not to make it all panegyric ; I have attempted to personate a mere stranger to you, perhaps with too much strangeness. But you must bear that in mind when you read it, and not think that I am, in mind, distant from you or your poem, but that both are close to me, among the nearest of persons and things.' 'But,' he concludes, 'it must speak for itself, if Gifford and his crew do not put words in its mouth, which I expect. Farewell. Love to all. Mary keeps very bad.'

The ominous hint that Gifford might put words into Lamb's mouth that he had never spoken was only too literally to be fulfilled. Immediately after the appearance of the *Quarterly,* Lamb writes again to his friend, this time in dismay : 'I told you my review was a very imperfect one. But what you will see in the *Quarterly* is a spurious one, which Mr. Baviad Gifford has palmed upon it for mine. I never felt more vexed in my life than when I read it. I cannot give you an idea of what he has done to it, out of spite at me, because he once suffered me to be called a lunatic in his *Review.* The *language* he has altered throughout. Whatever inadequateness it had to its subject, it was, in point of composition, the prettiest piece of prose I ever writ ; and so my sister (to whom alone I read the MS.) said. That charm, if it had any, is all gone : more than a third of the substance is cut away, and that not all from one place, but *passim,* so as to make utter nonsense. Every warm expression is changed for a nasty cold one.'

Lamb goes on to explain at some length the changes and omissions which Gifford had effected in his paper, and adds : 'I regret only that I did not keep a copy.' All readers of the letter, and of the review itself, will share this regret. The loss of the best piece of prose that Lamb had up to that time produced—seeing that the essays on Hogarth and on Shakespeare's Tragedies were already written—is indeed one of the calamities of literature. And even a cursory glance at Lamb's review confirms his account of what had happened. There is very little in it in respect of style to disclose its authorship. The thought—or rather the *feeling* —that pervades it is such as could have been shown by no man of letters of that date except Lamb, and in this respect the review is certainly characteristic; but of the *curiosa felicitas* of words which marks Lamb's prose when not tampered with by editors, it is significantly empty.

And this circumstance, no doubt, has tended to exclude the review from most surveys or histories of Wordsworthian criticism. Moreover, as Mr. Arnold has reminded us, Wordsworth has been fortunate in his eulogists. Most of those who have praised him have praised him well. Much has been written in the last twenty years of signal value in the appreciation and analysis of Wordsworth. Trained metaphysicians have delighted to pluck out the heart of his mystery, and to explain his unique message to the world. But all the more for that reason we should be thankful to one who, seventy years ago, could at once recognise the value of Wordsworth's message, while the world was still unworthy of it. For six years from that year (1814) of its publication, Bishop Wordsworth reminds us the English public was content with a single edition of *The Excursion*, consisting of only 500 copies. As late as 1827 another edition of 500 copies 'satisfied the popular demand for seven years.' All honour then to one who could feel its value, as Lamb felt it, when, as regarded the authoritative critical powers of that day, he stood almost alone. I say '*feel* its value,' and no true Wordsworthian will demur to the expression, seeing how large a share the heart bears in our judgments of this poet. For reasons we have seen, there is little of Lamb's distinctive charm of style in his paper; and he was neither a moral philosopher, nor a trained analyst, and we need not look for profound thought. Much of his praise may seem commonplace compared with that of a succeeding generation. It is the timeliness of his appreciation that should win our gratitude.

Listen to this passage, for instance : ' To a mind constituted like that of Mr. Wordsworth, the stream, the torrent, and the stirring leaf seem not merely to suggest associations of deity, but to be a kind of speaking communication with it. He walks through every forest as through some Dodona ; and every bird that flits among the leaves, like that miraculous one in Tasso, but in language more 'piercing' (Gifford altered this word into *intelligent*), reveals to him far higher love-lays. In his poetry nothing in Nature is dead. Motion is synonymous with life. ' Beside yon spring,' says the Wanderer, speaking of a deserted well, from which in former times a poor woman who died heart-broken had been used to dispense refreshment to the thirsty traveller:

> . . . Beside yon spring I stood
> And eyed its waters, till we seemed to feel
> One sadness, they and I. For them a bond
> Of brotherhood is broken ; time has been
> When every day the touch of human hand
> Dislodged the natural sleep that binds them up
> In mortal stillness.

To such a mind, we say—call it strength or weakness—if weakness, assuredly a fortunate one—the visible and audible things of creation present, not dim symbols or curious emblems—which they have done at all times to those who have been gifted with the poetic faculty—but revelations and quick insights into the life within us, the pledge of immortality.'

This passage, beautiful as it stands, was one of those which Lamb, in a letter to Wordsworth, bitterly complains of as having been mangled by editor Gifford, who had cut down 'more piercing than any articulate sounds,' into the tame and meaningless 'more intelligent.' But still we are able throughout to find sentences and phrases which are, in their essence, Lamb, and not Gifford; as when he says, 'In him [Wordsworth] faith, in friendly alliance and conjunction with the religion of his country, appears to have grown up, fostered by meditation and lonely communions with Nature—an internal principle of lofty consciousness, which stamps upon his opinions and sentiments (we were almost going to say) the character of an expanded and generous Quakerism.' Again, take his remark on the fourth book (*Despondency Corrected*), which he ranks as the noblest portion of the poem, that its versification 'is so involved in the poetry that we can hardly mention it as a distinct excellence.' 'The general tendency of the argument,' he goes on to say, ' is to abate the pride of the calculating *understanding*, and to reinstate the *imagination* and the *affections* in those seats from which modern philosophy has laboured but too successfully to expel them.' Again, here is a sentence with which we may be sure Gifford had little or nothing to do. It is Lamb's passing comment on the attitude of the village priest, in the fifth and following books, telling the simple story of those who slept in the *Churchyard among the Mountains.* I hope I may be forgiven if I first quote the corresponding comment of Jeffrey, from the *Edinburgh :* 'The sixth book' (*The Churchyard among the*

Mountains), 'contains a choice obituary, or characteristic account of several of the persons who lie buried before this group of moralisers : an unsuccessful lover, who finds consolation in natural history—a miner, who worked on for twenty years in despite of universal ridicule, and at last found the vein he had expected—two political enemies, reconciled in old age to each other—an old female miser— a seduced damsel—and two widowers, one who devoted himself to the education of his daughters, and one who married a prudent middle-aged woman to take care of them.' Let us hear Charles Lamb's comment upon the same book, with the matter or manner of which we at least are sure that Gifford had not meddled : 'In the resolution of these doubts, the priest enters upon a most affecting and singular strain of narration, derived from the graves around him. Pointing to hillock after hillock, he gives short histories of their tenants, disclosing their humble virtues, and touching with tender hand upon their frailties.   Nothing can be conceived finer than the manner of introducing these tales. With heaven above his head, and the mouldering turf at his feet —standing betwixt life and death—he seems to maintain that spiritual relation which he bore to his living flock, in its undiminished strength, even with their ashes, and to be in his proper cure, or diocese, among the dead ;'—a sentence, I think you will agree with me, worthy in nobility of thought and rhythm of Sir Thomas Browne.

I have only time to indicate by a few detached sentences how much that has become by reiteration almost the commonplace of Wordsworthian criticism was first spoken by Lamb—as it were in prophetic anticipation of that counter-criticism which *The Excursion*, above all Wordsworth's poems, was destined to call forth.   How admirably said is the following, where Lamb, after noting that Wordsworth's popularity is endangered by the very 'boldness and originality of his genius,' adds : 'The times are past when a poet could securely follow the direction of his own mind into whatever tracts it might lead. A writer who would be popular, must timidly coast the shore of prescribed sentiment and sympathy. He must have just as much more of the imaginative faculty than his readers as will serve to keep their apprehensions from stagnating, but not so much as to alarm their jealousy. He must not think or feel too deeply. If he has had the fortune to be bred in the midst of the most magnificent objects of creation, he must not have given away his heart to them ; or, if he have, he must conceal his love, or not carry his expressions of it beyond that point of rapture which the occasional tourist thinks it not overstepping decorum to betray, or the limit which that gentlemanly spy upon Nature, the picturesque traveller, has vouchsafed to countenance. He must do this, or be content to be thought an enthusiast.' He anticipates, moreover, the now common objection that the poet puts into the hearts and mouths of unlettered peasants thoughts and words unsuited to their humble capacities, and says finely that if the poet ' has detected, or imagines he has detected, through the cloudy medium of their unlettered discourse, thoughts and apprehensions not vulgar, traits of patience and constancy, love unwearied, and heroic endurance, . . . he will be deemed a man of perverted genius by the philanthropist, who, conceiving of the peasantry of his country only as objects of a pecuniary sympathy, starts at finding them elevated to a level of humanity with himself, having their own loves, enmities, cravings, aspirations, as much beyond his faculty to believe as his beneficence to supply.'

And lastly, Lamb disposes for ever of the critics who confuse poetry 'having children for its subject' with poetry that is 'childish,' and who, 'having themselves, perhaps, never been *children*, never having possessed the tenderness and docility of that age, know not what the soul of a child is—how apprehensive! how imaginative! how religious!'

In almost all the main issues, then, that so long separated, and, alas! still separate the reasonable lover of Wordsworth from those who sit in the seat of the scorner, Charles Lamb shows himself here, as in so many other fields of literature, almost unique in critical discernment. He was no partisan; he never writes as one holding a brief. He had the liveliest sense of Wordsworth's deficiencies and limitations. He is none of those 'fervent Wordsworthians' against whom Mr. Arnold has told us we must 'be on our guard' (a class, I venture to hope, not quite so large as Mr. Arnold would have us believe), who will have Wordsworth admired all round, or not at all. Lamb ventures to pick and choose, and to discriminate, even when he writes to the poet himself. And he can read and criticise on occasion without enthusiasm, and even with his own matchless humour. While he declares (may we not without presumption add, with what justice?) of the verse:

> And thou that didst appear so fair
> To fond imagination,
> Dost rival in the light of day
> Her delicate creation,

that 'no lovelier stanza, I think, can be found in the wide world of poetry,' he is not afraid to say bluntly that even the *Poet's Epitaph* is disfigured by the common satire upon parsons and lawyers at the beginning.

I do not think it would be a bad day's work for the

Wordsworth Society to print side by side these two essays of Jeffrey and Lamb that appeared in the two leading critical authorities of the time almost in the same week, when *The Excursion* was first submitted to the judgment of the world. It might be called, after Mrs. Barbauld's famous story, *Eyes and No Eyes;* but under whatever name, it could not fail to teach many lessons, both of encouragement and warning. There is an unpublished comment of Lamb's in the matter of another poet, George Wither, with which I may fitly close this paper. When an early copy of an edition of Wither's poems, with manuscript notes of Dr. Nott's, was submitted to Lamb for his further suggestion and criticism, he found that Dr. Nott had written against Wither's satire *On Ambition* the words—'A very dull essay indeed.' Upon which Lamb retorts :—

'Why double-dull it with thy dull commentary? Have you nothing to cry out but 'very dull,' 'a little better,' 'this has some spirit,' 'this is prosaic'? Foh !

'If the sun of Wither withdraw a while, clamour not for joy. Owl—it will out again, and blear thy envious eyes.'

If this is true of the 'sun of Wither,' how much more need is there to repeat the warning for those who have only eyes for the clouds that now and again steal across the sun of Wordsworth !

LORD HOUGHTON'S ADDRESS AS PRESIDENT, 1885.

LORD HOUGHTON'S ADDRESS AS PRESIDENT, 1885.

LADIES and Gentlemen, this is the third meeting which may (in a manner) be called representative of English verse, that I have had the pleasure of addressing this year. The first was the occasion of the unveiling of the bust of Coleridge in the Chapter-House at Westminster, a meeting which exhibited not only deep personal interest in the character of Coleridge, and in the honour he had received—the greatest honour which an Englishman after death can receive—that of a presentment of his image in the great national mausoleum, 'the Pantheon of the West,' as Mr. Tennyson —who himself one day will probably lie within those precincts—has called it. That meeting, besides that recognition, was a very interesting resurrection, so to speak, of the value and extent and power of Coleridge's philosophy. And it was remarkable that every speaker, I think, on that occasion expressed personal gratitude for the thoughts which had been imparted to him by the poet Coleridge, not only in the melody of his verse, but in the novel systems of thought of which he was the author in this country. The second occasion on which I had the pleasure and the honour of being present and presiding, was the inauguration of the bust of the poet Gray in the hall of Pembroke College, Cambridge, after more than a hundred years of silence as to his name in that University. That was a very interesting occasion, and although it originated chiefly in the interest in Gray which had been shown by his able biographer, Mr. Gosse, was nevertheless fully estimated and understood by the rest of the University and other representative men, of whom the most remarkable perhaps is Mr. Lowell, the American Minister, who took such an interesting part in your meeting last year. I only wish that he had tided over a little his departure from this country, and had been present with us here to-day. I look on this as the third meeting of that nature, and I may be permitted to say that I think gatherings, representative of literary homage, and also of personal interest in the poets in whose works we still take delight, are not only very just in themselves, but extremely useful in the cause of literature. We in this country are not too apt to keep alive the remembrance of literary men. I do not know whether we esteem them less, or whether on the whole their influence is less than among other nations, but certainly such a sensation as followed the death of Victor Hugo would be scarcely possible in this country.

The very occasion of our meeting here to-day almost precludes me from saying anything of especial interest, because whatever I might say with regard to the work of Wordsworth, to have any interest at all, must be of a critical character ; and although I know that this is not merely a mutual admiration Society, or even an individual admiration Society, yet nevertheless I do not conceive that any criticism, with such liveliness and liberty as makes criticism at all amusing, would be suitable at a meeting of this kind. Therefore I am driven, if I am to say anything different from the commonplaces of admiration with which we are familiar, to fall back on what I might call any possible personal connection

of my own life and mind with that of the great poet. And
I am enabled—I think fortunately—to introduce this subject
to you by reading the initial passage of the delightful little
book which I hold in my hand—Matthew Arnold's *Selections
from Wordsworth.* I owed most, if not the whole, of the
interest of what I had to say about Gray at Cambridge, to
the subtle and delightful criticism of Matthew Arnold on
Gray, in the edition of *The British Poets.* I will, therefore,
if you will allow me, read to you these few words of Matthew
Arnold as the foundation for any future remarks :—' I
remember hearing Lord Macaulay say, after Wordsworth's
death, when subscriptions were being collected to found a
memorial of him, that ten years earlier more · money could
have been raised in Cambridge alone, to do honour to
Wordsworth, than was now raised all through the country.
Lord Macaulay had, as we know, his own heightened and
telling way of putting things, and we must always make
allowance for it. But probably it is true that Wordsworth
has never, either before or since, been so accepted and
popular, so established in the minds of all who profess to
care for poetry, as he was between the years 1830 and 1840,
and at Cambridge.' I happened to be a member of Trinity
College, Cambridge, at that time, and I am delighted to confirm that judgment. My recollections of that period are
sufficiently vivid to enable me to say that I am very proud
of having personally, in some degree, contributed to that
great acceptance of and I might say enthusiasm for Wordsworth which was generated among the youth of Cambridge
at that time. When I look back upon that time, and the,
so to say, mental proceedings by which it was made important to the lives of all who shared in it, I find it somewhat
difficult precisely to comprehend the cause of that enthusiasm.

It was contemporaneous with a burst of interest in the poetry of Shelley and of Keats. With regard to Keats, of whose life I had afterwards the pleasure of being the recorder, we were very proud of having been the means of introducing to English literature the delightful poem of *Adonaïs*. A son of Mr. Hallam, the historian, who was the Marcellus of his day, and who, if he had lived, would have been a most distinguished name in English history—the Arthur Hallam of the *In Memoriam*—arrived from Italy at that time, bringing with him a copy of the *Adonaïs*, which had been printed at Pisa under the superintendence of Byron. That copy we reprinted at Cambridge, and, as it were, introduced into British literature.

The enthusiasm for Keats is, I think, very intelligible. He is essentially the poet of youth ; he is the embodiment, as it were, of youth and poetry, in the richness of the imagination, and in the abundance of melodious power. We also, I think, fully comprehend, now that Shelley has taken his just place among the poets of England, how delightful it was to our youthful interests, and I may say to our youthful vanity, to raise the name of Shelley from the obscurity, and I might almost say even the infamy, which at that time attached to it, to the high atmosphere of pure imagination in which it now exists in the estimate of all real lovers of British literature. But there was no such reason why we should have laboured to any similar extent for the elevation of the name and works of Mr. Wordsworth. The name of Wordsworth was familiar to the crowd at Cambridge in two ways. His brother was the Master of Trinity, a venerated and respectable old gentleman, the author of a very dull ecclesiastical biography, and who had not recommended himself to the undergraduate mind by any exhibition of geniality or especial interest in our pursuits, our avocations, or even our studies. We had at Cambridge, in the son of that Dr. Wordsworth, by the name of Christopher Wordsworth, a very eminent scholar and not unagreeable companion, but he manifested in youth the germs of that outwardly hard, though inwardly benevolent, character, which so much distinguished him as the learned, pious, excellent administrator, the Bishop of Lincoln. I had the pleasure of accompanying that distinguished prelate in those Grecian travels which are familiar to you all, and I wish I could show you in my books about me here the presentation copy of his Voyage to me, which not only confirmed our affectionate relations, but introduced me to a new Greek word, which I do not know is familiar even to such Hellenists as I see present. The book is addressed συνοδοιπόρῳ ἐμῷ. I do not know whether, if any of you had been asked to give me a Greek word for 'fellow-traveller,' you could have done that—I am sure I could not.

Let us look back therefore at what could have been the rationale of our faith and interest in the poetry of Wordsworth. I think I alluded to our juvenile vanity in rescuing the names of Keats and Shelley from the injustice which we thought had been done to them. Well, there was something of that sort, I think, in our patronage (such as it was) of the name of Wordsworth. When we came to read him seriously (as we did), we thought that the ridicule which had been thrown upon the name of Wordsworth and the publication of his pastoral poems was supremely unjust. We could see the causes of it; how that the extreme familiarity of the diction had in it something by no means congenial to the literary mind of that or perhaps any other period; not that England at that time was new to the familiar diction, because we had had it in the most distinct way in the poetry of Burns, where it had not only been willingly accepted, but was undoubtedly one of the causes of the ready acceptance of his verse among the people of England, and still more of Scotland. It was not that alone, but it was, I think, that this extreme familiarity of diction was accompanied by something that looked like vulgarity of thought. The sentiments which this diction represented were of a very ordinary character, connected with the ordinary peasant life of the country, and unaccompanied by any of those stirring, deep, and passionate emotions, with which the common language of Burns was saturated. There was, too, a certain indelicacy of thought in the sense of producing to the mind images of a very common character under circumstances of an almost ludicrous nature. And, looking back at this now at the distance we do, I think I can say that we felt this more strongly, from that one great deficiency in the faculties of Wordsworth—a total want of the sense of humour. No man with a sense of humour could have exposed himself to those occasionally just criticisms of the almost comic positions of some of his characters, verging on coarseness. I do not think that the lines of *Peter Bell,* which were thus cited as examples of almost comic verse, could have been written by any man with a strong sense of humour. He would have seen the position himself quite as strongly as his critics would have seen it. And at that time, whatever else we were, we were all humorists. Therefore there was something to get over in our admiration, and I think we got over it by a process which, looking back, seems to me to have been almost too good to be true. I do not think that, as a body of young men, at that time we were especially religious, or especially virtuous in any way, and therefore, I do not think it was the height of the morality of Wordsworth which attracted us; but still there was something that we saw (I do not know how) as to the moral elevation of that verse, in contrast with the reigning poetic power of that time, namely, the verse of Lord Byron. It was then not only fashionable, but almost indispensable, for every youth to be Byronic. Of course, though at Cambridge we had not either the energy, or perhaps the courage, to be Corsairs or Laras, yet nevertheless we enjoyed the poetry, and especially the later poetry, of Lord Byron, as something very cognate to our dispositions and tempers, probably not the best of either. But we did see that there was something in the poems of Wordsworth and of Shelley which satisfied what we knew to be our better and higher aspirations.

I daresay there may be some persons present who have heard of an event of undergraduate Cambridge life at that time, which has the peculiarity of tiding its memory into several future undergraduate existences, namely, the expedition from the Debating Society at Cambridge to the Debating Society of Oxford, to discuss and impress upon the University opinion of Oxford the superiority of Shelley to Byron. That expedition was remarkable as having originated in, and having been supported by, men who are still of living interest in this country. I think it was originated by Sir Francis Doyle, who afterwards became Professor of Poetry at Oxford; and it was certainly sustained by a name not unfamiliar to you, the name of Mr. Gladstone, by whom we were received at the railway station, and conducted to our abode. You know that, according to the formula of University life at Cambridge, you cannot be out for a night without what is called an 'Exeat'—a permission to be away

—which can only be obtained from the Master of the College, and I was deputed to obtain this from Dr. Wordsworth, the Master of Trinity, and did obtain it. I have always had some compunction in having done so, because I cannot think that that reverend theologian would have favourably given us the permission if he had known we were going to advocate the poetry of Mr. Shelley. I have always had a dim suspicion—though probably I did not do so—that I substituted the name of Wordsworth for Shelley. Nevertheless, I so wrapped up in my language the definition of our object—which was mainly, as I put it, the destruction of the wicked influence of Lord Byron—as to make Dr. Wordsworth believe that what we intended to substitute for Byron was not Shelley, but Wordsworth. However, we did go, and I have no doubt that with our laudation of Shelley we combined the laudation of Wordsworth, at the same time, in our representations to the University of Oxford. We were of course very much shocked to find that the name of Shelley was utterly unknown at Oxford; indeed, one of the speakers said he did not know a line of Shelley except

My banks they are furnished with bees.

We discovered he thought it was Mr. Shenstone, not the poet of world-wide reputation, we had gone down there to discuss. The expedition was interesting as a specimen of what I may call a very laudable literary enthusiasm, of which I shall be very glad to see more among the youth of this day. However these facts may be, it remains true that the undergraduate youth of my time at Cambridge did take that part in, I will not say rehabilitating, but enhancing the fame and power of the poems of Wordsworth in the University, and in the general world of letters of which he afterwards formed part. Of course at that time the wealth and the power of Wordsworth were increasing. Matthew Arnold says: 'The death of Byron seemed to make an opening for Wordsworth. Scott, who had for some time ceased to produce poetry himself, and stood before the public as a great novelist,—Scott, too genuine himself not to feel the profound genuineness of Wordsworth, and with an instinctive recognition of his firm hold on nature and of his local truth, always admired him sincerely, and praised him generously. The influence of Coleridge upon young men of ability was then powerful, and was still gathering strength; this influence told entirely in favour of Wordsworth's poetry. Cambridge was a place where Coleridge's influence had great action, and where Wordsworth's poetry, therefore, flourished especially. But even amongst the general public its sale grew large, the eminence of its author was widely recognised, and Rydal Mount became an object of pilgrimage.' It is very interesting to see in connection with Wordsworth's adoration of the beauties of Nature, that his name and fame are incorporated with the scenery of the Lakes, just as much as are the name and fame of Sir Walter Scott with the scenery of Scotland, of which he may be said to have been the creator. Mr. Arnold goes on to say: 'I remember Wordsworth relating how one of the pilgrims, a clergyman, asked him if he had ever written anything besides the *Guide to the Lakes.* Yes, he answered modestly, he had written verses. Not every pilgrim was a reader, but the vogue was established, and the stream of pilgrims came.'

I have been one of those pilgrims, and I can fully confirm with my personal observation the very interesting paper on the reminiscences of Wordsworth amid the peasantry of Westmoreland, of which you have a delightful record in the

last volume of our *Transactions*, by the Rev. Mr. Rawnsley,
whom I regret not to see here to-day.   I remember myself
talking to several old people about the matter, and they
used exactly the language which is here given about what
they call his 'going booing about.'   It must have been a
kind of vague poetical utterance to which they gave that
very distinctive and characteristic epithet.   And the peasantry of Westmoreland seem fully to have recognised that
deficiency to which I have already alluded—his want of
humour.   Here is a sample of what Mr. Rawnsley records.
' " Did you ever read his poetry, or see any [of his] books
about in the farm-houses ? " I asked.   " Ay, ay, time or two.
But ya 're weel aware there 's potry and potry. There 's potry
wi' a li'le bit pleasant in it, and potry sic as a man can laugh
at or the childer understand, and some as takes a deal of
mastery to make out what 's said, and a deal of Wudsworth's
was this sort, ye kna.   You could tell fra the man's faace
his potry would never have no laugh in it." '   It may be unjust to call that especially a defect ; but, nevertheless, it was
evidently a part of Wordsworth's mind.   And while it was
one of the interesting reminiscences of Voltaire to know
that Voltaire fully recognised the greatness and the superiority of English poetry over that of his own country—in its
high moral standard and power of thought—Wordsworth is
reported to have spoken of Voltaire as being a remarkably
stupid writer.

Well, his fame grew ; and in these letters from Wordsworth
to Kenyon—also published in our *Transactions* for 1884
—there is this very interesting passage, written in 1837,—

' I hear from many quarters of the impression which my
writings are making, both at home and abroad, and to an
old man it would be discreditable not to be gratified with

such intelligence ; because it is not the language of praise
for pleasure bestowed, but of gratitude for moral and intellectual improvement received.'

You have heard those beautiful lines—

> I 've heard of hearts unkind, kind deeds
> With coldness still returning ;
> Alas ! the gratitude of men
> Hath oftener left me mourning,

and I think I see in this passage the embodiment of that
feeling.

Beyond these vague personal impressions, ladies and
gentlemen, I do not know that I have anything to say. I
asked a man of letters to come here to-day, and he said he
believed he admired and enjoyed Wordsworth as much as
anybody, but still if he had come he should have had to
say that he could not put him in the first rank of English
poets, as he would a supreme poet of passion, or a supreme
poet of melody. Well, this may be so, and the same was
said of that other poet at whose celebration I attended,
that of Thomas Gray. In my remarks on that occasion I
stated the disadvantages under which the poet of sentiment
must always lie, in comparison with the supreme poet of
passion, or the poet of supreme melody. On the one hand
we may say that the poet of passion will always have a
depth of sympathy, almost we may say a violence of sympathy, to which the poet of sentiment cannot attain. And
this was, I think, the chief cause why the poem of Thomas
Gray—representing, I think, perhaps the poetry of sympathy
in its most perfect form—the *Elegy in a Country Churchyard*, took, nevertheless, almost a century before it became
part of the English language as it now is. Then, Thomas
Gray wrote little else : Wordsworth wrote much. And we

cannot leave out of consideration, in judgment of him, the poetical life, as it were, the poetic personality, which stretched over nearly a century. It is this which gives to Wordsworth a great specialty as the poet of sentiment—that he has, as it were, identified himself with almost all the great and general, and especially the domestic, affections of mankind. There is no poetry which can be said to form such a distinctive portion of our household literature as that of Wordsworth. Its interest in so many forms of familiar life, its interest in the common occupations of the world, and above all, its perfect enthusiasm for Nature, and from Nature to Nature's God—this gives to Wordsworth the assurance of a constant immortality, crowned, I think, by the production of some few poems which we may place at the very top of philosophic poetry. If I am asked—in that perfunctory way in which one is sometimes asked to write in a lady's album—What is the greatest poem in the English language? I never for a moment hesitate to say, Wordsworth's *Ode on the Intimations of Immortality*. That poem is to me the greatest embodiment of philosophic poetry, which may decorate youth, and childhood itself, with the years of grave and philosophic manhood. It comprehends the life of man.

I thank you for having listened to these desultory observations, and I only wish I had the time or means for producing something more worthy of your hearing.

WORDSWORTH AND TURNER.

By HARRY GOODWIN.

WORDSWORTH AND TURNER.[1]

THE painter of 'The Fighting Temeraire' and 'The Slave Ship,' and the writer of *The Leech-Gatherer* and *The Happy Warrior*, were men of genius, widely separated in art and life. Yet the leading feature in the work of each is alike: the art of both was marked by a greater love of Nature, and a return to more simplicity, than was characteristic of the period of severe traditional conventionality in which they worked.

Wordsworth shows, in his sonnets to Haydon, and to Sir George Beaumont, and in his objections to Sir Joshua Reynolds's 'mere portrait-painting,' that, outside his own special art, he was under the influence of the conventional traditions of his time; just as Turner, in his attempt to write verses after the manner of Pope and Rogers, proves that in the art of painting *only* was he freed from the narrow mannerism of the eighteenth century.

It is scarcely too much to say that landscape-painting received as great an impetus from the work of Turner as poetry received from Wordsworth. Both left old paths; both sought after new methods, fresh truths of nature, rarely hesitating to use the most homely incidents to illustrate their themes. Let us take, for instance, Turner's 'Church-yard in Kirkby Lonsdale, Yorkshire,' in which picture one

---

[1] Read to the Society in May 1885.

might have expected an incident given in the spirit of
Young or Cowley, had it been painted by one of Turner's
contemporaries; but the great master quietly ignores all
the unities, and paints probably exactly what he saw—viz.,
a number of boys, who have left their school-books among
the graves, have set up a mark on one of the tombs, and
are throwing at it, in all the abandonment of boyish mischief.
Over their heads the loveliest trees wave softly in the tender
blue.   Far away the river winds, and loses itself in the
mystery of the folded hills.   Without this exquisite beauty
of landscape, the picture would remind us more of the
poetry of Crabbe than of Wordsworth; but the beauty
elevates and sustains the commonplace, as the poetry of
Wordsworth often surrounds a seemingly trivial subject with
pure and noble ideas.   At the time it was painted, it was
as daring an innovation as the poem of *We are Seven* could
have been.   Both painter and poet seem to have said,
'Enough of weeping swains and funereal urns,'

> The common growth of mother Earth
> Suffices me, her tears, her mirth,
> Her humblest mirth and tears.

Turner's work, like the world of nature, has its delicate
mystery of detail, as well as its grand sweeping masses and
largeness of outline.   He saw and portrayed the sublimity
of light, and the grandeur of the forms of cloud.   But
Turner never forgot the human interest in any scene.   We
are made to see through his eyes the varied life of men, on
hill and in dale, in the city and on the sea.   Their toil, their
pleasures, all are given with the force of truth, sad and despairing as the toil may be; but above are the skies, and the
glory of the heavens transfuses all with surrounding brightness.   In the words of Goethe, as rendered by Carlyle :

> Here is all fulness,
> Ye brave, to reward you ;
> Work, and despair not.

Now in this is there not much kinship with Wordsworth's special insistence on the healing power of Nature, and the perfect fitness of the natural world to human life ?—

> For I have learned
> To look on Nature, not as in the hour
> Of thoughtless youth, but hearing oftentimes
> The still sad music of humanity,
> Nor harsh, nor grating, though of ample power
> To chasten and subdue.

One strong characteristic these two great men had also in common—their keen perception of, and sympathy with, the sad side of human life, and the mystery of pain ; but they both looked forward to the light.   They could say—

> Through love, through hope, and faith's transcendent dower,
> We feel that we are greater than we know.

Numberless instances may be given from Turner's work in illustration of this kinship.   Perhaps his 'Scenes in the Holy Land,' and his illustrations of Rogers's *Poems*, and of the Rivers of England and France, give a more vivid idea of this than some of his grander and more ambitious work.   In these 'Scenes in the Holy Land,' taken principally from sketches by other men (for Turner was never in the East), it is interesting to note with what imagination he connects the human interest of the event with the scene in which it happens.   Thus, in the drawing of ' Rama,' wolves are tearing the lambs among a flock : one poor sheep stands over the mangled body of a lamb.   In the ' Bethlehem,' one bright star in the evening sky, the solitary figure of a woman with a young child by the wayside, the tender mystery of the grey twilight—the loneliness, the poverty, and humility of the figure—tell us of what the painter's heart was full. Many of Turner's illustrations of Rogers's *Poems* have much greater affinity with *The Prelude* and *The Excursion* than with the dragging lines and stilted sentiment of the poems they were painted to illustrate. The design, for instance, intended for the shepherd 'on Tornaro's misty brow,' is perfectly fitted to picture to us the passage in *The Excursion*—

> But for the growing youth,
> What soul was his, when, from the top
> Of some bold headland, he beheld the sun
> Rise up, and bathe the world in light!

In Turner's drawing the sun is literally 'bathing the world in light;' the power and grandeur of the visible universe swallow up material existence, filling and satisfying the soul with its own supernal beauty. In the 'Datur hora quieti,' the peace of parting day, the rest and stillness, suggest the leading thought of *The Prelude*.

To those familiar with Turner's 'Shipwreck' in the National Gallery, these lines of Wordsworth's, from *Peele Castle in a Storm*, must, I think, seem like another illustration of the same thought—

> That hulk which labours in the deadly swell,
> This rueful sky, this pageantry of fear.

Wordsworth once said of Southey, 'Books are his passion, and,' he added, 'wandering, I can in truth affirm, was mine;' and 'wandering' certainly was Turner's. All over England, all over the Continent, he wandered, receptive and solitary, becoming increasingly absorbed in his Art, untiring in reproducing what he saw in Nature; and at last accumulating such a mass of work that it is difficult to believe it the creation of one man.

Turner did not take public criticism and disapproval with the dignified patience and quiet self-reliance that were so characteristic of Wordsworth; but neither did he ever lower his ideal to meet the views of any art critics.

On one occasion, while Turner was retouching a picture, an artist friend said to him : ' Well, now, I never saw anything like that in Nature;' to which Turner replied, 'Very likely; but don't you wish you were able to see it ?'

To conclude this parallelism—already too long in words and too short in circumstance—it has been said that there was in Turner's work a strange mingling of the sublime and the ridiculous ; and I believe that the same has been said of Wordsworth, from the days of the Edinburgh Reviewers to this present time. There may be a germ of truth in the criticism. Both men may have been lacking in a sense of the humorous—that saving grace of the nineteenth century ; but life was a serious thing to both. They had a message to deliver, and were straitened until it was accomplished. Wordsworth has said, ' I wish to be considered as a teacher, or as nothing.' And so what he says comes from his lips with a gravity not ill fitted to convey the truths he had to teach. Both Poet and Painter were at one in their endeavour to show to others all they could of that world of beauty into which they had access,

> A sense sublime
> Of something far more deeply interfused,
> Whose dwelling is the light of setting suns,
> And the round ocean and the living air,
> And the blue sky, and in the mind of man :
> A motion and a spirit, that impels
> All thinking things, all objects of all thought,
> And rolls through all things.

LORD SELBORNE'S ADDRESS AS PRESIDENT, 1886.

LORD SELBORNE'S ADDRESS AS PRESIDENT, 1886.

LADIES and GENTLEMEN,—When I was asked more than a year ago to preside at the Meeting (then to be held) of the Wordsworth Society, I felt, as I feel now, that I owed a debt of piety and gratitude to the name and the memory of Wordsworth, and to his work, which compelled me to do what I could to pay it by any means within my power. Last year I was prevented from doing so. This year I have consented upon one condition, which I hope you will pardon me for making. I said that if it was necessary to prepare an essay, or some elaborate work, for your interest or instruction, I did not feel equal to that. What should it be? Should it be criticism? Well, there were three reasons which made me unwilling to make that attempt. One was, that it would be a very laborious thing to do it with any possibility of giving satisfaction to you, or to myself; and I was not satisfied that other duties would give me the time to do what I should have wished if I undertook it. Another and perhaps as forcible a reason was, that I have been all my life a worshipper at the inner-most shrine of Wordsworth, and I do not think that the worshipper quite likes to undertake the task of dissection or criticism. And a third reason, also quite sufficient, was that I felt sure that the thing had already been very well done —perhaps as well as it could be, certainly better than I could expect to do it—by others at other meetings of the Wordsworth Society. So I thought that if I were here to-day, I must be allowed to be here upon the condition of rather speaking to you shortly, and in a conversational manner, so as to give my own impressions of Wordsworth, not new, and I have no doubt probably common to most of you, and already better expressed by others. But my own impressions have at least this to recommend them, that they are real, and they have endured almost the whole of my life.

Now the beginning of my personal acquaintance with the poems of Wordsworth, and, I may say, with the Poet himself—with whom I had some small opportunities (very much valued) of personal conversation—goes far back, to the time when I was an undergraduate at the University of Oxford. There it was my good fortune very soon to be honoured with the friendship of a distinguished man, the poet's nephew, and an ardent admirer, as he ought to be, of his uncle,—Charles Wordsworth, who is now Bishop of St. Andrews. Many a night did I sit in his rooms at Christ Church, hearing him read with that animation of which he was a master the specimens which he thought the finest, and most likely to interest and attract others, of his uncle's work. That was the beginning. There I was a pupil. Then I formed a very intimate friendship with a man younger than myself, also at the University, who also has left a name behind him, but is now gone—Frederick William Faber—who was distinguished, first in the Church of England, and afterwards elsewhere ; a man of ardent character and great zeal in everything which he undertook, and which he believed to be right, and especially an enthusiastic lover of poetry. He and I read Wordsworth together, as two lovers, rather than as pupil and master.

And I think in that stage of reading perhaps it came home even more than it did at the first. And having so begun, and having followed it for myself as opportunity has offered, until I became tolerably well acquainted with everything which Wordsworth had written, I speak no more and no less than the truth when I say that this acquaintance with the works of Wordsworth has been to me as great a power in the education of mind and character, after the Bible, as any that I have known. The Bible first, certainly. I think it has been so to all who have given it a chance. Certainly it has been so to me. I put no book in competition with the Bible. But, after the Bible, I trace more distinctly, with more certainty, and with less hesitation and doubt, to Wordsworth, than to any other literary influence whatever, anything I may recognise as good in the formation of my own mind and character. I do not mean to say for that reason that Wordsworth is necessarily the greatest of all the writers whom I have known, and from whom I have learned. I should hesitate, of course, to say that he was greater than Plato; and I should not hesitate to say—if we must make comparisons—that he was not altogether so great as Shakespeare. But, nevertheless, I have learned from Wordsworth more as an individual man than I ever learned from Plato, or even from Shakespeare. Nor am I unfamiliar with other great poets and great writers of ancient and modern times. I have mentioned those whom I should place the first, and therefore you may easily suppose that of the rest, great as they may be, I cannot say so much as I have said of these.

What was it, first and foremost, and most important, which one learned from Wordsworth? One learned, I say, more about Man, and more about Nature, and more about the union of the two, than is to be learned anywhere else. That was the lesson which I learned. The sympathy, the intelligence with which man is regarded and portrayed and put before his fellow-men throughout the works of Wordsworth is, I think, something unique in all literature. Man everywhere, man in all conditions—the great, the noble (I use the word, of course, in a moral and not in the lower sense)—the noble of the earth, the men called to do illustrious deeds and leave imperishable names,—Wordsworth felt with them and understood their vocation. But not with them chiefly—with common men, men in every condition of life, men struggling with infirmity, men struggling with temptation—and, of course, when I say men, I mean women too—men falling under vice, men bowed under sorrow, men almost cast out from the world. None were cast out from Wordsworth's sympathy. He saw that which was great, that which was divine, that which was beautiful pervading them all, in every condition ; and he could make the lesson of the old Cumberland beggar as touching to the heart as the lesson of Laodamia, or of Dion, or of any other great example of public or of private virtue. That, I think, was a great thing to learn, because there is in the world in which we live a wonderful amount of distracting force in the glory and glitter of worldly success, worldly ambition, and in the miserable inequality of ranks. I do not say this in any socialistic sense, but I say it in the sense of a man sympathising with his fellow-men. In all these things there is a great deal which tends to distract the mind and harden the heart, and make people forget, after all, that worth makes the man, the want of it the fellow ; and, as Pope said—

'All the rest is leather and prunella.'

Pope taught that in those verses—he said it, at least ; but

I am not at all sure that the moral of Pope's poems was very much calculated to carry the lesson home to the hearts of men. I thank him for the truth when he spoke it. Wordsworth speaks the truth, not as a man who comes down to ride the high horse of ethics over his fellow-men, but simply as a poet of human nature. He sets before them in all its varieties that same real nature which we have in common, and which we ought to recognise in all, wherever we meet with it. Now do not be frightened and offended if I may seem here or there even to drop something which may look like political allusion. It is not politics in any sense about which we are likely to differ. But it may be in the recollection of some of you that a great man—whom I will not name, for at present I do not agree with him, as I have often done before—in 1866 offended some people by speaking of the 'common flesh and blood' which we have with the general mass of our fellow-countrymen, as a reason why we should place that degree of trust and confidence in them which experience, the growth of opinion, the progress of circumstances, and other things in human affairs dictated when the time had come. I from my heart and soul felt the force of the expression, and was by no means one of those who was in any way offended by it. I do not, indeed, agree with the principle that 'the voice of the people is the voice of God,' although sometimes the popular instinct is not unlike that of women—I hope the ladies will pardon me if I pay them a compliment in one direction which may possibly not seem so in another,—who go straight to the point, passing over the intermediate stages, and are very often more right than men who go through them. But to suppose that to be true as to the whole range of human affairs—that they can by any possibility, because they have those generous, right

kind, true human instincts, always judge rightly about difficult matters—is not a lesson we are at all taught by Wordsworth, or by any philosophy which involves a true, a right,
a discriminating, as well as a deep sympathy, with human
nature. It is not by flattering people that you will best
show your fellow-feeling; it is not by telling them they
have qualities they have not; that they are what they are
not, or can be what they cannot be; but it is by making
the most of what you have in common with them as they
are. This is the way in which human sympathy will be
cultivated, and such good done as can be done by the
cultivation of human sympathy, and this Wordsworth teaches
us throughout his writing. He does not teach us by any
means to abandon our judgment in order to indulge our
sympathy. The over-seeing Power of which he is the
preacher is not a 'kindling' power only, but is also one to
' restrain.'

So far I have spoken of what one learns about Man.
Now, with regard to Nature, I will merely glance at a point
of the utmost importance, relative to Nature as well as to
man, of which I am reminded by seeing that we are to be
favoured with a paper by Professor Veitch upon a subject
certainly of great interest, and requiring to be handled with
that judgment which I have no doubt will characterise his
way of treating it—'The Theism of Wordsworth.' I have
not the least idea how Professor Veitch is going to treat that
subject, but I cannot help saying some words about it
myself. I am, as I daresay everybody present to whom my
name is not entirely strange knows, a profound believer in
the truth of the Christian religion. That belief has grown
with my growth. The whole experience of my life has
tended to confirm it. The more I meet with statements of

difficulties, the more I feel that these are not difficulties peculiar to Christianity, but that they are difficulties of a kind incident to the state of probation in which we live, to the nature of things, and from which, in one form or another, there is no escape whether you are a Christian, or whether you are not. But, at all events, I make this profession before you—not of course for the sake of making it, but for the sake of what I am going to say upon the subject of Wordsworth from that point of view. A man who can say with sincerity what I have just now said must know and be able to see whether or not there is anything contrary, anything repugnant, anything at variance with his convictions and his belief in the poetry of Wordsworth. I say confidently that there is nothing—nothing whatever. If there were a single point out of harmony with that Christian belief, I must have felt it. I say there is nothing of the kind. I mention two poems of which some people may take a view different from that which I take, poems to which, at all events, any one speaking upon that subject is likely to make some allusion. They are *Tintern Abbey* and the *Intimations of Immortality*. I have met with people who say of *Tintern Abbey*, ' This is Pantheism.' What do they mean by Pantheism ? Nothing is more easy than to use a word of that sort in a vague, unintelligible manner, without any accurate attempt to determine in what sense it is to be understood. It may possibly be meant only to signify that which every Christian believes. Of course I need not say that one of the universally accepted axioms of the Christian religion concerning that inscrutable divine nature in which every Christian believes (though no Christian pretends to define and comprehend it) is the omnipresence of God. The mode of that omnipresence, the conditions under which it exists, we do not know ; but every Christian, every theist, professes to believe in a Divine omnipresence. And that belief, beyond all doubt, is set before us in the most glowing, the most real manner in that poem of Wordsworth. Technical Pantheism means, if it means anything at all, the identification of all things which exist—what we commonly call matter (though I cannot define what matter is any more than I can define anything else)—with God. In other words, Pantheism means the assertion that the universe is God, and therefore everything is divine. Now there is nothing of that in Wordsworth. Philosophers may think that is true, or they may not think so,—just as Plato held the idea of a soul of the world, that is to say, that there was a central divine soul. He thought so of every one of the planets and fixed stars, and in what we call matter he saw the body to that soul. No ideas of that kind are to be found in Wordsworth ; but the simple idea of a universal, all-penetrating, all-present, divine power and influence is there. With regard to the other beautiful poem, the *Intimations of Immortality*, I have heard some very staunch upholders of orthodox dogmatic teaching find fault with it. All I can say is, I see nothing in it but this—though in some respects presented in a fanciful form—a recognition of the divine origin of the human soul. And if there is such a thing as a human soul, it has a divine origin, and whatever there be in it of true, beautiful, and divine, comes from that origin, and from that alone. All that I seem to have learned from Wordsworth. I do not mention it controversially, but I mention it as part of the education of my mind by the reading of Wordsworth.

Now to refer to our other subject. I do not like comparative standards in anything. I do not mean that one can help ranking poets in a certain order of greatness. If I were asked to name the greatest poets, I should refer to the general sense of Englishmen, and should place Shakespeare first—I am not speaking of Homer and the ancients; they belong to a sphere very distinct, and we should confuse matters by going so far afield—and I should place Milton (with some hesitation) second, because there is a certain greatness about him, which, with many defects, is not approached by any other writer in our language. And I should certainly put Wordsworth third. There is a completeness in the work he has done, a thoroughness, which I cannot recognise elsewhere. That may be, perhaps, because I have personally learned so much from him. I say it to express my own individual feeling. But as I began, so I conclude. I deprecate comparative standards. It has often happened to me to hear comparative standards applied to scenery. A person expresses his great admiration for some beautiful scenery. Somebody else says : ' But this is nothing like Scotland !' 'This is nothing like Switzerland !' I do not think a man who talks or feels so has a true sense for scenery. Of course there is an association which leads to a kind of comparison ; but I think that everything has its own proper beauty. I can enjoy the snows of the Alps, and feel their sublimity ; but when I come back to England, and see our green fields, our stately and beautiful trees, and all the other charms of our country, I confess I do not want to have Switzerland here ; I am content with England, or with Scotland, or with Wales, or with the Lake country, for they seem to me to have quite enough to fill one's soul with absolute beauty, and all the better on account of the variety in which it is portrayed. And so it is with regard to poetry. We ought to remember that, instead of its being necessary for one great poet to be like another, it is just the contrary. The great poet has his own special and separate vocation; and it is in proportion as that is true, and he realises and fulfils it, that he is a great poet. He must be, so far, unlike others.

I am disposed to admit what I suppose those who criticise Wordsworth would perhaps impute to him as a defect—that of all great poets he is perhaps the least objective; and, for that reason, he may sometimes show a want of form and colour in his poetry. I am not inclined to deny that—either the general fact, or that the other is, perhaps, its unavoidable consequence. But although I admit that he is perhaps the least objective, yet (if it is not a paradox to say it) I fancy that the poetry of Wordsworth educates the sense of beauty, especially in regard to scenery and natural objects, in a degree that no other poetry I know of does. The reason is not very far to seek. The essence of poetry is not in its outside, not in its form, not in its colour, not in its music. Although all of us feel that these are accessories—the clothing which ought to go with poetry, and that poetry is defective so far as it has them not, yet, after all, these are the outside. The essence of beauty is in its more spiritual part; and Wordsworth lays hold of the spiritual part of Nature. He never separates the two. The outward and inward eye see together. He sees with them both deeply, and he teaches and helps others to do the same. He is a true artist also.

Although I say that he is a true artist, I am not sure that I like him best when the artist is most obvious, or when the art of the artist is obvious. Criticism, whether it be self-criticism, or criticism of the form of one's own work, or of anything else in it, is rather an enemy to what is deepest and most genuine in poetry. The greatest poets are at their worst when they are most self-conscious. If we are to take it that Shakespeare's plays and sonnets came from the same hand, all I can say is, that I could not point to a better illustration of the difference in the degree of greatness between the poetry which is self-conscious and the poetry which is not. The sonnets are self-conscious, and I must say, to my mind, not self-conscious in the most engaging way; whereas the plays—those wonderful, many-sided, natural, and spontaneous outbursts of genius—they exhibit no self-consciousness at all. So it is with Wordsworth, and yet he is a very considerable artist. I do not think anybody can doubt that if we want examples of magnificent form, of magnificent colour, we may find them in *Tintern Abbey* and in the *Intimations of Immortality*, and not in those alone of his works. Surely there is no poetry of the kind which has ever surpassed them in these qualities. I may be thought a heretic by some (Mr. Matthew Arnold is not present, or I might be afraid to say it), but I can enjoy all the small things as well as the great ones. He seems like an artist going about, pencil in hand, taking wayside sketches of the smallest as well as of the greatest, of the most trivial as well as of the most sublime, of the pettiest as well as of the most splendid objects, and he brings them together in a way which would make many a critic cast this or that sketch aside with ' Trifle ! Not worth doing ! Very insignificant ! ' The person who will read them all, and endeavour to enter into the feeling of all — following the notes of the music instead of pulling it to pieces—may, I think, see the same true sense of real beauty, the same feeling of the beauty of Nature and humanity in all its forms, pervading his lighter and inferior as well as his greater work.

I have said all that I want to say. I feel that whatever is true in it you have heard before. If you have not heard it, possibly you have thought it. The only credit I can take to myself is that of thoroughly feeling and believing all I have said.

THE THEISM OF WORDSWORTH.

By JOHN VEITCH.

T

THE THEISM OF WORDSWORTH.

IF I were to seek to express the main characteristic of the poetic mood of Wordsworth at its highest reach, I should say that his mind was open equally to the world of sense —the finite, and to the sphere of the infinite which borders and surrounds this world of ours. Most reflective minds realise both worlds—that the finite is set somehow in the midst, and as but a part, of infinitude itself. Our own limitation suggests this. From the sense-world we go out to the boundless in space, in time, and in power. Our shortcoming in presence of the moral ideal links us by a personal bond to the conception of absolute duty and unswerving will. Each finite life truly lived passes under the shadow of infinity.

But to Wordsworth both spheres were equally real, or rather the infinite was the more real of the two. In the full consciousness of infinitude and the limitless, Wordsworth recalls Lucretius ; but there was this difference—with the ancient poet infinitude was unpeopled, ‘a melancholy space and doleful time,’ transcending and dwarfing human life and its powers, holding for it neither love nor sympathy, vacuous and inexorable : while with the modern poet it was the abode of living powers, even ultimately of one supreme Power of life, closely related to and influencing the soul and heart of man. Now this sense of the boundless, the transcendent in

limit, is one of the most powerful conceptions in Wordsworth's life and poetry.   And it is at the root of his theistic
view of the world.   It is by no means the whole of this view,
but without it as a direct conception his theism—any theism
in fact—is impossible.   This is the frame, as it were, in
which God is to be set ; and without this opening into the
transcendent, the finite world—the world of our experience
—must remain to us as the whole of reality.   But what does
he say ?—

> In such strength
> Of usurpation, when the light of sense
> Goes out, *but with a flash that has revealed*
> *The invisible world, doth greatness make abode,*
> There harbours ; whether we be young or old,
> Our destiny, our being's heart and home,
> *Is with infinitude, and only there ;*
> With hope it is, hope that can never die,
> Effort, and expectation, and desire,
> *And something evermore to be.*

Speaking again of the view from the ascent of Snowdon,
he says—

> There I beheld the emblem of a mind
> *That feeds upon infinity,* that broods
> Over the dark abyss, intent to hear
> Its voices issuing forth to silent light
> In one continuous stream ; *a mind sustained*
> *By recognitions of transcendent power,*
> *In sense conducting to ideal form,*
> *In soul of more than mortal privilege.*

There are several other passages which indicate the same
elevating consciousness, and the ennobling practical, moral
influence of it on his life and poetry.   It is especially in
these lines :—Hence

> an obscure sense
> Of possible sublimity, whereto
> With growing faculties she doth aspire,
> With faculties still growing, feeling still
> *That whatsoever point they gain, they yet*
> *Have something to pursue.*

This feeling was manifest in him even from earliest child-hood, 'the disappearing line' of the public highway

> that crossed
> The naked summit of a far-off hill,
> Beyond the limits that my feet had trod
> *Was like an invitation into space,*
> *Boundless, or guide into eternity.*

There is in a view of this sort the opening up of the deepest contrasts in human life, thought, and imagination. We find this brief life of ours standing out as but a small speck, now bright, now darkened, against the whole of the past and the future in time ; our individual experience and knowledge set against the boundless possibilities which time and space may unfold; our selfhood, our personality—mysterious, deep, and significant as it is—in contrast somehow not only with the impersonal in things, but with the great, perhaps ungraspable, conception of selfhood in the universe. This rising above limit in our experience is the first breaking, so to speak, with the finite world—the world of the senses—the sphere of purely earthly regards and earthly interests, and, in the very realisation of our own limit, there is revealed to us that far wider and higher sphere of being which holds for us awe, reverence, and rebuke, incentives to action here that can never allow us to rest in the mere contentment of earthly enjoyment or bounded prospect. Once this sphere dawns upon us, but not until it dawns, are we on the way, however devious and perplexing, by turns in brightness and in shadow, that leads to the Presence which men call God. The root-difference between the mind of the purely earthly man and the God-visioned man, not the whole difference, but the deepest, is just this point of the sufficiency or insufficiency of finite experience—or a bounded life in time. On this point Wordsworth and Pascal are at one. ' Man,' says the latter, ' was born only for infinity.'

This, then, is the first stage in the progress of the Poet's mind to his peculiar theism. But there is a second even more important stage. There is a sense, a consciousness of a power or powers in the infinite sphere which surrounds us, and of their presence, in some of our moods of mind, to the senses—certainly to the soul and heart—especially when the conscience is quickened or alert. There are of course ordinary passages innumerable in which a sense of powers higher than the world yet in it is indicated. For example—

> Ye Presences of Nature in the sky
> And on the earth ! Ye Visions of the hills !
> And Souls of lonely places.
>
> Moon and stars
> Were shining o'er my head. I was alone
> And seemed to be a trouble to the peace
> That dwelt among them.

But in this connection there are two passages especially which recur to the student of Wordsworth.

The first is the memorable passage in the *Prelude*, in which the Poet tells us of that night, when rowing alone on Esthwaite Lake, suddenly

> A huge peak, black and huge,
> *As if with voluntary power instinct*
> *Upreared its head.* · I struck and struck again,

> And growing still in stature the grim shape
> Towered up between me and the stars, and still,
> For so it seemed, *with purpose of its own*
> *And measured motion like a living thing,*
> *Strode after me.*   .   .   .
>
>   After I had seen
> That spectacle, for many days, my brain
> Worked with a *dim and undetermined sense*
> *Of unknown modes of being;* o'er my thoughts
> There hung a darkness, call it solitude
> Or blank desertion.   No familiar shapes
> Remained, no pleasant images of trees,
> Of sea or sky, no colours of green fields ;
> But huge and mighty forms, *that do not live*
> *Like living men,* moved slowly through the mind
> By day, and were a trouble to my dreams.

The other passage is when in the night he had thoughtlessly taken, as he tells us, 'the captive of another's toil.'

>   When the deed was done
> I heard among the solitary hills
> *Low breathings coming after me, and sounds*
> *Of undistinguishable motion, steps*
> *Almost as silent as the turf they trod.*

Let us note here the mingling of reality and indefinitude, a reality all the more and the more impressive because it is unaffected by human limits.   There was 'purpose,' 'motion,' 'life,' yet 'unknown mode of being ;' 'a living thing, that did not live like living men,' yet 'mighty,' boundless, uncircumscribable in its power, before which the individual—solitary, alone—confronting it, is as naught.   It is real all the while, yet it is a reality with which thought cannot cope, and which will cannot withstand.

In such circumstances an ordinary mind, if impressed at

all, would have been simply overcome with fear. Wordsworth's emotion was that of awe—the awe of a new revelation of the unseen—that cast its shadow over all his imagination, and solemnised and purified the inner heart of his moral life. Indeed, in both the instances referred to, the unseen power was bodied forth as an impersonation of a suddenly quickened and highly sensitive conscience. A link was formed between the moral world of the finite spirit and the unseen, as if the soul were in the presence of a higher, purer consciousness than its own, unknown until suddenly revealed.

In its essence this feeling was not new to Wordsworth; it was not new to him even in some of the aspects which he felt and delineated. 'Unknown modes of being'—mighty, limitless by us, surrounding, overshadowing this sense-world of ours; a consciousness of this kind had been a marked and powerful influence in the popular feeling and current ballad literature in the district from the Derwent to the Tweed. Its hills, glens, wide-spreading solitary moorlands had nourished it, for nowhere does a man feel his own littleness more, nowhere does he feel the aweing, purifying power of solitude and mystery greater than on the far-reaching, often mist-darkened, moorlands of 'the north cuntré.' We have it in the expressions of 'the darke forest, awesome for to see;' 'the dowie dens' and 'the dowie houms;' 'the brown' and 'waesome bent,' and even in 'the lee'—*i.e.* lonesome—light of the moon. This feeling very readily passed into a sense of supernatural power and presences surrounding the steps of the traveller, so that we have the common word 'eerie' expressing the emotion which comes from the felt nearness of the super-sensible and the unearthly, and we have all the long-cherished beliefs regarding that mysterious spirit-world and ' middle erd '—that ' other cuntré,' intermediate between heaven and hell—chequered neither by mortal change or calamity, nor cheered by mortal hopes, removed from agony and shut out from bliss, which yet might at any moment flash in weird shape on the lonely traveller on the moor. The shadow of this lay on the life of the earliest Border minstrel, Thomas the Rhymer, waiting his call through the years, and then calmly, resignedly passing, at the beck of the gentle white hart, to the mysterious land, by a way so awesome and weird :—

> O they rade on, and further on,
>   And they waded through rivers abune the knee,
> And they saw neither sun nor moon,
>   But they heard the roaring o' the sea.

In the fairy ballad of the young Tamlane there are circumstances and feelings delineated as experienced by the heroine not essentially different from the imaginative mood of Wordsworth, as depicted in the passages quoted :—

> Gloomy, gloomy was the night,
>   And eerie was the way ;
> And fair Janet, in her green mantle,
>   To Miles Cross she did gae.
>
> The heavens were black, the night was dark,
>   And dreary was the place ;
> But Janet stood with eager wish
>   Her lover to embrace.
>
> Betwixt the hours of twelve and one,
>   *A north wind tore the bent ;*
> *And straight she heard strange elritch sounds*
>   *Upon the wind that went.*

Do we not realise here a certain parallel to

> The conflict and the sounds that live in darkness,

or the

Notes that are
The ghostly language of the ancient earth,
Or make their dim abode in distant winds?

Obviously this emotional sense of the unseen in the soul of Wordsworth had its source deep down in a certain heredity of feeling, due to the past, and nourished by circumstances of scenery and of race. In him it was sublimed. What had been but a dim working through the ages on the fears of the older Cymric and Scandinavian people became in him, as he lived and grew with open and fervid heart, a revelation of moral and spiritual truth, and thus an inspiration for mankind. And this was at the root of his moral and theistic feeling.

Essentially connected with the consciousness of infinitude in Wordsworth is the tendency to seek to grasp the world as a whole, to rise to a point above details, to seek relation, connectedness, unity, in the phenomena of sense; to centre all phenomena, all appearances, in one—a Unity of Being. This with Wordsworth is not a mere unity; there is somehow the consciousness of a Spirit—call it infinite or absolute—which permeates all the forms of existence, all the world of created things, working therein as a power, and therein manifesting its nature. To this high sense or faith the whole education of his life, as described especially in the *Prelude*, unconsciously led him—unconsciously, I mean, as to its steps and process. In this conviction he found rest, consolation, practical power. It was not with him a process of conscious seeking; it was rather a process of conscious finding through the abandonment of himself to the gradual revelation of a Personality higher than his own, that hovered over him from his infancy, and spoke to him in many ways ere he knew the Speaker, and finally realised the Presence that filled the temple of earth and heaven.

The questions here arise—(1) What precisely was the nature of this unity, the sense or consciousness of which so powerfully influenced the thought and imagination of Wordsworth? (2) How generally did it arise in his mind, and with what guarantee or warrant?

Now, on the first of these points we must keep in mind that there are three, and but three, views of this world of our experience, and its relation to what may transcend it. We may hold, first, the simple independence of each fact in the world—that all is originally unconnected, single, isolated; any connection which now subsists has arisen through accident—call it chance, custom, association. In the words of David Hume, 'Things are conjoined but are not connected.' Laws would mean on such a system merely the common modes in which things have, without guiding principle, come to be uniformly associated. This is Atheism in the proper sense of the term. It is the absence or denial of the Θεός, Ultimate Principle, or God. This view is, I need not say, alien to the whole spirit of Wordsworth, who constantly proclaims the inter-connectedness of the outward world—the action and reaction between Man and Nature—and the unity of the scheme of which these are parts. In its moral and spiritual consequences this theory is not less opposed to the teaching of Wordsworth, for, in making each thing independent, it makes it self-sufficient, and it entirely ignores the question of origin, as it precludes any question of destiny. But what says the Poet?

I was only then
Contented, when with bliss ineffable
I felt the sentiment of Being spread

> O'er all that moves and all that seemeth still ;
> O'er all that, lost beyond the reach of thought
> And human knowledge, to the human eye
> Invisible, yet liveth to the heart ;
> O'er all that leaps and runs, and shouts and sings,
> Or beats the gladsome air ; o'er all that glides
> Beneath the wave, yea, in the wave itself,
> And mighty depth of waters.   Wonder not
> If high the transport, great the joy I felt,
> Communing in this sort through earth and heaven
> With every form of creature, as it looked
> Towards the Uncreated with a countenance
> Of adoration, with an eye of love.
> One song they sang, and it was audible,
> Most audible, then, when the fleshly ear,
> O ercome by humblest prelude of that strain,
> Forgot her functions, and slept undisturbed.

Every reader of the *Prelude* knows how powerful was the influence of Coleridge on the mind and heart of Wordsworth at the period of his life when that poem was written (1799 to 1805).   But there is no point on which Coleridge and his sympathetic rather than intelligent acquaintance with the rising Absolutism of the Germany of the time impressed Wordsworth more than in the matter of the transcendental unity of being.   He says, speaking of Coleridge and his superiority to the ordinary way of looking at things—

> To thee, unblinded by these formal acts,
> The unity of all hath been revealed.

And we have a characteristic passage of the so-called 'speculative' order in lines like these :—

> Hard task, vain hope, to analyse the mind,
> If each most obvious and particular thought,
> Not in a mystical and idle sense,
> But in the words of Reason deeply weighed,
> Hath no beginning.

The Poet's own good sense and strong concrete sympathy, fortunately for himself and his poetic work, speedily stayed this line of confusion between the relations in time and the beginningless beyond intelligibility.

In the second place we may admit—may be driven to admit—that there is more in things than accidental conjunction; that somehow one thing is through another thing; that there are essential connections; that there are ends, even purposes, reasons, in the order and arrangements of things. This leads us to the conception of a Power—a Power of some sort—transcending experience, yet, it may be, working in it. This is entirely opposed to the atheistic or atomistic view of the world. There is a Power above things, more than things—a Power which subsists while these pass; and through the working, unconscious or conscious, of this Power things are as they are. But here there are two subordinate views, for we may regard this one transcendent Power as unconscious or conscious. It is, on either supposition, a substantial or abiding Power; underlying all, working through all that is, has been, or will be. But if not conscious of itself and its workings, it is an impersonal force; and it matters little whether it be regarded as known or unknowable by us. On this I may remark in passing there has been a great deal of useless controversy; but it is obvious that no force which is allowed to manifest itself can be unknowable—even unknown; for in its manifestations it is, and these are known by us. It might be added even that that which does not manifest itself in some form is not, is never, actually. On the other hand, if the transcendent Power be conscious—conscious of itself, conscious of its workings—it is a personal power, with intellect and will—shall I say emotion? For I am not now speaking anthropologically, I am speaking analogically, and, as I hope to show, strictly in conformity on this point with the view of Wordsworth. I am simply using words which, however inadequate, are the best we have to indicate the character of the transcendent reality. This is the proper Theistic view.

Now the position of Wordsworth lies, as it were, within the scope of the last-mentioned view. He holds by a Unity, a transcendent yet manifested Unity, a Unity amid a multiplicity, yet not a blind or unconscious power ; a Spirit, Soul, Personality, yet not as the human—not a magnified man. This is the ground, the reason, the living, quickening principle of things—of Nature and Man alike. Of Him we may rise to consciousness, and He may become to us a source of inspiration, imaginative, moral, and spiritual, giving us

<blockquote>Truths that wake to perish never.</blockquote>

The other view, the Pantheistic, Wordsworth would have repudiated—not perhaps on what may be called speculative grounds, but simply from the feeling that it is utterly unsuited to our experience—in fact, contradictory of it. The speculative difficulties of it he might not have appreciated or even apprehended. That a formless, indeterminate force should be, and should pass, one knows not why or how, into the formed, definite, unending variety of the beautiful world ; that the conscious should rise out of the unconscious ; that the individual self-conscious, the personality of man, should spring from the abyss of formless, undirected energy, —all this Wordsworth would probably not have thought of. But brought face to face with facts, he would certainly have recognised the essental incongruity of the alleged worthlessness of the individual in the world; the indifference of his existence before the supreme Power ; his coming and going without care or love or concern on the part of the Absolute ;

the worthlessness, even absurdity, of individual effort after moral and spiritual progess, in face of the certainty of final absorption in the formless abyss out of which each one has come we know not how, and to which each one can but return and be no more—the evil as the good, the good as the evil. All this he would feel and recognise, for the one central conception of his moral theory was the worth of the individual—of man as man ; the deep sense of personal responsibility for character and effort ; above all, the conscious relation of the human to the divine.   Higher minds

> Are Powers ; and hence the highest bliss
> That flesh can know is theirs ; the consciousness
> Of Whom they are, habitually infused
> Through every image and through every thought,
> And all affections by communion raised
> From earth to heaven, from human to divine.

On the scheme of Pantheism, man—the finite, conscious spirit—is both an accident and an anomaly.   There is no reason for the being of a conscious personality on the hypothesis of an Absolute which is in itself unconscious ; and effort to develop this personality in the line of the higher, intellectual, moral, spiritual life is merely to violate the law of its being, eventually to court disaster and pain in the process of final absorption within the unconscious.   Individuality and freedom are the haunting shadows and the mockery of such a life.   Wordsworth's view, on the other hand, is that man, taken at his highest and best, is the nearest type to God, and that every step we take in nobler effort is a stage of assimilation with the Divine.

What I have said of the nature of the Theism of Wordsworth may be proved and illustrated by reference to passages with which all are familiar.   I merely indicate briefly the points in those passages which bear on the matter in hand. One of the strongest and most pertinent is in the first book of the *Prelude*, and therefore written as early as 1799, which begins with the lines—

> Wisdom and Spirit of the universe !
> Thou Soul that art the Eternity of thought,
> And givest to forms and images a breath
> And everlasting motion, not in vain
> By day or starlight thus from my first dawn
> Of childhood didst thou intertwine for me
> The passions that build up our human soul.;
> Not with the mean and vulgar works of man,
> But with high objects, with enduring things—
> With life and nature—purifying thus
> The elements of feeling and of thought,
> And sanctifying, by such discipline,
> Both pain and fear, until we recognise
> A grandeur in the beatings of the heart.

There is here the consciousness of a transcendent Spirit, a spiritual Power above and beyond the order of experience. It is Soul, living Soul or Spirit, analogous thus to us, to our spirit, yet in contrast to ours and all its workings, for it is 'the Eternity of Thought,'—not the mere everlastingness of successive thoughts in time, not the mere order of perceptions or thoughts ever going on, not a mere perpetual series of relations—but 'the Eternity of Thought,' the ground, the substratum, the very permanent in all thinking. It is in contrast to our finitude, to our successive thinkings, gropings, in time, until we get what we call 'the truth;' it is 'the Eternity,' the Soul or Consciousness above time and succession and finite effort or struggle, in whom all this is grasped and held, as it were, in one indivisible act. It is, in the language of Aristotle, the Θεός—the one Eternal Energy. And as Plato put intelligence first, and as grounding all things, so the Poet in his own method sets Man and Nature as grounded and inspired by the Eternal Soul.

But though transcendent in itself, in a sense above experience, it is not a *caput mortuum*, or empty abstraction. It is not even a power dwelling apart, set high up in the heavens, no one knows where or truly what. It lays its touch upon earth, on what we call the outward or material world, and on what we name the soul of man.

> Thou givest to forms and images a breath
> And everlasting motion ;

and through these—in a word, through the outward and symbolical world—this Soul that is the 'Eternity of Thought,' that gives breath to the passing scene around us—

> Intertwines for us
> The passions that build up our human soul.

And thus we share in its workings, are drawn into communion with the Transcendent Spirit, and 'pain and fear are sanctified for us,' and we no longer are mere passing, individual organisms, but a link in the life, the solemn life, within the fold of the Eternal Thought; and so we rise in the scale of being, and 'recognise a grandeur in the beatings of the heart.'

In the classical lines, *Tintern Abbey*, written about the same time (1798), we have the sense of the nearness, the immediacy, so to speak, of the mysterious Spirit of all emphasised—

> I have felt
> A presence that disturbs me with the joy
> Of elevated thoughts ; a sense sublime
> Of something far more deeply interfused,
> Whose dwelling is the light of setting suns,
> And the round ocean and the living air,
> And the blue sky, and in the mind of man :

> A Motion and a Spirit, that impels
> All thinking things, all objects of all thought,
> And rolls through all things.

I do not see that the Poet has given us any theory of the mode of this touch of the Eternal Spirit, the how of the connection between the infinite and the finite. In this he was right, eminently sound and healthful in feeling. Indeed obviously no such theory can be given on a doctrine which makes the touch that of a Power which is essentially super-human, and not to be formulated in the language of the modes of human consciousness. There is 'the burthen of the mystery of this unintelligible world;' unintelligible to the mere understanding of man. Of any such attempt there is but one or other of two results—the transcendent ceases to be God; or man, the finite, usurps the place of the In-finite, and becomes the only ultimate reality. There is either the degradation of God or the deification of man; and this is but another expression for the degradation of God. I know no theory of the relation of Infinite to finite which is not merely a wandering in cloudland. True philosophy is not that all things—*yes* and *no*—are true; sound ethics is not that all things—*good* and *evil*—are good; and true theology is not that God is all things—*Man* and *Nature*—or that all things is God. Yet no theory of the necessary emanation of the finite from the Infinite can escape these consequences; and unless it be necessary, it is not a reasoned or demonstrated theory; it is simply a matter of faith, of analogy, and probability.

I shall not take up your time with any detailed reference to the *Ode on Intimations of Immortality from Recollections of Early Childhood;* but it is impossible wholly to pass it by in this connection. In it we have the Poet's fullest, most explicit statement of the intuition of God, and, so far, of man's relation to Him ; the assertion of the pre-existence of the soul ; the hope of immortality ; the prefiguration of an unearthly life :—

> The Soul that rises with us, our life's Star,
> Hath had elsewhere its setting,
> And cometh from afar :
> Not in entire forgetfulness,
> And not in utter nakedness,
> But trailing clouds of glory do we come
> From God, who is our home.

There is 'the soul that rises with us, our life's star,' as if the body and the bodily life were simple accidents, conditions which allow the God-descended, God-given soul to accommodate itself to the brief passing through this time-limited world. It hath set before, to rise again with us, the individual. It is ours, and we are in it ; but it holds more of heaven than of earth, more of God than of us. It is but as a wanderer from its home, orphaned until it again returns to God, and dwells with Him in His presence, in that sphere of light, and knowledge, and love, from which it had so mysteriously emerged, almost fallen. Our relation to earth is represented very much as that of a guest, a wayfarer, to whom earth is kind :—

> The homely Nurse doth all she can
> To make her Foster-child, her Inmate Man,
> Forget the glories he hath known,
> And that imperial palace whence he came.

The impress of our origin and destiny is on us in the childhood time. The soul is not originally a mere *tabula rasa*, or blank sheet of paper, on which Nature has to write its impressions. It is not a mere receptacle for the tracings of the senses, so that the greatest reach of our knowledge afterwards is only the combining and generalising of these ; and the very possibility of the notions of God, and personality, and immortality, and all purely moral and spiritual conceptions is absolutely excluded even from our consciousness. From our very birth we have a certain community with God, and this is shown most in the simplicity of heart which is self-contained and self-contented, almost self-joyous, while

> Heaven lies about us in our infancy,

and ' the earth' and 'every common sight' is

> Apparelled in celestial light,
> The glory and the freshness of a dream.

But there is more than this : there is the feeling and the glimpse of a type or ideal over all our life, towards which, from this early revelation, we are almost constrained to aspire. Gradually the world comes in, and this ideal fades, but is never absolutely lost ; it never wholly dies, and we have as the very saving of our life all through this worldliness—

> Those obstinate questionings
> Of sense and outward things,
> Fallings from us, vanishings ;
> Blank misgivings of a Creature
> Moving about in worlds not realised.

It is thus

> those first affections,
> Those shadowy recollections,
> Which, be they what they may,
> Are yet the fountain light of all our day,
> Are yet a master light of all our seeing ;
> Uphold us, cherish, and have power to make
> Our noisy years seem moments in the being
> Of the eternal Silence.

Their issue, their final teaching, is—

> The faith that looks through Death.

Of the intensity of the Nature-feeling in childhood alleged by Wordsworth, it may fairly enough be said that it does not hold universally. But I set little store on this as discrediting or derogating from the importance of the feeling where it does exist. The physical organisation, with its peculiarities in individuals, has much to do both with the furtherance and the repression of natural intuition and feeling. Man is by no means a mere mind, and even the natural outflowings of mind are greatly modified and determined by bodily conditions. That a special feeling or form of intuition does not appear at a particular stage is no proof either that it is unnatural or that it has not a latent reality.

But this may be said, that the intensity of the Nature-feeling alleged by Wordsworth is not sufficient to found a proof, if we may use that expression, of its relation to former perceptions or intuitions in a previous state of existence. This reference, indeed, may be taken as a poetic way of putting the truth of the first fresh intuition of the outward world as fulfilling in various ways certain primary intellectual and emotional needs of our own nature—eliciting the free, fresh outflow of the faculties, soothing the heart, touching the imagination, giving us the impression that we have not been ushered into a strange land, uncouth and bewildering, but into a sphere where has been at work, and is still working, the same Hand which is felt in this inner, conscious life of ours. The Poet himself has touched this very point when he speaks of—

> that calm delight
> Which, if I err not, surely must belong
> To those first-born affinities that fit
> Our new existence to existing things,
> And in our dawn of being constitute
> The bond of union between life and joy.

And infancy or youth is here a relative term. We may not have the feeling in childhood ; it may come at a later period of life ; but when it comes, it brings with it youth—a new-born spirit, which will survive all through life as a glory which never fades, and a heart which never grows old. And every time we feel the presence of the Transcendent Power in things, there is a freshening of all the springs of life. I do not think I use exaggerated or inappropriate language when I say that to such a heart the journeying through this often arid and conventional world is as if by the banks of a river, the streams of which do glad the city of our God.

To a man of the type of Condillac or David Hume, to any one whose whole view and feeling of the universe is merely that it is a series of sense-impressions, sensations, perceptions—associated, generalised, transformed,—the gospel of the *Ode on the Intimations of Immortality* must appear simply meaningless drivel—in a word, ‘foolishness.’ Yet to Wordsworth the reminiscence and the intuition of the Divine Reality and the Transcendent Ideal are as real as any sense-impression, and a great deal more influential on the regulation of life, moral and spiritual, than either a series of impressions, or any prudential code of ethics generated out of them—any rules for the avoidance of pain and the securing of pleasure. Such a conception, such an ideal as that which overshadowed, solemnised, purified, and elevated the soul of Wordsworth in that immortal Ode, and in those other kindred utterances which might be quoted, withered to the core self-seeking and prudential calculation, and strengthened and beautified this earthly life with a wholly unique sense of the littleness and yet the grandeur of self, as a travelling not from grave to grave, but from God to God.

This Theistic view of Wordsworth is not, as I have

remarked, anthropomorphic in the ordinary sense of that word. While the essence of it is the recognition of a Spirit in the world, and in man, and above both, it is a long way removed from the kind of conceptions that ruled Greek and Roman mythology. The Spirit he feels has no taint of earthly passion, nor is it to be measured by human intelligence. It is not fashioned merely in this image. It is something above and beyond, yet in Nature and man. In the sonnet to the

> Brook, whose society the Poet seeks,

we have one of the finest and subtlest expressions of this relationship :—

> It seems the Eternal Soul is clothed in thee
> With purer robes than those of flesh and blood,
> And hath bestowed on thee a better good ;
> Unwearied joy, and life without its cares.

No word is more ambiguously employed than the term anthropomorphic. It is thought a sufficient objection to Theism to say that it makes God anthropomorphic. Anthropomorphic may be taken as meaning fashioned exactly as man is—conceived as to personality, intelligence, and will,—or as we find man to be, but somehow indefinitely or infinitely greater than man. If Deity be regarded as infinitely greater than a conscious personality, as above limit in intelligence, above law of thought and conceived law of being, then undoubtedly we have a contradiction ; for we cannot conceive either consciousness or personality wholly without limit, definiteness, or determination. And a God merely man, but indefinitely greater than man, is no true Deity. But anthropomorphic in the sense that Deity, as an object of thought, must be regarded in and through the highest conceptions of our experience—that is, self-consciousness, personality, intelligence, free-will, generally conscious activity—this every theory of Theism must assume. If Deity is to be held an object of knowledge at all, as anything more than a mere indefinite, limitless substratum of substance—a mere *caput mortuum*, or at best indefinable force—the conception must have in it those features, must reflect them in their highest reach and purity. We at least must think of Him through these, if we are to think of Him at all. Anthropomorphic, therefore, in this sense, Deity is, and is conceived by us to be. This is the true meaning of the scholastic phrase *ex eminentiâ* as opposed to *actualiter*. In a word, Deity, if cognisable, is cognisable only through relation or analogy to what is highest, best, most perfectly formed in our experience. This will be found to be mind—conscious being—in its ultimate ground of free power or self-activity. He is

A Power
That is the visible quality and shape
And image of Right Reason.

He is this, for the simple reason that He, the highest Power of all, cannot be less than we are or can conceive at our best. Wordsworth's view of the Eternal Soul, while it is opposed to a literal anthropomorphism, is not, as seems to me, opposed to the view that this Soul flows into and fills all our highest conceptions; but it is a fountain whose overflow no human vessel can contain.

There thus seems to be no incompatibility between the Theism of Wordsworth as expressed in his general poems and the views to which he gives utterance in the *Ecclesiastical Sonnets*. These, while breathing a pure, solemn, elevating spirit, have never appeared to me to be pervaded

with the native inspiration and characteristic suggestion of
the Poet's genius and imaginative growth.   They reflect his
historical and traditional feeling.   But the Church forms
and service, even the doctrines of the Personality of God,
His manifestation in Christ, the sense of sin and the
quickening of the Holy Spirit, are readily folded in the
embrace of the Poet's Theism.   This takes in all that is
highest in these, keeps it while it transcends it.   These are
for us the best and highest definite expressions of what is
necessarily transcendent, not adequate even to this tran-
scendency ; but they contain the profoundest symbolism for
us, and so thoroughly the essence of the true, that while in
the ages to come, in this life or in another, this aspect of
the highest reality, while it may be sublimed, will never be
contradicted by aught to be evolved.

After all this it may be said that this view of Wordsworth
may be only a peculiarity of his experience as an individual ;
it may be something which he has felt and known, but
which no one else is likely to feel or know.   It may, in a
word, be valid for the individual, but not for mankind.
This touches the question of the warrant or guarantee for
the view of the Poet.   Now on this generally I should like
to say that we ought to keep in mind one pre-requisite, one
condition of all knowledge, and that is the possession of a
certain degree of faculty, and the placing of ourselves in
circumstances in which this faculty may have play or exercise.   It is so in the sphere of the senses.   The eye must
be there to recognise form and colour.   For the colour-
blind, diversity in colour does not exist.   The ear must be
there to hear sound, and it must be attuned to harmony,
ere harmony exists for it.   The man who lives absorbed in
the material world knows nothing of the world of mind or

consciousness, its modes, forms, varieties, which nevertheless is his very self. A man may live all his days, and
never know what he is; never know the spiritual world
within him; never rise beyond organic impulses. Yet
there is a possibility of colour, and sound, and experience
of the spiritual world, whether the individual has the faculty
for the two former or not, whether he turn in upon himself
or not. It is possible even that circumstances, heredity, the
power of the organic life in us, may, partly through the
power of the past, and partly through the circumstances of
the individual, shut him out from a whole world of reality,
and that of the highest, purest, noblest kind,—nay, from the
knowledge of his true or highest self. And just as the
prophet, the seer of old, was needed to recall men to the
reality of things—the insight of moral and spiritual truths,
—so the seer-poet in these times may be needed to open
the eyes of mankind through his individual vision to what
is a universal reality, even the common though foregone
heritage of the race. This is what Wordsworth believed he
did, and I for one venture to think that he was right in so
believing. What does he say of his vision and himself?
In his solitary walks at Cambridge he felt

> Incumbencies more awful, visitings
> Of the Upholder of the tranquil soul,
> That tolerates the indignities of Time,
> And, from the centre of Eternity
> All finite motions overruling, lives
> In glory immutable. . . .
> I had a world about me—'twas my own;
> I made it, for it only lived to me,
> And to the God who sees into the heart. . . .
> Some called it madness—so indeed it was,
> If childlike fruitfulness in passing joy,

> If steady moods of thoughtfulness matured
> To inspiration, sort with such a name ;
> If prophecy be madness ; if things viewed
> By poets in old time, and higher up
> By the first men, earth's first inhabitants,
> May in these tutored days no more be seen
> With undisordered sight.

Again, poet, like prophet, has ' a sense that fits him ' to perceive ' objects unseen before.'

> Prophets of Nature, we to them will speak
> A lasting inspiration, sanctified
> By reason, blest by faith : what we have loved
> Others will love, and we will teach them how.

Wordsworth was what is known as individual or individualistic in the highest degree. There is not one personality as a writer in this century more singularly unique than his. But his individuality was not an idiosyncracy ; it was not abnormal, or merely subjective. Rather it was normal, and of the highest type. We speak of two selves in man, and we do so rightly. There is the lower self, finding its gratification in worldly interest, commonplace objects, and, it may be, low passion ; the everyday self, dwelling in its little world, its microcosm, which it mostly values for itself, and which finally encloses it as a bounded prisoner. There is, however, a higher self—unworldly, spiritual, reverential,—living under the shadow of the Unseen ; keenly alive to all suggestions from the transcendent and supersensible world ; seeing faces looking, as it were, through the veil of sense ; living more in this consciousness than in the ordinary worldly routine ; prizing it, in fact, as the true life. In most people this higher self is but a wavering ideal that comes and goes, with only a temporary influence. The characteristic of Wordsworth was that this was the highest, strongest, most constant power in his life. In this lay his individuality, but as such it was a typical individuality, normal in the highest degree; representative, not certainly of what is common among the individuals of the race, but representative of what is certainly the true type of human life, of what that life ought to seek and to be. And if such a man habitually, or even in his frequently recurring best moments, felt and knew a Transcendent Power in the world around him, in his own soul, as a divine but very real atmosphere of the higher life, we may well suppose that this is a catholic element, not a peculiarity of the individual, but open to every man who has singleness of vision and purity of heart. 'Blessed are the pure in heart, for they shall see God.'

Wordsworth had a strong feeling regarding intuitions or primary truths as a revelation and a strength to man. To these book-lore was in his view wholly secondary. This opinion was held by him even perhaps to exaggeration. But it is in this line that we are to seek what for him at least was the ultimate warrant of the faith in the one abiding Transcendent Power manifested in all things. And it is something to have the testimony of a pure, unworldly spirit to the consciousness, at least, of such a reality, amid the blindness, heedlessness, limited and noisy worldly self-content of our own time.

The Transcendent Power which held Wordsworth through life was not discovered by him, or got through a process of dialectical exercise; it was revealed to him as a Being external to himself, which laid its hand upon him absolutely, overpoweringly. The light which shone and the voice which called from heaven on Saul of Tarsus were not more distinctly influences which unconditionally seized and swayed the apostle than was the Power in the outward world which surrounded, revealed itself, and made the poet-seer its own, its daily vassal and its impassioned voice—

> Speaking no dream but things oracular.

On that memorable morning after the night's dance and rural festivity, when the dawn rose before him in 'memorable pomp,' he tells us—

> My heart was full ; I made no vows, but vows
> Were then made for me ; bond unknown to me
> Was given, that I should be, else sinning greatly,
> A dedicated Spirit.

Wordsworth, to sum up what I have said, seems to me to stand in two great relations to thought—past and present, to mediæval mysticism, and to modern science.

In the first place, what he felt and taught was not a mere mystical intuition of a God or Being apart from the world, leading to absorption in His contemplation, love, and worship, but the consciousness of the Divine as present in the world of sense, speaking through it to the soul, and thus directly regulating the life in the present—raising the actual world to the divine,—not depreciating it, or leading to its being regarded as worthless, something to be despised and crucified. His point of view is indeed the highest reach of the reaction of the modern spirit against that unhealthy phase of mediævalism, not yet extinct among us, which regarded the earth and earthly things of whatever sort as vile, to be eradicated and stamped out of human life. Wordsworth fused for us the spirit of worship and the spirit of imagination —religion and poetry. He saved us from substituting

A universe of death

> For that which moves with light and life informed,
> Actual, divine, and true.

In the second place, we may be disposed to ask in these times : Is science the only interpretation of Nature ? does it tell us all we can know about it ? Science is no doubt an interpretation in this way, that the intellect comes to the aid of sense, and discovers the relations among things, and the ideas which things exemplify. But we must keep in mind that those ideas, those relations, are not themselves sensible things, although without them these things are to us meaningless. Is it a great stretch to ask one to go a little further in the line of unpicturable relations, to rise a little higher above impressions to ideas, and to inquire whether the gathered uniformities of science are not themselves to be run back to a system ruled by an intellectual conception and dependent on transcendental power ? This would be to go above or beyond science, but the procedure is not unscientific; it is the simple carrying out of what science itself postulates for its own existence, the application of those unpicturable, even unverifiable, notions of time and space, and cause and end, without which science cannot move a step; for whatever is universal in truth is unverifiable in our actual experience. What Wordsworth found, what was revealed to him as an intuition—not an inference certainly,—was the simple correlative of the cosmos, of the ordered system, the one ordering power, the Θεός. His was the science of science, the knowledge of knowledge. In this relation one word more. Science, in its true essence, has always sought the universal. It has sought this by different methods and in different spheres, but always the universal; so Plato, so Aristotle. This, at least, was their common aim. With them it was the necessary, therefore the universal. Bacon sought the same thing by generalisation from particulars. There was still another form of interpretation left unapplied. This Wordsworth gave. He read the appearances of sense into moral or spiritual truths, thus finding in the individual, shifting forms of the sense-world ideas fitted to regulate and elevate the higher life of man, and so rising above not only sense but individual appearances to universal, unchangeable truths. He showed that those moral and spiritual lessons are in the outward things, are at least the product of the interaction of Nature and mind, are true and real meanings, are open and designed for us to learn, and that, as the prophet of old revealed new truth, so the seer-poet opens even to ordinary vision this constant, this profound, this all-hallowing revelation. And thus Poetry came to complete Science, to show that in and through phænomena there is a community of knowledge between man and God, a community of consciousness in 'the Eternity of Thought,' a fellowship even of moral and spiritual feeling.

There are many ennobling practical lessons and rules of life which flow from the theism and general religious system of Wordsworth. But among these, the highest, that which truly involves all the others, is the lightening of the 'burthen of the mystery' of the

> Heavy and the weary weight
> Of all this unintelligible world,

this world which for the understanding of man presents so many insoluble problems. It is the yielding

> That serene and blessed mood
> In which the affections gently lead us on,—
> Until the breath of this corporeal frame
> And even the motion of our human blood

> Almost suspended, we are laid asleep
> In body, and become a living soul ;
> While with an eye made quiet by the power
> Of harmony and the deep power of joy
> We see into the life of things.

Wordsworth does not here point to that sublimity of character which is found in a dignified and reasoned acceptance of the inevitable, yielding even a complacency which enables a man to turn to the sunnier side of things and break into song. He leads rather to the composure which arises from a faith whose reflective and scrutinising eye pierces 'the cloud of destiny,' and is nourished by what it feels is beyond and above it. There is all the difference between 'putting by' and seeing beyond.

> Faith in life endless, the sustaining thought
> Of human being, Eternity, and God.

Meanwhile let this be our rule of life :—

> Enough, if something from our hands have power
> To live and act, and serve the future hour ;
> And if, as toward the silent tomb we go,
> Through love, through hope, and faith's transcendent dower,
> We feel that we are greater than we know.

POETS WHO HELPED TO FORM WORDSWORTH'S STYLE.

By ALFRED AINGER.

POETS WHO HELPED TO FORM
WORDSWORTH'S STYLE.

ALL serious students of Wordsworth are well acquainted with those Prefaces to the Lyrical Ballads, in which he set forth and defended his famous theory of ' Poetic Expression.' We all know how admirable was the reformation he there defended, and also how somewhat rash and unguarded was the language he used in doing so. His friend Coleridge entered into the controversy, and we possess in his *Biographia Literaria* a criticism of Wordsworth's theories, perhaps of its kind the most searching, complete, and satisfactory in the whole range of critical literature. He maintains, as you will doubtless remember, that Wordsworth's practice was excellent, but that his defence of it was open to grave question. For Wordsworth had asserted that there should be no difference whatever between the language of poetry and that of everyday life, and Coleridge set himself to show (and I think we may say succeeded in showing) that the language of Wordsworth's poetry, even when it was simplest and freest from the conventional poetic diction of the eighteenth-century versifiers, was still far removed from the colloquial English of the humbler classes, which he yet claimed to have used without modification.

No doubt Coleridge was right : Wordsworth in his *Apologia*

had attempted to prove too much. His case reminds us of the famous advice said to have been given by a judge of long experience to one who was a novice on the bench : ‘Never give reasons for your decisions. Your decisions will probably be right ; your reasons will probably be wrong.’ Of course I do not make the sweeping assertion that all reasons Wordsworth advanced for his usage were wrong. But Coleridge saw, and we can see with him, that they prove too much. We shall admit this if we recall that even of good prose, the best prose of literature, it cannot be said that it is identical, or ought to be, with the prose of everyday life. When we sit down to write an essay or a story, we are bound to exercise a care in the use of language, and to introduce a more choice vocabulary than when we discuss the last evening’s entertainment over the breakfast-table of the morning. There is a fine line of Boileau’s in his *Art Poétique*, which seems to me to put the matter in a nut-shell—

Le style le moins noble a pourtant sa noblesse

(‘The humblest of styles has a nobility which must be respected’). In this, as in other spheres of human life and conduct, *noblesse oblige.*

It is possible, however, to make too much of Wordsworth’s statements in defending his theory of poetic expression. There is no doubt whatever as to what he meant when he denounced that poetic phraseology which for nearly a hundred years had cramped and hindered the development of true poetic insight in the verse-writers of England. From the time of Pope, those who passed for poets in England, with some eminent and noteworthy exceptions, had gone on copying, not from Nature, but from one another. ‘It is remarkable,’ writes Wordsworth in one of the Prefaces just referred to, 'that, excepting the *Nocturnal Reverie* of Lady Winchil-sea, and a passage or two in the *Windsor Forest* of Pope, the poetry of the period intervening between the publication of the *Paradise Lost* and the *Seasons* does not contain a single new image of external nature; and scarcely presents a familiar one from which it can be inferred that the eye of the Poet had been steadily fixed upon his object, much less that his feelings had urged him to work upon it in the spirit of genuine imagination.' Well, this assertion perhaps partakes of the exaggeration that too often marks Wordsworth's language in speaking of his predecessors, but we cannot deny that it is substantially true. And the practice thus described —of not looking at Nature with their own eyes, but of borrowing the aspects of Nature (or what were supposed to be such) from one another—this practice was of course at the root of that conventional language, that 'poetic diction,' which by Wordsworth's day had become vapid and nauseous beyond bearing. This was inevitable. As long as Nature is not watched and noted at first-hand, it is clear that the same words, epithets, and phrases will serve over and over again to describe her. Just reflect what this 'poetic diction' really was. Even from men of genuine poetic sensibility, even from Goldsmith, and Gray, and Thomson, we might compile a complete vocabulary or glossary of this poetic language. Out of this 'poetic diction' we might construct a poetic dictionary. Let us recall a few of such stereotyped words and phrases. In the poets I have in mind a girl is a *nymph*, and her lover a *swain ;* a poet is a *bard ;* a traveller always a *pilgrim ;* the air in motion is *the gale ;* a wood is a *grove* ; birds are *songsters* or the *feathered choir ;* any distant view in the country is the *landscape ;* a country house is a *bower ;* a person living alone always a *hermit*, and so forth ;

and a list of the poetic epithets that occur over and over
again, such as 'odorous,' and 'vernal,' and 'purling' could
be indefinitely extended. This was what constituted, in
fact, the stock-in-trade, the capital of any ingenious wit or
'eminent hand' who set up as poet; and the strong family
likeness among those writers, under the circumstances, is
not to be wondered at. Most of the minor verse of the
eighteenth century consisted in 'ringing the changes' upon
these substantives and adjectives, and many others like unto
them. And the secret (a very open one) of this poetic style
is certainly the direct antithesis of Wordsworth's. For it
lay in *not* using for poetic purposes the language of every
day. It lay in *not* calling a tree a tree, a field a field, a
wind a wind—in fact, in *not* calling a spade a spade.

We may sometimes have wished that Wordsworth had
been somewhat more explicit, and had told us how and
when he first made the discovery that the tyranny of long
poetic usage must be crushed, and poetry emancipated from
its fetters. Was he, we wonder, first struck by the vague
and vapid character of the diction of the eighteenth-century
poets, or by the vague and vapid character of their representations of Nature? The question is not of much consequence, for the two vaguenesses and vapidities are closely
allied and mutually involved. As long as men do not look at
Nature with their own eyes, the old names and epithets
answer all purposes. But when a poet begins to 'take
Nature for his teacher,' he must at once discover that the
old diction is inadequate. To a man who sees, for instance,
that a wood has a thousand different aspects under different
skies, and at different seasons, and in different moods; and
that the breeze of summer never twice breathes in his ear
quite the same message, it is impossible that he should be

content to go on labelling these things the 'grove' and the 'gale,' merely because his poetical godfathers have gone on doing so for a hundred years. To a man who looks on the peasant boy and the peasant girl with a true poet's sympathy, and hears in them the 'still, sad music of humanity,' it is impossible that he should not turn with loathing from such empty nomenclature as 'nymph' and 'swain.' It is the first-hand study of man and Nature that itself condemns and destroys that poetical diction which Wordsworth found himself constrained to abandon.

Now, who were the poets who had done this, in a measure, before Wordsworth, and pointed him out the way? He has told us in these Prefaces and elsewhere, and they are worth our noting. In a passage I just now quoted he mentions Thomson and the Countess of Winchilsea as being eminently distinguished for having watched Nature for themselves, and tried to reproduce in verse her infinite phases and changes. Of the latter of these writers, it is not too much to say that if English readers of poetry know anything about her, it is mainly owing to Wordsworth having singled her out for honourable mention in his Preface. Anne Finch, Countess of Winchilsea, lived between 1660 and 1720 (about), and thus was rather before Pope than contemporary with him. She began to write just as Dryden died, and before Pope had set the key and the stop for so many a wearisome versifier of that century. Mr. Gosse, in his Preface to the selection from this writer, in Mr. Humphry Ward's Collection, does not overpraise her when he calls her 'a poetess of singular originality and excellence.' She is not wholly free from a diction which was to become later on conventional, but her language is in the main as clear and pure as Wordsworth's own, and for the same reason, that her poems show unmistakably that she watched Nature for herself.   And it was this quality in her evidently which attracted the admiration of Wordsworth.   Her principal poem, mentioned by Wordsworth, *A Nocturnal Reverie*, is an attempt to describe the peculiar features, the sights and sounds, of a summer night in the country.   The poem is in the rhymed decasyllabic couplet, the heroic couplet, which Waller and Dryden had already done so much to make the favourite metre for descriptive and narrative poetry, and which Pope was to do yet more to impose as a yoke upon his successors.   And it seems to me quite certain that it was the recollection of this poem, and the amount of real first-hand observation of Nature contained in it, that led Wordsworth to write that early poem of his, *An Evening Walk*, first published in 1793.   The very title of it suggests comparison with Lady Winchilsea's *Nocturnal Reverie*, and this poem also is in the heroic couplet. It might appear strange that Wordsworth, already in full reaction against the school of Pope, should yet have chosen Pope's special couplet in which to write a poem based upon principles so different.   I cannot but think that it was Lady Winchilsea's example which here determined his choice.   And there is one slight instance of his unconscious obligation to Lady Winchilsea which, as far as I have seen, has never been pointed out.   The *Evening Walk* was composed by Wordsworth between 1787 and 1789—that is to say, when he was a youth of seventeen to nineteen.   But still earlier than this—in 1786 (as Professor Knight thinks probable)—the young Wordsworth had written a shorter but more remarkable poem—more characteristic of him in thought, feeling, and diction.   It is a sonnet, and has for its heading only the words, 'Written in very early youth.'

It will be found on page 2 of the first volume of Professor Knight's edition, and runs as follows :—

> Calm is all nature as a resting wheel.
> The kine are couched upon the dewy grass ;
> The horse alone, seen dimly as I pass,
> Is cropping audibly his later meal :
> Dark is the ground ; a slumber seems to steal
> O'er vale, and mountain, and the starless sky.
> Now, in this blank of things, a harmony,
> Home-felt, and home-created, comes to heal
> That grief for which the senses still supply
> Fresh food ; for only then, when memory
> Is hushed, am I at rest.   My Friends ! restrain
> Those busy cares that would allay my pain ;
> Oh ! leave me to myself, nor let me feel
> The officious touch that makes me droop again.

A remarkable production, in any case, we shall agree, for a boy of sixteen ; but remarkable also as showing how essentially the boy Wordsworth was father of the man.   The purity of the diction (a perfect example of his later practice and illustration of his protest) and the turn of the phrases, 'this blank of things,' the 'officious touch,' the 'harmony, home-felt and home-created,' are indeed absolute fore-shadowings of the Wordsworth that was to be.   But the one characteristic piece of Nature-transcribing that I meant to instance is that in the third and fourth lines—

> The horse alone, seen dimly as I pass,
> Is cropping audibly his later meal.

'*Cropping audibly.*'   Every one of us will recall how in the absolute tranquillity of a late summer evening in the country, the regular 'twitch,' 'twitch,' of a grazing horse is one of those few sounds that strike the ear at that season,

and only at that season, because of the otherwise perfect
stillness. Nothing could have been better chosen to em-
phasise that stillness, and bring the scene more graphically
before us. And it is at least noteworthy that Lady Winchilsea, seventy years before, had noted and preserved in verse
the same characteristic feature of '*night in the fields.*' In
her *Nocturnal Reverie* she has it thus—

> When the loose horse now, as his pasture leads,
> Comes slowly grazing through the adjoining meads,
> Whose stealing pace and lengthened shade we fear,
> Till torn-up forage in his teeth we hear.

This is coarsely expressed ; it lacks the transmutation of
that finer sense and touch which embodied the same observation in the lines—

> The horse alone, seen dimly as I pass,
> Is cropping audibly his later meal.

But so close a parallelism can hardly have been accidental.
Wordsworth had first been struck in reading the poetry of
Anne Finch with the power, in this instance, of a single and
most commonplace and unpoetical feature of a summer
evening, to bring Nature closer to us, and thereby to excite
our best and happiest emotions of delight in her. Lady
Winchilsea had helped, as he said Burns had done also, to
teach

> his youth
> How verse may build a princely throne
> On humble truth.

Of the other poet, the author of the *Seasons*, here chosen
by Wordsworth as an honourable exception to the 'poetic
verbiage'-mongers of the eighteenth century, less need be
said. Thomson is by no means free from the use of that

vocabulary which Wordsworth set himself to dethrone from its bad eminence. But Wordsworth had noticed that when Thomson most trusted to his own observation, and was most directly inspired by personal contact with Nature, *his* diction also cleared itself from the conventional taint. Wordsworth was an ardent admirer of Thomson, and especially of what he calls 'that noble poem,' *The Castle of Indolence.* We remember how he chose to write one poem in imitation of it—the lines 'written in a copy of *The Castle of Indolence*,' when he describes Coleridge and Tom Poole. We remember how, moved by Collins' *Elegy on the Death of Thomson*, he in turn was led to write his exquisite lines on Collins, 'composed upon the Thames near Richmond.' Wordsworth's general debt to Thomson he has himself acknowledged; and unlike as the two poets are in outward garb, and little as the author of the *Seasons* may now be read, we can understand how much of value and of encouragement Wordsworth found in that lover of Nature who preceded him. There is a noble stanza in *The Castle of Indolence*, which may not much remind us in phraseology of Wordsworth, but which might almost serve as a motto for Wordsworth's collective works :—

> I care not, Fortune, what you me deny :
> You cannot rob me of free Nature's grace,
> You cannot shut the windows of the sky,
> Through which Aurora shows her brightening face ;
> You cannot bar my constant feet to trace
> The woods and lawns, by living stream, at eve :
> Let health my nerves and finer fibres brace,
> And I their toys to the great children leave ;
> Of fancy, reason, virtue, nought can me bereave.

There is one slight but not insignificant proof of Words-

worth's careful reading and unconscious remembrance of
Thomson to be found in his well-known *Poet's Epitaph*.
Every one here could repeat that bewitching stanza—

> But who is He, with modest looks,
> And clad in homely russet brown?
> He murmurs near the running brooks
> A music sweeter than their own.

I must confess to having known Wordsworth's poetry
intimately before I knew Thomson's equally well, and in
those days I often wondered who was the individual in
'russet brown,' and where Wordsworth had met him.   One
ingenious critic, apparently sharing my then ignorance, has
suggested that Wordsworth had Charles Lamb in mind,
because of the old snuff-coloured suit which Elia once wore,
and which his friends knew so well.   But Wordsworth could
not have been familiar with the old snuff-coloured suit so
early as 1799, when the poem was written.   No.   Wordsworth had first met the modest singer, and no doubt forgotten the introduction to him, in Thomson's *Castle of
Indolence*, where he thus appears—

> He came, the bard, a little Druid wight
> Of withered aspect; but his eye was keen,
> With sweetness mixed.   In *russet brown* bedight,
> As is his sister of the copses green,
> He crept along, unpromising of mien.

In '*russet brown.*'   It is the very phrase, and was
suggested to Thomson, as he all but admits, by the parallel
of the sister warbler of the copses green,—of course that is
to say, the *nightingale.*   It is not unamusing that Philomel
was the real prompter of the epithet, and *not* Charles Lamb.

Too much, perhaps, has been made of Wordsworth's *un-*

indebtedness to books, and his obligations to Nature alone. We all know the charming story of the visitor who asked to see the Poet's study at Rydal Mount, and the old servant's reply, 'This is where master keeps his books, but he studies in the fields.' The answer was as true as it was witty. But not the less was the Poet under great and definite obligations to books. He himself, at least, never ignored it. Books are 'a substantial good,' he said, and most surely they had been to him 'a substantial good.' Burns (at least when writing in his own matchless dialect, for when he chose literary English as his model, he too often fell into the worst conventionalisms of poetic diction), Thomson, Lady Winchilsea,—these and a few more had taught Wordsworth that when Nature was closely loved and brooded over, she never betrayed her worshippers in this matter of style. Above all, from the ballad-writers; from Hamilton and the Yarrow poems; From Logan with his *Ode to the Cuckoo—*

> Sweet bird ! thy bower is ever green,
>   Thy sky is ever clear ;
> Thou hast no sorrow in thy song, [illegible]
>   No winter in thy year ;

from the touching simplicity of the *Children in the Wood*, the new-felt charm of which Johnson had in vain striven to laugh away—

> These pretty Babes, with hand in hand,
>   Went wandering up and down ;
> But never more they saw the man
>   Approaching from the town ;

from these, and such as these, Wordsworth formed his own noble and pellucid English. He was a student, and a close student, of other men's style. But in spite of certain Miltonic echoes in portions of his blank verse, he cannot be called the disciple, even when starting on his course, of any one English poet. Rather he had watched what the qualities of mind and soul were which had kept style pure, and had set himself to acquire these.

We part to-day. I have no claim or right to speak a farewell, but I should like to end this paper with the concluding lines of Hartley Coleridge's sonnet to Wordsworth, which speaks of the strong tie that should exist among all true Wordsworthians, and which this Society, we may modestly hope, has done nothing at least to weaken—

> Oh, what must be
> Thy glory here, and what the huge reward
> In that blest region of thy poesy?
> For long as man exists, immortal Bard,
> Friends, husbands, wives, in sadness or in glee,
> Shall love each other more for loving thee.

SPEECH BY AUBREY DE VERE.

SPEECH BY AUBREY DE VERE.[1]

I DEEM it a great honour that I have been intrusted with the pleasant task of offering the thanks of this Meeting to its honourable President. All who heard it will feel how admirable his address was. He stated in its earlier part how indebted he considered himself to the genius of Wordsworth, and the lasting benefit he had derived from it in his youth. I can only say that now, when he is no longer a youth, I think he has made an ample return for the obligation. Last year the Wordsworth Society was presided over by a poet who was an old friend of mine, Lord Houghton. I think it is not less appropriate that this Meeting, which is our last, should be presided over by such a statesman as Lord Selborne. Wordsworth's poetry is eminently that of philosophic thought ; and amongst other subjects of philosophic thought profoundly interesting he has left behind him many passages indicating that political philosophy was more studied by him than by poets generally. He has written several sonnets on what he considered to be the characteristics of the true statesman. There is one in which he considers the position of England at the time of the contemplated French invasion. He says—

> We shall exult, if they who rule the land
> Be men who hold its many blessings dear,
> Wise, upright, valiant ; not a servile band,
> Who are to judge of danger which they fear,
> And honour which they do not understand.

---

[1] In moving a vote of thanks to Lord Selborne, July 1886.

In another sonnet he speaks of the true statesman in these words :—

> Blest Statesman he, whose mind's unselfish will
> Leaves him at ease among great thoughts.

I believe he would have rejoiced in the thought that any meeting at which his poetry was considered should be presided over by a statesman, whose whole career has been marked by consistency as well as by justice.

Wordsworth was eminently a patriot, as well as a statesman. There is a sonnet in his *Memorials of a Tour in Italy* which illustrates this. When at Florence, he was shown a seat on which Dante had sat day by day watching the Cathedral while it was being built. Wordsworth regarded it for some time, full of awe, as if he had no right to stand thus close, as it were, to a poet he regarded as so much greater than himself. But Dante was a patriot as well as a poet. At last exclaiming, 'Whatever I may be as a poet, I am not less truly than he was, a patriot,' Wordsworth sat down on that seat, and

> For a moment filled that vacant throne.

Our President must allow me to say that the address he delivered this day seemed to me the most cordial, the most discerning, and, for that reason, the most satisfactory praise of Wordsworth which I have ever heard expressed. He does not, however, stand alone in holding those opinions. A great poet, Sir Henry Taylor, long since told me that he believed Wordsworth to be, not merely the greatest of modern English poets, but distinctly, without any exception, the greatest English poet since Shakespeare. The same belief I have heard expressed by my father, both a poet and an admirable critic. I consider Wordsworth to be a greater

poet than Milton. I do not say he often soars so high. I
do not say that his diction is as lofty, or his style as majestic
and solid; but he had a greater range of thought, and a
vaster sphere of human sympathy than any other poet,
except Shakespeare. Shakespeare alone can be compared
with Wordsworth in Poetry's humanities. Shakespeare is
the greatest of all humanists. Wordsworth, of English poets,
is the next greatest master of the human heart, and the one
who most profoundly sympathises with human nature both
in its joys and sorrows. He was also pre-eminently the
poet of Nature. Frederick Faber, the eminent Oratorian,
was a friend of mine. I was once on a visit to Wordsworth
(to have slept under his roof I regard as the greatest
honour of my life), and we had a conversation about the
different modern poets who had in late years described
Nature. He expressed a low opinion as to their success in
description. He took down several volumes, and he said,
'Here is a descriptive passage by ——. It is exceedingly
able writing, but it is not Nature. It is doubtless effective,
but it is the writing of a person who vainly endeavours to
blend together as much as he sees, whether congruous or
incongruous, into a single picture. This is the way in which
he did his work. He used to go out with a pencil and a tablet,
and note what struck him, thus: "an old tower, " "a dashing
stream, " "a green slope," and make a picture out of it.'
Then, turning to me, the old Poet added, with flashing eye,
'But Nature does not allow an inventory to be made of her
charms! He should have left his pencil behind, and gone
forth in a meditative spirit; and, on a later day, he should
have embodied in verse not all he had noted but what he
best remembered of the scene; and he would have then presented us with *its soul,* and not with the mere visual aspects

of it. . . . With the exception of myself,' he ended, 'I do not think I ever met a man who realised the inner meanings of Nature.' In this there was nothing of vanity, for he suddenly added, 'I should make one exception: there was one man—Frederick Faber—he not only had as good an eye for Nature as I had, but a better one—a much better. He used to walk with me on the mountains; and I was very much surprised at finding that, with all my great and manifold experience of them, he was constantly detecting certain *characteristic* effects which I had never perceived. He had a better eye for Nature than I have.'

You will all agree with what we heard from our noble President, and also from the gentleman who spoke on the Theism of Wordsworth, that the charge of Pantheism sometimes brought against his poetry is a wholly mistaken one. On this subject he had no confession to make of any change of opinions. Respecting it he once said to me: 'When I was a young man, I was very much occupied with several other subjects of thought, philosophical, political, etc. It was then that my imagination worked out for itself the channel along which it afterwards flowed. In my later life I became more and more impressed by the dignity and importance of Religious Truth; but my poetic habit had already been formed. Moreover, I thought it would be presumptuous in me to assume the office of a religious teacher, or often to write on that subject.' There is one particular poem to which I should like to refer the reader because it illustrates, not only the theistic, but the definitely Christian character of some of his most characteristic and beautiful poetry. His poem, *The Primrose of the Rock*, consists of two parts. The first part is a highly imaginative illustration of Wordsworth's philosophic genius in his dealings with Nature and with man; the second is an emphatic confession on the subject of '*Redeeming* Love,' that is, of Christianity, which in one of his later poems he has called 'the lord and mighty paramount of Truths.' Some persons have misunderstood Wordsworth, in part owing to the sense in which he commonly uses the word 'Nature.' They object that he magnifies Nature to such a degree that he seems to set aside the Supernatural as foreign to man. That is never his meaning. A line taken from one of his later poems illustrates his deepest convictions on that subject. He says—

> By Grace Divine,
> Not otherwise, *O Nature*, we are thine.

The Poet is not at war with the theologians as regards Grace and Nature. Wordsworth here affirms distinctly that it is only by 'grace divine' that we, in any adequate sense, belong to Nature. This is all-important. The Nature which he sings and celebrates is thus not a Nature contrasted with Grace; it is an ideal, if not an unfallen, Nature, the Nature to which we ought to belong; but to belong to which is only possible to a fallen race by the aid of Divine grace.

I believe, as I have already said, that Wordsworth is the greatest English poet, with the solitary exception of Shakespeare. I may seem to utter a paradox when I say that I think him, on the whole, more in moral harmony with Shakespeare than is any other English poet. They are, on the surface, obviously and eminently unlike. Shakespeare is the most self-forgetting of all poets; Wordsworth the least. The former is the most dramatic of dramatists; the latter could not, except in short pieces, such as *The Brothers*, adequately express himself in the dramatic form. But the great lyric, idyllic, and philosophic poet resembles Shakespeare more than any other poet in that which is the soul of all poetry—in his poetic reverence for humanity, and his imaginative appreciation of the connection between humanity and the moral and spiritual sense in man; although, being singularly destitute of many special dramatic aptitudes, though by no means of the dramatic faculty itself, his genius was fortunately compelled to select for its expression a poetic *method* (for Poetry, like Science, has its different *methods*) almost the opposite of Shakespeare's.

INDEX.

Printed by T. and A. CONSTABLE, Printers to Her Majesty, *at the Edinburgh University Press.*